Lovin' You Is Wrong

Lovin' You Is Wrong

You can't have your cake and eat it, too. Or can you?

Alisha Yvonne

URBAN BOOKS LLC
www.urbanbooks.net

Urban Books
10 Brennan Place
Deer Park, NY 11729

ISBN 1-893196-70-4

First Printing October 2006
Printed in the United States of America

10 9 8 7 6 5 4 3 2 1

This is a work of fiction. Any references or similarities to actual events, real people, living, or dead, or to real locales are intended to give the novel a sense of reality. Any similarity in other names, characters, places, and incidents is entirely coincidental.

Submit Wholesale Orders to:
Kensington Publishing Corp.
C/O Penguin Group (USA) Inc.
Attention: Order Processing
405 Murray Hill Parkway
East Rutherford, NJ 07073-2316
Phone: 1-800-526-0275
Fax: 1-800-227-9604

Acknowledgements

To my mother, Rhonda Brown: Your support is worth platinum in my heart. Thank you for believing in me and continuing to provide encouragement in all of our time of grief. Your strength is what helps me to shine. I love you.

To my siblings, Donna L. Smith, Gregory Savage, and Ronald Byrd: Thanks for your wonderful, enthusiastic outlook during the completion of this novel. You provided me with encouragement during the days when I'd start to have self-doubt. I love you and again, thank you.

To friends and family (Charles Brown, Barry and Penny Clark, Sherita Nunn, Tee C. Royal, Kendal and Eric Hubbard, Richard and Carol Holland, Jacki Miller, Patricia Perkins, the Tutwilers—Benjamin, Paul, and Martin, Royce Willis, Deborah Tuggle, Lillie Garrison, Florida Parker, Rachel E. Clark, Camela Dodson, Tisha Moody, Angela Bonner, Audrey White, Pam Small, Cardester McCoy): I'm excited that so many of you care. You have come out of the woodwork with support. I'm extending an open invitation into my heart so you can see just how overjoyed I am. *Sherita,* I'm proud that we are friends—thanks for all you do. *Uncle Ben* (Benjamin Tutwiler), I OWE YOU! *Royce,* I'm saying it again, you're the man! *Uncle Paul* (Paul A. Tutwiler), you were one of my first inspirations for the written word—now publish that book! *Kendal,* best friends don't come packaged better than you. *Grandma* (Lillie Garrison), you mean more than I could ever express. I'll just sum it up with I love you!

To some very special online and local book clubs (R.A.W. SISTAZ, Memphis-RAW, ReadInColor, Sophisticated Souls of Learning, Women In Sisterhood, Women Seeking Knowledge, Uchefuna, GFI-Mphs, and Unique Women Social Club): What can I say to such a wonderful group of people? Your support is every author's dream, and I thank you all for helping mine come true. Girl Friends Inc-Memphis, I'm waiting on the next party . . . and please remember to bake me some macaroni and cheese. ☺

To Urban Book's staff and my fellow supportive authors (Carl Weber, Roy Glenn, Robilyn Heath, Keith Lee Johnson, Thomas Long, LaJill Hunt and the entire Urban Books family), Cherlyn Michaels, Cydney Rax, Eric Pete, David Williams, Regina Neequaye, Margie Gosa Shivers: Did you ever know that you're my heroes and everything I'd like to be? In case you all didn't know, here it is written in black and white— you light up my literary world! Much success to all of you.

To my awesome editor, Chandra Sparks Taylor (Taylor Editorial Service):
Once again, your professional touch has helped me turn *Lovin' You Is Wrong* into the best novel yet. I've never forgotten your words, "Alisha, you know I'm

not going to let you put some mess out there." You held true to your promise—*Lovin' You Is Wrong* is DA BOMB. ☺ Thanks again for all your hard work, dedication, and patience with this project.

Dedication

In Loving Memory of Corry L. Richmond
29 June 1974–10 September 2003

A Letter to Corry . . .

A day I don't think of you hasn't come to pass. You are never forgotten and will forever live on in my heart. I can feel you smiling on me—what an incredible honor to have an angel such as yourself watching over me. I'm blessed, so you get your rest because we've got a whooole lot to talk about when I see you again.

Love,
Sis

P.S. Please put in a good word for me. Really don't want no trouble at the Gate. ☺

Lovin' You
Is Wrong

Chapter One

Fo' Yo' Info-may-shun

Am I even worthy of living? For the past two weeks I've had no other option but to stare at these same four walls and the mass of cards and flowers that accompany them. The anxiety I'm feeling is only adding to the thought that I should be dead. Every time that door opens, I get a whiff of what really should be fresh air, but instead it's the stale smell of blood and corrosion, which is a constant reminder that I now have the death of one too many people on my hands. And it was all a result of love.

One of the most complex things with which I've ever had to deal in my life is love. As a little girl, I knew one day I would have to grow up and perhaps meet the man with whom I'd want to spend eternity. But even at eight years of age, I knew I didn't want the kind of love my momma had with my daddy.

See, Momma always said a man doesn't love you unless he hits you upside the head at least a few times a week. It didn't seem right to me, and it sure as hell didn't seem like it had anything to do with love. Although I was a child, I had enough common sense to tell the difference between right and wrong. But see, this was all my momma had been taught. And somehow, in all her seventy-three years of life, she still doesn't feel any differently.

My daddy stands six-foot-two with a husky build and has long arms—strong enough to knock over a bull. Momma's slender five-foot-seven frame never stood a chance against his mighty blows. Although we were living in Charlotte, North Carolina, my daddy's extensive reach could draw back and swing a blow from Tupelo, Mississippi, to knock Momma off her feet. She would fly clean across the room to the opposite wall, taking everything in her path with her. Momma had conditioned me to believe this was what she wanted. So, two to three times a week, I would just stand there following my daddy's unmerited abuse on Momma and wait to see if I could tell whether she was still breathing. Extreme anxiety would come over me the times I saw her motionless for what seemed like forever before she could rise to her feet.

Now that I'm thirty-three years old and blessed with a daughter of my own, I should've come to the realization a long time ago that I've got too much ahead of me as a mother to be succumbed by despair. Men, jobs, or any other distractions shouldn't have played a pertinent role over raising my child.

Crystal, being the bright and artistically inclined preteen she is, certainly didn't deserve to have to endure all the stress I've dealt with over the last couple of years. Everyone knows that a child feels a mother's pain, and Crystal is definitely one who knows when something is wrong with me.

My position as senior financial analyst at the Memphis Metro Life Insurance Company had become overwhelmingly demanding. I knew time would be limited this summer with Crystal, so I finally permitted her to go stay with her father, Darius Coleman, out in L.A. for a while. He had relocated there with his mother shortly after discovering that I'd been serious about going on with my life without him. Crystal was very excited to go, and I knew this was something Darius had been hoping for since he left a year ago. It took much of the guilt off me for not providing the means for Crystal and me to have our family time. If I could, I would take it all back 'cause I'm definitely paying for it now. I just thank God that I've been given another chance to still be a mother to Crystal.

Back at the insurance company for which I'd had previous employment, New Vet Life, I met and worked closely with a very intelligent man, Roman Broxton. Roman was this smooth, suave, and "I know I got it going on" type of brother. He had so many women calling the office for him, all claiming to have questions about insurance, I talked with him about investing in a pager. He didn't want all of them to have his cell phone number, so he would have them calling the office to leave a message on his voice mail there. I had become totally convinced that Roman was nothing but a player and a womanizer. At least three women were coming to meet him at the office on different days of the week for lunch. I think he must've had these engagements mapped out in a calendar book somewhere. I really can't understand just how he kept up with each appointment for these sistas. The man was fine, though. His smooth, chocolate skin made my mouth long for a Hershey's bar! And oh my goodness, that shiny, charcoal-black, wavy hair of his was an eye-catcher, too. Although he kept his hair cut kind of low, I couldn't resist the temptation of rubbing my fingers across his head as I walked past him sitting at his desk. His body was ripped and buffed in all the right places, and I can't begin to tell you about what he looked like in a pair of jeans and a wife-beater T-shirt. Oh, my goodness! I can still remember the first time I saw him come to the company picnic looking so fine!

I was sitting with Crystal at a bench in the park, when here comes Roman getting out of his Lexus 430, marvelously enhanced with what the men of today like to call chrome dubz—you know, twenty-inch rims. Anyway, everyone would often hear him refer to his car as Black Onyx. All I know is, the man was black, his car was black, and I liked to call it black-on-black crime, 'cause it was a damn crime, a sin, and a shame how good that black-ass man looked anywhere near that car. Every man can't pull that off.

Well, he just kind of stood there looking over toward everyone with his domineering smile—a smile that didn't quite spread fully across his face, yet showed just enough of his pearly-white teeth to melt the ice off a woman's heart. His ass looked good in those jeans—Hilfiger, I think. Well I just know that whomever designed them had to have had Mr. Roman Broxton in mind at the time. Dark in color, neat at the waist, pockets on the ass, those jeans were definitely made for him! And that white wife-beater did nothing but complement his abs. I put my napkin up to my mouth 'cause I could feel myself drooling. Just when I was about to invite him to sit at the table with Crystal and me, my attention was drawn to his passenger car door as it swiftly swung open.

I could see a woman's foot hanging out of the car as she sort of leaned inward to primp in the mirror behind the sun visor. She was applying lipstick. I could tell by that shiny red, high-heeled pump hanging out of his car that she was just like the rest of his women—high maintenance! Come on now, nobody wears high heels of any kind to a picnic. For real! But, I wasn't mad, though. It only reminded me that Roman wouldn't want a sista like me and that he was too much of a player for me anyway.

Roman had come on to me before, but I immediately turned him down. I told him I don't date men with whom I work. He believed me, and he didn't say anything else to me about taking me out for a long while. He would ask me to hook him up with some of my friends, though. But how could I when I knew his caliber?

Now, there was one other brotha, Lance Ferrell. He was another man whom I had figured was unattainable. Lance was six feet with a sexy caramel complexion. He had hazel eyes, and kept a well-groomed goatee—he had a tight body, I must add. He was too good-looking! Back in Charlotte, a girlfriend and I came up with a term that we called *laissez-faire*, which means hands-off. This man was a prime example of laissez-faire. Although we knew this term was normally used in business affairs, we adapted it 'cause we meant business when we said hands-off. A man like

Lance in our eyes was *too* pretty to touch. The way we had it figured, if he was a laissez-faire man, then he could easily break your heart.

In our past experiences, my girlfriend Renee Hamilton and I found that men who had the essence of success, charm, and were damn near prettier than us, couldn't seem to resist letting all this substance swell their egos. Yet, Lance was so sweet and gentle when it came to women. I'll admit, he would always give women the utmost respect. He hadn't had a girlfriend for a couple of years, though. His last one somehow broke his heart, so he was taking time out from being tied in a relationship.

Lance was a brotha totally opposite of Roman, yet they somehow got along better than two blood brothers. I could never figure it out, but what I do know is Lance made any woman happy to be with him while Roman was out crushing hearts. Lance had a way of looking at you with a smile that could warm you on the inside while his eyes would undress you and say how much you meant to him. Now, that was some stuff! A woman can't help but love a man like that. At one time, I had thought his last girlfriend must've been young and dumb 'cause you don't come across a man as gentle as Lance every day. I soon learned that Lance had his share of faults, too, and that I could respectfully brand him with the tag *laissez-faire*.

Chapter Two
Ain't No Denying

I'm not one of those sistas who thinks her shit doesn't stink and that just 'cause I got a pretty face and a well-rounded ass, all men of the world owe me something, but I'll admit, something about working so closely with Roman and Lance, not to mention being their boss, was empowering within itself. C'mon feel me now—two fine-ass, educated, I-can-get-what-I-want-on-my-own black men, the kind a woman doesn't have to worry about him asking her to leave the tip after a dinner date. I know all of this because I reviewed their résumés and sat on the panel as both of them interviewed for their positions. I also had the privilege of providing input for their salary recommendations. As for going out with them, on several occasions I'd accompany them to lunch and to dinner after a late workday. Neither of them would ever hear of me paying for our meals, let alone leaving a tip.

Before I got my promotion to senior financial analyst, Roman, Lance, and I used to talk quite frequently while we would finish up last-minute paperwork. I knew so much of their business outside of the office. The two men were pretty close to being the same age as me, give or take a number or two, and I learned that both of them had had their fair share of women and faults with them. When I became senior financial analyst, I got my own office, as well as an abundance of detailed work that had to be done in solitude, so the guys and I couldn't rap to one another as frequently anymore. I'm sure that made some of the other female agents and brokers in the office very happy. They were jealous of my relationship with Lance and Roman.

Lance was very particular about with whom he shared personal business. He and Roman would make small talk with some of the other women occasionally, especially Roman. You couldn't expect anything different from him because amusing women was just a way of Roman being himself.

I enjoyed the talks we would have at the end of each workday, so when we could no longer converse on a personal level, I felt as though I was being left out of something. Furthermore, I couldn't even tell if the guys missed communicating with me.

I had been in my new position for about four months before I realized I hadn't done my homework properly. I was given a pay increase, but it wasn't nearly what it should've been, given my experience. My assistant's pay was just about equal to mine, and it didn't sit right with me for a while. She as well as the insurance agents in the office made commission, due to the contract agreement made at the time she was promoted. This put her salary in the same bracket as mine, yet she performed fewer duties and worked fewer hours. No one explained to me at the time of my promotion that I had the option to be senior financial analyst as well as make a percentage for continuing to write policies. I was told that I could only receive bonuses at the end of each quarter. When I went to upper management about my realization, it was explained to me that due to the salary we'd negotiated, I was no longer eligible for commission.

This was very unfair to me. I took on a lot of responsibility when I accepted that promotion, and although I shouldn't have had the added duty of writing policies, I did. There were times when no one else in the office was experienced enough to write certain policies, so I felt I had to handle them. Do you think I felt good about my job after learning that if I had done my homework I could be making more quarterly? Hell no! I continued to talk to upper management about what I felt was right, and they constantly ignored my concerns.

I started doing a little investigation of my own on other insurance companies in the area. After all the years I'd put in at New Vet Life, I had come to realize it was time for me to move on. I faxed my résumé to several interesting listings, and then I nervously waited and prayed for a call.

In the meantime, I spoke to Roman and Lance and made them aware of the fact that I was looking for other employment. I knew I could trust them, and I didn't want them to be caught by surprise once I began my packing.

"Well, baby girl, you just gotta do what you gotta do. You been talkin' with those tricks in upper management for what two, three months now? Sheee, it's time to move on." The sternness in Lance's tone was enough to convince me I was doing the right thing.

Roman seconded Lance's advice. "Yeah, boo. Don't trust they asses! They might try to beg, plead, and even get on their fuckin' knees to make you stay. You know what's best for you."

"Yeah, I know. And it's funny how people don't miss the water until the well runs dry. You know what I'm saying?" I responded.

Lance put on one of those warm smiles and answered, "Yeah, and hey, baby girl, I would be lying if I told you I wouldn't miss you, but at the same time, I can't do anything but understand."

"Thanks, Lance." It was all I could say at that moment. I was too focused on his flawless white teeth as he spoke. And his mouth framed them perfectly, too.

It had been a little more than a year since I'd been with a man. My ever-so-denied hormones caused me to take note of almost every sexual aspect about these two brothas. Lance had pretty lips and could lick them like LL Cool J when he spoke. Roman's thick eyebrows and well-groomed mustache gave off the same radiance as his wavy charcoal hair, adding fanatical definition and sharpness to his face. *Hpmh!* Yeah, my next thought was of how I was gonna miss them, too.

Roman and Lance had promised to take me out to dinner if I got an offer from another company. I was excited that they wanted to celebrate with me. In my mind, this meant that they, in fact, missed the talks we'd had as well.

After another month, I finally got the offer for which I was hoping. I let the guys know just before I turned in my notice. Upper management was dumbfounded. They responded in just the manner I'd expected.

Mrs. Emily Andrews, my senior manager, pleaded with me. "Holiday, please just give us a little more time before you make your decision."

"A little more time? A little more time? There is no more time. I've made my decision. That's why I'm turning in my notice now. I don't mean to be disrespectful, nor insubordinate to you, Mrs. Andrews, but I don't appreciate you calling me in your office now to speak on my resignation. If my moral was really a concern of yours, you would've addressed my pay issue months ago when I first asked you."

"I understand that, Holley, but please, just give me a chance to speak with some other members of management. I just know there has to be something we can come up with that could possibly keep you here. You're a great asset to this company. There's absolutely no one here more capable of doing your job. And quite frankly, I just don't see how another company could give you the job fulfillment that you expressed in your interview for this position."

I'd been standing the entire time we'd been talking. She hadn't tried to offer me a seat upon entering her office, so there I stood before her with my arms folded high up at my chest. I took a few seconds to fully observe the image of a pale white woman with green eyes and a neatly cut brunette hairstyle—moussed to the max. She had a look on her face I'll never forget. She couldn't deny being bewildered as she sat behind a gorgeous marble-top desk placed inside of an office that could neatly house my entire living room.

With all sincerity upon my face I responded, "I

would've loved to have considered anything upper management could've come up with two months ago, or maybe even two weeks ago, but for right now, I know without a doubt that I have to go with my gut instinct on this."

"And I even understand that, Holley. I just want you to think about your career and where it may be headed. You've been with us for eight years now. Just a few years ago, you began training Roman and Lance, among others, and helped turn them into some of the best insurance brokers this company has ever seen. Your talent as an analyst started here. I'm only trying to tell you as a boss and a friend, you shouldn't just throw away eight years for something that is uncertain. Forget about the money for a second and think about what if things don't work out with that company like you think. This is not just your life you have to consider, Holley. It's your daughter's life as well."

"Mrs. Andrews, please don't bring my daughter into this conversation. Crystal is my concern, and I have considered her life. What you possibly don't understand is that I'm moving on faith. Now, I know you may not want to hear that, but I know that my time is up with this company. You value me so much, but taking a look into the pay situation was too much to do. And why? Was it because you have plans of promoting my assistant—a little twenty-two-year-old white girl with less experience?"

No answer. The room housed so much silence I had to rethink my question to Mrs. Andrews. All I could hear was the low hum of other employees talking as they passed on the other side of the door. I continued with my mild interrogation. "Or, is it that you can't stand to see a dominant black woman with such authority given a prominent salary?"

Again, Mrs. Andrews could only stare at me in amazement. She had never seen this raving side of me before. Her silence only infuriated me more, however, I knew that forcing her to tell the truth wouldn't make me feel any differently than I did at the time, so I let her off the hook when I spoke again. "You don't have to say a word. I know the answer."

Finally, Mrs. Andrews found some nerve that would allow her to open her mouth to speak. "Holley, it's really not what you think. I apologize that management's actions have given you this false concept of racism and discrimination among us. To tell you the truth, I don't believe there are any members of management who are racist. I wish I could say something to make you understand."

Agitated from having to stand so long, I shifted my weight and posture so that Mrs. Andrews could tell I was not pleased with being in her presence. However, I had one more thing I needed to discuss before leaving her office. "You know what, Mrs. Andrews? While we're having this little talk now, I'd like to take this opportunity to make you aware of something else that has bothered me."

"Sure, go ahead, Holley."

"Oh, it's about what you've just called me. I've never liked it when members of upper management thought it was cute to call me Holley. My parents named me Holiday in honor of my precious birth, bright and early on Christmas Day, which is called a holiday, not Holley. Something as simple as getting my name right has been disrespected around here for years. Why I ever expected any of you to pay regards to any other concerns of mine, I don't know."

By this time my head and left hip looked as if they were trying to meet each other halfway. My right hand was stuck on my hip like it had been affixed with glue.

Mrs. Andrews cleared her throat before speaking. "Holiday, I can see that you're quite agitated with this company, but please just hear this one last thing before you go. I want you to know that I've always heard your concerns. It's just that I've never been in a position to do anything about them. It's not my decision alone, you know. Maybe you're right. If your time is truly up here, then everything that has happened isn't a mistake. And it's more evident to me now that your mind is made up, so I won't waste any more of your time. Holiday, I do wish you all the best."

"Thank you, Mrs. Andrews," I said as I reached to shake her hand.

Chapter Three
A Different Beginning

Not knowing what the future has in store can cause sure anxiety for some people. I basically told Mrs. Andrews I only feared fear itself, but being honest with myself is to admit my nerves were on edge, and I prayed nightly for all to go over well.

A few more weeks went by, then I moved on to the new company, Memphis Metro Life Insurance, which is where I'm currently employed. From the very beginning, it was everything I prayed it would be. I caught on to all the new procedures quickly, and I was even given a salary I didn't expect. After my probationary period, upper management realized my potential to add more positive developments to the company, so my salary was increased by an additional two and a half percent.

I knew that everything I had to endure with New Vet Life had begun to pay off with this new company. I applied those eight years of knowledge to Memphis Metro Life, and members of upper management were extremely impressed with my skills. I also had been introduced to the best staff for whom anyone could ask. They were all very cooperative and ready for a change. It didn't take much to convince them to trust whatever I suggested to help bring more success and bonuses to the company. It was hard to believe at first, but I soon got use to the idea that this company had far more to offer than where I'd previously been employed. There was no turning back for me.

Roman and Lance would call me up to see how I was doing from time to time, and I'd call them every once in a while to catch up on things in their lives. I missed them more than I ever knew I would. I'd seen and communicated with those guys daily for close to three years. I had no idea I'd long for the times I'd have to crack the whip and make them get a move on with their tasks. Lunch just wasn't the same with a different staff, but with things going so smoothly, I knew I would survive.

Crystal didn't care one way or the other about me changing jobs, but what could I expect from a daughter turning twelve? She only cared that I kept her in the latest fashions and that I kept up with her beauty shop appointments every two weeks. She did, however, want me to come in every evening to check her homework, put dinner on, and talk about what happened at school.

As for the weekends, Fridays were our nights. We would go skating or shopping or just do whatever. We had to choose Friday nights because on Saturdays Crystal wanted to be with her friends or with her cousins on her daddy's side. They'd go to the movies or spend time playing with the PlayStation 2.

I've found it even harder to get Crystal to listen to me the closer she got to her teenage years. I mostly tried to tell her what I know I should as a mother. As for anything else, I just watch her closely and make sure she's making wise decisions. When I see it's time for me to put my foot down, I will. Crystal can be a little stubborn like her daddy, but in the end she'll come to me and say, "Mommy, I'm sorry." Now that's the kind of kid I'm proud to be raising.

Chapter Four
Let's Call It a Date

It was about eight o'clock in the morning when my telephone rang, waking me up from a fantastic dream—Denzel Washington had left his wife for me, and we'd just cuddled close to engage in a passionate kiss. Damn! Anyway, I took Crystal over to spend the night with her cousins the night before. I thought that maybe it was her calling to ask me for something.

"Hello?"

"Hey, boo! What's going on?" a male voice on the other end said.

"Who is this?"

"Who you want it to be?"

My voice was groggy as I answered, "Well, it's pretty early in the morning, and it just so happens that I really don't feel like playing games. Now, if I don't know who you are in about three seconds, I'm going to hang up."

"Damn! It's Roman. What the hell is wrong with you today?"

"Oh. I'm sorry, Roman. I haven't gotten up yet. I was just half asleep, and I couldn't catch your voice."

"Well, who else calls you boo?" His voice was cheerful. I could tell that he felt like playing with me.

"Nobody, just you. I told you I was half asleep, but I'm up now. What's up, though?"

"I was just talking to Lance, and we were trying to figure out when you gon' let us take you out to dinner. It's Saturday, you know, and you don't have to work today. Tonight, you couldn't possibly be too tired to go out like you've been claiming lately, now could you?"

I sighed with a deep breath. "Where's Lance?"

"The negro better be at home. I just got off the phone with 'im."

"Call 'im on three-way for me, then."

"Aah-ight. Hold on." Roman knew he could tickle me with his intentional broken and southern dialect.

After about three rings, Lance picked up and answered in a low, seductive voice. "Yo, whaddup?"

I jumped on the opportunity. "You, baby boy!" Hearing him answer the phone in this manner had stimulated a reflex action to my brain.

"Now, you had me to call the man on three-way, and then you wanna start the conversation. How you gon' act, boo?" I could tell by Roman's harsh tone he was frustrated.

"Oh, my fault! Go 'head, Roman! My fault." I chuckled.

"Yeah, anyway what's up, man?" Roman replied.

"Oh, I see you got Holiday on the phone, huh?" Lance asked.

"Yeah. She ain't actin' right, though, man."

"Is that right? Well give me a short synopsis on her."

"I can't really call it, man. I think things are probably to the extent of her missing me bustin' her upside her head, or something. Is that what's wrong with you, boo?"

"Oh no, you didn't go there. Don't even play with me like that, Roman!" The guys laughed. "Y'all just don't know. I've got real issues with those type of words. You need to take that back, Roman."

The guys' laughter ended abruptly as they could tell my tone was serious. "My bad, Holiday. You know I'm just talking," Roman said.

"Mm-hmm," I responded matter-of-factly.

"Holiday, what's up with ya? If you scared to go out with us, baby girl, just say so. We'll cut you some slack," Lance insisted.

"You guys are a trip! What do you have up your sleeves? Somebody's got something planned, resorting to trickery in order to get me to go out with you."

"Now you trippin'! What even causes you to make such a crazy accusation?" Roman asked with agitation.

"Well I know I'm not stupid. Y'all trying to pull some reverse psychology to get me out? Like I said, what do you have up your sleeves?"

"Holiday, we've been calling you for a year now trying to get you to kick it with us, and you keep coming up with excuses. Tell her, Lance."

I didn't give Lance a chance to respond. "It hasn't been no damn year! Stop your lying, please! And Lance doesn't have to tell me anything. You keep trying to make me look bad. I haven't been making excuses. Shoot, I've been tired. What's wrong with that?"

"Nothing. If you think being a wallflower is okay, then we'll accept that. Won't we, Lance?" Roman asked.

"See, there you go again with that reverse psychology crap. If I'm a wallflower, then it ought not to make you any difference, seeing how I would be the opposite of anyone you'd like to hang out with. Roman, I bet your ass was a psychology major in college, weren't you?"

"Mmm, no comment."

"Just what I thought. I knew you were 'cause you're good at that shit. And guess what? I *am* going to take you up on your offer. What time do you want me to be ready? And, where are we going anyway?"

"Whoa, one question at a time, baby girl. We haven't decided where yet. We weren't even sure we were going to be kickin' it anywhere tonight," Lance responded.

"So I was the deciding factor, huh?"

"That's right. We had to be sure you weren't gonna be scared this time," Roman responded jokingly.

"*Ha ha ha!* Enough with the scared jokes, Roman. I'm about to prove to both of you I'm not afraid of you. Okay?"

"Where're your fine friends. You could invite somebody along, you know?"

I wasn't surprised at Roman's suggestion.

"Uhn-uhn, Roman! I thought this time out was for us old pals to be kickin' it. I didn't know you were just using me to get to my friends."

"Girl, shut up! You know I don't even know your friends."

"Yeah, and I got your girl! You need to quit playing and figure out someplace for us to go tonight." It had become obvious that Roman wasn't going to give up on trying to aggravate me.

"Umph, now ain't that something? You don't seem to mind when Lance calls you baby girl. What's up with that?"

"That's different, and it doesn't concern you. Now hurry up and think of somewhere for us to go before I change my mind for real."

We all laughed at my cynicism. "Where's Crystal?" Lance asked.

"She's spending the weekend over to Shaundra's, her cousin on her daddy's side."

"Then I know it's on and poppin'!" Roman said.

"Boy, please. It ain't that *on*. I don't indulge in those type of parties," I exclaimed to Roman to make certain he knew I meant it.

"Mm-hmm, and I got your boy, too." I'll admit, he got me back on that one.

"Roman, man, don't forget Holiday has a curfew," Lance said, trying to get me riled up again.

"Whatever! We'll see," I responded.

"Have you been to The Peabody Place yet, Holiday?" Lance asked.

"Now you know I haven't been anywhere."

"I think we should go there. That place has plenty of things to do. There's Jillian's, which has an all-adult atmosphere after ten. There are places where we can bowl, dance, or just chill down there if we want. Oh, and when Isaac Hayes's place is open, The Peabody Place is the best spot in Memphis! The whole facility seems to be jumping with people. I just can't remember what else to mention right now. We won't get to do it all tonight anyway."

"Lance, don't forget there's a movie cinema there,

too. And if any of that doesn't sound enticing enough or float your boat, once we get down there, then we could head one block over to Beale Street. I'm sure that between the two places, we'll find something to do," Roman informed us.

"Oh, you know what? I just remembered, man, there's a place on North Main Street called Precious Cargo Coffeehouse. It's one of those joints with live music and open mic nights for poetry and everything. Every time I've gone, the atmosphere has been extremely friendly. I'm certain you'll like the jazz you'll hear there, Holiday. The band Cry Out is the best I've heard anywhere lately. The walls are covered with some wonderful original artwork, and I'm telling you, you'll experience that special ethnic vibe you love so much, baby girl. Roman, did you get to check that out when you were downtown last?"

"Naw, man, but that's cool, though. It sounds like something you'd have to go to the lower east side of Manhattan to experience. So, it has one of those urbane atmospheres, huh? I think we'll enjoy it. What about you, Holiday? I know you get down with jazz."

"You know I do. Don't tell me any more. Shoot, I'm getting excited."

"Ya shoulda been excited a long time ago," Roman said, using his playful voice once again. The guys were having too much fun trying my patience it seemed.

My hormones were unbalanced, and it was getting more difficult not letting it show. "For what, Roman? I think you're lying anyway. I believe you're taking me to your designated spot, the place where you play those little mind games with all of your women. I wouldn't be surprised one bit if the managers and everybody there knows you."

Roman spoke in a mild baby tone as if I had hurt his feelings. "Ooooh, now that's cold. That wasn't nice to say at all, Holiday. Do you really believe that?"

"Please, negro, your feelings aren't hurt. If anything's wrong with you, it's just that you're stunned by the fact that I know the true you, player. Now tell the truth and shame the devil."

"You ain't ever told a lie. The fact remains, I am a player playah," Roman responded as if that status was the best in the world to hold.

"Listen at him, Lance. He's real proud of it, too."

"Hey, don't hate the player, hate the game," Roman went on to say.

"Save it, player! That saying went out of style just after your wave nouveau. Now what time are we meeting?" I knew that making a false reference about his good hair would hit him hard, so I shot a question at the end to lighten the blow.

My question didn't get answered right away. Lance was too busy cracking up at the wave nouveau thing, and Roman was busy trying to talk over Lance's laughter, explaining that he'd never had any type of chemicals in his hair.

I started to feel bad for cracking on him like that, so I apologized, "Wait, wait, wait. I'm sorry, Roman. You know I'm only teasing you."

"Yeah, I was about to say, as much as you've stuck your fingers in my hair, passing by my chair at work, you ain't ever felt grease in this head!"

I had to cut his rambling short, or else sit and listen to him go on and on. "I know. I know, now give me the name of the place where we'll be meeting tonight, please." This was good thinking on my part 'cause Roman sounded as if he was going to start his little fit of how he'd come to be born with this naturally good hair.

"Meeting? Baby girl, it's too dangerous out there for you to drive downtown at night by yourself. Not to mention you'll have to find parking and walk to meet us. Naw, just let me pick you up around eight o'clock tonight," Lance stated, being the gentleman I knew he'd be.

"Shiiitt, in that case you can pick me up at seven-thirty then," Roman said.

"Alright, man," Lance said as we all laughed.

"So, I'll see you guys tonight." I was so enthused. I was about to prepare for a night on the town!

Chapter Five
Prove It to Whom?

I felt like a high school girl getting ready for a first date, except this was more like a double date, minus one female. I immediately jumped out of bed and went straight to the closet to find something to wear. I had some trouble picking the perfect outfit, so I went on a spree of talking to and answering myself.

"Okay, Holiday, what about this one?"

"No, not sexy enough."

"Well, what about this dress?"

"It's not too flashy, not too sexy, but the color is wrong, though. Come on now, Holiday. I know you've got something in this closet you've forgotten about that's going to make the guys wonder what they've missed all this time."

I found my outfit. It was an intriguingly sexy, body-fitting dress. It was one of those little black numbers that said, "watch out now!" to a man's imagination without being too suggestive. I thought it complemented my satin brown complexion as well. I was pleased with my selection, so I jumped back into bed. It was still early, and I had all day to do nothing.

I found myself just lying there, though, daydreaming about what the night would be like and how the guys would react to me in a night scene environment. I imagined Roman would be getting up close all night, filling my sinuses joyfully with his Burberry cologne. I imagined Lance would be winking and flashing me that gorgeous smile just after licking his lips and repeatedly telling me how stunning I look in my made-for-me-only dress.

Damn! Thinking of those men had me sooooo horny. I lay there contemplating pulling out the silver bullet. My bullet was a small toy, but quite capable of giving me ultimate satisfaction. I slid my hand into my panties to discover a heap of wetness. My mind raced with thoughts of Lance's face between my thighs, sucking me dry. I quickly got out of bed and opened the nightstand drawer. After retrieving the bullet, I turned it on. At first there was a low vibration, and then there was nothing. My sex toy had died on me. I could kick myself for not purchasing a new pack of batteries the last time I was at Wal-Mart. Now I was truly in need because I had never conquered masturbation with my own hands before, and I wasn't about to try.

I went into the bathroom, washed my hands, and started the shower, but then my phone rang. I turned the water off and managed to answer the call on the fourth ring.

"Hello?"

"Hey, girl. It's Erika. What's going on?"

I met Erika Peebles several years ago while attending Lemoyne Owen College here in Memphis. Although we had different majors, we managed to become friends because we seemed to end up in the library at the same time when papers were due. One day we noticed the coincidence and started a discussion. In doing so, we learned we had a lot in common, so we decided to keep in touch. This turned out to be good for me 'cause I didn't know anybody, and Erika knew everybody. She also became a shoulder for me to cry on about Crystal's father, Darius. Up until I'd met her, I would only call his kin people here in Memphis and whine to them about the grief Darius caused me. I was blessed to have Erika be there for me.

"Girl, you won't believe what I'm going to do tonight!" The excitement in my voice could've easily made Erika think I was about to pick up a lottery check.

"What?"

"Remember me talking about my ex-coworkers, Roman and Lance?"

"Yeah, the fine ones. Oh yeah, and Roman attended Lemoyne Owen when we were there, right?"

"Uh-huh, but he graduated before us, remember? Anyway, they just called and asked me to go out with them tonight. We're going to Precious Cargo downtown on North Main Street."

"Girl, you're lying! You're going with both of them?"

"Yes. What's up?"

"Nothing, but can I go? I think you need some help!" Erika said, laughing.

"No, trust me, I don't need help. I got this! Anyway, I kind of told them I wanted this to be an old pals going out 'cause we missed each other kind of thing."

"Oh, sure! Whatever! Lucky bitch!" Erika said teasingly.

"Luck doesn't have anything to do with it, sweetie."

"Really? Well what's the operative word needing to be used here?"

"Skills! Try the word *skills* 'cause I don't have luck, I have skills!"

"Yeah, alright, skills." Erika laughed a little harder than before.

"No, I'm just playing, girl. Maybe next time I'll invite you to come along. I'm sure Roman wouldn't mind that."

"Yeah, I forgot you told me he's the whore of the two."

"Erika, he's proud of it, too. We just got through discussing it on the phone. He's so smooth that I believe women just somehow overlook his whorish flaws."

"I don't know how, Holiday. I couldn't overlook them. I want my man for myself."

"But Erika, those women don't appear to know what he does."

"Well, he must only mess with really dumb women then. He couldn't pull that crap over on me."

"On me either, Erika. I don't care how fine he is, if he plays around, he's got to go. I've let many go before, and after all that Crystal's father put me through, if I could let him go, I can let any man go. I share a bond with Darius. Crystal is that bond, but if I'm not willing to put up with his crap, then there's nothing that I'm willing to take off another man, period."

"I feel you, girl. You don't have to. I know Darius must hate at this very moment that he lost you."

"Erika, he called the other day. I don't know, but he must've been drunk or something. He says he's been sober for ten months now, but anyway, he wanted to reminisce. I wasn't feeling him. I don't need a trip down memory lane. It isn't the same for me as it is for him. He's the reason I live in Memphis right now. He had me following him down here, with a promise of marriage and being a family man. I can't believe that I trusted him. I'm actually offended that he'd even call me trying to reminisce. I'm still trying to get past all the beatings and all the cheatings, all the drinking and all the lack of respect, period. Not to mention the fact that the bad outweighed the good by ninety percent. If it weren't for me talking to Crystal and letting her know that Darius had a problem, I don't know if she would've been able to forgive him. I'm happy she loves her father in spite of the difficult times we've experienced, and I'm working on leaving all of that in the past, too. But forgiving him doesn't mean that I have to go back to him. No, my sista! I am lovin' the distance between me and that man!"

"But Holiday, you have to remember, you're the reason for you and Crystal being in that predicament for so long. A man will only do what you'll allow him to. If you had gone on when I was telling you to, some of the mental anguish that Crystal had to endure could've been avoided."

"Erika, it's easier said than done. I didn't understand my momma putting up with my daddy, either, and then I had to walk a mile in her shoes. My baby was just like me. She loved her daddy regardless of what was going on between him and me. And although I lived every day afraid for my mother's life, I, also, feared that if we left my father, I'd never see him again."

"You shouldn't've wanted to see him again!"

"Erika, that's not fair for you to say. He was brutal to her, but he never laid a hand on me. It wasn't until I was about twelve years old that I learned my mother felt helpless, and that she couldn't leave my father. Despite my talking to her and trying to convince her we'd be all right if we left, she didn't want to leave. She didn't like the abuse, but she also felt that deep down, he loved her."

Erika's background was different from mine. Her mother was raised to believe that she didn't need a man to define her, so when her father became abusive, they fled from him. Erika believes that since her mother was able to successfully get away from an abusive marriage and raise three young children on her own, that it should be just as simple for all women.

"Erika, in a lot of ways I can see I'm like my mother. I've allowed far too much abuse to go on in my life, and just as Momma didn't have very many family members in Charlotte, I didn't know anyone in Memphis except Darius's folks, until I met you."

"Yeah, but Holiday, don't start making excuses. You know better than I do how it feels to see your mother being abused. True, you got out, but Crystal had seen far more than a little girl her age should've by the time you left."

"I know, but, Erika, we all make mistakes. The first one was trying to stay and make that nigga love me."

"Oh, I give you your props, though, my sista. You're a strong woman. At least you haven't let any of those rough times in your childhood and the no-good-ass men you've dealt with break you. After leaving your family behind in North Carolina to follow Darius, you kept your head up and finished school. I definitely commend you."

"Thanks, girlfriend, but I have to wonder, what's next? I'm still young, you know, and I do want some affection from time to time."

"And I know that's right! Keep living. We'll get the right man for us someday. Hey, I don't mean to change the subject, but what are you wearing tonight? " Erika asked abruptly.

"Check this out. I pulled out this sleek little black dress I've never worn before. I believe you were with me when I bought it about a year ago. I think it's time to pull it out and put it on now."

"Mmhmm, I know you do. What are you trying to do, gain the attention of one of them, or both of them? 'cause I'm gonna tell you something, heifer, with that body of yours that I despise so much, one of them is going to holla if not both of them."

"Oh, girl, stop!"

"No, I won't stop. You know you're trying to be slick, showing off those long legs and perfect figure with the watch-me-work-it-now booty in that dress. I remember seeing how great you looked when you tried it on at the store."

"Erika, I'm not trying to catch either one of those men for myself. They aren't right for me, and I'm hardly their type. I do have to confess though that I'm extremely attracted to them, but I don't have to worry about them wanting me."

"Yeah, but my sista, with that dress on, you'll be their type tonight. And let's talk about that Pocahontaslooking hair of yours, which attracts the hands and fingers of both men and women. Are you going to wear it down tonight?"

"Yes, I think so. The guys have never seen me with my hair down. I just want them to see that I do have it going on, you know. They've never seen me outside of work in attire for partying, either. This feels like sort of a first-impression thing for me. Once they've seen me in my club wear, I won't have to prove anything to them anymore."

"Well, alright. You just be careful tonight. It's not like you're use to any of this."

"I know that's right. I might get out tonight and lose my mind or something."

"You know what I mean, Holiday. No matter how you try to hide it, you're missing some type of male companionship in your life. From what you tell me about these guys, they're good-looking, they're hot, they're smooth talkers, and you haven't been with a man in a while now. I've seen it happen before with women. They'll have enough drinks to where all is right in the world. You don't want to end up sacrificing the friendship with them for one night of pleasure, do you?"

"You really feel like you need to have this talk with me?"

"No, but you know me, I'm always trying to be somebody's momma, sister, friend, and all that stuff." We laughed.

"Well, Rome is the one who's slick, but believe me when I tell you I'm not his type. As for Lance, he's a gentleman."

"Girl, aren't these the same two men you were telling me call you boo and baby girl?"

At this point I felt kind of ashamed 'cause I realized that answering Erika would just further prove her argument about Roman and Lance being crafty when it comes to women. Reluctantly I said, "Yeah, but it's because they think of me like a sister."

"See, that's the mentality I'm talking about. Holiday, you're one of the smartest women I know, but right now you're being very naïve. Calling you pet names like that makes them smooth and slick talkers. Both of them."

"Okay, I can see what you're saying. I'll be careful. I'll tell you what, when I get back home, I'll just give you a holler."

"That'll be fine. Be sure to have enough fun for me, though," Erika said.

After hanging up with Erika, instead of showering, I decided to go for a run downtown on the riverwalk, my favorite location. I thought a lot about the things Erika said. She made a lot of sense, but this was my night. I figured I'd try to set something up later so that Erika could hang out with the guys and me. She would see then why I value these men as friends. Plus, despite what she said about desiring to have a body like mine, Erika had very few flaws with her own. I knew for a fact she was Roman's type. He liked his women overly exaggerated with clothes, hair, and makeup. Erika's a beautiful light-skinned black woman. She's high maintenance, but that's her choice. We just differed in that way when it comes to personalities. I like nice clothes, but they don't have to be Donna Karan or Chanel the way Erika's fashions are.

My run was just what I needed to get my day pumped up. After a long, hot shower, I took off in my snow-white Mercedes Benz to enjoy more of the sunshine. On the ride out, I couldn't help but think of how deserving I was of a good time. I didn't have anything else planned, and Crystal was away; therefore, I didn't need a baby-sitter. It couldn't have been more perfect!

Chapter Six

How Ya Like Me Now?

Nervousness caused me to have to fix myself a couple of drinks before the guys came to pick me up. They showed up on time, and I was ecstatic when the doorbell rang. When I opened the door, to my surprise, I was overdressed. The guys had on pullover sweaters and dark khakis.

"Maybe we should've discussed the dress code," I said timidly and full of embarrassment.

"No, Holiday, you look great!" Lance tried to reassure me.

"No, Lance, you're going to have me stepping out of here looking like a fool."

"How so?" Roman asked.

"Because! I'm overdressed!"

"And so, you think you're going to look like a fool?" Lance asked with a puzzled look.

"Yes! I'm going to change."

"No, Holiday, please don't! You look stunning, and I would be honored if you would accompany us tonight dressed to kill." Roman spoke with a smirk on his face, giving me puppy-dog eyes.

"I don't know. I just wish you guys would've told me the dress code."

Then Roman replied in his convincing baritone voice, "I'm sure there'll be people dressed from one extreme to the other, so stop being self-conscious. I don't care one way or the other what anyone else has on anyway. They're not out with me tonight. You are."

"Now, did you hear that? Let's go! I can hardly wait." Lance gave me a wink as he reached out to grab my hand.

Roman drove, and I sat in the front while Lance sat in the back. When we arrived at Precious Cargo, I thought for a split second that with Roman being the driver, he'd be the one to open my car door. I thought wrong. I pretended to be looking for something in my purse, hoping that he'd come around to my side of the car and open my door. Lance was still inside of the car as well, putting on his jacket. I looked through the driver side window and observed Roman standing in place, looking down at himself, and brushing off his jacket. That was my clue that he wasn't going to be a gentleman as I had hoped. Lance proceeded to get out of the car, so I closed my purse and reached for the latch on the door. Just as I started to open it, I felt it pull away from me. It was Lance. How could I have expected anything different? After all, Lance was the one who opened the door so I could get into the car. I shouldn't have expected Roman to be anything different than he'd always been.

"Look at downtown Memphis! Memphis is stepping up." I was totally amazed at my new hometown.

"Yes, I'll give it that. Memphis was pretty much a do-nothing town until Precious Cargo Coffeehouse opened here near The Pyramid," Lance said, glancing at the building.

"I can't believe the crowd that's lined up to go inside the building," I responded.

"And why not? Once people visit this place, they tend to go and recommend it to others. That's how I found out about it. You know, I think with the opening of The Peabody Place and Precious Cargo being downtown, Memphis is about to be on the map!" Lance gave one loud clap of his hands and nodded at the improvements as he looked around.

"So what do you guys think about taking a walk around downtown first? Or, are you both ready to get in line?" Roman didn't seem too anxious to go inside.

"Oh, we can go ahead and get in line," I said. I had become a little nervous about what the atmosphere would be like. I just wanted to get in there and see if I liked it, and if not there would still be time to do something else.

It didn't take us very long to get up to the front of the line, though. It seemed to have moved pretty quickly. Had it not, I wouldn't have minded. The night air was so beautiful. It was a warm, but breezy August night. I started to have second thoughts about taking that walk around downtown first. But, since we had gone so far up in the line, I didn't bother to mention it to the guys.

While waiting to get in, I noticed the dress of the

other people standing outside. Everyone was in casual bar attire. Some women had on low-rise pants and cute little fitted tops. Some even had on a simple blouse, Capripants, and sandals. I started to worry, but I played it off with the guys and just kept talking. I could hear the band while we stood outside in the line. The smooth mellow jazz tones flowed right outside, adding to everyone's excitement. I had become very anxious to get in and have a seat. The line started to move a little faster, and then we were in.

"Oh my goodness. I *am* overdressed. Look at these people in here. No one is dressed for a night on the town! Unh-unh, I'm ready to go."

"Holiday, so what, these people aren't dressed up. We're first-timers. We couldn't have known the dress code without coming here first," Roman said.

"Lance has been here before! Or was that you, Roman, who said you've been here before?"

"Holiday, I've never been here." Although my tone was elevated and tense, Roman still responded cool and collected.

"I believe you have, Roman, with your lying ass!"

"Whoa, whoa, whoa! Why all the hostility?" Lance asked with a look of surprise.

"Because I'm not comfortable, Lance. Please, let's leave."

"Holiday, it was me who said that I'd been here before. We didn't know that you were intending on dressing so beautifully, but once you opened the door, you looked breathtaking, and we didn't want you to change. Just forgive us this time and try to relax. I promise you're going to have a great time."

When a man responds to your antagonism so

calmly, you have no choice but to just straighten up. "Alright, I'll try. And I'm sorry for venting at you, Roman."

Roman looked at me for a few seconds then nodded before responding. "Just relax, okay?"

"Okay. We can go on and get a table."

We found a table in an excellent spot. We could see the jazz band perfectly from where we sat. The hosts had begun taking requests from the guests to participate in the open mic sessions. I wanted to make a move to the mic, but I hadn't mellowed enough yet. I knew it would only be a matter of time though.

Chapter Seven
Mic Check

"So, what do you want to drink?" Lance asked me.

"I think I'll have a margarita," I said, going in my purse for some money.

"Well, I'm going over to the bar and get our drinks 'cause from the looks of it, it's going to be a minute before we can get a waitress over here," Lance said as he pushed away my hand, which was extended with money in it.

"Okay, well hey, man, you get this round and I'll get the next round," Roman replied.

"Oh, that'll work," Lance said. "Cool. You know what I drink. Right, man?"

"Oh, no doubt. No doubt. I'll be back shortly. You just make sure that Holiday doesn't get too bored before I get back."

"You don't have to tell me anything. I got this," Roman said, smiling at me as Lance walked over toward the bar.

"Oh, really?"

"Yes, really," Roman replied.

"So, what do you drink?"

"I drink what every man of the career world should be drinking."

"And, what's that?"

"Bourbon and Coke."

"Bourbon and Coke? That's what today's career man should be drinking?"

"Absolutely."

"Why?" I asked with one eyebrow raised. I had never heard anyone state this before.

"It's a drink that soothes a man's mind and enables his body to mellow. Men of today are generally overworked, so bourbon is the answer to chilling out. Unfortunately, I only chill out on my off days." He laughed.

"You know what? I think you've been watching a little bit too much television. Now which one of your favorite movies did you hear that on?" I laughed.

"I didn't hear that on television or anywhere else. I just know how the drink makes me feel. I believe it's the solution for any man to have a calming evening."

"Well, you should've just said that at first. It makes more sense than what you said about today's career man being overworked." We both shared a laugh that time. "Man, Roman, I just keep feeling like people are staring over here at us."

"Holiday, boo, please try to relax. People are staring over here, but it's not for the reasons you're thinking. We're a few new faces to this spot, and you happen to be with two of the finest men Memphis has to offer. Why else would everyone be looking over here? Huh, boo?"

"I guess I'll agree with that. Just give me a little time to warm up to this place. I'll be all right."

"I know you'll be all right. Holiday, boo, you're with me. I'm gonna make sure you're all right every time you're with me," Roman said in a sexy, yet convincing tone.

"Well, that sounds promising." I did like the sound of it coming from him.

"And, believe that it is," he said.

"So how many is it now, Roman?" I began to be inquisitive after talk of him keeping me happy for the night.

"How many what?"

"Women. How many do you juggle now? You know it's been a while since we last had this conversation, and I'm just playing catch-up."

"Let's put it this way, I still don't have anyone to call my own."

"No, shit? Roman, tell me something I don't know. Or, better yet, try answering me. Was the question too hard for you or something?"

"You know, I've seen a lot of feistiness in you tonight. I think I like it. It goes extremely well with that little sexy black number you're wearing."

"Forget it, Rome. Forget I asked. I see you're not going to answer me, but you could've told me it was none of my business, you know."

"Yeah, I think I like it with that little sexy black number. And by the way, you should call me Rome more often. You just made it sound so damn good coming out of your mouth."

"And you're so full of . . . well, never mind. I said that I was going to chill out, and I am."

"That's right. We're going to enjoy this night.

There's no telling when you're coming back out with us again."

"Oh, shut up. I just might be back out next weekend."

"Oh yeah, which day?"

"Don't be trying to make me commit to a day, Roman."

"You said it, not me."

"I was thinking about next Saturday because my girlfriend Erika wanted to come along tonight, but I kinda told her that it was just an old friends night out."

"You told her right, but she's welcomed to come along next weekend if we decide to go out again."

"I'm sure you'll be thrilled to have her come along."

"Stop that! See, there you go again. You just can't help it, huh? It's just in you to keep throwing my mannish ways in my face, right?"

"Yeah. I guess you've got a point, Roman. When I'm around my pastor, I make constant mentioning of the Bible. When I'm around you I tend to think of male-whorish topics. Yeah, I can see what you mean about it's just in me." I smiled on the inside, watching for steam out of the top of Roman's head.

Roman played cool. "I see you're not going to be so easy to deal with tonight, but I can handle the pressure."

"Okay, okay, I'm through. I only wanted to fan some flames your way for a minute, but I can see I didn't succeed. Maybe I'll just be nice from here on out."

I sat there and just waited on Roman to spark up the next conversation. I felt kind of bad about having such a raw attitude for no real reason. Erika's comments of being careful forced me to put my guard up way too high. There was brief silence then before we knew it, Roman and I were back to laughing and having good conversation.

"Whoa, do you hear this saxophonist? He's remarkable. I've got to find out who he is," Roman said.

"Yes, he is outstanding. I guess I've been missing out on a lot, huh?"

"Well, I guess that includes me, too, Holiday. I've never been to this place before, contrary to what you believe."

"I don't know. Maybe I shouldn't have said those things about you. I apologize for offending you, Roman."

"No, apology needed," he replied, gazing into my eyes.

"Thanks," I replied, gazing right back.

I was really caught up in that moment. This man had so much sex appeal, and he seemed to know all the right things to say. Erika said letting one of these men get to me could happen. She was right 'cause I was feeling something inside of me I hadn't felt in a very long time. The strange part about having this feeling was the fact that I hadn't had anything to drink. I knew then that I my guard couldn't be let down. Roman was starting to really turn me on with his suaveness. I was so relieved when Lance returned with our drinks.

"So, what've I missed?" Lance asked.

"Man, Holiday claims she's going out with us again next Saturday," Roman told Lance.

"Damn, man, you *are* good! How long was I gone?

Shit! I wanted to take part in showing you a good time, too, Holiday. I guess it took me too long to get the drinks, huh?" Lance said jokingly.

"Stop! No, I really haven't committed to a day. I only said that I was thinking about it. I have a girl-friend that I'd like for you guys to meet."

"Is she as fine as you?" Lance asked.

"I think you'll like her."

"Is she as intelligent as you? What about her charisma? You two are friends. She's got to have the same appeal as you," Roman said.

"Well I'd say so."

"Baby girl, does she have it goin' on as half as much as you do?" Lance asked.

"I think you'll like her. What's up with this line of questioning? And Roman, you never seemed to care about any of those things with women before. Intelligence? Charisma? What's up with that?"

Roman tilted his head to the right, raised his left eyebrow then answered, "Come on, boo. Answer the man straight up. You know the answers to these questions. Women judge each other all the time. Now, tell us what's really going on with this friend of yours."

"I said I think you'll like her. Now, let's just enjoy the music and the poetry that's about to come up next."

"Don't you just love this side of her? We didn't get it when she was our boss," Roman stated to Lance.

"Yeah, I think I do like it. It fits her whole persona tonight," Lance answered.

"That's what I said. See, Holiday, if the two of us are saying the same thing, there must be some kind of truth to it."

"Oh, and so that makes it the Gospel 'cause it's

coming out of the two of your mouths? Is that what you want me to think, Rome?" I asked.

"Man, you sure are hard on a brotha, but did you just hear how sweet she called my name?" Roman asked Lance.

"It's all good though, boo," I responded matter-of-factly.

"I think you may've met your match, Roman," Lance said, laughing.

Roman leaned over to get closer in my face before he responded, "I believe you just might have a point there, Lance. I'm starting to think so myself."

The moment he leaned over and spoke, I sort of backed away because I wasn't sure what he was trying to prove with this move. However, I managed to get a whiff of his breath with that bourbon on it, and surprisingly, it turned me on. Something about that smell was very sexy and masculine. I even had thoughts of kissing him. It sounds crazy, but it was one of those moments that one would have to actually be me in order to understand it. I couldn't speak just then; I had too many thoughts playing in my mind, and if I had spoken, I'm sure I would've told on myself. I managed to play it off with a half smile, one in which I didn't have to show any teeth, but just sort of spread my lips in an upward motion to show a pleasant approval. I noticed Roman and Lance staring at my lips. I imagine they were only admiring my new shade of lipstick, Raspberry Frost.

"Boy, this music is right on time tonight," Lance said.

"I know. We talked about that while you were gone. That man on the sax has some talent, doesn't he?" I asked.

"The whole band does. I think this is definitely going to be my new spot," Lance replied just before taking another sip of his drink. Roman wasn't playing around with his either.

"Hey, I tell you what. I'm about half done with this one, and I still don't see a waitress trying to make her way over here," Roman said, looking around the club.

"Would you like for me to go and find one?" I offered.

"No. I see one I'm going to beckon. Excuse me, miss, do you know who's supposed to be waiting our table?" Roman asked a waitress walking past our table.

"Yes, but, she's very tied up at the moment. We're running around here like crazy women, trying to get caught up. I'll let her know that you're ready to order, but I think it'll be a few minutes before she'll be able to make her way over here," the waitress said.

"Well, we're just needing to order more drinks right now. Do you think I should just go over to the bar and order?" Roman asked.

"Yes, sir. Most of our customers are ordering the drinks at the bar 'cause of the mad rush of people in here tonight. I do apologize, and I'll still let her know you've been waiting," the waitress responded before walking away.

"So, I guess you heard that. Are you extremely hungry, Holiday?" Lance asked.

"No, I'm fine. I wasn't sure what kind of place this was, so I ate before I left. I just really wanted to come and drink and maybe dance."

"Well, I'm fine right now, too. I can wait to eat," Lance said.

"Okay. I'll just go on over to the bar and get another round of drinks ready. I'd like to have them sitting here, waiting, once we finish these," Roman said as he got up from the table.

"Baby girl, I've *got* to go find the restroom. Will you be okay?" Lance asked as he stood to leave the table.

"Sure. I'll be fine."

I sat there for about two minutes thinking to myself that the night wasn't so bad after all. The margarita wasn't bad, either. The lyricists that I'd heard so far were excellent, and everything just had me wedged into the moment. The next time a staff member came around with the clipboard to sign up for open mic, I was really feeling it. I signed up before the guys came back to the table.

"Lance, I still can't believe you left this beautiful woman at the table all by herself," Roman said when they returned.

"Man, you're drinking bourbon and Coke just like I am. I know you know when it's time to go, *it's time to go*!" Lance responded making fun right back.

"Yeah, I do know! I'm just trippin', having a little fun, that's all." Roman laughed.

"So, Holiday, I see you over there groovin' with the music. That margarita must be all right 'cause you've mellowed out big time, baby girl," Lance said.

"You ain't lying. I feel goooood."

"How good are you feeling?" Roman asked.

This time I tilted my head to the side and raised one eyebrow before responding. "Not that good, doggonit!"

"See, look at you. Get your mind out of the gutter. That's not what I meant, boo. I'm just saying, are you relaxed?" Roman asked, putting his mellow baritone voice on me.

"Yeah, and you're going to see how relaxed just in a minute."

Roman and Lance both looked at each other in wonder. I smiled and kept sipping on my margarita. A few moments later it happened. The emcee stepped to the microphone.

"Now we've been hearing and seeing a lot of the same faces. Well, guess what? We have a newcomer to the mic, and she's going by the name of Lady Day. Come on, show some love for Lady Day, y'all!" the emcee announced.

The band kicked off playing a smooth, mellow jazz tune. Everyone, including Roman and Lance, were applauding and looking around for Lady Day. I took another sip of my margarita, and I proceeded to get up from the table. Roman and Lance looked at me, taken aback.

"How's everyone doing tonight?" I asked, upon grabbing the mic. The audience responded cheerfully. "All right? Well first of all, I want y'all to overlook my dress 'cause I'm not here to impress. Tonight, I've been inspired with a burning desire to put your hearts on three-alarm fire. Now would that be all right? I said would that be all right?" The crowd applauded enthusiastically. "Good! Now I wrote this piece about a year ago with the intention of never letting anyone hear it, but I feel compelled to share it with you tonight. It's called 'Dream Motion'. And it goes something like this . . ." Before I started, I looked at the band to let them know to pump up the melody.

I found myself staring at the wall, when up popped a
*   photo play of each and every day,*

Of my life.
Moving in sloooow moootion.
I couldn't move, I sat so amazed, and so I gazed
At this enormous screen with a movie scene,
And yes it seemed
Like an Oscar-winning act, when it was really a fact
Of my whole existence just like that.
It played before me, continuing to scorn me, but what
    could I do?
This was my life, and in a daydream, too.
Now, while I'm glaring, there's so much comparing
Of my life to the big silver screen,
If you know what I mean.
Well, let me break it down for ya.
While I play the main character, my family and com-
    rades complete the cast.
Of course, there are villains—you don't even have to
    ask.
Although the plot is still uncertain, the climax is
    explicit for all.
The main character—remember me—suffers from a
    number of rises and falls.
For what I'm gon' share with you next, I really hope you
    get my drift.
'Cause this is something serious, and I know everyone
    needs a whiff.

This message is, I'd fall down, but praise God, I'd get
    up
My calamities in this show were so depressing, I'd had
    enough!
I sat there with tears welling in my eyes, I looked up to
    the Heavens
And yelled, "Father, please hear my cries."

*I immediately fell to my knees 'cause I was weakened by
    my pleas.*
*I asked the Mighty Master on High, "Lord, help me ac-
    cept your deed."*
*When I arose from my moment in prayer, indeed the vi-
    sion was still there,*
*But I didn't let this discourage me 'cause He knows my
    every care.*
So, check this out!
*Now, I know you can't pause a motion picture, looking
    at it on the big screen,*
*But I'd seen far too much, and after all, this was my
    daydream.*
I pressed rewind and fast-forward as much as I needed,
*I edited that picture down to the last glitch, until I suc-
    ceeded.*
You should've seen me on top.
*My elevation of appellation called for concentration for
    domination 'cause*
My designation was messing with my individuality.
Naw, not really!
*It was just all still a part of my illusion, and now I'm
    coming to the conclusion,*
*That this flick, is this week's pick, and it gets four stars
    and two thumbs up!*

The crowd went wild. You would've thought I was
some kind of celebrity or something. I never thought
that putting that poem to jazz would make it so much
more momentous. I received a standing ovation, and
Roman and Lance rose to their feet as well, receiving
me back at our table with hugs and kisses. I really
thought I had it going on then. All the women in the
whole place saw these two strikingly attractive men
hug and kiss me on both my cheeks. We took our

seats, and the emcee went on to compliment me further. I looked over at Lance. He sat there gazing at me with astonishment. Roman seemed flabbergasted as well. I felt so on top of things. I had managed to show them another side of me that they'd never known. Not only that, but I'd succeeded in leaving them with nothing but admiration for me.

We sat and listened a little while longer, then we danced. Lance and Roman really went out of their way to make me feel good that night. They danced with me one at a time, as well as together. Dancing with both of them at the same time was my favorite part of the night. I could feel envious eyes on me while we danced.

Precious Cargo turned out to be the best place to go to relieve myself of some unwanted stress. The owner had done well with creating a site for local talented artists to openly express themselves. I couldn't wait to run tell somebody else I knew about my whole enjoyable experience there.

The night started growing cold, and we didn't want it to end. I suggested to the guys that we go back to my place and have one more drink then call it a night. They agreed, and we headed out of Precious Cargo. It didn't seem to take us long to get back to my place because we talked all the way there. You know we were still buzzed and pumped about the amazing night we'd just had. It felt like it wasn't real. I actually got up in front of people and expressed a piece of my original poetry. And for a while, I thought it was a part of my imagination, but I felt like the guys were diggin' me more and more as the night progressed.

Once we got back to my place I fixed us another

drink and turned on some music. We talked the night away. Before we knew it, it was five o'clock in the morning. At that point, I had to call it a night. I had every intention on making it to the eleven o'clock Sunday morning worship. Roman and Lance understood, so I walked them to the front porch and told them to call me once they each made it home safely. Roman stepped up and planted a very sweet kiss on the right side of my face, and then Lance followed suit on the left cheek. I couldn't help being flattered. I watched them drive off, then I took a shower and waited on them to call me once they'd made it home.

I made sure to give Erika that buzz to prevent her from worrying. She couldn't believe that the call was just coming at almost six o'clock in the morning. Needless to say, I overslept for Sunday morning worship.

Chapter Eight

Club Raina's Got it Goin' On

It was Thursday night, and there we were again, on the phone making plans to go out Friday night. I had talked to Lance and Roman almost every day since we last went out. Roman would call me, and I would call Lance on three-way. I had started feeling like we were supposed to all talk every day. Roman had even called me on his lunch break that Monday afternoon, talking about us going back to Precious Cargo soon. They made me feel like I was somebody worth keeping in touch with.

I talked to Erika earlier that Thursday afternoon about going out with us the next night, and she made plans to do so. We were going to try another spot out east called Club Raina's. This was a club where Friday nights were called "Fantastic Fridays." This meant something extra was going on. Well, all we'd heard was that Club Raina's was the spot to be on Friday nights, and that we'd better get there early or we might not be able to get in.

"Girl, I hope the guys are on time like they were last week," I said to Erika.

"Relax. I'm sure they will be. They know I'm here," Erika replied with a cynical smile.

"I guess I'm just nervous about you meeting them after all that I've told you about them."

"Don't be nervous. Shoot, it's just a date, not a job interview. Calm down, girl." Erika was being her usual self. I don't think anything could make this lady nervous.

"Well, at least I know I'm not overdressed this time. I called this place myself and found out the code."

"Well, what did the receptionist say a Fantastic Friday is?"

"You know, I really forgot to ask about that. I wish I would've thought to question tonight's activities."

"It doesn't matter. I just want to be able to get up in there, okay?" We both ran toward each other with hands in the air to slap a high-five.

"Is that a car I hear pulling up?" I began wringing my hands.

"Yeah, it sure is, and there are two very attractive men about to get out of a silver Cadillac Escalade," Erika responded, peeping through my chiffon curtains.

"That's Roman and Lance! So, they decided to take Lance's vehicle, huh? I'll get the door," I replied as I started toward it.

"Hey, boo, what's going on? You look beautiful once again." Roman hugged me then kissed me on the cheek.

"Thanks, Roman. You look stunning yourself," I told him as he embraced me a little longer than expected. I didn't mind though. His body felt so good close to mine, and his cologne had quickly begun to be spellbinding. I noticed he wasn't wearing his usual fragrance. Although I didn't ask him what cologne he was wearing, I'm certain it was Obsession. I had briefly dated a man almost a year before who use to put the capital O in Obsession when he had it on. He turned out to be the wrong man for me, but I never forgot that hypnotic scent.

"Let her go, man. I need some love, too. Hey, baby girl. I agree with Roman. You are absolutely beautiful tonight," Lance said smoothly as he reached to hug and kiss me as well.

"Thanks, Lance. You've got it goin' on yourself, man!" I invited them inside for a minute to get acquainted with Erika.

"Well, could this pretty lady be Erika?" Roman asked as he reached for her hand.

"Yes, I would be Erika," she replied, grinning from ear to ear.

"Hello, I'm Lance," he said, also reaching to shake Erika's hand.

"I'm pleased to meet both of you. Finally, after Holiday speaking so much about the two of you, I have faces to place with the names." Erika turned to give me a sly wink.

"I don't know about you guys, but I'm ready to roll out!" I exclaimed impatiently.

Lance was the first to second me. "Well, I don't see a reason why we shouldn't leave, so come on."

We did make it to Club Raina's in time to get in, and we were able to get a table as well. It felt kind of strange to me because I didn't know if we were out on a double date. I just kind of rolled with the flow until somebody said something. I was sitting back waiting on one of them to make their move on Erika. I figured it would be just a matter of time, so I was anxious. Erika wasn't saying anything, but I felt at that time, she was waiting on the big moment, too.

While we were eating, we discovered what Fantastic Fridays was all about—male dancers. I was totally shocked because I was the one who mentioned to the guys that we needed to go to this place. I didn't want them to be disappointed.

"Oh, my goodness! If I had wanted to see some men shake their thangs, I could've asked a few of the fellows I know to come over to my place and get down like that. I could've saved you gentlemen some money and got *that* at home." Erika's tone was discouraging.

"Is that right? Oooh, so you've got it like that, huh?" Roman asked her.

"That's exactly right. I've got it just like that. Holiday, I thought you told these guys about me."

"Hey, you guys, I'm sorry. I don't know why my coworker suggested that we come down here tonight. She knows that I'm not like that. This is terrible. I really can't believe this. I'm so sorry, you guys," I said full of shame.

"Holiday, it's not as bad as you think. Hey, the waitress said the show is not that long. We can hang in there and allow you ladies to have a good time," Lance offered.

"Yeah, so stop apologizing. I'm kinda looking forward to seeing who's going to get flipped in the air. I hope all the ladies with these sexy dresses got on some type of panties tonight. I've been at one of these shows before. I've seen some women get embarrassed 'cause they weren't prepared. I just wish I had known earlier so I could've brought more of my one-dollar bills. I just might be inclined to pay some of these women to give me a private show." Roman was laughing as he talked, but I could tell by looking in his face he was serious.

"I should've known you would be looking forward to the show." I smirked at Roman.

"So do you ladies suggest we go somewhere else when we finish eating?" Lance asked.

"No. It's probably too late and too crowded to get in somewhere else," Erika stated.

"Ladies, it won't be so bad. You'll see. We're going to have a great time here. It may be after the show is over, but we'll still have a great time. Ain't that right, boo?" Roman asked, looking at me.

"Yeah, I trust you."

"What's this 'ain't that right, boo?' " Erika asked, frowning, surely confused.

"Oh, Holiday knows what I told her the last time we went out, don't you?" Roman winked at me. I almost couldn't look in his face to answer him. The wink he sent my way was a gesture that surprisingly caused me to blush.

"Roman promised me that whenever I'm with him, I'm gonna be all right, and I believe him," I managed to somehow respond without giving away my admiration for his flirtation.

"Well what did Lance promise you?" Erika pondered.

"He didn't have to say anything. His actions told it all, and that was the promise of a good time," I said.

"That's right! And don't you forget you owe me a slow dance tonight. You gave Roman the last dance last Saturday," Lance said.

"Well, I ain't gon' be no hater. Lance, you go right ahead and get the last dance tonight. I just want to be able to get a dance in period," Roman stated.

"Unh, I just wish I could be in Holiday's shoes for just one minute tonight. You have got to be extremely flattered right now," Erika said.

"Actually, I am. These are my friends, though. They seem to know just what to say to make me feel good."

"Yeah, but it's no act, though," Roman answered.

I don't think I'd ever blushed so hard before. The guys had my nose wide open. I expected them to be kind, but this was beyond niceness. It was almost as if they were trying to prove a point of some type. I just didn't know what it could be.

"So, since you ladies insist you don't want to see the show, the two of you can just sit right here, and we'll entertain you with our naturally charming conversation. But, if we ever go anywhere and some ladies are giving a show, expect us to be going down front on the floor," Lance assured us, giving Roman a brotherly handshake.

"That's fine. I wouldn't have any problems with that," Erika replied.

"Okay, I'm glad we've got that understood." The smirk on Lance's face said he didn't believe her.

The dancers were called the Black Knights. The shows weren't very long at all. I was amazed at how fast time went by sitting there chatting with Erika and the guys, and trippin' off some of the things we had seen the men do to the women on the floor. Lance and Roman seemed to have been enjoying our company though during the show. Once it was over, the two men seemed to be fired up. They ordered more drinks, and they were ready to party. That was fine because so were Erika and I. We couldn't wait to dance with the two of them.

"Oooh yeah, that's my song. Come on one of you. Who's ready to dance?" Roman asked when the disc jockey began to spin "On and On" off Janet Jackson's *Velvet Rope* album.

"Oh, it doesn't matter. Go ahead, Erika." As much as I loved the song playing, I just wasn't ready to dance.

"No, you go ahead, Holiday. I can wait until the next dance."

"Look, the two of you aren't shy, so quit pretending. I tell you what: Lance, you can have the first and last dance with Holiday tonight. Come on, Erika, let's party, babe," Roman said.

"Well, since you put it that way, Holiday and I will have the first dance. Come on, baby girl," Lance said, pulling me on my feet.

We all headed for the floor and danced to about five songs nonstop. I looked over at Erika and Roman, and it seemed as if they were having a good time. However, I will admit that the last time Roman and I went out, he displayed more enthusiasm while dancing. Lance and I were having a blast. The two men were very good dancers the weekend before, but I wondered why Roman seemed like he just wasn't into the music by the second song. A short time later, we switched partners. Suddenly, Roman seemed to be feeling the music again. I had to really groove to keep up with him. We switched partners one more time, and I was exhausted. Those guys had worn me out.

Once the fast songs ended, a slow one came on. We just stayed paired up with whom we last danced. Lance grooved with me as though he was in love. It kind of made me wonder, though, if he had something extra on his mind like taking me to bed. Lance held me as though we were partners in life, and I belonged to him only. It did feel nice to be held that way. I quickly analyzed Lance's actions, believing he was just buzzing and feeling great. I looked over at Roman and Erika to see if they were having a good time. Roman was watching Lance and me. I smiled at him and just got back in the moment with Lance. I couldn't have been more pleased.

When the song ended, we made our way back up to our table. I couldn't believe that there were two couples sitting at our table. We had left our belongings there to indicate we had not gone anywhere, yet there were still people there. Erika and I had walked off the floor before Lance and Roman. I think they were standing back a little bit, taking a moment to admire some women they saw once we headed off the dance floor. I believe that this must've made the couple at our table think we were alone.

"Excuse me, but this is our table," I politely said.

"You're excused, and this *was* your table," one of the men stated.

The man's reply surprised me. I figured these people wouldn't be happy about having to move, but I hadn't thought they would elect not to get up.

"No, this was and still is our table, so if you don't mind, I'd like to sit down," I replied in a voice that let him know I wasn't easily intimidated.

The women at the table, along with the other man began giggling. By this time Roman and Lance must have been heading our way and heard some bits of the disagreement.

"You can sit down, but you better take your shit and sit your ass somewhere else 'cause we ain't getting up," the man said.

"Man, what the fuck did you say?" Roman's voice rumbled over the loud music, and everyone within viewing distance could see the wrath on his face.

Initially no one responded. The man who had cussed at me had an "Uh-oh, I done fucked up" look on his face. His eyes bucked, and his eyebrows raised up as far as his hairline. The shock had caused this man's mouth to widen and round into a perfect letter O. In the moment of silence, I took the opportunity to step closer to Lance.

Roman spoke out again. "What did you say to her? Nigga, you done lost yo' mind! I will bust yo' ass! You don't talk to her like that!"

"Man, y'all been gone a long time from this table! How you gon' be gone all that time and don't expect somebody to sit here," the man angrily said.

"The same way I expect that this is a mutherfucking restaurant and club and people are going to eat, get up and dance, come back, sit back down for a break, and then get up and dance some more," Roman exclaimed.

"Man, all I'm sayin' is . . ." The man wasn't allowed to finish.

"Man, I'm not getting ready to debate this shit with you. Number one, you wrong 'cause you disrespected my girl. The table is secondary right now. I'm about to get into yo' shit about having the wrong attitude. Fuck the table." Before anyone knew what happened, Roman flew across the table at the man.

All of us women screamed in horror as Roman lunged with severe rage. I had never seen this side of him before. I couldn't believe he had just turned gangsta right before my eyes. Luckily, Lance was able to grab Roman before he got to the man 'cause I believe Roman would've seriously hurt him. Erika and I just got out of the way. Roman kept screaming obscenities, and the man screamed a few back. Lance continued to hold on to Roman, but he was swearing at the man as well.

I heard Lance tell the man he ought to let Roman whip his ass 'cause he deserved it for being such an asshole to me. It didn't take long for security to come over and put us all out. They followed us to the parking lot to make sure a fight didn't break out there, either. I'll tell you, Roman must've put some fear in that man's heart 'cause on the way to our vehicles the man apologized to me from a distance for being disrespectful to me. Roman still had a look of fury. I don't think there was anything this man could've done at that moment to change the way Roman was looking or feeling. I was just as surprised as Erika 'cause I had never known Roman to be that upset about anything.

Speaking of fear, I believe that Roman managed to place terror in the rest of our hearts as well. I know that I was afraid. We all walked to the car in dead silence. Besides, the man's apology reverberating across the parking lot, all you could hear were our footsteps in the night.

After finally getting over what Fantastic Fridays were all about, the night actually had started shaping up to be wonderful. I couldn't have ever predicted an altercation in this very public place involving my friends and me. Erika and I were left baffled. Lance kept quiet, too. We kind of all just waited on Roman to break the ice and have something to say.

"Before you crank up, Lance, I need to take this time to apologize for getting so angry and getting us kicked out of the place. I hope you guys understand why I got so upset. Holiday, you're my girl. I got your back on whatever! He disrespected you, and I couldn't handle that. I apologize that everyone had to see such a terrible side of me. Erika, I hope this doesn't shatter your image of me either. I don't have a bad temper or anything. I just couldn't take hearing that asshole talk to Holiday that way. I hope you'll forgive me and still all go out with me again." Roman's regret seemed sincere.

Erika sort of put on a half grin and replied, "We're all okay, and nobody got hurt. That's the important thing. We all have our limits, and it's unfortunate sometimes when we get pushed in places or among people who we wouldn't want to see that side of us. I totally understand, Roman."

"Thanks, Erika. Boo, do you forgive me, too?" Roman asked, giving me playful puppy-dog eyes.

"There's nothing to forgive. You stuck up for me; therefore, I need to say thank you. Thank you, Roman."

"You're welcome, and I'd do it again. So would Lance while he's sitting here playing innocent. Lance was angry, too. Y'all just couldn't hear him."

"Oh yes, I could hear him, too," I said, nodding at Lance and Roman.

"Man, I wanted to whip that boy, and I wanted you

to whip him, Roman, but I just couldn't let either one of us go to jail tonight. At least, not in front of Erika 'cause she doesn't know us very well. I wanted her to think we could keep our cool, you know?" Lance explained.

"Well, it's no secret that you two care a lot about Holiday. I think that's awesome," Erika said.

"Hey, it's still early. We can't call it a night this soon. Why don't we go back to my place? I've got a career man's drink and some margarita mix. We could put on some music and have a party," I offered.

"I'm down for that!" Lance said.

"Then why you ain't cranked up yet? Let's go!" Erika stated.

I learned that just because a man is educated and in his thirties doesn't mean he's let go of those teenaged urges to fight whenever he doesn't like something. Although I was happy to know Roman had my back, I also felt he should've been man enough to walk away. There is a contradiction in wanting Roman to stand up for me on one hand and wishing he would've controlled his temper on the other hand, but having mixed feelings about the outcome at Club Raina's was one of my first signs that I had somewhat of an infatuation with thug love.

After finding out that Roman's characteristics included ruggedness, he was deemed him sexy as hell in my mind! The fact that a desire for Roman even partially ignited truly shocked me. I wondered if I even knew myself anymore. Time for rediscovering the new me was shortly to come.

Chapter Nine

A Little Bump and Grind

We switched seats, and Roman and Lance sat up front and talked. Erika and I sat in the back still trippin' off what had happened. Erika said that despite everything, she still had a very nice time at Club Raina's. I asked her which guy she was diggin', and she replied, "Shoot, both of them!" When I asked her which one had come on to her, she said neither had—yet. We continued to gossip and giggle some more in the backseat, but the guys couldn't hear us because we were whispering. Roman and Lance did a little whispering of their own. There's no telling what those two were saying. They turned up the radio, so we wouldn't be able to hear their conversation, either.

I noticed something the entire time. Up to that point, Roman's cell phone was continuously lighting up. He had the ringer off. It really didn't bother me, but I know that whoever she was, I imagine she was somewhere hurting. Roman would look at the phone then clip it back to his side. Later, Erika told me she noticed that, too. I also remembered that Roman was doing the same thing the first time we went out. Lance would answer his phone, but Roman would just let his voice mail pick up. As suave and debonair as Roman was, that was another reminder that he couldn't be my man.

We drank and danced some more at my place. Then, about half-past midnight, Erika realized she had a long drive ahead of her, so she decided to go on home. I was a little disappointed, but I understood. Lance, being the gentleman he was, offered to trail Erika part of the way home. She agreed, and they left my house before one o'clock. Roman, on the other hand, was not ready to leave. I was cool with that because I wasn't ready to end the fun. Shortly after Lance and Erika left, I asked Roman if he'd mind staying over because we were having one drink too many, and I didn't want to have to drive him home so late. He agreed, then I asked him to excuse me for about fifteen minutes to take a shower. It was late, and I didn't want the night to slip away from me. When I came back into the living room, Roman was looking through my CD collection. We continued to play music for a while, and as the night grew older, we realized that it was going to be another long night like the weekend before. I didn't have anything to do the next morning. I wasn't even scheduled to pick Crystal up from her cousin's until one o'clock the next day.

Roman went and took a shower, and I gave him a pair of my big sweatpants and a large T-shirt. I like to wear too-big clothes around the house. Roman and I had selected five CDs to put in the stereo before he had gone to take a shower, and they were still rotating by the time he came back. The moment he stepped into the living room the *Waiting to Exhale* soundtrack started playing. We sat and talked through the first few songs, then we slow-danced on Aretha Franklin's song, "It Hurts Like Hell." I must admit I was really into him at that moment. He was stroking my hair and gazing into my eyes as we danced. I wanted so badly to question him about why he was being so gentle with me, as if I were his woman, but the moment just felt so right that I decided to just relish in it.

"So, you think you're slick, don't you?" I asked, giving him a shame-on-you look. I dropped my head a little, squinted, and poked my lips at Roman.

"Excuse me? I don't quite understand."

"You told Lance that he could have the last dance, and you've tricked me into dancing with you after he's gone."

"Tricked you? Tricked you? Is that really how you feel?"

"No, but it just seems kind of strange that once Lance thinks that he's had the last slow dance with me for the night, you had to go and ask me to dance."

"You could've declined, but you didn't, did you?"

"If I had remembered, then maybe I would've."

"Could've, should've, would've. It's done and over with now. I won't tell Lance if you won't. Deal?"

"You are slick. I'm gonna start calling you Slick Rick."

"You better not! What I would like for you to start calling me though is Rome. I've never heard a woman say it as sexy as you. Besides, Roman is pretty much my business name. You and I are on a personal level right now, and I'd like very much for us to keep it personal from now on." Roman was gazing into my eyes, giving me a feeling of enchantment. I stopped dancing. I wasn't quite sure I'd heard him correctly.

"What are you saying, Roman?"

"I'm saying that I'm very much into you, Holiday. I know you can feel that. I want to be a part of your world. I want to experience a life with you."

"Roman, now I know for sure that you're buzzing. Did I make the career man's drink too strong or something?"

"Holiday, I may be buzzing, but it has nothing to do with the fact that I want some Holiday in my life. This past week, I've grown closer to you, and I feel like I know you on a different level, and I'm really into it. Hell, surprised me, too! But it's a feeling that I can't shake. I only thought I wanted to be a player, but, after having these long, in-depth conversations with you every day, I've realized that I want something different now. This life policy of yours that we discussed earlier this week, about giving love only to get loved, that's what I want to share with you."

"Roman, I can't! I have just been through too much over the years. I can't commit to a relationship with anyone. I'm just not ready. Although we've been talking every day lately, there's still so much I feel I don't know about you."

"Shit, that's easy! What do you want to know?"

"You don't talk about your mother. All I ever hear is how much you love your father. Why? Where's your mother?"

"She passed away when I was seven years old. My father never wanted to keep one woman long enough to make her a mother to me. What else do you want to know?"

"Yeah, but why is it that I've never heard this before? What's making you hold back this information? I've talked about my folks and my childhood with you. Why is it that you won't share more with me?"

"Because I don't like talking about it. Okay, you're a stronger person than I am. You've accepted your childhood pains, but I'm not there yet. It doesn't have anything to do with the way I'm feeling right now, though. I want to be a part of your world. For real!"

"My life isn't as simple as you think. Besides, how do we know that we can trust each other? We don't know that yet, so let's just remain friends for the time being."

"So what happened to your life policy?" Roman hadn't stopped gripping my hands.

"Nothing. I shared that with you because I feel one day I'm going to be with a man who can show me nothing but love, and I, in turn, will show him the same thing. Right now, I know that I'm not ready to put my trust in a relationship."

We fell silent for a moment, which enabled me to hear the shuffling of my CD player searching for a new track. When the song began to play, Roman grabbed me around the waist. "Kissing You" by Faith Evans seemed a little too right for the moment, and Roman took advantage of it.

As Roman pulled me closer, he softly spoke into my ear. "Do you hear this song, Holiday?"

"Yeah."

"It's talking to us," he said as he slowly kissed my face then my lips.

"Roman . . . Roman, please wait. Wait a minute. Roman . . . Roman." I spoke between breaths as we alternated short and long kisses.

"Rome. Call me Rome, babe. Say it. Say it, Holiday. I wanna hear you call me Rome. Let me hear you call me Rome, boo," he kept pleading in a soft, masculine voice as he slowly kissed my face and neck, caressing my breasts with his strong hands, soon making his way down to kiss me between my thighs.

"Rome, stop."

"No, not 'Rome, stop.' Just Rome. Call me Rome, baby," he said as he slid my panties aside and began to French-kiss my vagina.

"Rome. Rome." I couldn't help but moan his name as a reflex of the heat he was causing me.

"Un-hmm. Come on, boo. Let me hear you say it again. Call my name, boo." He continued to make his requests between my moans.

"Oooooh, Roooome!" I had reached a much-needed but much-too-soon climax. I hadn't intended to go there so suddenly, but my body wasn't use to the attention.

"How do you feel? Did you like that? 'cause that's the way I'd like to hear you call my name every time. Come on, let's go in the bedroom and finish what we've started."

"Hold on, Rome. Do you have any condoms?"

"Of course I do."

"Then, I'm ready if you promise to be gentle. It's been a very long time."

"I promise, Holiday. I'll be as gentle as you need me to be. All I want you to do is remember to say my name how I like it, relax, and enjoy what we're about to share, but wait . . . don't move. I wanna carry you into the bedroom."

"What? You don't have to do that." Roman confused me with his offer.

"I know, but this is about to be more of your night than it is mine."

Roman picked me up and carried me into the bedroom. I was so not use to the attention, I almost felt ashamed to let him be this affectionate toward me. He put me down on my bed. This time he took off every stitch of my clothing, and the first thing he wanted to do was taste my juices, which he had caused to flow. I was totally taken into ecstasy by this man. I knew right then that this wasn't going to be a one-night stand or just a fling.

Chapter Ten
The Morning After

Daylight came before we knew it. Our indulgence through the night was intense, off and on, as though we were a couple madly in love. As for me, I allowed this to happen because I hadn't been intimate with a man for pretty close to a year. Although I knew that Rome was a manipulator and a whoremonger, it really didn't matter. He was with me for the night, and he was providing me with everything I felt I needed.

As for that stuff about a relationship, I just really couldn't see it. After all, this was Rome. I knew too much about his dirt. This made it hard for me to even want to consider having him as my man.

"Good morning, boo."

"Good morning, Rome."

"Did you have a good nap?"

"Yes, but I haven't had enough sleep yet. Turn over and go back to bed."

"No, I think I better not. It's about nine o'clock."

"So?" I couldn't believe that after a night like we'd just had he would be ready to leave so soon.

"So, it's Saturday, and I've got some things I have to take care of today."

I didn't really believe him. "Yeah, like explaining to that woman or those women calling you where you've been all night? Look at your phone, Rome! It's lighting up as I speak! There's no telling how many missed calls you have on that thing. Oh, why don't you check your voice mail? I'm sure it's full. And you want me to consider a life with you? I don't think so!"

"Holiday, I had my ringer turned off on my phone for a reason. That reason being, because I was with you. And I only wanted last night to be for you. Now, I'll agree that there may be a number of women who could've called and left messages, but you could at least give me credit for not electing to be obtainable for them. I thought I'd made my purpose for the night clear, but I guess I didn't."

"Rome, I'm just scared. You can't blame me for that, can you? I know you a little bit too well. I really feel you aren't ready to change. Overnight, Rome?"

"Holiday, everything in my heart right now says change. All the women that I've gone out with lately haven't shown me anything that said they could've been Mrs. Roman Broxton. You, on the other hand, have shown me plenty that says I would be a fool if I let you get away. You're ambitious, family-oriented, and I just love your inner drive. Give me a chance, boo. All I want is just one chance. I promise you won't regret it. Can you know what a love between us can do if you don't give it a try?"

I sighed. I could see he wasn't giving up. "Rome,

what are you envisioning when you think of a life with me?"

"Long-term commitment with you, as well as with Crystal. Family-oriented activities for the three of us. I see me discovering new and better ways to show you ladies how deeply I feel for you as time passes. I can adhere to all your concerns by doing whatever is necessary to make the situation comfortable for all of us. Boo, there'll be so much love that it'll result in a lifetime for us. I just know that I want to share true love with you. How about that, huh?"

"Rome, it all sounds good, but what about a relationship with God? Can you see that? Can you see going to church with me and becoming an active member?"

"Absolutely. I'll start by going this Sunday."

It was sort of understood from that point that we were what you'd call an actual couple. I did, however, ask Rome not to mention it to Crystal yet. I just wasn't ready to explain to her that I was including a man in my life. I wasn't sure how she would take it. She wasn't so pleased about me going out that Friday night with my friends. After all, Friday nights were supposed to be ours. I totally understood from where she was coming, but I had been hemmed up so many nights with work that I thought I deserved one Friday evening to do something I wanted. I guess now I realize that the best thing to do would've been to decline my friends and choose Crystal instead.

Still, I preferred that Rome and I kept our love affair a secret from Crystal for as long as possible. I needed to be sure that we could last. This thing we had started out was on a trial basis for me. If I discovered early that I couldn't trust Roman, then letting him go would be easy, and there would be no attachment to my child. I was ready to closet this relationship for a very long time if need be. A woman's gotta do what she's gotta do.

Chapter Eleven

Sisters Forever

Erika called me about noon. Rome had been long gone by this time. I was nervous about breaking the news to her of my relationship with him, so I just kind of told her that I couldn't talk long 'cause I was just waking up from a nap and I was running late to pick up Crystal. This wasn't totally a lie. I was just waking up, and I did have to soon head out to pick up Crystal on the other side of town. So, you see, there was some truth.

The fact that Roman was my man was still soaking in with me. I couldn't tell Erika just then, but I felt an overwhelming need to let the cat out of the bag, so I called my best friend, Renee Hamilton, back in Charlotte, North Carolina. I knew Renee would be more understanding.

Renee and I were in the fourth grade when her family moved into the house next door. She didn't have siblings and neither did I, so it was easy for us to become best friends. We got along like sisters, and we could always be seen together in many places. Renee and I resembled each other in many aspects. We were about the same height, had the same satin-brown complexion, and long, dark hair. People were always asking if we were kin.

"Hello, Renee. It's been a couple of weeks since we last talked. What's going on with you?"

"Holiday, what's up, sis? You finally put the paper·work down long enough to call your old friend, huh?" Renee asked. She knew that I often engrossed myself with homework from the job.

"Oh, whatever. We've gone longer without calling each other, Renee."

"Yeah, but last time was so brief I hardly had time to find out how things are really going with you."

"Sorry about that. I have time to talk now though."

"Okay. Where's my niece? It's too quiet. I don't hear Bow Wow playing in the background." Renee laughed.

"Well you know Crystal. She's going to spend as much time with Darius's people as she can. It is the weekend, remember?"

"Holiday, since when did you start letting Crystal spend Friday nights with them? This is something new to me."

"Oh, I really haven't started anything like that. Crystal and I agreed to exchange our family night for this evening. That's part of what I've called to talk with you about."

"Uh-oh. What's up, Holiday?"

"Renee, would you believe me if I told you I got me some last night?"

"Say what? No, I wouldn't believe you. Girl, shut your mouth! I know that didn't happen. Not to you,

Ms. I-ain't-got-time-to-be-bothered-with-no-man," Renee said, mocking me.

"Renee, you make me sound so bad. Give me a little credit. I do have feelings."

"So, you really got you some?"

"You still don't believe me? Whoa, maybe I have been sounding like a bitch with my nose stuck up in the air."

"Holiday, I wouldn't say all of that. I know you've been through a lot in the past years with men. I also know that you're not very happy with your father right now either, so I haven't been judging you."

"Have you seen my parents lately?"

"Now you know I still live right next door. I see Mr. Simmons out there mowing the lawn every Monday evening. I see Mrs. Simmons as I leave to go to work. She still likes to sit out on the porch to catch a breath of the fresh air in the morning."

"She's wearing that old rocking chair out I bought her a few years ago, huh?"

"Are you kidding me? That chair *is* worn out. I can hear the squeaking before I get out on my doorstep."

"Renee! I know you ain't lettin' my momma rock in nothing like that. Why you haven't bought Momma a chair?"

"I offered, but she won't let me. She's proud of the fact that you gave her that one. You better hurry up and send her another one. That's all I'm gon' say about that."

"Hmph! A'ight, but I called to tell you about my experience last night."

"Oh yeah. G'on, girl. Who is this man?"

I went on to tell Renee the details of who, why, and what happened. She expressed some concerns, but overall she was happy for me. I asked her to continue to look after my parents, and then we hung up.

Renee moved back into her childhood house after her mother passed away. She says she can't bear to sell it, so after a few renovations, it's home again for her. Renee never knew her father, and it was too bad that I couldn't offer her mine. He was never anyone I could look up to, and Renee experienced some of my pain the times she was allowed to spend the night. Company was never an excuse not to beat Momma when my father felt like it. Renee would sit in the corner and pray with me. I wanted God to strike my father dead with a massive heart attack in the middle of one of his blows to Momma's frayed body. God never struck Daddy down, but the fact that He spared my mother's life each time, kept me from being angry with Him.

Chapter Twelve
My Life Is Your Secret

A few days passed by then I called Erika. There was no sense in hiding my relationship with Roman from her. Eventually, she'd have to know.

"Erika, what's up, girl? Are you busy, on the other line or something?"

"Naw, I'm not doing anything. What's going on?"

"Girlfriend, I need to talk to you. I just don't know how, though."

"Holiday, this sounds serious. When have you *not* been able to talk to me about anything?"

"I know what your response will be. I'm just not sure that I'm ready to hear it."

"Try me, girlfriend. Damn, how bad can it be?"

"Well, here goes. I kind of got myself in too deep with a situation."

"Oh yeah, what kind of situation is this?"

"The kind that you're not going to agree with."

"Girl, if you don't stop beating around the bush," Erika exclaimed.

"Okay, okay. After you and Lance left Friday night, Roman stayed over a little longer—well, much longer. It was late, and I felt that we'd had too much to drink to be driving, so I asked him to stay for the night. And he did." I squeezed my eyes shut tightly, waiting for her response.

"Mmhmm, I'm still listening. I know there has to be more by the sound of your voice," Erika replied.

I swallowed hard and continued to speak. "Sure, there's more. I kind of allowed Roman to sleep in my bed. With me. At the same time."

"Holiday! You had *sex* with Roman! Tell me you *didn't.*"

"Mmhmm, and it was good, too," I responded sort of timidly.

"Holiday! You have got to be kiddin' me. You're damn right you got caught up, in too deep, or whatever the hell you said! Oh, that's messed up! Real messed up! So now what? Have you even heard from him since?"

"Yes, I have! He called on Saturday. He wanted to come back over."

"Oh, he wanted some more booty, huh?" Maybe Erika didn't know it, but she had just belittled me.

"No, Erika! If you would just let me finish, you'll understand why he called me on Saturday."

"Oh, well I'm sorry. Please continue." Erika's tone was sarcastic, and I was starting to be pissed off.

"He called to see if he could spend more time with Crystal and me, but I didn't want him to. I had Crystal swap our family night to Saturday so that I could go out with y'all on Friday. I wasn't about to let him infringe on Saturday as well."

"Well, has he called you since Saturday?"

"Yeah, he's called every day since. We haven't seen

each other though. My evenings are too consumed with making dinner, helping Crystal with her homework, and my take-home assignments from the job." I was speaking fast, running words together, trying to make Erika believe that she had nothing to be concerned about.

"So, is this going to be a long-term thing or what?"

"Well you can put it like this: It wasn't a one-night stand."

"Then what is it?"

"We kind of made a commitment."

"A commitment? Girl, what kind of commitment do you think Roman is going to keep with you? You're starting to talk real silly right about now, Holiday!"

"I'll admit, it *does* sound kind of strange, but Erika you would've had to have been there in the moment with us to understand how and why."

"Girlfriend, pardon my saying so, but you are not ready for something like this. Even if Roman could be committed to you, you just aren't ready, sweetie. You've been through too much to try to be dedicated to someone right now. You understand where I'm coming from?"

"Yeah, but Erika, what am I supposed to do? Continue to harbor all the pain from the lack of affection my daddy had for me? Hold on to the shame that I gave my all to a no-good-ass baby daddy whom I came to learn never even gave a shit about me? Just what do you think I should do, Erika?" My voice was weak and trembling as I tried hard to fight back the tears.

"I'm not trying to hurt your feelings, Holiday. And you know without me even telling you, that regardless of who the man in your life is, you'll never be able to divide the past from the present. You've tried before, remember? It only cost you the three very short relationships you had just after Darius Coleman."

I didn't like it, but she was right. "Okay, the first one did say that my lack of trust for him was the cause of our breakup. The second one's voice was too harsh. Every time he made a point, the sternness reminded me of the control my father had over my mother and me. But the third one, hell, that wasn't my fault. He couldn't accept the fact that Crystal came before him in my life. Now, I couldn't fix that."

"Yeah, but did you even hear yourself about the first two? I'm only saying all of this because I'm concerned, Holiday. For some reason, you've completely changed from the person I know, and it's scaring me. Just last week you wouldn't have fallen for a guy like Roman. Honey, if the sex was good, okay. I can understand that better, but don't go confusing good sex for a decent man to call your own."

"Well, I guess it was only meant for him and me to understand 'cause certainly no one else could've been there to know how this came to be."

"What does Crystal think about this?"

"She doesn't know yet. I'm not ready to tell her. As a matter of fact, I don't know if I'll ever tell her."

"What the . . . And you say this is supposed to be a long-term commitment?"

"Yeah."

"Then how do you figure Crystal, as smart as she is, won't figure this out? I'm serious, Holiday. I'm worried about you now. You're just not thinking rationally."

"Okay, but I was just thinking that if Roman and I can make this last, then we'll tell her. But, for right now all she needs to know is the man named Roman is Mommy's friend from work, and he goes out with us sometimes."

"Here's my guess: It probably won't work. And don't be stupid, Holiday. I just wish you'd share with me what it was that Roman said to you, giving you the feeling he could be the one. His 'Smackavelli' personality has just completely won you over. It's kind of sad, too. You shouldn't be so desperate."

"I'm getting ready to let you go! I've been trying to ignore all the insults, but I think I've had enough now. I wouldn't have ever said anything like that to you. If you think what I'm doing is called being desperate, then keep thinking it. I know, Roman knows, and God knows what it is for us. I'm *not* getting ready to stop seeing him. I don't care what you or anybody else thinks of me. If it doesn't work, it doesn't work. But, I betcha I'll find out through experience this time. I've turned down plenty of men thinking I wasn't ready. Now, I'll know for sure. And on my own!" I was fuming. I knew that Erika would disapprove, but I hadn't counted on her having so much to say.

"I'm sorry you feel insulted, Holiday. You're my best girlfriend, and I refuse to hold back on anything I feel could help you. I just don't want you to let Roman be the same man to you that he has been with other women in the past. What did he say about them? Is he willing to let go? Did you think about discussing this with him?"

"Erika, what do you think? Yes, we've discussed it. He no longer wants that type of life. Just have a little confidence in me. You're making me feel like you think I'm some type of dumb-ass, gullible fool for love or something. Really, Erika. I'm a big girl. I can handle myself, okay?"

"All right then. It's your life. I'm still your friend, and I'll be here for you."

It upset me that my girlfriend thought that I had poor judgment in choosing Roman to be my man. Kind of made me wish that I hadn't ever told her all that junk about him in the first place. I knew I would just have to show Erika that everything was going to be okay. I didn't want her to have hard feelings for Roman despite the fact that he hadn't done any of his dirt to me.

I still had to wonder why I had gone against everything I first felt before all of this occurred. Maybe there was some truth to Erika's logic. Maybe I was just settling because I was tired of not having a man to call my own. And, I know the sex definitely played a big part in the whole decision. Little did I realize that I was still a big hypocrite.

Although I wanted Rome to put God in his life, I had no intention on stopping with the sex. I felt that I had been deprived too long, and after that first night with Roman, my body was giving me signs of dependency. I wanted this man just about five times a week. When I couldn't have him, I became irritable.

Chapter Thirteen

Let 'im Know

A couple of weeks later, I met Roman and Lance for lunch. It had been on my mind whether Roman had told Lance about us, and what, if anything, Lance had to say about it. When we met at the restaurant, I was looking for signs in Lance's face that he and Roman had been discussing me. I couldn't tell. There were no signs. This made me very nervous for some reason. I guess I was just perplexed as to why Rome hadn't told Lance, his "boy," about us.

"Baby girl, what's up?"

"Oh nothing, Lance. Just all work and no play."

"Well, we'll have to see if we can change that, now want we?" Roman said, giving me a look of seduction.

"I guess so," I replied with a smirk.

Lance looked confused. "Did something just fly over my head? I *know* I just missed a word or two." He continued to look back and forth at Roman and me.

"Oh, Lance, I know that we haven't had a whole lot of time to talk, and I've definitely neglected to tell you some things. Last Friday night after you left, Holiday and I had a lot of time to get personal. A lot of time, if you know what I'm saying," Roman explained.

Lance paused before he spoke, looking at Roman, perplexed. He even set down his glass and coughed as if some water had gone down the wrong way. After a brief moment, he cleared his throat and sat looking at Roman for an awkward ten seconds. I couldn't understand just what was going on, so I felt the need to break the ice. Just before I started to speak, Lance glanced at me. I threw a huge smile on my face and nodded in agreement with what Roman had just said.

"Of course, I know what you mean. Are you guys like a couple now?" Lance responded cheerfully, although astonishment was still on his face.

"Yes, we are," I responded, maintaining my smile of contentment.

Lance took a few seconds to sip on his glass of water again before responding. "Man, that's great! That is really great! I never would've thought it, but I think it's cool though. Roman, I'm happy for you, man. You've got yourself one hell of a woman. You better be good to her."

"Yes, I know. I have every intention on making her the happiest woman alive." Roman rubbed my back with long, sensual strokes.

"Good, I should hope so," I said to Roman, reaching for his hand.

For about two months, things were working out like I had expected. Crystal continued to spend

Fridays with her cousins, and Roman would take me out on Saturdays. Sometimes Lance would come along, and I was totally cool with that. He was still our friend.

Something got strange about Lance's behavior at times, and he wouldn't ever try to bring a date along when we'd all go out. I noticed that his cell phone wasn't ringing as much when he was around Roman and me, either. All of this bothered me. Lance didn't appear to be as happy as he once seemed. I left it alone though. I figured that whatever it was, it would surface soon.

Roman didn't seem to notice the change in Lance. He wasn't talking much about Lance or what he knew of his best friend's private life. It seemed a little out of place for me to ask my man about what was going on in his friend's life, so I waited and hoped that whatever it was, Lance would be okay.

Time was flying by with the romance between Roman and me. We had only been together for a little more than two months, but since we would spend every weekend together, have lunch, and talk a lot over the phone, it seemed as though we had been together more than a year. Roman would also go to church with Crystal me on Sundays. Erika attended my church as well, so this was a good way for me to show her that Roman was serious about me.

Erika wouldn't bring up Roman or Lance when we'd talk. I couldn't tell if she was approving of my relationship with Roman at that point. It bothered me quite a bit, but I refused to broach the subject with her. I just didn't care to hear any more of her opinions. For the first time in a long while, I was happy.

Erika soon slacked up on calling me. My feelings were hurt, but what should I have done? Leave my man alone because my best friend was acting silly? No, me having a man should not have bothered her the way it did. Erika was a beautiful woman, and she could get her a man. As a matter of fact, she could get any man she wanted, if she really wanted one. As far as it mattered to me, Erika would simply have to stay strong on her own.

Chapter Fourteen
A Family Affair

"So, Crystal, what kind of grades are you making right now?" I heard Lance ask.

"I'm still making the honor roll, Uncle Lance," Crystal answered.

"What? You mean to tell me you've got the smarts like that? What grade are you now?" Lance asked.

"The sixth grade, Uncle Lance," Crystal responded as if Lance should have already known.

"So, that would make you eleven or twelve?"

"Eleven going on twelve," she exclaimed.

"Oh, excuse me, Miss Lady. I'm sorry. I just asked 'cause I don't ever remember making the honor roll when I was your age. I was just a hardheaded little boy who didn't care much about homework or anything. My mother had to beat my butt to make me do my schoolwork. I think it's really great that you care a great deal about your grades. As a matter of fact, when does the next report card come home?"

"Oh, I think it should be in a few weeks."

"Good. Show me your grades and I'll give you five dollars for every A you make. How about that?"

"That'll be great," she answered, grinning from ear to ear.

"So remember, if you have a B in any subject right now, you still have time to push it up to an A," Lance said, smiling at Crystal.

Roman decided to add to her excitement. "I can make the deal even sweeter. I'll match anything Lance gives you for your good grades."

"You mean, if I make an A in four subjects, Uncle Lance is going to give me, let's see five, ten . . . And if you match that I'll have forty dollars!" Crystal stated, jumping up and down with joy in her voice.

"Boy, just think what you could do with that money!" Roman stated.

"Mom, hey Mom! Get in here! Uncle Lance and Uncle Roman said they would give me five dollars for every A I make on my report card. I'm gonna have so much money 'cause I'm gonna try to make all A's. Watch and see."

I was delighted to see the joy on my baby's face. "You guys better start saving your money 'cause I'm gonna see to her making the principal's list!"

"Okay, it's a bet," Lance said.

We were all getting ready to go see a movie. It was Friday night, and Crystal didn't seem to mind at all that Roman and Lance were going to hang out with us. As a matter of fact, she had become quite fond of the two men. This made it very easy for me to invite them over during the week to eat dinner with us, or to just have them bring me something from the store so I wouldn't have to go back out. Crystal thought nothing of it. It got to the point where Crystal just looked at Roman and Lance as two very good friends of mine who wanted her to call them Uncle. I was content with this. I didn't have to explain anything to her about my love affair with Roman.

I awakened, feeling great. "Hey, baby. It's Saturday, and I was calling because Crystal's gone until tomorrow night again. She's away for cheerleading camp this weekend. So, what are we going to get into?" I asked Roman the next morning.

"Oh, boo, I didn't mention it before because I didn't want to spoil your week, but the company is sending me to Jackson, Tennessee, to help out at the office there. It seems that someone has screwed up some policies, and no one working in that office knows how to straighten them out quickly enough," Roman explained.

"Rome, you were just with me last night. All that time at the movies, you didn't think about telling me once that you were going to Jackson this morning?"

"Boo, I've told you, I didn't want to spoil any other moments earlier this week, and last night started out so great that I just couldn't find a way to bring it up. You've been in such a good mood lately, I didn't know how to bring myself to tell you. And I know that our quality time together means everything to you. Please, boo. Just let me make it up to you later."

"Were you going to even call me and let me know you were leaving?"

"Holiday, come on now! How would it look if I were gone a whole day without letting you know?"

"You've pulled it with other women, remember?

Anyway, I didn't realize that those branches were even opened on Saturdays."

"Holiday, let's not go there. Boo, we were doing so well. If you'd like I can give you the office number. Later on you can just call me to confirm I'm there."

"No, I don't want the number. If you're lying, it'll definitely come back to haunt you."

"Boo, please take the number. Come on and write it down. It's area code . . ." Roman began to quote the phone number for the Jackson office.

"I don't want it, Rome."

"Then, if you won't take it, I'll just call you later. You've got caller ID. I just want you to see that I'm not being deceitful, boo."

"Rome, what am I going to do today? Can't you come back tonight?"

"From what I hear, I'm gonna have to work pretty late. So rather than drive back tired and sleepy, I've reserved a hotel near the office."

"Mmph! I could just cry. I don't know what I'm going to do tonight. You know Erika and I don't hang out anymore. We don't even really talk that much nowadays."

"Then I think this would be the perfect time to call her and play catch-up. She may be dying to hear from you."

"I don't think so. She sees me at church and speaks to me as though we're just sisters in Christ who happen to attend the same church. She doesn't act like someone I've been friends with for years now."

"Holiday, call the woman."

"Nope, I won't do it. I'll be bored first. I didn't do anything to her. Right after you and I hooked up, I still kept trying to call her and talk like we use to, and she was dodging my calls and kept telling me she was busy. I know how to take a hint."

"Okay, how about this. Hold on a second," Roman said just before he clicked to the other line to dial up a number on three-way.

I became curious. "Rome, who are you calling?" I asked when he came back.

"Hold on. You'll see."

"No, don't tell me to hold on. I wanna know. And it better not be Erika, either."

Then I heard another male voice speak out. "It's not Erika, baby girl. It's Lance." Lance had heard the tail end of our conversation just after picking up to answer.

"Oh, Lance, I'm sorry. Rome and I just got through talking about Erika, and I thought he had dialed her number."

Rome spoke out. "Holiday, you're trippin'! Where would I have gotten Erika's number?"

"I don't know! You speak to her at church," I reminded him.

"Uhn-huh, and you figure that I would get a phone number from her? I don't know what to say about you now. You've completely confused me."

"I'm sorry, baby. I'm just frustrated." I knew I had disappointed him with my lack of trust.

"What's wrong, Holiday?" Lance asked.

"Man, she thinks I'm lying to her about having to go to Jackson today."

"Thanks, Holiday! I didn't know you had changed your name?" I said to Roman sarcastically.

"My fault, boo. Go on. Tell 'im what's wrong with you."

"I understand that you have to go take care of business, baby. I really do. It's just that you've spoiled me. I'm use to having something to do every weekend. I guess I'll just have to manage tonight."

"Hey, Lance man, why don't you take her out for me? She doesn't want to call Erika, and I don't know anything else for her to do."

"Sure. Holiday, do you want to go out with me tonight?"

"Oh no you don't, Lance! Don't you go feeling sorry for me."

"No, Holiday. Seriously, I would be honored to go out with you tonight. Come on now. Aren't we still friends, too?" Lance asked.

"Yeah, but are you sure, Lance? I don't want to be any bother to you. You might've had plans or something."

"Boo, what kind of question is that to ask the man? Of course, he's sure. Lance, you have any place in mind? I'll pay for it."

"It's really up to Holiday. I'm game for whatever she wants to do tonight. Holiday, I really didn't have anything planned for tonight. Whatever you have in mind for us to do is fine."

"Oh, I don't know. Let me think."

"Well, whatever you two decide, I'll be happy to pay for it when I get back. Right now, I need to be getting out of here," Roman said.

"Man, don't worry about anything. I'm sure I'll have enough, and if I don't, Holiday can just wash some dishes or something," Lance joked.

"Umph! I can see myself now, clothes wringing wet from all the suds and water splashing on me." I laughed.

"Okay, so then it's settled? 'Cause I really need to be leaving now," Roman said.

"Oh, go on, man. I'll make baby girl decide what she wants to do some time today. Be careful on the road, too."

"Yeah, baby. Have a safe trip. Call me and let me know you've made it."

"All right, you guys. I'll talk to you later," Roman said and hung up.

Chapter Fifteen
Premier Night

Later that afternoon, Roman called me from the office in Jackson to let me know he'd made it, but I knew he was also confirming that he was actually there. He continued to call me all afternoon on into the early evening. Rome was doing everything possible to make me comfortable with the fact that he was working. I heard the voices of guys in the office in the background discussing some of the policies. Rome even called my cell phone so that I would have the office number on that caller ID. I felt proud to have my man go these extra lengths to help me feel comfortable. He was proving to me that all he had expressed to me in the beginning was true. He said that whatever the concern may be, he would do his best to rectify the situation. He did just that.

About seven o'clock that night, Lance rang the doorbell. He and I had decided to dress casually for the evening. The weather was rainy and sticky, so I wasn't in the mood for dressing up.

We had planned a night out at The Premier Night-club. Steve Harvey was going to be there after his show at the Orpheum Theatre, and I wanted to see if I could get an autograph. I had been to The Premier a few times before, so I figured we'd enjoy ourselves. Lance was able to get us VIP passes. He said he knew Curtis Givens, the man who owned the club. I never asked how he and Curtis knew each other. I was just happy to get the passes.

Once Lance and I left my home heading to the club, it began to rain a little harder than it had been earlier. We didn't let that stop us from going though. Lance pulled his Escalade into the parking lot, and members of security met us with an umbrella while valet parked the truck. We didn't even have to stand in line. Lance flashed the passes, and we were escorted to our table. I was very impressed.

The club had changed since the last time I remembered. The VIP section was roped off from the rest of the public. The couches were made of soft red velvet and were positioned in front of a gorgeous wall-unit fish aquarium. The club's beauty left me in awe.

Though the atmosphere was lovely, it was not enough distraction for the trouble I had on my mind. It shouldn't have come to me as a surprise that Lance noticed.

"So, you're awfully quiet. Are you disappointed that Steve Harvey hasn't made it yet?" Lance asked with a concerned look.

"Oh no, that's not it. I'm sure Steve will be here soon. I just have something on my mind that's causing me to be in kind of a funk."

"What's that? Or do you care to share it?" Lance inquired.

"Sure. It's just that ever since we left to come here, I've been calling Rome to get his phone number to the hotel, and he's not responding."

"What's happening when you call?"

"No one's answering at the office, and he's not answering his cell phone. I've left several messages, but he hasn't responded to any of them."

"Are you just concerned, or is it that you need to talk to him?"

"I kind of wanted to be able to reach him tonight when I get in. He never gave me a number to his hotel room, so the only means of contact would be on his cell. I'd really be worried, though, if I couldn't reach him once I get home."

"Well, you've got the cell number. Just continue to try him there."

"It's not that simple, Lance. Something just doesn't feel right." I began to frown. Lance could tell by the look on my face that my worry was far deeper than I had explained.

"I tell you what. I'm sure he's fine, so just hold on a minute. I'll see if I can reach him for you."

"Thanks, Lance, but I'm telling you, he's not answering."

The rain began to pour down even harder than it had before we'd entered the club. At times, I could hear the thunder hammering louder than the deejay's music. Some time had passed since Lance began listening to Roman's cell phone ring, so I looked over at him to confirm that it would be okay if he just hung up. Just as I raised my hand to wave for Lance's attention. He dropped his head and spoke into the phone.

"Hello, Roman? What's up, man?" My jaw damn near hit the floor. "Yeah, I've picked up Holiday. We've been here for about a half hour now." Lance continued to talk, then there was a little bit of a pause.

"Oh, so he picked up for you, huh. Okay. Okay," I said. I couldn't have been more agitated.

"Man, I really think you need to talk to Holiday. Just say something to her." Lance was trying to whisper as he got up from the table to continue talking to Roman.

The little bit of conversation that I'd heard between the two made me sick to my stomach. I wondered how Roman could be hurting me that way. He had become one of my best friends. Just earlier that day he was trying to prove to me that he wasn't doing anything deceitful. Then, a few hours later, I couldn't even get him to speak to me when he *knew* I was sitting just right across from his voice on the phone. Lance came back to the table, and I wasn't sure if I was ready for him to.

"Baby girl, I'm sorry. Roman says to give you his love, but he can't talk right now."

"Shhhooot! Why couldn't he talk? What else did he say?" I didn't mean to be hollering at Lance, but I was.

"He said to tell you that he would try to see you tomorrow."

"Hmph! *Whatever!*"

"Are you okay?" Lance asked. Tears had started welling up in my eyes.

"How can you sit there and look at me like that?"

He didn't answer, but I knew he understood exactly what the question was about. I pointed my finger in his face and said, "You actually have a guilty look on your face. It's like you know something, yet you keep looking at me as though you're wearing the perfect mask. I can see all through you, Lance. I know Roman was your friend before he was mine. I don't expect you to tell me anything. You really don't have to. Common sense answers my questions." My voice was trembling, and I didn't have control over how my words came out. All of the pain and tears had taken over.

"Holiday, I'm not trying to wear a disguise at all. I'm looking at you because you seem to be so torn by this, and I'm just concerned about you. The look of guilt must be because this is very awkward for me. You're my friend, too. I have a sense of loyalty toward both of you, but the best I can do right now is listen to you." Lance's voice was sympathetic.

"I'm sorry, Lance, but will you take me home? I promise we can do a rain check or something. I just need to leave right now." My throat was dry, and I couldn't swallow. I had no idea that I would be feeling such pain so soon into the relationship with Roman.

"I understand, baby girl. Just let me get the check for our drinks, and we can leave."

Chapter Sixteen

Squirrels Always Get a Nut

The ride home was silent, all except for my sniffling. I had pleaded with Lance not to turn on the radio—I didn't feel like hearing music, be it fast or slow. It was taking us longer to get back to my house because of the stormy weather, and I could tell the quiet between Lance and me was not as calming for him as he drove. Still, I wouldn't allow him to turn on the radio.

The two of us were in total disbelief about Roman's actions. I could feel Lance looking over at me with remorse for what I was going through. I continued to cry because I couldn't believe I had allowed Roman to come into my life and corrupt it worry and heartache. I was content with things the way they were. Then, here Roman comes offering me a way of living that I thought could be more sufficient. I went for it, and with him of all people. I cried out of sheer pity for myself.

"Lance, you're welcomed to come in if you'd like,"

I said when we arrived at my house a few minutes later.

"Well, I wouldn't mind coming in for a little while just to talk to you and make sure that you don't cry yourself into a deep depression," he replied.

"I guess I do need someone to talk to. I just don't know if I want to talk about *him* though."

Lance opened his car door and started to get out of the car as he spoke. "That's cool. We can go through your DVD collection and find something to watch or talk about something else."

"Maybe we can find something funny, and that can make up for having to leave the club before Steve Harvey could show up," I said, opening my car door.

"Baby girl, why did you do that? You know I hate it when you open your own door. I know you've got things on your mind, so I'll excuse you this time."

I forced myself to smile. "Thanks, Lance. I'm sorry. I'm not use to a gentleman such as yourself. How did you get to be this way?"

"Learned behavior, baby girl. Learned behavior. My father use to open doors for my mom until he became ill and passed away," Lance explained as I turned the key then stepped into the house to flip on the lights.

"Oh, I'm sorry. I do remember when he passed away. We all got together at the office and sent flowers for the funeral. How long ago was that?"

"It's been close to three years now. I still miss the old man like it was yesterday, though. Pops taught me so many good values. Especially on how to keep a good woman."

"My folks are just about a thousand miles away, and it's almost like they're dead because I can never see them. Work is always getting in the way. My daddy won't allow my moms to have long distance on their phone. They're on a fixed income. I talk to them twice a month since I'm the only one who can reach out and touch someone. Money has been funny, so I've only been able to go visit about every two years. Not being able to see them for years at a time has been hard on me."

Lance stood. "I see what you're saying. Hey, just keep talking. I'm gonna browse through your DVDs to see what we might wanna watch."

"Try to pick something old; like something we might not have seen in a while, so we can trip. Do you want me to fix you a drink?"

"Sure, why not? Why don't we order some takeout, too? I'll go pick it up real quick. The rain has slacked off some. It wouldn't take me very long at all."

"Sounds good to me. Maybe this will be a better night after all. I'm starting to cheer up already."

We sat and tripped off a couple of Martin Lawrence movies while we ate shrimp fried rice from Ming's Chinese restaurant. Later on that night we had a couple of drinks while we sat and talked in the dimmed lighting. The television was turned off, and we had decided not to play any music. The conversation we began leaped from one thing to another, digging into some deep issues. We were totally into each other's opinions.

"Oh, so what you're trying to say is that men are not only stronger than women physically, but also mentally and emotionally?" I shook my finger at Lance as I spoke.

"Yeah. Contrary to popular belief, men have better willpower than women."

"Better willpower to do what, Lance?"

"Anything. For one thing, like walking away from anything we know is going to be bad for us in the long run."

"Are you talking about relationships?"

"Relationships and then some." Lance kept sipping on his bourbon as he spoke.

"Hell naw, Lance. Put the career man's drink down 'cause you're trippin'!" Lance couldn't avoid laughing at my response. "I think you're just looking for a certain reaction out of me, and I'm going to give it to you, too, brotha. Even the strongest men get weak, so I beg to differ with you on that."

"Really? Well differ, then."

"I know plenty of weak-minded men."

"Mmhmm, like whom?" Lance asked, sipping his drink again.

"Okay, well we can start with Adam since he was the first man around. Even a strong man like Adam became weak in many ways."

Lance's voice escalated. "Come on now! You can't blame the man for eating that fruit. Eve influenced him! You know you women have a way of making us men get into a lot of shit we ain't supposed to."

"Oh, so if she had told him to go stand under water holding on to boulders, I guess he would have done that, too, huh?" I kept my face serious, holding back my laughter.

"What kind of fruit was that anyway?"

"I take it that you didn't want to answer my question? I can't remember right off. I'll have to pull out the Bible to answer you."

"Naw. That's okay," Lance snapped as if he feared me beginning a sermon.

"Well, to answer your question, let's just call it an apple like most people, for the sake of this conversation."

"Okay, but listen to this. Adam wasn't thinking about that apple until Eve brought it up to him."

"And now you're about to help me prove my point. Even a strong man such as Adam couldn't resist temptation. He fell weak."

"But I keep telling you she influenced him. Temptation is hard to resist. And anyway, it's human nature to be weak."

"A cop-out if I ever heard one! Well, why is it that nowadays, no one has to tell a man about the apple, he just goes and picks one. And no doubt he'll eat it, too!"

"Baby girl, I don't know what you're talking about. I can't identify with that. I don't even like apples! I eat oranges!" There was a pause. Lance's breathing was heavy as though responding in such a serious manner had taken a lot out of him.

Finally, I burst into laughter. He wasn't making sense just then. "Now, what does that mean?"

"I don't know. Just thought I'd throw that one out to get you off track. You were winning the argument." We both continued laughing.

"I have really enjoyed our little talk tonight. You've gotten all philosophical on me. We should talk like this more often. I've got another question for you, though."

"Okay, shoot for it," Lance responded.

"What's been going on with you lately? I mean, you use to have as many calls as Roman would get on his cell, but now I don't see you dating as much or anything. What's wrong with that picture?"

"Uhmph. You mean you've noticed?"

"Yes, and I didn't want to say anything. I was just kind of hoping you'd talk to either Roman or me about it. Lance, what's going on? Are you okay?"

"Holiday, I'd like to talk about it. I just don't know if I need to."

"Lance, why? You know I'll talk to you about anything, don't you?"

"Yeah, it's just that it kind of involves you."

First silence fell on me, then I shook my head in confusion. "I'm not quite sure I understand, Lance. Come on, tell me. You can talk to me. I don't care what it is."

"Holiday, I love you."

"And I love you, too, Lance. Come on! Talk to me."

"You don't understand. I just did. I just told you. I love you. I really do, Holiday. I've fallen in love with you, and it's hard on me because you're my best friend's woman."

I had to clear my throat before I could speak. "Lance, how? Now, I'm really confused."

"Ever since that night we went to Precious Cargo I've felt something special for you. You stood there on that stage with all the lights and focus on you in the sexiest dress I've ever seen. Your body with all its magnificent curves accented that dress the way I know that no other woman could. I'd never seen you look so beautiful. I didn't realize that your business attire sheltered such a glorious body. And, baby girl, I must add that when you stood up there and took a look out into the audience with an empowered expression before you spoke, that had a heartening effect on me as well. Then, you rang out with a great deal of power and not to mention vast meaning. The only thing that came to mind when you gracefully walked down from that stage was, *Damn, what a woman!* I knew that night I wanted you to be a part of my life. I just didn't know how to tell you."

"Lance, I'm-I'm speechless. Really! I don't know how to respond. This is what's been weighing heavy on your mind?"

"Yes. It's affected me so much that I had to ask my female associates to give me some space. I asked them not to call me anymore. All I'd do while I was out with any of them is think of you and what you might be doing at that moment. It's very hard on me. I can't be serious with anyone right now. I mean, I know that you're my best friend's girl, but I really can't help but think about you every day."

"Lance, what were you thinking when Rome and I told you that we were together? You told me you were happy for us."

"Baby girl, I put on a game face, and I lied. I was hurt. You didn't see the look that I gave Roman? What I was really thinking was, *Oh, no! This can't be. This just can't be happening to me.* But, despite your relationship with him, I can't change the way I feel. I've tried. I just can't."

"What do I say, Lance? What do I do? This is blowing my mind right now."

"One of the reasons I feel I can't let go is because I know without a doubt that I'm the better man. This wasn't supposed to happen. Roman should've never had a chance with you. I'm not saying that you aren't smart for choosing to be his woman. I'm saying, between the two of us, I can love you better."

Tears came to my eyes. "Maybe I'm not so smart. You see what he's doing to me right now, don't you? I knew this man's track record—better than anyone knew, I think. He's been a very good friend *and* lover to me up until now. I just fooled myself into thinking that he could change for me. I'm sorry for crying on you, but this was unexpected, and to think, I've given him my heart when I wasn't willing to give it to any man. Now he's crushing it. Lance, go on and tell me. He's with another woman right now, isn't he? One of the women from the Jackson office, right?" As I continued to sob, Lance hesitated before speaking. I don't know if I really expected him to tell me the truth at that point.

"Holiday, I'm not going to tell you what we discussed when I talked to Roman. I'm still saying, however, that I'm the better man. It's tough, but it's reality. This could cost us all our friendships, and I don't want to lose either one of you. Roman is all I've known for years as a friend, and outside of his womanizing, he's not a bad person. Just as I learned my values from my father, Roman learned his ways from his father. I believe that not having a mother there to raise him is what caused him to be so numb to the fact that he's caused a lot of pain to a number of women. He just can't help it right now. But, you're a damn good friend as well, Holiday. What's a man to do in this situation?"

"Be a friend to me now, and give me some advice. What do I do about him? What do I do about you?"

"Right now, Holiday, I don't believe I could give you the best advice. What I want to say may be a little selfish. I want you to someday be Mrs. Ferrell. I do have a suggestion, though. Why don't we just be oblivious about Roman and have our moment for right now."

Lance came closer and spoke with lustful eyes. Since the relationship with Roman, I hadn't taken the time to notice how attracted I was to him. The thought of wanting him slapped me in the face so hard that it quickly became a rude awakening. I wanted to take back the expression that I'd just given Lance as he came closer, drawing deeper into my soul with his eyes. But, I knew there was no denying the lust I had equally begun to feel.

"Lance, I don't think I can. I'd feel terrible the next time I talk to Rome. I know he's probably not doing right by me, but I do have a conscience. I'm sorry. I'm sorry, Lance." I lowered my head and more tears started to flow.

Lance sat motionless for a moment. It was hard for me to tell what he had begun to think. Though I wanted to see what his expression might have been, I couldn't bring myself to lift my head. My hurt and anger had filled me with so much sorrow. I just sat with a bowed head, hoping that he would just get up and leave. Just as I had that thought, Lance slid even closer to me and put his hand under my chin. He looked me in my eyes without blinking as if he was studying a book. His next move yielded my heart. He started from my chin and worked his way up, kissing my tears from my face. He was so gentle and cautious to catch every tear flowing down each cheek. My heart wouldn't let me reject him. It felt so good and so right. But, I knew I was wrong, and so was Lance. Our moment had come at a time when I was vulnerable. It's not an excuse; however, it is the reason I allowed it to happen.

"Holiday, let me make love to you," Lance pleaded to me in a soft, but adamant voice.

"Lance, I-I-I," I tried to speak but couldn't because Lance had begun to kiss me.

As we were kissing he began to slowly lie back on the couch, pulling me down on top of him. My mind, believe it or not, was actually saying *no*, but, my body was screaming *yes*. He kissed me as though my lips tasted like buttery sweet toffee. Imagine that. I didn't want him to let go. And believe me, he didn't. As we continued to kiss, he started gripping my butt and slowly, but firmly grinding against my body, which was screaming *hell yes*, so rejecting him had totally faded from my mind. I felt his nature beginning to rise. As it got larger and larger, I started to think that maybe this was something I shouldn't do. I tried to pull myself up, but he wouldn't let go.

"Baby girl, what's wrong? Are you okay?" Lance maintained that soft and sensual voice while looking up at me.

"Yeah, but we shouldn't do this, Lance." I was actually trying to convince myself.

"Hey, I think you want to. I can see it in your face. It's okay. Come on. I have condoms."

"No, that's not the problem. And Rome's not the problem either." I pulled myself up and slid down a bit on the couch.

"Then, what's wrong?"

I was thinking that he was too much "man" for me. I was embarrassed to tell him, so I just kind of played it off.

"Nothing. I'm just nervous. I think I want to."

"Are you sure?" Lance asked me out of politeness, but I'm almost certain he was hoping for a yes.

"Yes, I'm sure."

I was wishing that I'd had the courage to say, "No,

I'm not sure! You've got too much going on down there for me," but I just tried to relax as he pulled down his pants. I then took off his shirt. Once he got the condom on, he laid on the couch once again. This frightened me because I knew that this meant he wanted me to ride on top of him. I said to myself, *Holiday, tell this man you can't do that! He's going to hurt you, girl, and you'll be lying up in the hospital somewhere. You better tell him you can't handle this!* But, silly me, I just went on to take a deep breath and then climbed on top of him. I was right! It didn't even want to go in. He started to grind to help loosen me up. That helped. So, once it was in, I was afraid to move. I didn't even look at him. I stared up at the ceiling so Lance couldn't see my expression while he held my hips and penetrated me. I was so ready for it to be over, and it had just begun. He was actually doing all the work. He was gentle, but it didn't matter. When a man has that much tool to work with, he doesn't have to try to hurt you. He just can.

Lance realized that he was too much for me, so he tried a different approach. He asked me if we could go to the bedroom. I approved, so we headed in that direction. Once we got in there, he positioned me on the bed, then proceeded to get on top of me. Once he was able to work it in, it actually started to feel good. His dick touched every wall and reached every corner. I couldn't believe it. I had never experienced this much pleasure before. No man had ever been able to make me feel this way. I was use to a climax stimulated by kissing or fondling my clitoris. Lance was able to reach and touch spots I didn't even know I had. He was totally satisfying me, and he hadn't even gone "downtown" on me, yet. I was starting to think that I would definitely be back in this predicament of being in the bed with Lance again. How could any woman deny herself the best sex she'd ever had? You can't! You just can't!

Lance never went downtown that night. I was beginning to wonder if he was into doing that type of thing. It didn't matter because I was very much satisfied with the entire act. I thought about something Lance had said: He wanted me to someday be Mrs. Ferrell. Although this was flattering, I really didn't like the way Mrs. Holiday Ferrell sounded coming out of my mouth. It just didn't have a nice ring to it. This was not the reason that I couldn't see marrying Lance. I just felt that he was saying all of that stuff out of lust.

I didn't know how or if I would even try to break the news to Rome. I still loved him even though I felt he was spending time with another woman. Love just doesn't fade like magic, but it sure will appear unexpectedly like magic.

Chapter Seventeen
Secrets in the Dark

The night I'd had with Lance was beautiful, and no one could take it away. But, it was time to face reality. I had just slept with my man's best friend. The man that I loved so dearly. The same man who was able to make me commit to a relationship with him when no other man could. However, this was also the same man who wouldn't even speak to me on the phone when he knew I was sitting right in front of Lance when they were talking. Who did he think he was fooling? Besides, I still didn't receive a phone call all night. Not even to say, "Hey, boo. I'm okay." I could've been lying up all night worrying about Roman. He wouldn't have known because he never called to find out.

Waking up to a new day after having slept with Lance proved that the night of bliss was not just a dream. The moment I opened my eyes, the soreness between my legs screamed *mercy*. I slowly rose up to slide out of the bed in which I had slept solo. I begged Lance to leave after repeatedly making love. I knew that turning to see him lying next to me once daylight came would greatly affect my conscience. I had hoped it would be some sort of relief if Lance's naked body had disappeared, but I was wrong. Though Lance had left, my conscience was there to keep me company.

It was Sunday, and I hadn't called Erika in a while by this time. I was starting to miss talking to her, but I refused to phone her. If she wanted to speak to me, she would have to call me first. I felt I didn't do anything to her, and if I did, I didn't do enough to deserve her treating me with silence.

Crystal and her cousin Shaundra returned from the weekend cheerleading camp early Sunday. I made an agreement with Crystal's aunt that I'd be the one to drop the girls at camp if she'd pick them up. Crystal and Shaundra got ready for church faster than I could and kept calling to see if I was on my way to pick them up. Roman distracted me with early contact.

"Good morning, boo. How are you?" Roman talked as though everything was as fine as it was before he'd left for Jackson.

"Fine," I said matter-of-factly. I couldn't believe he was trying to act as though nothing happened.

"Did you have a good time last night?"

"Yes."

"What time did you and Lance get in?"

"I don't remember."

"Is everything okay? You seem to be answering me rather shortly."

"Really? Well, I'm fine."

"So, you did enjoy yourself last night, didn't you?" Roman was trying to get me to open up to him.

"Immensely!" I continued with my deliberate short responses.

"Okay, Holiday. I'm serious now. Do we need to talk? What's going on with you this morning?"

"Roman, I think you know. Don't try to play ignorant with me. It's not working. You're too smart for me to believe that. Yes, we need to talk. Just not right now. I'm trying to get ready for church, and I have to be on the other side of town to pick up Crystal in less than an hour. So, if you don't mind, I'll get back with you later."

"No, I don't mind, but do you mind if I still go to church with you? You sound like you don't want to be bothered with a brotha."

"Hmmph, you're starting to act like Darius now. Every time he knew he'd done something wrong, he'd try to pacify me by offering to do something he knew I'd want him to do."

"Hey, lady, you're wrong for that! I've attended church every Sunday now with the exception of one or two. Don't even start trying to compare me to your baby's daddy."

"Whatever, Roman! I've got to go. Show up for church if you want to. It's a free country. I can't tell you where to worship."

"You don't want to see me there?"

"Bye, Roman! Don't make me hang this phone up in your face!"

"Why are you doing this? Why are you being so cold to me?"

" 'Cause I've already said too many times that I

need to get off the phone, and you're still holding me up. I'll talk to you later!" I knew he got the hint. I had too much harshness in my voice for him not to understand.

I managed to make it to church on time for Sunday school despite the hold–up. Worship started on time for a change, which was great, but if Roman was going to show, he had already missed the first fifteen minutes of the service. I tried to decide what I was going to say to him, but the night before kept lingering in my mind. I knew that sleeping with Roman's best friend was more than enough to send him over the top. Heck, it's flat-out betrayal, and I never knew a man who would just grin and bear such a thought. Instead of listening to the sermon, I began carefully collecting words in my mind for my talk with Roman.

Rome finally showed up. He crossed over several people so that he could sit next to me. Once he was seated, he kissed me on the cheek. I didn't respond. I didn't even look at him. He leaned over closer to me and put his arm around my shoulder to share my Bible during scripture reading. I was a little agitated, which was bad, because this was God's house.

About halfway through the service, I was drawn to look over to my right. For about the last fifteen minutes, I could see someone in my peripheral vision kept leaning forward as if looking down the pew at me. I couldn't stand it anymore, so I looked that way when it happened again. I discovered it was Erika. She was busted. She tried to play it off by smiling then looking away, but she was caught.

After worship, while everyone was participating in fellowship, I walked over to her and spoke. I didn't want to discuss our differences at church, so we hugged, and she asked me to call her later that evening. I agreed that I would, but before I walked off, Roman approached us.

"Hey, ladies. What's going on?" I didn't particularly care for him to be standing there with us, and my face showed it. That didn't make him leave though.

"Roman, how are you today? You're looking nice as usual," Erika stated. I couldn't tell if she was flirting or just making conversation. Roman wasn't looking his best that morning. Erika and I both had seen him look far better.

"Am I? I don't know. I'm not feeling too well this morning. I had assumed it showed in my clothes." Suddenly I felt Roman must've deliberately ragged himself, hoping to get some sympathy since he knew I was angry with him.

"Naw, you look great! I hope you feel better, though." Erika was just gassing up his head. I knew my girlfriend. She wasn't blind, and she knew he could look better.

"Erika, I'll call you. Crystal, Shaundra, come on let's go."

Roman proceeded to follow me as though he had come in with me. Once we got to the church parking lot, we went in two directions. I got into my car and cranked it up. I had to sit still before pulling off because of traffic. When I looked over to the left, I noticed Roman watching me from where he'd parked. It kind of spooked me for a second, but I got over it pretty quick. I figured he was just waiting to see me pull off safely; however, his expression was kind of eerie. I couldn't quite understand why he had such a look on his face. I kept glancing in my rearview mirror to see if he was following me. Something about my instincts told me I needed to be cautious.

The girls were out of school on Monday for a teacher in-service day, so Crystal had asked to spend the night at Shaundra's house. I called Darius's sister, Melinda, and asked if she'd mind. She didn't have a problem with it so we went home to get Crystal some more clothes. As we were packing, the phone rang.

"Hello?"

"Boo, are you ready to talk now?"

"No. Actually you're gonna have to wait. I have to take Crystal back on the other side of town, but when I get back, I'll call you."

"How long do you think it'll take you?"

"I don't know. If you let me get off the phone, I could leave and get something done."

"Alright, Holiday. I'll just talk to you later."

As I was driving, I was contemplating what I would say to Roman. I didn't know how I was going to let him know about Lance and me, but I knew that I was going to break up with him. Not to be with Lance. I just felt that I needed to put my guard up because of what happened when I couldn't reach Roman. That hurt me. I didn't want to get hurt anymore. Besides, I figured once Roman heard about Lance and me, he'd break up with me and hate me forever.

I had almost made it back home when I looked up in my rearview mirror and spied a car that looked like Roman's. It was remaining a safe enough distance behind me to where I couldn't distinguish the man driving. I tried to slow down so the driver would catch up, but he only slowed down as well. I was really starting to feel eerie. I decided to turn down a different street to see if the driver would follow, and he did. I figured by this time it had to be Rome. Why he was following me was a complete mystery.

When I finally made it home, I called Roman like I'd promised. "Rome, I'm home, and I'm ready to talk." I maintained my level of agitation in my voice. I wanted him to know that I was serious.

"Okay. Do you mind if I come in? I'm parked right outside anyway."

I wasn't surprised. I knew he had followed me, but I do have to admit that for a second I was speechless.

"What? I don't know, Rome. I wasn't intending on having company." My first mind said not to mention the fact that I knew he'd been trailing me, so I went along with that instinct.

"Holiday, boo, listen to you. You sound as though I'm not your man. Boo, this is your man you're talking to. Why are you being this way to me? Come on now and open the door."

"Alright. I guess we do need to talk face-to-face, but Rome I'm not intending on you being here long."

"Damn! All right. Just come open the door then."

I went to open the door, and when I did, he gave me a long kiss. I wasn't pleased about that, but I figured I'd better play it cool. The fact that I was alone with this man is what made me decide to take on a different attitude. He'd already been following me, and that put a touch of fear in my heart. Besides, one thing that my mother taught me about a man is that you can never tell what's on his mind. I didn't see any point in irritating Roman before I'd told him about Lance and me. That was going to be enough news by itself to upset him.

"Rome, thank you for such a sweet kiss, but we really need to talk."

"I'm listening, boo." He was so calm.

"While I was out with Lance, I couldn't enjoy myself for thinking of you. You made me feel good at first by trying to confirm for me that you weren't away doing anything deceitful, but then I went to call you back to see if I would be able to call you before I went to bed, and I couldn't even reach you. Now, I don't know who you thought I was, but apparently you had me mixed up with one of the hoochies you're use to going out with. You did just what you thought was enough to pacify me—calling me, probably so I wouldn't call you—then you went on to doing your merry little thing."

"Holiday, boo, where is this coming from? I wasn't expecting this. I really wasn't."

"Oh yeah. Then what were you expecting? Huh?"

"I don't know, but I wasn't expecting this. Boo, I thought you'd trust me. If I had known this would bother you so much, I would have told management to exclude me from the trip this weekend. I've told you, I can only see a lifetime with you and Crystal. There's no one else out there for me."

"Then, why the hell wouldn't you speak with me when Lance called you? Because, you were with another woman! That's why!"

"Boo, no! Please, don't do this to me. Boo, I love you so much. I don't know where you're getting this. Didn't Lance tell you what happened?"

"No. What do you mean?"

"We were in the manager's office when he called. We were trying to wrap up a meeting about possibly working next Saturday. Before that, we had spent the bulk of the time back in the file room. Well, I didn't know it at the time, but our cell phones couldn't pick up reception back there. I saw that you had been trying to call, but I couldn't talk during the meeting. I knew that you guys were out having a good time, so I told Lance to just let you know that I love you and I would see you this morning for church. Boo, there's no other woman. I wish I had called you last night before I went to bed. Maybe you wouldn't be so angry with me this morning, but I didn't want you to think I was paranoid about you being out with Lance. I just figured you'd have a good time and we'd see each other this morning. Boo, I'm so sorry I didn't call you back. Forgive me, please? This is simple. We can get through this." He had begun to embrace me about halfway through his speech.

Do you know what a screeching car sounds like when it's trying to make a sudden stop? You know that *eeeeerrrrrrk* sound. Well, that's what I felt like. My mind was trying to come to a sudden but *complete* stop. I couldn't believe what I was hearing. *Does this mean that Lance deceived me?* I wondered. I was taken aback. Tears began to well up in my eyes.

"Roman, I-I—," I wanted to say something. Anything. But I couldn't speak. What was there to say after hearing his innocence?

"Boo, what's wrong? Why all the tears?"

"Rome, I believe you, but we still can't be together. I'm sorry." I figured that before telling him about the night before, I'd better assure him that we shouldn't be together. I don't know why I thought breaking up with him first would make telling him about Lance and me a lighter situation. It was just a thought on impulse.

Roman looked at me with such amazement. He couldn't understand why after his apology I'd still say he and I shouldn't be together. "Help me understand, Holiday. You're hurting me right now. What's going on with you?"

"We couldn't *possibly* be together now, even if I wanted to. I've done something terrible. The unthinkable! I can't believe . . ." I started trembling with hurt and pain, and also fear.

"Holiday, calm down and tell me what you're trying to say to me."

"Roman, I-I-I've already cheated on you." I was afraid to look into his eyes, but I forced myself to.

He stood there motionless, barely even blinking. He had a look of hurt and disappointment all over his face. The silence filled the room, and it was killing me. We stared at each other for at least twenty seconds, which seemed like an eternity, before either of us made a move. Finally, it happened. Roman shed some tears. He slowly took a seat in my wing chair, bent over, and cupped his face with his hands. At that point he began to weep like a newborn baby. He may as well have stabbed me in the heart with a butcher knife because my heart felt pierced anyway. I was torn to see him so hurt.

"It was Lance, wasn't it?" he asked softly.

"How did you know?" My face was also filled with tears.

"You didn't have time to be with anyone else, Holiday. Something told me to call you back last night. I should've followed my instincts. But I told myself that since you were with my *boy*, everything was all right. Damn it! Damn it, Holiday!"

"I'm sorry, Rome! I know it's a little too late for that, but I really am."

"How could you be so gullible? Whatever the hell he told you to make you have sex with him couldn't have been the truth, and you fell for it. I've *never* known you to be that weak. One of the reasons I chose you to be my woman was 'cause I knew you were tough. I knew you had a good head on your shoulders and couldn't easily be persuaded by anyone. How could you've allowed this to happen?"

"Rome, I was hurting. I thought you were with another woman, and Lance said—"

Rome interrupted me. "Lance said I was with another woman?"

"No, but he wouldn't tell me what was said between you two when he called you. I was misled! I can't believe this!"

"You can't believe this! You can't! Holiday, you are a much stronger woman than this. Do you want me to believe you didn't plan for this to happen? You wanted this to happen, didn't you?"

"Rome, I'm telling you the truth. I thought I was a much stronger woman than this, too. I'm very disappointed in myself. I still love you, Rome. I know that's not going to make much of a difference now, but I just want you to know that I still love you, baby." I fell onto the couch, bawling.

"Holiday, you couldn't see that all he wanted to do was get a piece of ass? And, you provided him with just what he wanted. This man was my friend. I know him. But, he didn't have to pick you to do this to."

"I know. That's why I don't feel like I was just a

piece of ass to him. And, you need to stop belittling me by saying so. I know you're hurting, but don't stand here in my house and try to make me out to be a whore. I know you know that I'm not. I've said it, and I'm saying it again. Roman, I'm sorry."

"Holiday, I'm sorry, too." Roman turned and walked out on me.

Chapter Eighteen
No Game, No Gain

Roman left me weeping and feeling sorry for myself on the couch. I balled up into a knot, and I didn't want to come out of it either. My phone was ringing off the hook right next to me, but I wouldn't budge to answer it. The answering machine would record the messages and I could hear them. Several of them were from Lance. Roman had gone over to talk to him. Lance said that he just wondered if I was okay, and for me to let him hear from me. He sounded concerned, but I was in no mood to discuss anything with anyone the remainder of the night.

The next morning, I called in to work. I knew that would put me behind on my projects, but I felt like I just couldn't face the world. I still wouldn't answer the phone, either. Erika had called, wondering why I didn't phone her like I had said I would. Lance left more messages saying that he just wanted to check on me. I was sickened by his voice. I wanted to unplug the answering machine, but I was afraid Crystal would need me. Not once did Roman call me, though. That made me sick as hell.

By late that afternoon, I had started to feel somewhat better. I'd sat most of the morning rethinking the whole situation. Later that evening, I had a whole new outlook on everything. I no longer felt like I was totally at fault. I had started to realize that Rome actually had turned everything around on me. I remembered Rome's track record and had begun to think that he may not have been so innocent after all. Lance had his share of mischief in the time I had known him, but I started to have a gut feeling he didn't intentionally deceive me for a night of passion. Not the Lance I knew. And we were better friends than that.

I went to the phone late that evening when it rang to look at the caller ID. It was Rome. He wanted to know if he and Lance could meet with me to talk. I invited the two of them over, and to my surprise they drove up at the same time. We sat and had a heart-to-heart talk.

"So, is it true, Lance? Was I just something you were doing the other night?" I wanted to know.

Lance replied in a voice deeper than I ever remembered. "*Absolutely not!* What we shared was very special to me, and if I had my way, it wouldn't have just stopped there. That was your decision. You asked me to go home. I wanted to stay over afterward, but you started feeling guilty, remember? I'm appalled that you would even think such a thing of me."

"Well, it's not just me. I had a little help in thinking so. Isn't that right, Rome?" I asked.

"You were *my* woman! He was my best friend in the whole fuckin' world, and you've fucked him! What kind of shit is that to do to me?" Rome asked, outraged at the thought.

"Rome, you're trying to flip this whole thing around on me. I don't appreciate it one bit. You won't admit to it, and I'm sure Lance will *still* protect you so I won't even ask him, but I know you were up to no good Saturday night."

"Holiday, no matter what I say to you, you're still going to think what you want." This was Roman's opportunity to prove me wrong, and he chose to beat around the bush.

"Well, why don't you try her? Tell her what you told me on the phone Saturday night," Lance insisted.

"Man, why are you even going there?" Roman even looked busted.

" 'Cause you got me looking like a total villain in this woman's eyes. I look like the biggest dog who ever lived on the face of the Earth right now. Holiday, you know I'm not the type of man who fucks 'em and leaves 'em. Even if I was, you would never be a victim." Lance's confidence and the sincerity in his eyes convinced me he was telling the truth.

"Then tell me what was said on the phone when you called him the other night, Lance." I just thought I'd try it one more time.

"No, I'm going to leave that up to Roman's conscience. But, I know you're smart enough to read between the lines, Holiday."

"Lance, man, like I told you yesterday, people make mistakes. I still love you like a brother. It hurts like hell, but I can't let this come between us. We've shared too many years of great friendship for me to believe that you've never been a friend to me.

Holiday is a hell of a woman. I understand why being alone in her presence could be tempting. I'm willing to try to get past this, but I want my relationship with Holiday to work—even if that means you can't hang out with us anymore. In plain terms, man, you're going to have to back the fuck off."

"And like I said, I still love you like a brother, but if you can't be the man that Holiday needs you to be to her, then *you* need to back the fuck off," Lance said.

The two of them stared each other down, not even once blinking. I wanted to cut through the tension that had begun to thicken at that moment, but I knew I didn't own a tool sharp enough. Once they left my place, the only thing that we'd established was that each of us was wrong in some way or another. I told Rome to give me some more time. I had to think about things and see if I could determine what was best for me. I wasn't so sure anymore that a relationship was what I needed. A lot of extra stuff comes along with commitment. I still didn't trust Rome, and I was almost certain that he no longer trusted me.

Chapter Nineteen
The Secret is Out

I finally returned Erika's call.

"Holiday, what's been going on? I know we haven't talked in a while, but I still care. How have you been doing, girlfriend?"

"Girlfriend's got problems, as usual." I could only speak dryly.

"Well, I said I'd be here for you, and I meant it. You can talk to me."

"Roman and I broke up."

"Oh no! When? What happened?"

"A lot happened, and I don't believe I'm going to discuss it. I just called to give you a holla. We broke up Sunday evening, so I wasn't in the best of moods when you called and left that message yesterday."

"That's understandable. I still say that if you need to talk to someone, I'm here for you. I have my share of problems, too. I'm in no shape to judge anyone else."

"Erika, I feel so stupid. I can't seem to know when

I'm being naïve. If you tell me, then I'll understand it perfectly, but why can't I determine it for myself? It just makes me feel so dumb!" The frustration was starting to flow through my voice then.

"Holiday, you're not dumb. You're one of the smartest women I know. Hell, you might even be smarter than me. The problem is, you're human. You're subject to any of life's tribulations just like any of us."

"Yeah, but how do you explain me hurting Rome?"

"You hurt Roman? How?"

This time I put on my voice of shame. "I bet you can't guess."

"No, but the sound of your voice is starting to worry me. What happened?"

"I slept with Lance." There was a pause before I could continue. "But before you say anything, I know I was wrong. I know that Lance and I are both scum for stooping so low, but it occurred for a reason. The reason is not an excuse, but it's why I allowed it to happen."

I continued to explain the circumstances to Erika, hoping she'd understand. We talked for almost two hours on the phone. She had some encouraging words for me, but she scorned me as well.

"Holiday, I knew when we all went out that night, both of them had a thing for you. I could tell by the way Lance was playing with your hair while the two of you were dancing. And when we were back at your place, neither one of them could seem to take their eyes off you."

"Erika, I didn't see any of that."

"That's because you weren't as in to them as they were in to you. I noticed 'cause I couldn't help but pay attention to both of them. I remembered how slick you described them as being, so I watched their every move. They wouldn't have given me the time of day if I'd wanted it. I should've told you to be careful, those slick bastards!"

"So, do you think both of them played me?"

"No, I'm not saying that at all. I'm just saying that I'm not a bad-looking woman. I know I'm not, but I couldn't get either one of them to pay me any attention. And you know me, I'll flirt with a man—even if I don't like him. They couldn't hear my cunning words for being all in to you."

"Erika, that's not true. They were very nice to you. Anyway, what's that got to do with whether you think they played me or not? "

"They were nice. And although I believe them to be players, somehow I don't believe they'd ever choose you to do their bullshit to. They seemed to genuinely care about the friendship."

"Okay, then since you could tell they cared a lot about our friendship, how could you say that when we were all out, their feelings were greater than I perceived." Erika had me more confused.

"Simple. While I was dancing with one, he was busy watching you with the other. It was kind of uncomfortable, but you can't say that I didn't tell you that something like this would happen."

"I just can't believe that. Not that you weren't uncomfortable, but it's hard to believe that they paid so much attention to me."

"Well, they did. Believe it or not." Erika sighed.

"Okay, once we were alone, it was obvious. But I just couldn't see it at first. Right now, I'm not speaking to either of them. They've been calling me off the hook, too."

"What are you going to do?"

"Be by myself. You were right. I wasn't ready."

Erika and I got off the phone, and I tried to continue on with my life as it was before all the drama occurred. I just acted as if I never slept with Rome or Lance. This kept me from going into a deep depression. Besides, I had Crystal to think of.

Chapter Twenty

I Want You Back

A couple of weeks went by before I was willing to try to talk to Rome. He and Lance had been trying to contact me either at work, by cell phone, or at home. I conveniently made myself unavailable so I wouldn't have to deal with them. I guess Rome decided he'd had enough. He showed up on my job a few days later.

"Rome, what are you doing here?"

Roman never showed a hint of a smile. His eyes spoke a language that disturbed me a bit. "Holiday, if you're gonna keep avoiding me, I want to hear it from you face-to-face. Don't leave me to assume it, boo. That's tacky, and I know you're a better woman than that."

I set the stack of files that I'd been researching down on my desk. "Okay, it's lunchtime. Why don't we get out of here and talk?" I stood to walk him out. He was looking fine as usual. I didn't want any of my coworkers to get ideas, so I escorted Roman through the office so they knew he was with me.

"Do you want me to drive?" Roman asked when we finally made it to the door.

"No, just let me meet you. Give me about ten minutes to wrap up first."

We discussed where we'd meet for lunch then he left. As I headed back to my office, I stared straight ahead. There were speculating looks from many of the women, and I didn't want to answer questions about Roman. I explained to my staff that I might be back from lunch a little late, and I finished up the last-minute details and headed out to meet Roman at A & R Barbecue.

"Holiday, have you spoken to Lance since we last talked?" Roman asked the minute I sat down at the restaurant.

"Is that the first thing you want to know from me? You haven't seen nor heard from me in more than two weeks, and the first thing you want to know is have I spoken to Lance?"

"Well, it's not the only thing, but I do want to know, if you don't mind."

"Well if it makes you feel better, I haven't spoken with Lance since the last time I talked to you."

"Then I do feel better. At least now I know it just wasn't me that you had a problem with."

"What are you talking about, Rome?"

"You weren't answering my calls, so I figured you had something against me."

"No, and I don't want to sit and talk about the past either." The look I gave him made it evident that I hadn't come to discuss what happened between us, but he ignored it.

"Holiday, do you have any idea how this has affected me? How can you sit here and deny me answers that could make me feel better?"

I sighed deeply. I had compassion. I just didn't want to talk about my faults. "Roman, I really don't want to go through the motions."

"In other words, you're gonna be selfish and consider your feelings first. Harboring what really happened is what makes you feel good."

I took a long look at Roman and said, "Fine, what do you want to know?"

"Did Lance say that I was with another woman?"

"No, he never said that. That was my assumption. If he had told me anything even remotely close to that, I wouldn't be sitting here with you now."

"See, Holiday, that's strange because I think and feel enough for you to wanna still communicate with you. Why is it so hard for you to deal with me?"

"I've been through soooo much in my life, especially the last five years, that I'm just not willing to take anything off anyone right now. We've shared enough time together for me to still care, but if you feel the need to be with someone else, I can let you go on."

"Holiday, don't be so tough on me. I need you. Still. The last couple of weeks have been hard. I know I still love you, and we can work this out. Let's give it one more chance. Please." Roman held my hand and gave me a heartrending look.

Despite his efforts, my heart went unchanged. "Rome, you're making me feel uncomfortable right now."

"How so? 'Cause I'm holding your hand?"

"No, because I feel as though you're begging me, and I don't want you to do that. I really don't feel I can be the woman you need me to be. Better yet, I don't feel you can be the man I need you to be."

"Boo, you're still my boo. I don't want to have to let go."

There was another pause. I rubbed my hand across my face, and said, "Okay, how about this—let's still communicate every day and take it one day at a time. This way I won't feel attached to a relationship. Will that work?"

"Holiday, is there someone else? Are you thinking of Lance or something?"

"No. I'm sorry it seems that way, but the answer is no."

"Then, help me figure out how you could spend as much quality time with me as you have and not think enough of it to wanna preserve it? Huh? Help me understand that, boo."

"It's not you, Rome. It's me. Erika tried to tell me I wasn't ready. That's the only reason I could have allowed that to happen between Lance and me. I don't want to be in another relationship until I know for a fact I'm ready."

"Okay. Fine, Holiday. One day at a time. At least, do you miss me?"

"Of course I do!"

"How much?"

I kind of figured where he was going with this, but I just played dumb.

"Roman, what are you tryna get me to say? That I wanna give you a sneak peek of my panties?" I laughed.

He didn't laugh with me. Only licked his lips. "Boo, how much time do you have on your lunch break?"

"I have some time. Why do you ask?" I put a huge grin on my face.

"Let's hurry up and finish eating. I've got some time, too." Roman gave me that sexy-ass wink that I love so much. I could feel myself getting moist.

Well, I didn't know it when I first woke up that morning, but by noon, I was back at my house in bed with Rome. Our sex was intense, too. He cried. I cried. He had multiple orgasms. I had multiple orgasms. He succeeded in making me realize that I, in fact, had needed him. Rome had a way of making me feel like I was all that and then some. Everything I thought I needed, he made sure I got it. He acted as though he felt there was no excuse for me not having all the "good" life has to offer. While he may have been a whoremonger, he managed to show me that when he was with me, he was with me. Nothing else seemed to matter to him. I'd never had that in any other relationship before. Not even with Darius, Crystal's dad.

Though I originally wanted to take it slow, Roman and I went on to have what we thought was a beautiful relationship for a while. He took me to meet his father, Mr. Charlie Broxton, and to my surprise they looked nothing alike. I also got a glimpse of Roman's mother on a painting hanging over the fireplace. He was the spitting image of his mother, only the male version. Roman said his father absolutely adored the fact that he looked so much like his mother. I think this was a comforting sign for Mr. Charlie that Roman's mother had left him a part of her.

* * *

Shortly after Roman and I got back together, the tragedy of September 11 struck, affecting the entire world. Roman and I grew even closer. We spent every moment we could together. I still couldn't bring myself to let Crystal in on our secret, but there were times when she'd say something to let me know that I wasn't fooling her. After all, Roman began to spend a great deal of time with Crystal and me.

Christmas 2001 came and went. Roman and I exchanged very loving and thoughtful gifts. I wasn't sure if Roman had been speaking to Lance or not, and I didn't ask. My guess is they were still communicating, given the fact that they still had to work together. I never regretted the night Lance and I shared, but I was very sorry to be the damaging factor between two friends. After working with them for so long, I never would've thought it would come to all that it had.

Chapter Twenty-one

Once, Twice . . . Who's Counting?

Late January 2002, Crystal was away attending the final weekend of cheerleading camp, preparing for the upcoming annual competition. I took advantage of the time to do some early spring cleaning. I went through Crystal's dresser drawers, her closet, and pulled her mattress up to flip it. I discovered a diary in the midst. I put the mattress back down and sat on Crystal's bed staring at this bright red journal. It wasn't locked, and the urge to look through it grew stronger the more I sat and held it. I sighed deeply and decided against it. I've always taught Crystal not to look through my personal journal, so I felt I owed her the same respect.

Roman was at work, but I was expecting to see him later. When the phone rang, I hurried down the hall to the living room to answer it. I thought maybe it was Roman, so I was caught off guard when I noticed Lance's cell number on my caller ID. He hadn't attempted to contact me in several months. Surprised, I didn't know what to do, so I let the phone continue ringing. I pushed the vacuum aside and stepped closer to listen to the answering machine. Lance hung up without leaving a message. As soon as I reached to turn the vacuum on, the phone rang again. It was Lance once again. I thought, *Well maybe he's calling back to leave a message this time.* I don't know what came over me, but before the answering machine could finish talking, I picked up the phone.

"Lance? Hello, Lance?" I was hoping that he hadn't hung up.

"Holiday, you answered." He sounded surprised.

"Yes, I'm here."

"I was going to leave you a message. I just wanted to see if you ever found my sunglasses. I had told Roman some time ago when you guys started seeing each other again to ask you if you'd seen them. I guess he keeps forgetting."

"Well, I haven't, Lance. I'm cleaning up today and I haven't seen them. Where do you think you might've left them?"

"I was sitting on the couch that day all of us went to the movies."

I walked over to the couch and started feeling around between the cushions. "Oh, you know what? Here they are right between the pillows. You're lucky they aren't broken."

"I'm in the neighborhood. If you don't mind, I'd like to come by and pick them up."

"Well, I guess it's okay."

We hung up the phone, and I went to put on some decent clothes. Lance must've been in the neighborhood as he'd said because it didn't take him long to get over to my house. I barely had enough time to change clothes before the doorbell began ringing.

When I opened the door, my knees almost buckled at the sight of him. He had on the finest suede suit I'd ever seen. It was khaki colored, and he had a derby to match. His goatee was neatly groomed as usual, and his caramel complexion seemed flawless, reflecting off the tone of his garments. I cleared my throat and spoke. "Lance, you must've been around the corner."

"Actually, I was at the Radio Shack not far from here. Being so close made me think of calling you."

I stood holding the door open, looking into his eyes, but not really hearing what he'd said. When he finished his sentence, it was obvious, because I didn't respond immediately.

"Well do you want to come in for a minute?" I only asked after looking over at the clock on the wall and remembering that Roman was still at work.

"Sure I do, but I hope I'm not disturbing your cleaning."

"I was about finished when you called." I beckoned him in and closed the door. The breeze from shutting the door caused his scent to rise into my nostrils, bringing to mind old memories of the one night we'd shared. "So, how have you been?"

"I'm okay, actually. I've been doing well. I've been wanting to know how you're doing, though."

"I'm alright. I've been doing okay myself." I was trying to go with the flow without showing too many emotions. It seemed as if Lance was, too. He kept nodding while staring at the floor.

"How's he been treating you?" Lance asked.

Once again, I had to clear my throat. I didn't know exactly what he was looking for when he asked me a question like that. I tried to play it off though. "We've been doing great. Yeah, great. We've been doing great."

"Are you sure?" This time Lance conjured up the strength to look me in the eye.

"Lance, what are you looking for? What is it you want me to say? Are you trying to tell me something?"

"No, I'm not. Actually, I wouldn't know anything. Roman will never tell me his business like that again. I'm sure of it. As a matter of fact, someone has been placing prank calls to my mother for a couple of months now, I've had my suspicions, so Roman and I don't speak."

"Prank calls to your mother?" I was confused.

"Yes, to my mother. She's phoned me at least twice a week in the past two months, frightened someone has hurt me."

"Is that what the prankster told her?"

"Yes, and I believe that prankster to be your boyfriend," he replied, looking at the floor.

"I certainly hope Roman wouldn't do anything like that, Lance. Please get your mother's number changed. That's horrible for someone to do to her."

"I'm working to get her a private number now."

Lance continued to look down while we both searched for another topic.

"Roman's working at the Collierville office today. Why aren't you there?" I asked.

"They had enough volunteers, and I didn't want to give up my Saturday this week. I helped out the last two weekends."

"Lance, I probably shouldn't open up a can of worms, but I have to know. Why do you take up for Roman? He makes you look bad in doing so."

"Because Holiday, I want you to see that I genuinely love you. I don't want you to feel like I used Roman's faults to get you. If I'd told you the things I knew before we slept together, you would've been saying that I used that as an edge. He would've thought so, too. We made love, but it was what we both wanted. Roman still insists that I must've told you something to make you go there with me. I didn't want that. I wanted genuine lovemaking from both of us. I hope you didn't do it because you were mad at Roman."

"Not by any means. I loved the way you made me feel that night. I was mad at Roman. Maybe that aided in my ability to go through with it, but you made me feel special. Like you cared. And I wanted it."

"How do you feel about me now, Holiday?"

Lance stepped closer in my face. I looked up into his eyes as his six-foot frame overshadowed me. I wanted to swoon. He was so damn sexy, posing in that masculine stance and chewing on his favorite winterfresh gum. I could smell it on his breath as he stood there waiting for me to answer.

"Lance, I do, but here we go again, opening up a can of worms. Let's leave that alone. I love Roman very much, and I don't want to hurt him like that again." I turned to walk away, but he grabbed my hand and pulled me back toward him.

"I didn't ask you to open up anything, baby girl. I just wanted to know the answer to my question and I have it. I'll leave now."

I would be telling a lie if I said I was relieved Lance said he would go. Part of me wanted his company, but another part of me wanted him to keep moving on his way out. I walked him to the door and handed him his sunglasses so he wouldn't have another excuse to come back.

Lance turned to look at me with my hand outstretched as though I had read his mind. He shook his head in amazement and reached for the Versace shades. Once our hands touched, I looked in his eyes and he looked into mine. Before I knew it, we were kissing. While locked in a passionate embrace, he pushed the door shut and began to back me up toward the couch. As I started to lie back, he gently hovered over me, continuing to kiss me with all the care in the world. We took turns artistically placing the gum he'd been chewing back and forth into one another's mouth with our tongues. I truly enjoyed swishing around the taste of it mixed along with Lance's own flavor, but I soon asked him to get up. Of course he wanted to know why.

"I just can't go through with this. I can't hurt Rome like this again. Are you trying to get back at him for something?"

"Baby girl, no! I have a conscience, too, but I've been longing for you, Holiday. I miss your company. I miss seeing you. I love you, and the feeling isn't going anywhere."

"But what about Rome?"

"Baby girl, I swear I won't tell him. If he finds out, it's because you told."

At that moment, I was hot and bothered, and I started to remember how good it was the last time. I couldn't say no. I led him back to the bedroom where he began to undress me. I sat on the bed like he'd asked me to, and I watched him take off his suede jacket and place it on the dresser. After placing his gum onto a piece of old mail lying on the dresser, he stepped over to me and kneeled to take off my slippers. He began to kiss my feet and tell me how much he'd missed me. Once he'd had enough of that, he slowly began to work his way up my legs, kissing them softly. Before he could make his way up to my knees, I reached for him. I wanted to undress him with care. He refused, telling me to let him do all of the work. Lance proceeded to take off his clothes. I sat watching, getting more and more stimulated by the sight of a hard six-pack, a pair of sexy brown nipples, and his beautiful buff chest as he lifted his shirt over his head. Lance began to lick his lips as he stood looking down at me. He asked me to spread my legs and let him take a look. As I did, he continued to lick his lips and began to massage an already enormously aroused penis. It was amazing to me how his handsome body could be the same smooth caramel complexion from head to toe. He kneeled once again, but this time he provided a pleasant surprise.

"I've missed you," he repeated softly and seductively as he leaned forward to put his face between my legs.

All I could do was moan in ecstasy. I had previously thought he may not have been the kind of man who would do that sort of thing, but Lance proved me wrong as he held me down while I climaxed, being certain he didn't let anything go to waste.

Once Lance got up to put on a condom, I couldn't move I was so weak from the multiple orgasms. Just when I thought I couldn't take anymore, he inserted his penis. It took a minute for me to get used to him, but once I did, I realized I had missed him, too.

"Baby girl, tell me this won't be the last time," he seductively whispered in my ear as he penetrated me.

"I-I don't know, Lance."

"Not the answer I want to hear." He began to stroke me more vigorously. I moaned with erotic pleasure.

Lance asked me the question again: "Will this be the last time for us, baby girl?"

"Lance I-I—," This time he didn't let me finish.

"Not the answer I want to hear." He continued to make love to me passionately. He asked me once more during another climax. At that point, I had to say we could do it again. I don't ever remember climaxing so intensely. I felt it start from my womb and grow up into my chest. It made my legs shiver while my lips quivered. It left goose bumps on the back of my neck and scalp. Lance knew he had me, too. I couldn't say no to him during a climax like that.

Chapter Twenty-two

An Early Out

It was about four in the afternoon and still no call from Crystal. I knew she was okay, but I still expected to hear from her. Rome had said he expected to finish work around five or six and that we could go and see a seven-thirty movie. Lance and I showered together and dressed. We stood in the living room for about ten minutes kissing and talking about how intense our lovemaking was. Neither one of us wanted to let go. I finally walked him to the door to say good-bye.

As I unlocked the door and opened it, to my amazement, Roman was standing there. How afraid was I? He had that same look of fury on his face I'd seen that night when we were at Club Raina's. I was terrified! He'd already seen Lance's silver Cadillac Escalade parked outside, and there was no denying what we'd been doing because I had forgotten to comb my hair. I still tried though.

"Rome! Rome, baby, it's not what it looks like."

Roman began to make his way into the house. He slammed the door behind him and took a long look around the living room. He looked at Lance, then he looked at my hair before saying anything.

"What the fuck is he doing here?"

"I came to—" Lance tried to talk, but Roman cut him off.

"I wasn't talking to you! I'm talking to my woman right now! Answer the question, Holiday."

"Rome, baby, Lance just came over to pick up his Versace sunglasses. He was just leaving."

"Do you have 'em?" Roman asked Lance, looking down at his empty hands.

Lance couldn't say anything at the moment. And, honestly I was speechless. I thought at that moment we were definitely caught. I was trying to think of something to say to play it off, but when I looked over at the couch, not only were Lance's sunglasses there, but his hat was lying there, too—a definite indication that he'd been over for a while. We both had forgotten that his derby came off while we were on the couch kissing, but I was not about to be defeated this day.

"Oh, here, Lance, you're about to forget them again. They're going to get broken if you keep leaving them over here." I picked up both the hat and the shades and handed them to him.

"Thanks, Holiday. Take care," Lance said as he started for the door.

"Okay, Lance. You, too." I was still attempting to play everything off.

Roman didn't respond. He just stared Lance down until he couldn't see him once the door had closed. He turned and looked around the living room once again. This time he noticed the flashing light on the answering machine. He went and checked the messages. I heard Lance and my voice, and my heart started pumping overtime. I had forgotten to turn the answering machine off when Lance called. I couldn't remember all we had said on the phone, so I could feel my chest pounding. It turned out to be innocent though. All Roman heard was Lance and me discussing whether I'd seen his sunglasses, and that indeed I had found them. It's a good thing my answering machine didn't tell the date and time of someone's call. Roman would've discovered that Lance had been over for a few hours.

Before Roman did any more research, I couldn't resist asking him about the calls to Lance's mother. There was no safe way of approaching the topic, but I longed to know. It angered me there was a possibility of some truth to him being responsible for this madness.

"Baby, Lance told me someone has been placing prank calls to his mom," I said carefully. Roman did a double take. I continued. "His mother is elderly like my mine. She really doesn't need that kind of aggravation. Did Lance ever mention this to you?"

Roman put his hand up to his head and began rubbing his hair in circular motions. I walked up to him and placed my hands around his waist.

Sounding frustrated, Roman replied, "No, he never told me."

Relieved to get an answer, I held him tighter. I wasn't off the hook just yet, though. Roman didn't allow me to cling to him very long. He peeled my arms from around him, then walked back to the bedroom and discovered that the bed was totally destroyed. As he went closer, looking at it in disbelief, I tried to come up with a lie about not making it up that morning, but he remembered talking to me earlier on the phone while I was making the bed. I was forced to think a little harder.

Roman glanced over at the dresser and spotted Lance's chewed-up gum, which he'd placed on an old piece of mail. I thought he was going to say something, but he didn't. Roman knew I'd never bought blue winterfresh gum before, and he was ever so aware that it was the only kind Lance chewed. I wanted to say something to soothe over the moment, but there was nothing that could be said. As I racked my brain for another lie to tell, Roman walked into the bathroom, which was semi-steamed and smelled of fresh soap from the long shower Lance and I had taken together. I couldn't lie any longer. I went ahead and confessed. Roman sat on the bed for a second and dropped his head.

"Roman, I don't know what to say, except I'm sorry."

"Sorry? Sorry again, Holiday? You know you're starting to be sorry just one time too many." Roman's expression said that he was ready to knock my ass into a somersault. I was starting to wish Lance hadn't left me alone with him.

Still, I knew nothing comforting to say. "Well, what do you want me to say, Rome?"

"Nothin'! You don't have to say a damn word. Look at this bed! It looks like he done spent the whole day here just fucking the shit out of you! How long was he here, Holiday?" Roman asked as he suddenly got up off the bed in disgust.

"I don't know, probably not as long as you think."

"You're a damn liar! No need in lying to me now. Tell the truth! You want to play stupid with me, right? Don't try to spare my feelings now, Holiday. If you really didn't want to hurt me, you wouldn't have had that nigga in this house. No, better yet, you wouldn't have had him anywhere."

"Baby, you're right. About everything. I guess I'm just not ready to be committed like I thought. I'm so sorry, Rome."

"Yeah, you're sorry all right. I'ma tell ya like Ike told Tina, 'you bout the sorriest muther.' " Roman was quoting Ike Turner from the movie *What's Love Got to Do With It* as he turned to walk out on me. His voice was fading into the living room and then I heard the door slam shut.

I was relieved that Roman didn't open up a fresh can of whup-ass on me. His face had fight all in it. I wasn't pleased that he was hurt, but I also felt more nonchalant than I did remorseful. I went to my nightstand drawer and pulled out my favorite pen and journal. Then I went over to my chaise longue chair to relax and release. After a brief moment of meditation, I wrote "Matters of the Conscience."

How can love be more than just a word?
When is sound worth something being heard?
Why isn't every heart's rhythm beating the same?
What type of mind puts thought into a name?

Yes, all the answers should matter to the
    conscience,
But who can reply with little to no nonsense?
I really don't know, but I'll offer an educated
    guess.

My answers are what I feel when I'm at my best.

Love is much more when it can be felt down
    deep,
Like an inhabitant of the soul that won't let you
    sleep.
Sound is greater when it's light and can freely
    flow,
Much like whispers of kindness and musical
    notes.
Though I sway at a different pace and rare inten-
    sity,
I know it's a part of the plan and God's creativity.
Always think before speaking, it's a definite must.
Foolishness gets ignored, but intelligence wins
    trust.

I spent nearly half an hour releasing through written expression; however, I didn't bother to write
about what I may or may not have felt for Roman. My
mind was at a loss for what could be next for us. I
really didn't know if there would even be any more
Roman and me. I just kind of told myself to be prepared for whatever.

Chapter Twenty-three
Guess Who's Back

A week went by and Roman hadn't called me. I just couldn't bring myself to pick up the phone, either. The possibility that he didn't want to hear from me was more than obvious due to his spell of silence.

Lance, on the other hand, kept in touch. Although I had explained that there couldn't be any type of commitment between the two of us, he was actually cool with that. As long as he could have some of my time, Lance wasn't complaining. For me, it was just a booty call, but Lance expressed that he was just waiting until the day when he'd finally win me over. His thoughts bothered me because I knew I couldn't be what he deserved me to be: a true lover.

Looking back, it seems a little childish, but I just wanted to keep that space open—in case I got tired of Lance. I felt I needed to have room to send him packing without having to give a real explanation for it. I refused to give in to Lance and let him get use to me only to begin the same horrible treatment as my past boyfriends. Keeping my guard up was the thing that kept me mentally healthy. I also realized at that point that I cared a lot about Lance, but I felt I loved Rome more.

I had to call Lance at work one day. He'd said that he would pick Crystal up from cheerleading practice that afternoon for me, but I got a call from her saying that he was late. When I called Lance's cell phone, I got the answering service. This was the third time that he'd been late picking Crystal up for me. I couldn't understand what was going on, and it really began to bother me. My next instinct was to call Lance's job. Someone at the office had put me on hold for a minute, and Roman answered the phone. I was too afraid to talk, so I just hung up. Next thing I knew, my phone was ringing. I had forgotten that those office phones had caller ID. I was busted. I was too afraid that it was indeed Roman attempting to call me back, so I didn't answer. I didn't have the courage, so I just let it ring.

Lance did show to pick Crystal up from cheerleading practice. Crystal later told me Lance explained that his last daily appointment delayed him. After he dropped Crystal off at a study buddy's house, I made plans to meet him at his office for dinner. Since Lance had told me Roman wouldn't be there, I felt eased about going to my old workplace. I made it a point to be there an hour or so before Lance and I were to leave. I figured it wouldn't hurt to stop in just to say hello to a few familiar faces.

It was approximately 4:50 P.M. when I arrived. Rome's car was not in the parking lot, but neither was Lance's Escalade. A little nerve began to pump in my forehead as I became angry. I told myself that Lance's tardiness wasn't due to anything I should be worrying about, so I took a deep breath and calmed down before entering the office. Besides, I could just talk with Lance about the way I felt later. After checking my watch, I figured it would be perfect to get all of my socializing and reminiscing done before Lance got there. This way once he arrived, all we had to do was pack and head out for dinner.

Upon entering the building, heads came up from paperwork and acknowledged me. I was proud to be looking so enchanting in my business suit, which I'd just bought the day before. It was a black-and-white pinstriped jacket and skirt. The jacket had a white lapel and cuffs, and big single-breasted silver buttons down the front. My shoes were black-and-white slingbacks, and the heel was about three inches. I also had on silver accessories. I had dressed as nicely when I'd worked there before, but it was important to me for my ex-coworkers to see me in some new attire. It seemed to be an excellent way of showing them that I was doing all right for myself.

As I made my way around the office, I noticed that not much had changed. I passed by Rome and Lance's work area and it seemed to be the same as well, with one exception. I didn't quite remember Rome's desk being so plain. As I continued to make my way through the building, people were complimenting me on how good I looked and telling me how they'd missed me.

I was just walking through the areas skinning and grinning, haw-hawing and hee-heeing. After I had raised up from having a good laugh with one of my ex-colleagues, Cheryl, I spied Rome standing in the doorway of one of the side offices, peering at me with an unapproachable look. I refused to show intimidation, so I stared back without blinking. I noticed that the sign on the door had two titles on it. One of the names was his. Roman had been promoted and was sharing an office with one of the managers of compliance reporting. Without an invitation, I cautiously walked toward him.

"Hello, Holiday. I see you couldn't even be a big enough woman to ask me if you could speak to your man," he said sarcastically as I approached. "You didn't have to hang up in my face. I wouldn't have had any problem letting Lance know there was a call waiting."

"Well, first of all, congratulations on your new position. And second of all, I didn't realize you were aware I was still seeing Lance. I didn't want to cause any trouble."

"I didn't know, but I do now. When they called Lance to the phone, I decided to take a message for him since he was out of the office. I happened to glance at the caller ID before picking it up and discovered your number. Tripped me out."

"Well, I would apologize, but you've already let me know what you think of my past remorse," I lied. I thought the kind thing to do would be to let Roman think I wanted say I was sorry. I continued. "So, where's your car? I didn't see it outside."

"When I realized that I wouldn't have to be in the field, I let a coworker take it to the shop for me. I'm getting some more tint put on the windows, and with all the work I have to do around here this evening, I knew I wouldn't have time to wait for it."

"Oh, the factory tint wasn't good enough anymore, huh?"

"Naw, not really. This is Black Onyx we're talking about. My baby deserves the best." Roman winked.

"Well, who is this privileged coworker? You didn't even let me drive Black Onyx."

"You didn't ask."

"And you didn't volunteer," I snapped.

"Look, do you have a minute to step in my office? I want to ask you something."

I looked around the area then at my watch. "Well, I guess it wouldn't hurt anything." We walked inside, but I didn't close the door behind me. "Go ahead. I'm listening."

"First of all, I want to know if you've ever loved me, and if so, do you still love me? I find it real hard to believe right now that you've ever cared anything about me."

"The answers to your questions are yes and yes. Don't even go there with me, Rome. I've done plenty to prove to you that I love you. And, I love you for a lot of reasons. I don't think we have time to discuss them right now, though. But yes, Roman, I really did and still do love you."

"Give me one reason then. Let me hear one reason you still love me."

"Rome, you've been a friend when I needed one most. You've talked to me and brought me out of a shell that was very damaging to my spirit."

"Looks like I've done too good of a job getting you out of your shell."

"That's not true. I won't let you totally blame yourself for this."

"So, what is it? What makes you feel you can't love me without Lance being in the picture?"

"Lance adds something different. He brings everything to my life you do, but he also brings his meekness. He opens car doors, he takes off my shoes and massages my feet whether I'm tired or not. And he even makes my bath water—with bubbles—and takes the time to pamper me while I'm in the tub. Most of the time a woman needs that tenderness in her life."

"So, you're saying I didn't bring enough to the relationship to keep you happy?"

"Rome, you're what I would call a roughneck. You get hot headed and you don't take any stuff from anyone. This part of your personality usually comes into effect at the right times, like when I need you to be a protector. You're also what I call a bad boy. That's when another part of your personality comes into play—the player mentality. I can deal with the roughneck. Shit, sometimes I even need a little of that excitement, but the bad boy—player mentality I just can't deal with. I've had enough of that already to know I can't put up with it. You say that you've let that part of you go, but you've forgotten with whom you're dealing. I'm a grown-ass woman, and I don't have time for the games you want to play. I've learned that you have another part of you that knows how to love with your heart. You've shown me that from the start. This type of love has been so awesome that it keeps me from ever wanting to let go. But you give it on your terms and on your terms only. Now, I believe you when you say you're hurt about Lance and me. To be quite frank, I'd be hurt and pissed off, too." Rome stood looking in my eyes deeply as I spoke. "But remember, you started this charade. You lied and lied until your lies ran out. You can't pull that wool over my eyes any longer, Rome. I'm smart enough now to turn your ass around at the door when I see you coming with that same piece of wool."

I made sure that my tone would assure him that I meant what I was saying. He looked dumbfounded for a second. I even sensed a little frustration. He knew I had sized him up too well.

"So, are you saying you love me, the good and the bad, but I just need to learn more about how to love you the way you need to be loved?"

"Rome, you haven't been listening. Yes *and* no! To put it plain and simple, I'm saying that every man is different. I've realized that I love the two of you for your differences. Both of you love me in ways I'm not so sure I want to give up. Lance can't give to me what you have, and you can't offer me the love Lance has. I'd almost rather not be with either one of you than to have to choose. It's tough to swallow, but Rome, you opened that door for me to get out there like that. Lance just happened to be the sentinel, standing on the other side of the door, waiting for me to try to escape so he could seize me. *You* made him the lookout. But all the while, he found time to look in. You should've taken care of your landscaping at home, instead of going to see if the grass was greener somewhere else."

"Okay, Holiday! When you say it like that, a brotha can't help but get the picture. I kind of already knew all of that. That's how I can still hang in and look at you, and still want you. I've told Lance, I can't hate you two. I just wish that none of this stuff ever happened."

"Now, may I ask you something?" I could see in his eyes this made him nervous.

"Sure," he said.

"Is it true what Lance has told me lately about him expressing an interest in me to you long before we ever made love the first time? He said that he'd told you he thought a lot of me and didn't know of a way to tell me. Is this true? He feels as though he was stabbed in the back first."

"Holiday, I won't lie. Yes, it is true. He mentioned to me how much he admired you, but so did I. Just because he mentioned it first doesn't mean I didn't feel something for you first."

"I don't know who felt something first, but with your track record of being deceitful, I would have to say you were being selfish. Lance may have even told you that he was getting ready to approach me with his feelings, and you didn't care."

"Holiday, this is my best friend we're talking about. I didn't deliberately take you from him. First of all, you weren't in a relationship with him. You didn't even belong to anyone at the time. I already had feelings, and I chose not to share them with him. I knew that he wouldn't take it too well, so I just kept it to myself when he told me about his feelings. After you and I were left alone that night, I couldn't hold back anymore. I'm very sorry he felt betrayed, but I did what I felt was best for me at the time."

"Like I was saying, you were being selfish."

"Yeah, I guess I kind of was. It's why I can't be too hard on him, though. Anybody else, I would've whipped ass and asked questions later."

Lance walked up on us during the tail end of that conversation. His eyes were filled with disappointment. He, like I, didn't expect for Rome to be in the office when I got there, and it was just as discouraging to see me standing in Rome's office holding a conversation. I knew Lance couldn't have heard anything but the last part of what Rome said, so I didn't panic. I just played it cool and asked him if he was ready to leave.

Rome started making regular phone calls to me every day. I still wanted to hear from him and see him, too. I was trying not to play Roman and Lance against each other, but for three months that's how it felt. Rome was well aware that I was still sleeping with Lance, but Lance had no idea that Rome and I were still speaking to each other. Lance and I weren't in any type of relationship, so I felt it was okay not to tell him I was keeping in touch with Rome. Okay, Rome and I were socializing, and we not only spoke verbally, we communicated sexually, too. This was the problem. Two different men on a regular basis were sexing me for the entire three months. I needed a break.

One Saturday morning, Crystal and I got into a little spat. She was being adamant about spending the rest of her weekend over at her cousin Shaundra's house. I, on the other hand, felt Crystal had been spending too many weekends away from home, so she blew up at me. I approached her about my concerns as she was lying in bed.

"Crystal, honey, when it's all said and done, surely you agree that we haven't had very many weekends together lately," I said, sitting at the foot of her bed.

"Ma, what's the big deal? At least I'm with my kin.

I see you every day. It's not fair that you want to keep me from spending weekends with my daddy's people." She threw the cover over her head.

"Now, Crystal, that's not true. I've always given in to your pleas to see your family. As a matter of fact, Shaundra is welcomed to spend the night with us this weekend. How about that?"

Crystal snatched the cover from her face and yelled. "No! Why can't I just get away from the house for a day?"

Though surprised by her reaction, I managed to keep my cool. "Crystal, sweetie, Mommy's gonna have to ask you to watch your tone. I don't know what's gotten into you, but we need more quality time, and it's gonna begin today."

Crystal raised up and threw her pillow onto the floor. "Oh, what do you care? Since when did you wanna start choosing me over your boyfriends?" She ran into the bathroom, pushing me aside in the midst.

I couldn't believe my ears. My mind was totally bogged. I thought I had done a wonderful job of making Crystal believe I only had a friendship with Roman and Lance. What had I been thinking all of that time? Crystal was turning twelve in a few months and no longer a baby, though I mostly clung to her like one.

My heart ached, and tears filled my eyes. I knocked and pleaded with Crystal to talk to me. The thick wood on the bathroom door didn't muffle her whimpers. I longed to hold and console her. I continued to plead and ultimately resorted to lying.

"Crystal, it hurts Mommy that you would say such things. Honey, Lance and Roman are only friends. Ex-actly what has made you believe otherwise?"

I stood outside the bathroom door and talked until my spirit was drained. Nothing I said moved Crystal, so I felt it necessary to give in to her demand. When I told her she could spend the night at Shaundra's, she came out and ran into her bedroom to pack. This was the first time I had been in a predicament of Crystal being this upset with me, and I didn't like it. I definitely didn't know how to deal with it. We rode all the way to Shaundra's in silence.

Chapter Twenty-four

A Consequence for Every Action

Crystal left me brokenhearted, and I felt my best medicine was to go out to keep my family matters from depressing me. I called Lance, and we decided to chill at Fat Tuesday. We had been there for about an hour when I went to the restroom. I don't know how, but I managed to leave my cell phone on the table with Lance. Apparently, it had been ringing while I was gone because Lance's demeanor was distant when I returned. I leaned on his shoulder, hoping it would make him speak out in some sort of way. Then my phone began to ring to the tune of Sade's "Is It a Crime," and this caused Lance to go into a glaring zone, waiting for me to respond to the call. I tried hard to play it off, but Lance kept insisting that I might want to answer it.

"Hello . . . Mm-hmm . . . Yeah . . . Okay. Then I'll just call you later. All right, bye." I rushed the conversation on the phone, hardly keeping a straight face.

After hanging up, I looked over at Lance. He just

stared at me for about ten seconds before he spoke. "Who was that?" It was clear he was agitated.

"A friend of mine, Lance. Why?"

He stared at me for about another five seconds. "Look at my face. Look at it good. Do you really think that I don't know who that friend was?"

This time I did the staring. "I'm sure you do know, Lance. Is there a problem?"

"Come on, let's go." Though his voice was low, he was clearly pissed.

We left a whole lot earlier than I'd expected. Roman had asked if I was with Lance. He also wanted to know if we were at The Peabody Place since that was my favorite spot and whether I thought I could see him later. I tried to keep my answers short and sweet, but Lance was already one up on me.

Once we got back to my place, I expected Lance to walk me to the door then turn around, but he didn't. He came inside, reluctant to talk at first. Soon, he opened his mouth and let the frustration flow.

"Holiday, I know we're not in a relationship, but I have to say this. I'm still disappointed. I kind of figured you'd want to see Roman. I was just hoping through time spent with me, I could change your mind."

"So, has this made you lose your desire to keep company with me?" I wanted to know.

I cared whether Lance wanted to leave me alone. I felt I needed him in so many ways. However if he would be the one to break things off, it would've been a lot simpler for me. Though I knew he deserved someone more dedicated, I didn't have the emotional strength to force him to move on.

"I don't want to stop seeing you, Holiday. Is that what you want?"

"No. I'm just curious to know how you're feeling at the moment. If there's anything I can say or do to make you feel better, I'll do it. Don't you think I care anything about what you're going through right now? I haven't just been playing you, Lance. I love you." It was the truth. I did love him, but not enough to give up my other half.

"Good, then make it up to me now—by making love to me. And tonight, I want you to do all the work."

I smiled and said okay, but I was really thinking, *Oh shit!* Roman was expecting me to call him back so we could hook up. I think Lance kind of sensed that, so he conveniently asked me to be intimate with him. I couldn't turn Lance down, though. He had the sweetest look on his face. His eyes were dancing, which immediately turned me on. Also, I'd just spoken of how much I loved him and that I'd do anything to make him feel better. I turned the ringers off on the phones and led Lance back to the bedroom.

He spent the night with me. When we woke up Sunday morning, it was nearly noon. We had spent the entire night making love, talking, holding, and caressing each other. Although Lance had asked me to do all the work, he let me be the aggressor for about an hour and then it was fair play.

Making love with Lance, I knew what I could expect—and it was all good. There was never a bad moment in lovemaking with Lance. Every aspect about it was totally for pleasing me. Of course he was satisfied as well, but he made love as if his only agenda was to put me on cloud nine.

Roman, on the other hand, would make love to me as if he was trying to "get his" first, and if I didn't "get mine" in the midst, he'd just have to make it up to me later. That seemed to be his attitude on it. Oh, Roman would apologize, but he'd also let me know that I was just that good, and he couldn't help himself. Just an excuse to try to pacify me for not waiting on me. I got real tired of our lovemaking only being intense when we were trying to make up.

I felt pretty bad when I turned on my answering machine and heard Crystal's voice wanting to know what time I would be picking her up for church. I had promised Crystal I would arrive early to take her and Shaundra to Sunday school. I didn't know what I was going to say to her. Until I had started going out with these two men, I was on time for her extracurricular activities, I would be on time to pick her up for church, and I would even call her at night before she'd go to bed over to her cousin's house. I had begun to slack up on all of this, and it wasn't until I heard her pitiful message on the answering machine that I realized how much things had changed with me.

"Mommy, wake up. Mommy, I hope you're awake and on your way to pick us up. We're ready, and Shaundra's been standing in the door looking out for you. Mommy, please! Please wake up. I guess she must already be gone, Shaundra. She didn't pick up the phone." Crystal's voice began to fade out just as she was about to hang up the phone.

"Holiday, are you okay?" Lance asked after he'd

been standing there watching my demeanor change as I listened to Crystal's message.

"No. What am I gonna say to her? Partying too late is not an excuse, Lance. Those kids were awake, dressed, and ready to be picked up. I, on the other hand, was laying up from getting laid up!" I was on the verge of crying, and my voice was trembling.

"Baby girl, don't say it like that. Crystal is more understanding than you think. You don't have to tell her why you overslept, but just make sure you apologize to her."

"Lance, it's not that simple. Crystal and I had a little dispute yesterday. I've come to learn that she knows there is more to you and me. And even to Roman and me."

"Holiday, are you serious?" Lance seemed extremely shocked.

"Oh, yes. I'm very serious. Crystal even accused me of choosing you and Roman over her. I can only imagine what she may be feeling right now. Lance, I don't want to lose my baby's trust. She's growing up, and we should be developing an even closer bond by now, not growing apart."

"I can understand. You should definitely be careful of developing a distant relationship with your daughter. If this means that we can't spend as much time together, we'll just have to make the sacrifice. Crystal needs you."

"I'm glad you understand, Lance. Thank you." I walked over to kiss him. It was a brief kiss, but Lance continued to hold me at the waist. "Oh, by the way, I had several messages from Rome. He's not too pleased with me right now."

"So, are you going to call him back?"

"Lance, you shouldn't ask me questions you don't want to know the answer to."

"Baby girl, you should know that I have the answer. I just wanted to hear it come out of your mouth. Holiday, I can't stop you from wanting Roman. You laid right there in that bed last night and told me that you can't choose between the two of us. That didn't cause me to quit making love to you, did it? You know why? Because I'm not giving up that easily. I've told you before, I'm the better man, and I'll just have to make sure you understand it. That, or either Roman's gonna mess up big time for you to see it. But guess what? I'll be right there in the end. With you."

"You're that confident, huh?"

"I am. Confident enough to know I need to just hold on and be patient," Lance said.

I called Crystal to apologize. I took Lance's advice and just told her that I had overslept, but I was very apologetic. She was still disappointed, but she also told me that she forgave me. That's all I needed to make me feel better. I just wanted to know if she would forgive me for not being the mom I use to be. I promised her that she would see a change. I hung up with Crystal and gave Lance a smile of relief.

I took a step outside to see how the weather had shaped up for the afternoon. After getting up so late, I hadn't remembered to get my Sunday morning newspaper. *The Commercial Appeal* had called several weeks ago with a deal I was unable to pass up, so I got a subscription to the local paper.

Upon stepping onto the porch, what I saw next left me flabbergasted. I stood on the top step unable to speak, with one hand on my chest and the other hand over my mouth. Lance's beautiful silver Cadillac Escalade had black paint sprayed all over it. It wasn't just painted. It had a pertinent message for both Lance and me. The message was, GUESS WHO? HAVING FUN? NEXT TIME PARK THIS SHIT ELSEWHERE, NIGGA! I couldn't close my mouth. My lower jaw could damn near touch my chest. That message read from one side of that vehicle to the other. Top to bottom. I ran back inside.

"Lance, Lance! Come here, baby! Look outside at your Escalade," I yelled to him in pure panic.

"Why? What's wrong?" Lance ran right past me, heading to the door to look outside.

Lance came back in after carefully examining his vehicle, swearing. I just sat with my head in my lap crying. I couldn't believe Rome had stooped that low. I mean that was so elementary of him.

Lance didn't like using cuss words in front of me. I give him credit for trying his best to refrain from profanity as he cut those words short. "Mutherfu— Shh—Umph! It's on now! When I see his ass. Umph! I'm gon' kill 'im!" I had never seen Lance so enraged. His face had turned red, and he was spitting when he spoke.

"Lance, baby, try to calm down. I know you're upset, but it's just a vehicle. Baby, I'll pay for a new paint job. Try to calm down."

"No, it's not about the paint job! It's the principle of the thing now. Roman knows 'cause we've talked about this. You don't mess with a man's ride! If he got some stuff he needs to get off his chest, he needs to step to me with it. He's acting like a little bitch spraying paint on my damn ride!" I don't think

Lance even realized he had let a couple of his forbidden words slip.

"Baby, I understand. I really do. This has just taken me by surprise. I never would've thought Roman could be so cruel."

"Play back the messages. I want to hear them. I know he had to have said something incriminating on the answering machine."

"Okay. Hold on." I couldn't remember if Roman had said anything damaging to himself or not when I'd listened to the messages. I only remembered the calls escalating, making me extremely uneasy.

The first message from Roman wasn't so bad. "Hey, boo. It's getting kind of late, and you haven't called me back yet. I know how you are about being out too late, so I was just wondering when you were gonna come in and call me. I miss you, girl."

The second message sounded like he was a little disturbed. "Are you gonna call a brotha back or what? I've been trying to reach you for an hour. Give me a buzz when you get this message."

The third one hinted that Roman knew Lance was over. "Look, I know you're having a good time and all, but all it takes is a little common courtesy to call and say you're not gonna be able to see me tonight. Holla!"

The fourth message was a definite indication he knew Lance was over. "I'm sure this nigga is making you happy, but what you're ignoring right now is the fact that I'm your happiness, too. You could at least call me back and say something. Give me a buzz!"

The fifth call was simply a plea for me to just contact him. My ringers were off, and I was too caught up to know anything else. "Holiday, I ain't gon' even lie to you. I'm upset with you, boo. You're disappointing me. I just wanna hear your voice. I thought you would've called me by now. You want me to believe you love me, but you taught me better than anybody that love don't act like this. Call me, boo!"

In Roman's final message, he made sure that I understood his point. "I can't believe it's three-thirty in the morning and I'm still calling yo' ass! I could've been with any woman I wanted right now, but no! I been waiting on you to call me. What I expected you to say, I dunno! 'cause it ain't jack you can say to me right now. Oh, you ain't off the hook, boo. I'm not finna let you go just like that. This muthafucker can't have you just like that. No way! I'm not finna let it happen. Tell his punk ass I said you still my boo and gon' always be my boo!"

Lance was fuming. "Call the police! I'll see what he thinks of my punk ass when I press charges and send him to jail!"

I was expecting to see smoke coming out of his ears at any given moment.

"Lance, listen, I'm just as angry as you are about your truck, but this is my second time listening to those messages. Rome was drunk. And hurt. Now you know that being drunk and hurt is a hell of a combination. He said some things I'm sure he didn't mean. I'll still call the police if you want me to, but I'm just asking you as a friend to just let me talk to him first."

"Holiday, baby girl. I'm sorry you feel for him right now, but I've got to take some type of action. If I don't, I might take the law into my own hands, and

I know I could seriously hurt Roman right now. I really hate you can't understand that." He began pacing.

"No, I do. I understand, Lance. I'll call the police." I was reluctant though.

It sounds silly to say, but I felt compassion toward Roman. He was hurting. Had I known he was leaving those messages like that, I would've sneaked into another room and called him back. Though Roman had tendencies that proved him to be a roughneck, I know every man has feelings. If the shoe were on the other foot, I would've wanted Roman to find a way to call me back.

When the police got there, they examined the Escalade and listened to the messages. Although it was somewhat obvious Rome was the only one who would've maliciously defaced Lance's truck, the police said the messages weren't enough to arrest him. Roman never incriminated himself. They did, however, suggest that Lance get a protection order of some kind against Roman. Lance refused to do so because he and Roman still had to work together, and he didn't want to mess around and lose his job trying to enforce a restraining order. The New Vet Life Insurance Company had strict rules against employees with restraining and protection orders. If it involved two employees against each other, the bosses would just find a way to terminate both employees. I guess they didn't want the headache nor the burden of trying to make sure the employees stayed away from each other.

Once the police left, Lance decided to leave to see if he could get some estimates or even get a company to paint his Escalade right away. I walked him out to the sidewalk and tried to give him some words of encouragement. He wasn't feelin' me though. He never said a word while I was talking—just looked at me with a blank stare. I almost started to cry then because I knew that once I got back in the house I was going to call Roman. Not just to let him have it over what he'd done, but to also try to explain why I hadn't called him back the night before. I felt guilty that they both were victims of my selfish quest for what I needed in a man. I refused to make either one of them leave me alone.

Lance kissed me softly to reassure me that he still loved me, despite my feelings for Roman. I told Lance I would call him later, but he never said a word. He nodded and walked away to get into his Escalade. As he drove off, I watched until his truck got farther and farther away. I headed toward my front door and took one last look back. Just then, I spotted what looked like Roman's car speeding off, trying to make a quick turn to avoid me seeing him. My heart was beating fast, and my breath got short. I'd begun to wonder if I ever knew this man. Was this the same man I'd worked with over the years? All the women he kept, all the suaveness, he never displayed this side of him. It was eerie knowing Roman had watched all of the events beginning with me walking out of my front door viewing Lance's truck and ending with Lance and me standing outside kissing until he decided to drive off. I hurried into the house and locked all of my doors and windows. I was too afraid to call Roman back right then, so I talked on the phone with my best friend, Renee, instead. However, talking with Renee didn't keep me from wondering what was on Roman's mind.

Chapter Twenty-five

Romey Don't Play Dat'

I decided to call Roman Monday morning to set up a lunch meeting somewhere very public. I wanted to talk to him to see where his head was, but I also wanted to be cautious. I didn't know if I could trust that he wasn't going to flip on me. Roman and I had agreed to meet at a restaurant centrally located to both of our work areas. Once I pulled into the parking lot, I noticed him standing at the entrance waiting for me.

I extended my hand to greet Roman with a handshake, but he caught me by surprise with a quick yank of my arm, pulling me into a bear hug. I was speechless, but Roman sure had enough to say.

"I'm sick of you treating me like some type of stranger. When is the last time you've seen me, huh? Huh?" Roman's eyes were red like fire. The sight of them was enough to keep me silent. "That's what I'm talking about. You can't remember. So where do you get the nerve to offer me a handshake?" Still, I couldn't answer. "Don't ever do that to me again."

Roman finally let me go. He opened the restaurant door and motioned for me to go in before him. I wanted to run back to my car, but since I could see that the place was crowded, I felt my safety wouldn't be at stake. The hostess led us to a center table and then Roman made another gentlemanlike gesture.

"Thanks for pulling my chair out for me, Roman. That's not something I'm accustomed to from you."

"Yeah, I figured maybe if I tried to be more like your boy Lance then perhaps you'd give me a little more of your time." Of course he felt like being sarcastic.

"You know what, I'm just gonna cut right down to it! Spray-painting Lance's Escalade was very immature. Help me understand how a thirty-four-year-old man could still be interested in playing games like that."

"Whoa, whoa, whoa! What are you trippin' on?" Roman began playing the great pretender he is by acting like he didn't know what I was talking about.

"Here we go again, Roman. I've told you not to try and play me stupid! You could've gotten your ass locked up doing some mess like that!" It was difficult trying to keep my voice down.

"Holiday, all I did was try to reach you through a few phone calls while you were laid up with him. I don't have time to be out doing crazy stuff like vandalism!"

"So you do admit that it was crazy, huh?"

"Absolutely. I mean I'm pissed off at your boy, but I wouldn't play with him like that." No matter how Roman tried, he couldn't mask his guilt.

"Then, who do you suppose sprayed all that crap on Lance's SUV?"

"I don't know, but I have a few ideas."

I was surprised to hear him say that. "Oh yeah? Let me hear them."

"Well, some of those women he just up and stopped seeing because he was so in love with you weren't too pleased with him about that. He told me one of them said she didn't know if she'd ever forgive him for just dropping her for no reason."

"Bullshit! The message left on that truck was far more personal than that. Lance's ex-girlfriends don't know me. He wasn't even serious enough with any of them, so what you're saying couldn't possibly be true. There's no one else out there with more motive than you, Roman. Try again!"

"Boo, listen to you. You're all uptight about your boy, aren't you? The questions shouldn't be directed at me right now. I'm not guilty of anything. You're the one who's guilty of something, and that's lying to me."

"I didn't intentionally lie to you, Rome. I just got caught up with time and what was going on between Lance and me the other night."

"You know, you've been doing a lot of getting caught up lately. Am I supposed to just excuse you once again? I mean, would you like for me to keep accepting that Lance and I both offer something different to your heart that keeps you unwilling to give one of us up?"

"I don't know, Roman."

"Sure you do. You'd love to keep having your cake and eating it, too. That stuff you've been talking about your father didn't do you right, your baby's daddy didn't do you right, it's all got to come to a head. You need to stop making excuses and let go of the past. I'm not allowing you to take that shit out on me anymore. You've got to choose, boo. Me or Lance?"

"How do you think you can tell me how to live my life? I still care for you. You know I do, but you're not ready to be the love I need you to be, Rome. I'm not totally choosing Lance, but when he's not around, I miss him. I need him, and I need you. The lack of affection from pertinent men in my life is not an excuse, but please accept it as a reason."

"Excuse. Reason. Same damn thing to me, Holiday. Well, it's not good enough anymore. I'm never gonna accept you spending more time with Lance than me. Yeah, those calls I made to your answering machine were a bit rude, but I'll do it again if the situation ever occurs another time."

"Well, you shouldn't take your frustrations out on Lance."

"Fuck that nigga!" Roman banged his fist, causing the table and silverware to rattle. I wanted to hide my face. People had begun to look in our direction.

"Shhh! I don't need the extra attention, Roman."

"I'm sorry, but I'm getting pissed off." He picked up his glass of water, trembling with anger.

"And please tell me how you've managed to become so gangsta all of a sudden."

"Oh, I can suppress my hard feelings until I feel I'm being fucked over."

"Well, I know for a fact that now is not the time! I came here to talk and have a sensible lunch. I don't want to hear your obscenities. Save it for the streets."

"Yeah, and here you go running things again. You

tell me not to dictate what you can or cannot do, but I'm suppose to do whatever the hell you say?"

"Roman. Hmph. Later for that, okay? What I'm trying to tell you is that the two of you still work for the same company. You need to keep the ties at least kosher enough to have a working relationship. Has Lance already approached you about anything?"

"No. He can't provoke shit on the job. I imagine Lance will be ready to talk soon, but he better come correct when he does!" Roman banged his fist once again.

"How did I ever fall in love with you?" This side of Roman was very unattractive.

"What? What kind of question is that to ask me?"

"I mean this! I actually fell in love with you without ever knowing this side of you. It's not becoming of you, Rome."

"Like I said, I feel I'm being fu—" Rome was starting his obscenities again, so I interrupted him.

"It doesn't matter! You've still got to respect my wishes and anything that involves me if you want to be a part of my life. I'm sorry I can't offer you more than a little time here and there, but it's the same for Lance. I don't see how you could be so serious about being with me anyway. Before me, you were a playa-playah, remember? I haven't done all that much to influence you to want to settle down. As a matter of fact, you really haven't. I'm no fool! You're still out there like that. So, you want to know what I really think it is?"

"What do you think? Yes, what do you think, Holiday?"

"I think it's about power. Power and principles.

You have made this out to be a game, which is so ironic 'cause that's what I've been pushing so hard to prove to the two of you that it's not. It's never been a game to me. But, right now you guys are going back and forth trying to prove who's the better man. That's the name of the game. Who's the better man? I'm gonna tell you right now, Roman. No one's going to win. I'm smart enough to recognize when I'm being used as a pawn." My blood had begun to boil.

"Yeah, I know you're smart. You certainly are. Did you tell Lance the same thing, though? Does he know you're never going to choose between the two of us?"

"I've said it to him more times than I've said it to you."

"Despite what you think, Holiday, it's not a game. At least not for me."

"And you want me to believe that? Coming from the same man who'll sit across the table from me, look me in my eyes, and tell me he didn't have anything to do with putting that graffiti on Lance's truck?"

Roman was speechless at that moment. He just sat and picked up his glass to have a few sips before he decided to answer. "I haven't even seen Lance's Escalade. He didn't drive it to work today."

"So . . ." I opened my mouth to say something, but before I could finish the first word I was interrupted by an unexpected, but recognizable voice.

"And you expect for me to believe you? That you didn't even bother to take a drive down Elmhurst Road looking for my truck in front of Holiday's house last Saturday?" Lance was approaching our table, and he had heard Roman's last comment.

"Lance, how did you know we were here?" I asked. It was definitely a surprise and totally out of character for Lance.

Roman began to explain, looking carefully at Lance. "Like I told Holiday, I did make a few phone calls to try and reach her. There was no need for me to drive down her street if she wasn't gonna answer my phone calls."

"So, now I'm Boo-Boo the Fool, huh? You think I don't have sense enough to know you're lying, Roman? After all the years of knowing you, man, I've never known you to be this selfish. You knew I wanted Holiday, yet you still made a move on her first. She doesn't deserve a lowlife like you, Roman. Give it up!"

"Lowlife? Look who's talking. Despite what I did to you, she was actually my woman. You crossed the line and slept with her, man. Come on now! I know you know that! Regardless of anything, you were still my boy, and you were wrong to sleep with my woman."

"And, you know what? I'm not so sure you wouldn't have done the same thing, given my situation," Lance assured him.

"Well, I really don't even know why you're here right now. This was supposed to be a private lunch. Ain't that right, Holiday?" Roman asked, looking at me. Again, I opened my mouth to speak, but I wasn't allowed to complete my thought.

"Holiday didn't invite me. She didn't even tell me where you two were meeting. I invited myself. I pulled one of those old Roman Broxton routines by looking on the caller ID at work. When I found out it was Holiday I heard you discussing lunch with, I followed you. Pretty smart, huh? I learned from the best. You taught me well, man."

The tension around us was very thick. This whole predicament made me feel uneasy, and I just wanted to get out of there. I stood and spoke out. "Well, look. I'm starting to feel very uncomfortable right now with everybody staring at our table, so I'm just gonna find the waitress and ask for the check," I said, looking around the restaurant.

Lance grabbed me by the hand. "Holiday, wait. I still have some time on my lunch. If you have any time left, please, let's just go somewhere and talk for a minute. We really need to talk."

Lance was pretty much pleading with me. I didn't know how to answer him with Roman sitting there. "Uhmm? Well, I—"

"See, this is the shit I'm talking about. This is the boy who's trying to make this into a game. Hey, don't be jealous 'cause I had the opportunity to have lunch with Holiday today. You've had your turn." Roman stood and slid back his chair.

"Roman, come on now, man. Not in here like this. Why don't we just go outside?" I was really beginning to worry at this point 'cause Lance had responded to this a little bit too calmly.

"Oh, we can go! We can go outside!" Roman stepped in Lance's face.

I stood between the two men with my hands placed on their chests to hold them back.

"No! No! Stop this, you guys! This is silly! You guys are not about to fight! Come on now!"

The two men were way too strong for me. More words were said then punches were thrown, with me in the middle. I'm not sure, but I'm almost certain

Roman threw the first blow. All I know is between the two of them, someone hit me upside my head causing excruciating pain in my right ear. I also had a bloody nose and a bleeding lip. I screamed and hollered in terror and pain. Some gentlemen working for the restaurant came to my rescue. Somehow they managed to pry Lance and Roman apart long enough to pull me from between them. I yelled at Roman and Lance to stop fighting and get the hell out of the restaurant before the police came. They yielded to my concern and fled from there. The manager suggested I pay the bill and leave, too. The police would want to know what happened, and I didn't want Roman and Lance to get in trouble. Hmph, ain't that something! Even with a bashed-up face at the hands of those two men, I still cared enough to not want them to have to suffer. I'll admit, I helped to make my own life a trip.

Chapter Twenty-six
Love Goes On and On

I took the rest of the day off to try to get the swelling in my lip to go down before Crystal got out of school. Explaining something like that to her would be difficult. Looking into her eyes with my bloody lip would especially be hard since I'd promised her that my lifestyle would change. The manager at the restaurant had given me some ice before I left, so I had placed it on my lip and face from the start.

I was very ticked off. I thought that either Roman or Lance should've been the bigger man and just walked away, especially since I was standing between them. And, what really topped the cake was the fact that I didn't recall seeing any blood nor bumps and bruises on either man before they left. There I sat in my room most of the evening trying to hide from Crystal, and neither of them had to lose a day of work or anything because of the fight. It ticked me off!

I received a phone call from Lance later that

night. "You know what, Lance? Don't call me, 'cause you're sad. You're sad just like Roman. You just couldn't stay away. If you were angry enough to want to fight the man, then why didn't you just keep your distance? You embarrassed the hell out of me! I feel like all of Memphis knows my business now. I'm so disappointed in you!"

"Holiday, I didn't call to argue. I understand you're gonna be mad at me for a while. I just wanted to make sure you were okay."

"Well, I still have a tremendous headache, and my ear hurts from me being hit upside my head. But other than that and my pride being scarred, I'm all right." I huffed into the phone.

"Baby girl, I'm sorry about that. I don't think I hit you though. If I did, you know it wasn't intentional."

"It doesn't make any difference whether it was intentional or not! I was trying to keep the two of you from going to jail. One of you should've been the bigger man."

"I'll agree with some of that. But are you sure it's not just the fact that you didn't want to see the two men you love get into a fight?"

"Bye, Lance!"

"What? Why?"

" 'Cause you're pissing me off! I didn't think it was appropriate for the two of you to be fighting period, let alone inside a public restaurant!"

Lance sighed. "I'm sorry. You're right. I apologize for not being the bigger man, and I'm very sorry you got hurt."

"Alright, whatever! Let me get off this phone and check Crystal's homework. We got a late start tonight."

"Will you call me back after she goes to bed? I'd

like to stop over for a minute—just to see you. I just want to see you face-to-face, long enough to get a hug."

"Well, we'll see. I'll call you back."

After Crystal went to bed, I called Lance back so he could come over for a minute. It didn't take him long because he was already out riding, waiting for me to give him a call. I opened the door to a pleasant surprise. Lance stood there holding what seemed like the biggest bunch of roses I'd ever seen.

"Lance? What's this?" The roses were shielding his face.

"Baby girl, I just couldn't resist seeing you tonight. I feel so bad about everything."

"These roses are more beautiful than any flowers I've ever seen. Where in Memphis did you find them?"

"Oh, don't you worry about that. I just wanted to give you a token to say I'm sorry. I know it doesn't make up for what happened today, but I do apologize."

I couldn't help admiring the roses and sniffing them. Lance could tell he'd definitely made a good decision in giving them to me. They smelled so wonderful, and I was totally captivated by the beauty of their color. Two-dozen roses along with the baby's breath and greenery made them look like the largest bunch of flowers in the world. They stood in a huge vase, and once I set them on my coffee table, they blocked my television and everything else in the vicinity.

"Lance, what color are these roses? Lavender?"

"No, baby girl. I was told they're silver."

"Oh yeah, I can see that. Thank you so much. I love them." I gave Lance a kiss on the cheek.

"Baby girl, I've been thinking that maybe I should just back off and let Roman do his thing."

"Stop talking foolishness, Lance. I've told you, if I let one go, I'm gonna let the other go, too."

"You don't think you could ever love just me? What does Roman have to do with what you and I got going on?"

"Nothing. It's just that I would feel so guilty having to choose or even to cause one of you to have to do so. I can't do it. I just can't do it."

"So you still have a selfish attitude when it comes to my or even Roman's feelings, huh?"

"Lance, I can't believe you're even talking this way."

"Do you love one of us more than the other?"

"No. Honestly, I can't say that I love one of you more than the other. At one time I thought that I had more feelings for Rome, but I soon realized that I only felt that way because I had been with him first. You give me the love I need, too. I can't love one more than the other. I'm sorry if that's not the answer you want to hear."

"Are you sure you even love me?"

"Very sure. I am so sure. I've been praying about it and everything. I haven't told you, but I've even lost one of my best friends because of this trio situation. Erika totally thinks of me as less than a woman now. If it were that simple to just change the way I feel about you and Roman today, I would. I'm going through a great deal of pain as well. And, I don't take pride in hurting you both."

"Baby girl, I'm sorry to hear about your friendship with Erika. How did you find out that she felt this way?"

"Guess. Sister Nelson, one of my church members, told me. She loves to be the bearer of bad news anyway. She told me about Erika telling a lot of members that they needed to pray for me. I got called out in worship and everything. One Sunday another sister, whom I've never known to be a prophet, got up in front of the congregation pretending to prophesy about a female member who's fornicating with two men who are best friends. Just putting all my business out there in church like that. Well over half the stuff the woman said couldn't have come from anyone but Erika. Erika told everyone I hardly call her anymore, and that I'm less of a mother than I use to be."

"Oh, that's messed up! You didn't need her, Holiday. Erika shouldn't have done you like that."

"I know. It's all right. I'm gonna straighten my life out soon, though."

Just then the phone rang. It was late, and I almost didn't answer it, but I didn't want the ringing to awaken Crystal.

It was Roman on the line. "Um, I don't mean to interrupt your little late night cap, but I was hoping to be able to talk to you for a minute. Will you ask your little boyfriend to step into another room and let us talk? That is, if I'm not already interrupting something important."

"Roman, are you outside my house?" I ran over to the window to look out.

"Oh, see this has gone too far. Holiday, tell his ass to come in," Lance said.

"No, I can't do that. Crystal's home asleep and that would be too dangerous. No!"

Roman's voice sounded agitated. "Holiday, I don't

want to come in. Tell him I'm through fighting, but that's not gonna make me stop seeing you though."

"Is he trying to do anything to my rental car?" Lance asked, heading to open my front door.

"No. He just drove off," I said.

"I see now that I'm gonna have to pop a cap in Roman's ass about this foolishness he keeps doing. All of this damn stalking is unnecessary." This was the second time I'd seen Lance pace.

Roman hissed, "I told you to tell 'im I'm through with that nonsense. All I'm asking is for my share of time in this relationship with you. I'm your friend, too, remember? That's all. Lance doesn't even matter anymore. You're what's important to me. I ain't trying to lose what little involvement we do have over trippin' with his ass. By the way, tell Lance I said the roses make a nice gesture, but I'm the one you love."

I heard Roman, but it was just hard to believe he meant everything he said. I just wondered if he had anything else up his sleeve. I didn't bother telling Lance about Roman's comment of the roses and my feelings. The tension was heated enough without repeating those thoughts. Roman was becoming a nightmare.

Chapter Twenty-seven
Ready or Not

I'd begun to feel like I was watching my life in a movie. It just didn't seem real. I wondered how I had gone from being celibate and only being dedicated to my Lord Jesus Christ and my loving daughter to having not just one worldly man, but two. It just didn't seem real. Many people probably think I've made all of this up, but the truth is, I haven't! And, it gets even more unbelievable.

I continued to juggle both men for about another four months. They both had a sense of it, but they just kind of stayed out of each other's way. I was very careful not to mention one while I was with the other. Although they were still working in the same establishment, Lance had complained to me of someone destroying the files of his largest clients. I worried about whether Roman was involved, and Lance certainly had no problems placing the blame in his former friend's direction. Lance threatened to take such harassment to upper management, but I pleaded with him not to do so. I feared for both men's careers.

I guess sometime around October 2002, strange phone calls started coming in frequently. At first there were one or two calls a day. The person on the other end would just hold the phone and say nothing. Eventually, the calls progressed to about fifteen a day. I asked Roman and Lance if they'd given my phone number to anyone, but they both denied it. Crystal was worried that it was some type of maniac or something. I got real tired of the aggravation, so I had my home number changed. I made sure it was private and couldn't be easily found on the Internet. That helped for about a month, but the person decided to start calling my cell phone. I knew then that this was something personal, but I couldn't figure out whether it was Roman or Lance or Erika. These were the only people who I felt would be willing to play this type of game with me.

Christmas was approaching, and the children were out for winter break. Crystal, of course, didn't want to stay home for the entire vacation, so she and I came up with a compromise so she could spend time with her other family. Besides, I had to work, so it was a help for Crystal to stay with Shaundra. We did agree, however, she would be home for Christmas Day. Her dad had sent some gifts, and Crystal knew it was going be a grand holiday, given she knew what I had planned to get her. After giving her lessons on my ten-speed bike, Crystal asked if she could have a bike of her own for Christmas. She and I talked about being able to go biking together. It pleased me to see Crystal so excited about the holiday, and I enjoyed decorating the tree with her before she left.

I had hoped that in the spirit of the Christmas season, Roman and Lance would be at least cordial in the work environment, but neither man would let up on the hostility. After having to plead for his job before a review board with a panel discussion about the missing files, Lance was about ready to kick Roman's ass once and for all.

December 21, 2002, I'll never forget it. This was the day that New Vet Life Insurance had its Christmas party. They had rented a ballroom at the Rivercity Renaissance Hotel near the airport. This also marked the day that after all the months of contentment with the relationship between Roman and Lance and me, I got my "face broke." I found out I had been played.

Lance had invited me to the Christmas party, but when I really think about it, I believe it may have been a set-up. There were warning signs proving this, but somehow I managed to overlook them all. I decided to take Lance up on his offer since Roman hadn't mentioned anything about the event to me, and I couldn't even reach him for a couple of days. Lance mentioned having seen Roman at work in the previous days, but he didn't know whether Roman had plans to attend. I tried to call Roman the evening of the party, but my calls went unanswered. I didn't want him to be surprised by me accompanying Lance to the event.

Lance and I arrived in his truck. The valet opened the door for me, and I stepped out flawless. There were three women I'd never seen before standing at the door staring me down. Once Lance got out of the truck and came over to me, we proceeded to go inside the building. The women were sort of blocking the entrance, so I gave Lance a look as if to say,

"Never mind them, open the door." He caught my expression and went over to hold the door for me. I gracefully strutted past the women with my head in the air. I heard them rambling about something, but it all sounded like murmur. I wasn't quite sure if it was directed toward me, although I could feel them watching me. I never turned to look back.

Lance had color coordinated with me. We were both dressed in red and black. My silk Japanese dress was long, body-fitting, and strapless, with a split up the back. The basic color was red, but it had black and gold in the Japanese designs. It was cold and rainy, so I had to wear a black silk wrap to cover me until I got inside. The shoes and accessories matched perfectly, of course. I had to wear my hair in an updo, though, 'cause that was the only thing to complement my entire look for the night.

Lance wore a red tuxedo jacket with black lapels. His pants were black with a black satin stripe down the sides. I wasn't so sure that I liked his fashion, but I rolled with it. His goatee was neatly groomed the way I liked it, and the cologne he was wearing had me pining for him as usual.

The first thing I wanted to do was take pictures before we partied too hard. I felt the best snapshot would be just after we had arrived, and I was right. They turned out beautifully. I put them in my purse 'cause I knew I was going to have bragging rights once I returned to work.

New Vet Life gave away great door prizes and surprise Christmas bonuses, too. Everyone who had exceeded quota expectations received recognition. I proudly watched as Lance walked down front to accept his award. Roman's name had been called also, but he was not there to collect his earnings. The two of them had previously thanked me for being a major factor in helping them reach that quota. Before I left the company, I made sure I told Roman and Lance everything I thought they needed to know to continue succeeding in the business. They deserved those bonuses though, 'cause they went the extra mile that year.

I had been dancing with Lance when I noticed Roman strutting through the door. He didn't see Lance and me, so after the song finished, I asked Lance if he would mind if I went over to speak. Lance expressed concerns, but I assured him I'd only take a minute to say hello. I left Lance sitting at our table.

Roman had been talking just off the side of the dance floor to one of the women I had passed standing at the entrance. His back was to me, and he seemed a bit startled when he turned to see me just after I tapped him on the shoulder. Roman had shock written all over his face. He threw his head back, squeezed his eyes shut for a few seconds, then opened them again. I smiled, waiting for Roman to say something, but he seemed to be speechless.

"Holiday, I didn't know you would be here," Roman stated.

"Well, I tried to call you. You're one hard man to catch up with these days." I tried to ignore the rude woman glaring into my face as I spoke.

"Oh, sorry about that. I've been kinda busy lately," Roman said, disregarding the fact that he'd been talking with someone before I walked up.

"Roman, aren't you going to introduce me?" the woman asked.

"Later," he replied, clearing his throat.

The woman's eyebrows went together as she frowned in confusion. I'm not certain what I looked like, but I didn't know what Roman's answer was about either.

"Excuse me? I don't understand." I refused to let him off the hook with such a short reply.

"Holiday, where's Lance?" Roman asked.

"Over at our table." I pointed to the area where Lance had been holding our seats.

"Good. Do me a favor and go chill with him for a minute. I'll be over there shortly."

I really didn't like the sound of things. Roman's voice was apprehensive, and he looked unhappy. It was strange to me that though he hadn't seen or talked with me in a few days, he never smiled the whole time I stood in his presence. I went back to the table with Lance and tried to ignore the conversation that had just transpired between Roman and me. Eventually, Roman came over to chat.

Lance wasn't thrilled about Roman taking a seat at the table with us, but he permitted it for my sake. Roman conveniently omitted picking up our conversation where it had left off, and he was up and down from our table all night. When I'd ask Roman to dance, he gave me excuses. I stopped accepting them when I heard "It Hurts Like Hell" playing. It was our song because we'd danced to it the night Roman first expressed his feelings for me. So there wasn't an excuse in the world good enough to deny me a dance at that moment.

Lance had gone to the restroom, so I took Roman by the hand and led him on the dance floor. Until that moment, you couldn't tell which man was mine. Due to Roman's disappearing acts the entire night, we all only looked like good friends. I'd had a few drinks, and I was feeling good. I tried to be careful not to hurt Lance's feelings, though. This was the first time the three of us had been cordial in a public place since our friendship fell apart. Lance tried not to watch us. I began to think of ways to explain being on the dance floor with Roman, but my mind was blank. Once I noticed Lance wasn't paying us any attention, I took advantage and began rubbing my hands in Roman's hair. Playing in his wavy hair felt like silk upon my fingers. I kept trying to make Roman give me eye contact while we danced. I wanted to make the moment feel like it did the first night.

"Roman, what's wrong? Are you feeling uncomfortable with Lance sitting over there? He's not looking, baby."

"No, I'm fine. I haven't thought about Lance."

"Then, what is it? I can't seem to make you get in this moment with me. What's up with that?"

"Nothing . . . I don't know. Maybe it's Lance. I'll try to relax, though." Just then Roman's eyes told me he realized I was way too smart to believe anything else.

"Well, I'll just try not to play in your hair then. How about that?"

Roman took a second to think and then he said, "You know what? Fuck it. It's Christmas, and I love you, girl. You can rub in my hair, boo. I am your man. And don't you forget it, alright? Bump what anybody has to say about it."

Well the final sentence in his statement should've been my clue. I should've taken my fist and busted Roman in his face as hard as I could after he said that. He had basically told me there was someone at the party he and I should be worried about. His uneasiness was confirmation that the someone was a woman. Then, she walked up to Roman and me as we danced.

"Excuse me, Roman! Roman!" one of the females that had been standing at the entrance said, tapping him on the shoulder.

"What?" Roman answered her with extreme harshness in his voice.

"You want to tell me who this is—and this time, tell me the truth 'cause I know damn well this is not Lance's woman. She's dancing this close to you, rubbing all in your hair like that. Come on talk to me, baby."

"Rachel, this is Holiday. Holiday, this is Rachel." Roman's voice was reduced to almost a whisper.

"No, tell it right. It's Rachel E. Clark, if she just has to know."

By this time all eyes were on us. Roman still had his hands around my waist, and we were standing in the middle of the dance floor. Ms. Rachel E. Clark stood there about five-foot-six, looking at the two of us with her big chestnut-brown eyes, her swollen belly aimed at us, and her hands on her hips.

"And you ain't told me jack. So, Holiday, do you mind telling me who you are and what you're doing with my man?" Rachel's hands were still positioned on her hips.

"Actually, Rachel, I kinda thought this was my man. As a matter of fact, we've been together off and on for a couple of years now. How he got to be your man, I don't know."

"Oh, so Roman, this is the one you told me about

several months ago? You told me you weren't with her anymore. You said you wouldn't take her back 'cause she cheated on you." Rachel began to tap her foot. "Oh! So now I know why you've been so sneaky tonight. And, why did you swear to me this was Lance's woman?"

"Wait a minute! Roman told you that?"

"He sure did," Rachel answered.

I couldn't help noticing how high Rachel's belly sat. "I don't mean to be rude, but I just have to know. Are you pregnant, Rachel?"

"Yes, I am. I'm exactly six months today. You didn't bother to tell her you had another woman pregnant, Roman? And, I can't believe you had the audacity to bring her here, knowing full well I'd be here!" Rachel's right hand never left her hip.

Rachel shook and bobbed her head with rhythm as she spoke. Roman continued to stand there motionless. He even looked as if he was being careful not to breathe for fear that either Rachel or I would tag him with a right hook.

I couldn't stand to hear any more. Lance walked toward me with my wrap, which I'd left at our table. I threw it around my shoulders then headed for the door. Roman and Lance both followed me. Once we were just outside the door, Lance grabbed my arm.

"Let me go! I don't want to look at either one of you right now." I was feeling so much pain. Some of it 'cause I sort of thought I had deserved this.

"Holiday, let me explain, please," Roman pleaded.

"You don't need to explain anything to me. Your shit is self-explanatory. Almost the whole time you were giving Lance and me grief, you had another woman. And then she's pregnant with your baby.

Why the fuck didn't you just leave me alone, then? That's sick! Real sick, Roman! How did I know not to stop using condoms with your ass? Huh? 'Cause I'm smart like that, that's why! But, what makes me even more ill is that I've been putting my mouth on you, and you've been sticking your naked dick in another woman. I should find me something out here on this ground to pick up and lay your sorry ass out!"

"Boo, calm down please. That damn baby ain't mine. I was using condoms! You think I would jeopardize you like that? You heard her say she's six months pregnant. I haven't even been messing with her that long. She's only been employed here about four or five months at the most."

"Great! And, that's suppose to make me feel better?" He was too ignorant to realize he had still told on himself. "You're stupid! That's what you're sounding like right now. Real stupid!"

"Excuse me, valet. I'm ready for my vehicle," Lance said, standing there with one arm wrapped around me. I jerked away.

"I'm not riding home with you. You knew about all of this, and you only brought me here to have it thrown in my face. I can't believe you wanted to see me hurt this way, Lance." I tried to fight the sensation of despair, but the feeling of being misused had become too much to handle. I could no longer fight back the tears.

"Baby girl, I couldn't tell you. You had already said that if you couldn't be with one of us, then you wouldn't be with the other. This was a failed attempt of pulling you closer to me. What do I need to do to show you how much you mean to me?"

"That's dirty, Lance. You know I'm not in a mind

to choose, yet you still brought me here to hurt me."
I'm sure they could barely understand me 'cause as I
spoke, I was bawling as if I had to make up for some
old stuff I hadn't cried about.

"Baby girl, this went all wrong. I hadn't thought of
things turning out this way."

"Boo, let's just go back to your place and talk
about this," Roman suggested.

I shaped up real quick and started to dry my tears.
"No. Hell no! I'm never talking to either of you
again!" The two of them looked at each other in disbelief. "Stay the hell out of my life!" I started strutting off, away from them into the cold and drizzling
rain.

"Come on, Holiday! You can't walk home in this cold
weather. And it's dark, baby girl!" Lance kept yelling
to me, but when he realized that I wasn't going to
stop, he and Roman ran to catch up.

"Leave me alone, and go see what your pregnant
woman wants!" I screamed. I had turned around to
see Rachel and her entourage swiftly approaching us
in the parking lot.

"What is it now, Rachel?" Roman asked.

"What the hell do you mean, what is it now?"
Rachel asked.

"Look, I'm gonna take this opportunity to be real
honest with you right now. Holiday is my boo. That's
the way it's gonna always be. Rachel, that baby ain't
mine. I haven't really been sweatin' you about it
'cause every time I try to say something, you get hysterical. I didn't want to be the cause of you miscarry-
ing, so I figured we'd address it once you'd given
birth," Roman explained.

"Oh no you didn't! No you ain't denying my baby!" Rachel began swinging and kicking at Roman.

Roman wouldn't hit her nor stop her from hitting him. All he did was try to block the licks. Well, I peeped this out once she first lunged on him 'cause he immediately threw his arms over his face. She only had the opportunity to hit him a few times, though 'cause I came to his defense.

"Aw hell naw! Step the fuck back!" I swung at Rachel then I pushed her away from Roman, into the arms of one of her friends. "Now let me tell you one thing! I know you're hurt! And you can go ahead and say whatever the fuck it is you think you need to say, but you're gonna keep your hands, feet, purse, and everything else to yourself. He's not gonna get in your face and I know he won't hit you, but I will whip your ass if you swing just one more time! Okay?"

"Fuck it! Nigga, don't say shit to me at work! Just talk to the judge at family court after the baby's born." Rachel rolled her eyes at me before she turned to walk away.

I wondered if the harassing calls had been made by Ms. Rachel. Although she claimed Roman lied about continuing to see me, I still had a suspicion she was the prankster. There was no real way of confirming my belief, but Rachel's embittered behavior toward me roused my curiosity.

Chapter Twenty-eight
Heading for Self-destruction

Some men have patterns with regard to the type of women they'll date and some don't. Roman only cared about beauty. Rachel didn't look anything like me. She had a stout frame and the night of the Christmas party, she wore some black boots with three-inch heels. She knew how to walk in them, too. I don't have to remind you that she was pregnant. She had neatly styled twists that complemented her face, dark skin, and chestnut-brown eyes, which all gave her a neo-soul look. From what I could tell, she took extra time to keep her nails manicured. I noticed that she didn't have on any nail polish. They were in fact her real nails, and they were very long and beautiful. But I know that Roman wished at that time they weren't. Rachel left him a couple of long scratches on his neck to remember that night.

I felt terrible about swinging at Rachel, but I never had a chance to apologize. I let too many emotions control my actions that night. I didn't take time to consider that she was pregnant and that I could've actually caused harm to her unborn baby. The thought of that made me realize how low I must've been feeling in order to ignore her pregnancy. What I probably should've done was just let her beat the dog out of Roman, but at that point he just looked so helpless.

That was the start of my Christmas being messed up. I knew, after all I'd learned, I should be through with Roman and Lance forever. Strangely, I still couldn't let go. And, my love for them hadn't changed. My whole outlook didn't change. These were the first and only men in my life to give me so much attention. If what they claimed to have felt for me wasn't real, I really didn't know the difference, and at least they knew how to fake their love. Crystal's father wasn't even very good at pretending. For the first time in my life, I felt wanted. Roman and Lance said they loved me, and in my mind, they both did. If I couldn't be with Roman, I didn't want Lance either. It's still very difficult to explain, and even now I'm left baffled.

December 23, 2002, I was contemplating picking Crystal up to bring her home. Before I called to see if she wanted to stay with Shaundra one more night, the phone rang. The caller ID read UNAVAILABLE. I went ahead and answered it 'cause a lot of my long-distance calls would still preview that way.

"Hello?"

"Tell yo' man he dun fucked wit' the wrong one now!" It was a creepy male voice on the other line.

"Hello? Who is this? Hello?" The phone line went dead.

I was so afraid. I started to have a gut feeling that

wouldn't go away. I decided I wouldn't pick Crystal up until the next day. Something about that call left me leery. Even though I wasn't pleased with Roman about Ms. Rachel Clark, I called him and asked if he'd come over to stay with me. I explained about the phone call, but he didn't seem worried. He figured it was just somebody Rachel had put up to playing on the phone. She must've found a way to get my new number.

Roman did come over to stay with me. I gave Lance a buzz to be certain he would not be coming over. He said that he was going to be out with some friends all night. That's all I needed to hear to put my mind at ease about having a good night with Roman.

"Boo, where's the mistletoe?" Roman asked later that evening.

"What mistletoe?"

"You mean you don't have any mistletoe in this house?"

"No. Do I need some?"

"Well, I just wanted a reason to kiss you all night long from head to toe." Roman stepped closer to me with a cynical grin on his face.

"You have a reason. At least I thought."

"Oh yeah, what's that?" he asked.

"The fact that you love me, dummy!" I said jokingly. "You do still love me, don't you?"

"Ummm, let me see." Roman put his hand up to his head as if he had to think about it.

"Uhn-uhn, don't play with me like that! You love me, mister." He grabbed me, laughing, then began kissing me passionately.

We were standing near the Christmas tree because

I had just clicked the lights on it. We stood there holding and kissing for another two minutes, then a big crash came through the window. Just after my reflexes caused me to jump, I looked in the direction of the window, and a big ball of flames hit the tree. We fled to the back door of the house and made our way around front. We never had a chance to see who or what had thrown something through the window. Immediately, I began accusing Rachel Clark. I couldn't think of anyone else who might've wanted to cause me harm.

Once the firemen had put the flames out, there was entirely too much damage to ever stay in that house again. All my clothes, Crystal's belongings, our Christmas gifts, everything was destroyed either by fire or water. I was so upset. I sat on the sidewalk rocking and throwing up from shock. My stomach ached, my throat was dry, and even my face hurt from having used so much energy when crying from the fright of everything.

Lance had made it over 'cause Roman called him after failing to calm me down. I was hysterical. The distress was too much. Eventually, I was taken to the hospital and given a shot to help me relax. I couldn't believe so much was happening to me. How was I going to explain this to Crystal? What about her Christmas gifts I'd purchased, wrapped, and put under the tree? I had insurance, but you know how long it takes to get paid from that. Hell, I worked at an insurance company, and I knew there was no way that I would get anything before Christmas Day.

Despite what happened, I recognize God was on my side. He gave me that strong instinct to leave Crystal where she was that night. He also blessed me to come through the fire alive. And He didn't just stop there. He enabled others to come through for me as well. My job took up a handsome donation. My church collected money for me, and Roman and Lance pitched in to replace everything Darius and I had bought Crystal for Christmas. God was definitely in the blessing business when the tragedy of losing my home occurred.

Crystal and I had Christmas at Darius's sister's house. People offered us a place to live, but I declined because I sensed that Crystal wasn't comfortable staying anywhere except her aunt's house. We just kept what little we'd begun to buy in a rented storage room. Shaundra was very happy to have Crystal living with her for a while.

"Cheer up, Mommy! It's not so bad. God has blessed us to still have each other," Crystal said, presenting me with a gift Christmas morning. "And happy birthday, too."

My baby gave me a quarter-carat diamond pendant on a sterling silver chain. The clarity of the stone surprised me. It was awesome. I wondered how Crystal had paid for it, but she replied before I could ask that she'd been saving her allowance and report card money. It was a miracle that Crystal had taken my present with her to Shaundra's house for wrapping. Given how excited she seemed to have a gift for me, Crystal would've been upset had the fire destroyed her surprise. Crystal is the most humble kid I know. After sensing my pain, she was selfless enough to offer me encouragement. I just wish it could've been the other way around.

Chapter Twenty-nine
Experience Is a Good Teacher

It got kind of rough having to live with someone else. Though I felt welcomed to live with Darius's sister, it was obvious it still wasn't our home. On top of that, the insurance company wasn't in any hurry to give me a disbursement for the fire since everything was still under investigation. Depression started settling in because my birthday and the holidays had passed and I hadn't been able to enjoy either of them. Despite all the help people were giving me, I still managed to feel hopeless. I didn't even have Erika to talk to anymore.

The Sunday following the fire, Erika came over to me at church and told me she was sorry to hear about what happened. I just stood and looked at her. Maybe I was wrong, but I was going through a lot at that time, and I just wasn't feeling up to communicating with her. We still hadn't squashed the deal with her talking behind my back. I couldn't just stand there and fake things with her.

After talking with my best friend, Renee, for a few days about the tragedy with my home, she was able to finally convince me to call my parents. I had hesitated because I didn't want to worry them. But, as Renee pointed out, there was a chance my parents would try to contact me at my old residence, so I called them and sugarcoated everything.

It dawned on me that I could at least be working on looking at some new houses, so I immediately called the Realtor I'd dealt with when I bought my first home. I had called him back in November with some questions because I was thinking of buying a house in the Southaven area, but I didn't keep in touch because I had felt I wasn't ready. He started running the information I'd given him on the type of house I was looking for and faxed me the printouts. Within a week I was looking at open houses in Southaven.

I found a home I was certain would work. I waited until Crystal got out of school, and we met the Realtor at his office. As we were driving to Southaven, I started to wonder how Crystal was going to adjust to the change. This meant she would have to change schools and meet new friends. Although I knew she was a very smart and a growing adolescent, I still worried about her adapting to new situations. She hadn't experienced anything this dramatic since her father and I broke up.

We made it to the house, and at first glance it was everything I had expected. I tried not to show too much excitement because I wanted Crystal's reaction to be genuine and not one that she thought I would want her to have. She stood and looked around the neighborhood then she took another look at the house. She looked up at me with a smile that I understood very well. It meant she was pleased. I gave her a wink and proceeded to follow the Realtor toward the front door.

It was a one-story brick home with a two-car garage sitting a little farther to the left rear of the house. You would have to pull on up into the driveway to see the garage. The landscaping was impressively well manicured. The homeowner had managed to keep his grass looking its finest despite the cold and rainy winter we'd been experiencing.

We started into the house and the first thing I noticed was the dynamic vaulted ceiling. There was a charming fireplace, new wall-to-wall carpeting, a huge kitchen with a breakfast area, and a dining room with a handsome chandelier. I continued to walk through the place in awe. Crystal was getting more and more excited. We went farther into the house, and I stumbled upon the first bathroom. It was off the hallway leading to the three bedrooms. The master bedroom was so huge that I didn't think it was a bedroom until I saw the large walk-in closet and the master bath. The other two bedrooms, to my surprise had plenty of space as well. As we headed to see the backyard, I pretty much knew right then this was the house I wanted.

The cost wasn't any problem. I had only bought my first place as a starter home and only intended to stay there long enough to build up more salary and credit in order to buy the place I had in mind. The Realtor worked on the offer right away. I was excited when I learned the owner had accepted the ten thousand dollars less I'd offered since he had to sell right away.

In March, Crystal and I moved into our new home. It was great to see Crystal so excited. She was even happy to be attending a new church home, which was not far from the house. Unlike our old congregation, there were more kids Crystal's age in Sunday school.

I had begun to spend more quality time with Crystal during the week. Some evenings, after she'd finish her homework, we would ride our bikes, or I'd take her on my five-mile runs. There wasn't as much traffic in our new neighborhood, and Crystal had started taking an interest in some of the things I liked to do.

I found her listening to my jazz some evenings while finishing homework, and I had seen poetry written in her English journal. She never ceased to amaze me. She even took up a love for cooking, so I allowed her to help me in the kitchen. I began to really enjoy this newfound time with Crystal.

I had been dodging Roman and Lance. I told them to give me a little space and I would call them when I was ready to talk. It wasn't hard at the time because I was going through a funk, and I didn't want to be bothered.

A former coworker told me Roman and Rachel were constantly at each other's throats. They were taking turns vandalizing each other's property and trying to get each other fired. There was never enough proof on either of them that they'd done any type of harassment, so neither was fired nor went to jail.

Lance was seen by one of my coworkers having lunch with another woman. It bothered me a great deal, but I sucked it up and never called him about it. I did ask him for space, so how could I call him inquiring about something that was none of my business?

I was at a point in my life where I thought I would be fine without either man and that just maybe this would be the time when the two men would realize they didn't need me. They didn't know that I had bought a new house, and I didn't intend on telling them. Every now and then, they'd call me at work or on my cell phone. I would just tell them I was okay and that I couldn't talk right then.

"Holiday, what's up, girl? Don't you think you've dodged us long enough now?" Lance's call on my cell phone caught me by surprise.

"Lance, I'm on the other line. Can I call you back?"

"Baby girl, seriously, I need to talk to you. Why don't you just take a few minutes to speak with me?" His tone was deep and sexy. "Just tell the person on the other line you'll call 'em back. Please?"

"Alright, hold on a second." I pretended to click over then I returned to the line with Lance. "I'm back. What's going on?"

"Baby girl, I know what you're trying to do, and it's not working. I still need you. I still love you very much."

"Is that right?" The first thing that came to mind was his lunch date.

"Yes! That's right, Holiday," he exclaimed.

"Then how do you explain your little lunch date with another woman? Were you pretending she was me?" I tried but I couldn't resist bringing it up.

"Baby girl, I knew you were trying to give yourself a chance to see if you could live without Roman and me, and I respected that. Although it hurt, I just tried to accept it. It was tough coping, though. Actually all that woman managed to do was make me realize she wasn't you. I couldn't have sex with her or anything. I want my baby girl back. Don't you miss me at all?"

"Yes, I miss you. I'm just being cautious right now. I'm still very fragile, and quite frankly, Lance, I'm afraid. I don't need the drama that goes along with a relationship to add to my problems. I just know it would do more harm than good."

"Have you talked to Roman lately?"

"No, I haven't had time to talk with him either."

"Well, where are you staying now?"

"Why?" I figured he'd get around to asking me that, but I wasn't ready for him to know.

"Baby girl, because I care. I care, that's all."

"I'm fine, Lance. I promise you. I'm fine. No need to worry."

"Hey, wait a minute. Here's Roman at my door," Lance said.

I couldn't hear everything that was said, and I knew that Lance had muffled his phone so that I couldn't distinguish what he and Roman were saying. Only a couple of minutes had gone by before Lance put the phone back to his ear.

"Holiday, are you there?" Lance asked.

"Yeah. What's going on? Why is Roman there?" I wanted to know.

"I'm gonna let him speak to you." Lance put Roman on the phone without confirming that it was okay with me to do so.

"Boo, how are you doing?" Roman sounded anxious to talk to me. He spoke as if he was out of breath.

"Good, Roman. How are you?"

"I'm missing you. I just showed up to speak to Lance about us trying to call you. I thought perhaps if he and I were together when we called then maybe you'd be more willing to speak to us. I know you like it when Lance and I are getting along. I've been worried about you, too. Why are you being so distant with us now? When are you gonna let us see you?"

"I just explained it to Lance, so when we get off the phone why don't you talk to him about it?"

"Where are you?"

"I have my own place now."

"Really! When did you do this? Is it an apartment or a house?" I could tell Roman was getting his hopes up very high about his chances of visiting.

"Well, it's home. That's all I want to tell you right now."

"Boo, why are you doing this? My love for you is real. I thought you understood that. Will you at least give me your home phone number?"

"I don't have a home phone, but you can still call my cell phone. I won't change the number," I lied.

Please explain to me why I didn't just tell them that I had a home phone, and that I didn't want them to call me on it. I sat there and lied to Roman about not having an alternate number, and shortly after that, the phone began to ring in the background. Roman heard it, too. I couldn't say anything. I wanted to just hang up on him, and I should have. A few seconds later, Crystal came in the room with the cordless phone and said very loudly, "Mommy, telephone!" Okay, I was so outdone. I hung up on Roman for real that time. I turned the ringers off on all the phones to prevent Crystal from being tempted to answer them.

Lance's number kept appearing on my cell for hours. I didn't want to discuss things with either of them anymore. I just wanted the men to understand that I needed to move on with my life. Only time would tell if they could respect my choice.

Chapter Thirty

A Rude Awakening

I couldn't believe it when several days went by without the guys trying to reach me. I really expected them to show up on my job, or call there at least. They never even bothered to call my cell phone anymore after that night. I found this to be odd, but I carried on with the rest of my week.

The weekend arrived, and Crystal and I had a lovely Friday night. She still had her heart set on going over to Shaundra's house on Saturday though. This really bothered me. I wanted Crystal to ask Shaundra to spend time at our house, but she was adamant about leaving home for the rest of the weekend. This was the second time Crystal blew up at me.

"I'm just tired of being at home, Mommy," Crystal said, pouting.

"I think your problem is that I've given you the upperhand a little too much. Do you know how many kids wish they could just go somewhere every once in a while?" I spoke up before Crystal could respond.

"Plenty. When I was your age, I never got to go places. You need to start counting your blessings, little girl."

"Well, what am I gonna do at home? I'm sick of playing Scrabble, and I can't keep up with you on our bike rides." Crystal folded her arms and poked out her lips.

"This is the first time I've heard you say these things. You never seemed to have had any problems with our activities before. You're scaring me. What does Shaundra have going on over to her house?"

"Nothing."

"Good. It's settled. You're staying home."

Her next response caught me by total surprise. "Arrgh! I hate you!" Crystal sprinted into her bedroom and locked the door.

"Crystal," I yelled and banged on the door. "Crystal, open up right this minute."

"Go away," she cried.

"Honey, why does it upset you so when I don't let you go to Shaundra's?"

"You don't care! I wish you still had your boyfriends. I bet you'd let me go then," Crystal yelled.

Her words cut like a knife. It hurt so much to hear her say that. "What are you saying? I've been spending a lot of time with you. I haven't been putting anyone before you. Why are you acting this way?"

Crystal swiftly pulled open her door and stood blocking me from entering her room. Tears streamed down her face as she spoke. "You caused my daddy to move thousands of miles away from us. He didn't care that he couldn't live with us anymore. He just wanted you to be nice to him when he came around. But, you weren't, so he left me. You're nice to other men. Why couldn't you be kind to my daddy?" Crystal cried harder than I'd ever seen her cry before.

"Sweetie, I never knew you felt this way. Can we sit down and talk?" I reached for Crystal's hand, and she jerked from me.

I couldn't believe what had just happened. I wondered if Crystal's actions meant she really hated me. We both stood in the doorway to her bedroom and cried. I think it was my tears that finally moved Crystal. She reached for my hand and pulled me into her room.

I sat on Crystal's bed and listened. "Mommy, all of my friends have both of their parents at home. I'm the only kid who can never talk about the things I do with my daddy. It hurts," Crystal said, sobbing.

"Sweetie, do you really believe it's my fault your father moved so far away?"

"Daddy says he loved you and that he only wished you would've been nicer to him when he came around."

"Crystal, that does sound like something your daddy would say, but I don't think he meant it the way you're perceiving it. What your father may have been trying to say is that he realized too late how I mattered to him. I was rude to Darius a few times when he came over to see you, but it was only because he was rude to me first, in my own home. My actions of speaking out like that to your father was too much for him because it confirmed in his mind that he and I were truly finished."

"But why did he have to move so far away? Mommy, I don't understand." It was very difficult to see Crystal with this much sadness.

"Sweetie, this is a question you'll have to ask your

father. I can only guess that losing me may have been a lot for him to handle, but he still has you here. Even as adults sometimes, we just don't make the best choices in life. And haven't I always told you that everything happens for a reason?" I wiped Crystal's tears as they fell.

"Yes, ma'am."

"Then you hold your head up, baby. There's a lesson in this separation we'll all pick up on eventually. Your father and I get along better with the distance between us, you know."

"Yes, ma'am. I know," Crystal said, looking into her lap.

"Sweetie, I need to ask you something, if you don't mind."

"Okay. What is it, Mommy?"

"This is the second time you've blown up at me, and you've brought up my former coworkers Roman and Lance. Why? What about my friendship with those men angers you so much?"

"Awe, Mommy. Do we have to talk about that?"

"Please, Crystal. Your feelings matter to me. I'd like to know."

Crystal sighed. "Mommy, I really miss my daddy. I understand why you and he can't be together, but I don't understand why you love spending time with those two men."

"Crystal, they are my friends."

"Yeah, some friends. They'll do anything you ask them, and they buy you everything. Mommy, please don't pretend with me anymore."

"Okay. Well, if you promise to be upfront and honest with me from now on, I promise to always tell you the truth."

"Mommy, do you know that Uncle Roman—I mean, Mr. Roman—doesn't love you?" Crystal sprung this comment matter-of-factly.

I wasn't expecting such a grown-up comment from Crystal, so it took me a moment to answer. I giggled when she proved she's always known better than Roman being my friend by correcting herself as she stated his name to me. She seemed a bit relieved to not have to call him Uncle Roman anymore. I dropped my head and shook it before replying. "What? Why do you say that?" I asked.

"The times he went out with us, I heard him on the phone with other women. He thought he was speaking low enough to keep me from listening, but one time I heard him tell some lady he missed looking into her beautiful chestnut-brown eyes."

I could've blown steam from my ears. Finding this out pissed me off, but I tried not to show it. "That Roman is something else. This doesn't surprise me, Crystal. Why didn't you tell me before?"

"Mommy, you kept trying to hide your relationship with those men. I was afraid to talk to you about my feelings."

"I understand, sweetie. I'm not angry with you. I'm just disappointed with myself."

"Do you still see them? I liked Mr. Lance."

"Really? What made him so different?"

"I don't know. I could just tell that he isn't all stuck on himself like Mr. Roman." We both laughed. "And he was very nice to me. He was the first of the two to offer me money for my good grades, he didn't mind picking me up from cheerleading practice, and on the ride home, he'd always ask if there was anything he could help me with on my homework. He even gave me the money to buy your Christmas gift."

"What? When? How did Lance sneak the money to you?"

"We talked about it the last time he gave me a ride. We went to the mall, and he helped me pick the diamond pendant and chain. I didn't have enough cash from my allowance, so Uncle Lance—I mean, Mr. Lance—charged it on his credit card."

"Hmph. Wow. I certainly didn't know that. Well, both you and Lance have a great sense of charm," I stated, reaching to hug Crystal.

Hearing Crystal say what she felt about Roman and Lance came as a surprise. I realized my child was not the little girl I thought her to be. I knew Crystal's feelings would definitely play a part in how I dealt with the two men from then on.

Crystal promised me that she and Shaundra would spend the next weekend at our home, so I allowed her to stay the night with her cousin. I had plenty of work I figured I could catch up on anyway. And if not, I would just finish hanging the wallpaper in the half-bath in Crystal's bedroom. The thought of serenity all day Saturday and Sunday had actually started feeling good.

Chapter Thirty-one
Silence Is Golden

I came back home from dropping Crystal off at Shaundra's to kick back for a minute. Later that day, I did a little homework from my job. I didn't spend a lot of time on that though. I took some time to go shopping for the house at the Super Wal-Mart, not far from where I live. Once I got back, I set up the things that I'd bought for my kitchen and the master bathroom. By the time I finished, it was late in the evening. I went and curled up on my sofa with a bag of jellybeans and watched the Lifetime Movie channel. It was shortly after seven when my doorbell rang. I couldn't imagine who it could be, especially after dark. I was a new resident, and my neighbors didn't know me well enough to come so late. My heart was beating so fast and hard enough to jump out of my chest. I started to look out the window for a car, but I was too afraid that whoever it was would shoot at me or something. After the investigators confirmed the fire at my last home was indeed arson by means of a firebomb, I was very paranoid.

I finally went and looked out of the peephole. It was Roman. I contemplated whether to open the door. I stomped and pouted like a toddler having a temper tantrum. It wasn't a surprise Roman had found me, but I had hoped it would take him much longer than it did to pinpoint my location. I made up my mind that speaking to him on the porch would be the easiest way to get rid of him quickly.

When I pulled the door open, I kind of stood there a few seconds sizing him up. At first, neither one of us could say a word. Roman's appearance was disturbing enough without him having said anything. There was more hair on his head than I could ever remember, and his face could use a good trim, too. His blue jeans were extremely wrinkled, but so was the once white, long-sleeve Oxford shirt he wore. Roman stood there holding a bag of groceries in each arm. I finally broke the silence.

"Roman, what are you doing here?"

"I came to kick it with you like old times, boo." Roman started to make his way into the house.

"Uh, I don't remember inviting you in." I placed my hand up to his chest to hold him at the door.

"C'mon, boo. You know I hate it when you treat me this way. You're acting like I'm somebody you never cared anything about." Roman knew saying something like that would get next to me. "Holiday, I just want to see you and spend a little time with you."

"How did you find me?"

"Boo, you know me. I have my ways of getting what I want. Now quit standing there asking questions.

These bags are weighing down on a brotha's arms. Let me in, boo." Roman started past me again, but I stopped him before he could get into the house.

"Roman, you can't come in," I said, blocking him from entering.

"Why? Who's in there?" Roman replied defensively.

"Nobody. This is my home, and I say you are not welcome here."

Roman tilted his head, closed his eyes, and bit his bottom lip. Before I realized what happened next, he had stormed past me, making his way into my home. He slung me fiercely, causing me to fall into a pile of champagne-soaked groceries and broken glass. I jumped to my feet, staggering, and ran into the house yelling for him to get out. Roman ignored me as he continued to search every room, every closet, and underneath anything that could possibly shield a man. Once he realized he would not find anyone there, Roman calmly strutted to the front door without saying a word. I followed him, screaming obscenities and telling him not to come back. Roman kept silent. Even when he slipped and almost fell on the wet paperbag on my front porch, I didn't hear a sigh from him. He just caught his balance and continued to walk to his car without looking back.

I locked my doors then ran to my sofa to sulk. I didn't know what I needed to do about Roman's behavior. I thought about getting a restraining order, then I dismissed the notion after having an idea to only threaten him with legal action. I felt telling Roman I would get the authorities involved would quickly straighten him out.

I needed to talk about what happened, so I called

Renee. I talked to my best friend for at least a couple of hours. I loved the way Renee could listen and offer all the right advice. Releasing over the phone to Renee proved helpful the way our talks had always been.

"Holiday, I sure didn't know that things had gotten this drastic in your life. I thought that maybe after you'd gotten settled into the new home, things would be okay. That damn Roman is something," Renee said.

"I don't know what to do about him, Renee. I sure know how to pick 'em, huh?"

"Well, you sure could've done better. I mean, what was that fool thinking when he put his hands on you? He needs to be sent to jail. Did you get cut on the broken glass?"

"No. Thank goodness!"

"Something needs to be done about Roman. You've had to move once already because of him."

"No. I moved because some idiot firebombed my house," I reminded Renee.

"Yeah, but there's a grand possibility that idiot is someone, particularly a woman who was reacting to Roman's deceptions. He can't just go around breaking hearts and thinking there'll never be consequences or repercussions. It's so sad, but I feel you were the recipient of what was really meant to hurt him."

"You're right. If it was Rachel or some other woman, she didn't care who was in the way. She just wanted to teach Roman a lesson. I sure learned, but I don't think Roman got anything out of me losing that house."

"You know what's odd to me?" Renee paused and then continued. "Roman really didn't seem to be as upset as he should've been about that firebombing. If he loves you so much, why hasn't he been vowing to get revenge or something? Why hasn't Lance?"

"Oh, look now, Renee. You're digging too deep now, sis. I don't want any blood shed over me losing that old house. I'm okay. Everything turned out for the better."

"Yeah, but you can't tell me that crazy-ass Roman wouldn't kill someone over you."

"Now see. You really shouldn't be talking like that. I don't wanna hear no stuff about somebody being killed. Roman ain't that crazy. He's just a little special, I think." I began to laugh hysterically. Renee didn't find it funny.

"Oh, *special* is an excellent word to describe Roman," she said.

"You know. Despite all the drama Roman is putting me through, I still have strong feelings for him. I really don't want to see him with another woman."

"Holiday, you're like true kin to me, and I love you. But yo' ass is as crazy as they come, too. There's no way in hell I would be trying to have anything to do with Roman after all the crap he has done. What are you thinking about, sis?"

"I guess I just understand better than most people what it feels like to love someone so much, but no matter what you do, they'll never love you the same. I feel for Roman. We shouldn't have ever gotten involved. I wasn't ready and neither was he."

"Well do I need to remind you of something you taught me back when we were teenagers?"

"What? What are you talking about?"

"My old boyfriend, Rick Davidson, use to stalk me

after I decided we needed to break things off. I kept thinking I should just ignore him until he got over it, but then you said something I've always remembered."

"What was it?" I pondered.

"Love doesn't act like that," Renee quoted. "Holiday, you and Crystal mean the world to me. I don't know what I would do if anything were to ever happen to you. You *can* let Roman go. It may seem hard right now, but trust me. Experience has taught me that time heals all wounds."

I choked back my tears. "Renee, you said a mouthful that time. I need to get off this phone and go meditate on some things. I'm under a great deal of stress. I love you, too, sis. I hope you know that."

"Sure, I do. We can talk later. Take care of yourself, Holiday."

I know that I told Renee I needed to meditate on some things, but I really didn't want to spend the rest of my night focusing on matters at hand and what should be done about them. I went to the hall closet and got all the materials for hanging the wallpaper in the half-bath in Crystal's room. Upon entering her room, I noticed Crystal hadn't made up her bed completely. I set everything down on the carpet and went to straighten her covers. While tucking the sheets, I bumped my hand twice into the journal I had discovered underneath her mattress a while back. After bumping it a third time, I decided to pull it out.

I stood looking at the cover, contemplating whether I should satisfy my urge to look through it. I decided that reading a few pages shouldn't be harmful to anyone, so I opened the book in the middle and began to read.

December 5, 2002 6:00 P.M.

    Who does she think she's fooling? I heard her talking to each of them on the phone today about what she wants for her birthday and Christmas gift. I heard her say diamonds are a girl's best friend. I really don't think either of them will get her diamonds, so I guess I'll spend my allowance to buy her some type gift with at least one stone. I should be able to afford that. Maybe she won't be too sad once she sees her boyfriends didn't get her what she asked for. I don't like it when Mommy cries.

I couldn't stand to read anymore. That one paragraph was enough to scar me deeply. I never thought Crystal had been keeping tabs on the events between Lance and Roman and me. I could just imagine if she'd felt it necessary to write about that time in my life, then all of the events involving those two men and me were most likely written in that journal. I refused to cause myself any more pain than I had already, so I hurriedly put the journal back underneath Crystal's mattress. I went into my room and cried myself to sleep.

Chapter Thirty-two

The Best Holiday Ever

I thought that admitting my selfishness and all my wrongdoings would aid in the attempt of letting go of the past. It didn't work though. I only kept feeling sorrier for myself. I continued to rationalize why I needed both Roman and Lance in my life. All of the spoiling me, making me feel like a woman and like I was very necessary contributed to my unwillingness to let them go.

A few weeks after Roman busted up groceries on my front porch and stormed through my house, I began accepting his phone calls at work and on my cell. I let him know we would never pursue a relationship because it just wouldn't work. I had seen another side of Roman that made me uncomfortable with the thought of him actually being my man. I didn't mind him calling to check on me, but Roman felt this wasn't fair. He admitted he wanted more out of me and that he would only accept talking over the phone because I hadn't totally dissed him from my life. At times I wanted to renege on accepting his calls. He would anger me severely with talks of a relationship when I had explicitly told him times before that we shouldn't be together. I could never say anything to make Roman understand.

I had also spoken to Lance a few times between then. I went on vacation for a week to treat myself to some relaxation, but Lance surprised me by offering to take off a few days with me. I thought about it then agreed to share time with him after spending the first half of my vacation alone. Crystal still had to attend school, so leaving town wasn't an option. Lance and I spent three days doing things I enjoyed doing in my spare time. He didn't mind going to a day spa for pampering and massages. The next day, we went to the Memphis Zoo and Aquarium and had an awesome visit. Lance took time to teach me about many of the animals living there. I never knew he had an interest in zoology. He acted as my personal guide. I was thrilled about his knowledge of the animals. The final day of my vacation, he pleaded for permission to share Crystal's junior cheerleading competition with me. I said no to him several times before making a final decision. My Christmas gift and all of the good things Crystal had to say about Lance came to mind, so I gave in and allowed him to join me.

Shortly after arriving at Crystal's school gymnasium, I began to have second thoughts about inviting Lance. I remembered her diary, and I wanted so badly to ask Lance to leave before Crystal could see him, but I didn't. Lance looked so happy to be there. I watched him sitting next to me in the bleachers, fumbling with his camera and the five rolls of film he brought with him. Once the competition began, he laughed, pointed, and snapped pictures of almost every cheerleading squad. It was difficult for me to enjoy myself because I worried that Crystal would be angry after looking into the bleachers to see Lance sitting next to me.

The time came for Crystal's team to compete. I sat and watched as her squad entered the gym. Crystal didn't look in our direction right away, but as soon as she did, I put up a nervous wave, slowly raising my hand into the air, and wiggling only my fingers as if to say hello. The squad was in formation, and I knew it was against the rules for Crystal to respond to me. My eyes were fixed on her though. She had begun to stare in another direction. I needed her to look at me just one more time. I had hoped that I could see some type of affirmation in her eyes that she was okay with seeing Lance and me in the stands together. While the team waited for the director to get the music ready for their routine, Crystal peered in our section again. This time Lance waved at her. I was relieved to finally see Crystal flash a beautiful, contented smile at us.

After the competition, Crystal ran over to Lance and me with a huge first-place trophy. I let her know how proud she'd made me then we all went out to dinner. Crystal made Lance feel welcomed by telling him she was glad he made it to her competition. Hearing her say that made my heart smile.

The next morning was Crystal's first day of tae kwan do. She was in the back getting ready when the doorbell rang.

"Hi, Lance, what are you doing here?" I asked. Lance had come over on Saturday, but never as early as he did this day.

"I wanted to see my baby girl. Anything wrong with that?"

"No, but didn't you just leave me after dinner last night? Besides, you never come without checking to see if Crystal is home first. You know what I'm going through. I don't want her to start making any assumptions, Lance."

"Oh, I forgot. For some strange reason I was thinking she went to stay at her cousin's last night."

"Well, she didn't. I know I told you that I might take her last night after we finished our game of Scrabble, but she reminded me of her tae kwan do lesson this morning."

"Well, do you mind if I ride with you guys?"

"Hmph. I guess it will be okay. Just do me a favor and ask Crystal before we make a decision that you should come along."

"Sure. No problem. I really should've called first," Lance responded.

"Crystal, are you about ready to leave? Someone is here to see you," I yelled.

"Yes, ma'am! I'm coming!" Crystal yelled back.

It was a very nice day for late March in Memphis. I was expecting it to be much cooler than it was, but we'd been blessed with some good weather. The sun was shining full blast into my Mercedes-Benz as we rode. Lance and Crystal talked all the way to her tae kwan do lesson. I could barely get a word in. Lance clung to everything Crystal had to say. He even let her feel like she had the upperhand in the conversation. Crystal seemed to enjoy trying to make Lance feel he wasn't a youngster anymore.

"I guess I'm just way behind the times. I feel like an old man. I was playing with the Atari 5600 when I was coming up. You mean to tell me I can't go into the store and buy any games for my Atari?" Lance teased.

Crystal laughed as hard as she could. "That even sounds crazy! What kind of system is an Atari 5600? It sounds like something weak! Mom, did you have one?"

"Yes, I sure did. And it was the bomb back in the day. We played Pac-Man, Frogger, Centipede—"

"Mom, we have those on PlayStation 2 now. But the games are on a disc, not that thing Mr. Lance was talking about."

"I told you. You make me feel like a little old man with gray hair." Lance shook his head at Crystal.

"You don't have to feel like that, Mr. Lance. You don't even have gray hair, but I think I saw one growing in your mustache earlier." Crystal laughed.

It was good to hear Crystal sound so cheerful. We dropped her off about nine-thirty. Lance had asked me if I wanted breakfast, but I declined because Crystal and I had a big breakfast just a couple of hours earlier. I still had a few errands to run, but Lance didn't mind riding along.

I hadn't heard from Roman by that time, and it seemed a little odd to me. I became a little concerned because I received a call from him late the night before. I wasn't able to get the phone in time, so the voice mail picked up. I waited to see if he'd leave a message, and he did. Roman was terribly drunk though, so I decided against returning his call. I had a notion to ask Lance if he knew of Roman's whereabouts.

"Lance, did you talk to Roman last night," I asked, driving toward the mall.

"What makes you ask me a thing like that?"

"I was just wondering. He left one of his famous drunk messages on my voice mail last night. I'm worried if he's okay."

"I know he had a late night out with some of our mutual friends, but he should be fine. Don't worry about that grown-ass man."

"Lance! You'd want me to care if the shoe were on the other foot."

"Baby girl, you don't ever have to worry about me calling you while I'm intoxicated. Hell, Roman ought to be ashamed to let you know he got that drunk."

"Well, I still don't see the harm in caring about what happens to him."

"You only have one child, Holiday. Save your energy for her."

I made a right turn into the mall. "I won't be in here long, Lance. I'm not shopping for myself." I laughed.

"That's fine. Whatever you need to do, it doesn't matter. I'm on your time today, baby girl. I just wanna be near you."

"Oooh, that's sweet!" I leaned over and kissed him on the lips after I parked. "I'm just returning this outfit for Crystal. It's too big and I've been driving around with it in my trunk for days."

We went into the mall, but it was empty. It had just opened and not many people were in there yet. This was fine with me 'cause I wasn't feeling up to dealing with a crowd. We found the store, exchanged the outfit and were headed back to my car, all in less than fifteen minutes.

"I'm glad I've gotten that out of the way. Crystal is

going to be thrilled I finally exchanged this outfit. One of Darius's sisters bought it for her good report card." I was walking fast and running my mouth as we headed out of the mall.

"It is cute. Does she always have to have a matching purse?" Lance asked.

"Yeah. She get it from her momma." I thought that little quote was cute, so I laughed my head off until I stumbled upon something familiar.

"Lance! Look! Over there! Isn't that Rome's car?"

"Where?"

"Over there!" I left Lance standing in the mall lot as I started walking swiftly toward what I thought was Roman's car.

"Girl, I swear! You will spot a man's car a mile away. Come back here. You don't know if that's really his car," Lance said, following me.

"Oh yes, it is his car! That's a Shelby county tag on the rear, and it's personalized. Right now I have a sick feeling." My stomach did a flip when I discovered it was Roman's Lexus, but I turned and headed back toward my own car.

"Baby girl, what are you thinking? Just put the outfit in the car and let's go. He may be here looking for something to buy you."

Lance was a quick thinker. He knew that despite my testimony of why I didn't need to be with Roman, I wasn't exactly ready to know that Roman had found another woman either. Knowing would only force me to totally give him up, and I didn't want to. When Roman was good, he was good. That's why I fell in love with him in the first place.

"Yeah, you're right. You guys have been extremely nice to me lately." I got in my car and cranked it up.

Lance was fidgeting, and I tried not to take notice. "Why are we still sitting here? Baby girl, let's go."

"Wait! I just want to see if he'll answer my call." I couldn't resist the temptation of dialing Roman's cell.

"What? Baby girl, you've got to be kidding me. I know you ain't gon' disrespect me like this."

"Disrespect? Lance, hush. I'm not in the mood to argue with you right now."

"Holiday, now you're being ridiculous. I didn't tag along with you to watch you be upset. Whatever Roman is doing in the mall is his business. He ain't yo' man, and you gon' mess around and get your feelings hurt tryna keep up with him."

"Lance, you know something, don't you? And you're not telling me!" I screamed, waiting for Roman to answer his cell phone.

"Baby girl, all I know is what I told you earlier. He was out with some friends last night. I only know this because a mutual friend told me. Roman and I don't kick it like that anymore."

"Yeah, but he was recently at your home talking to me on *your* phone," I replied tensely.

"You think I invited that nigga over? I wish you'd realize I'm not as stupid as you make me sound, Holiday."

"Yeah, and my name is Sally Sausage Head!"

I immediately turned off the car ignition and opened the door to head back into the mall. Roman hadn't answered his cell, and I knew in my heart what this meant. Being with another woman would be the only reason Roman would not answer my call. Otherwise, he would've picked up before the phone could ring twice. Though it would hurt me, I felt I just needed to see Roman with this woman for myself.

"Holiday. Holiday. Come on, baby girl. Don't do this to yourself. Come back," Lance yelled as he tried to catch up with me.

I responded to Lance without looking back. "Lance, right now you need to stay behind me and let me do my thing. If I'm wrong, I'll suffer the consequences later. As for right now, I've got to do this."

He followed me, huffing and puffing from the power walk I'd forced him to do to keep up. I was determined to search every inch of that mall until I found Roman. I knew he couldn't have passed right by me on his way out as Lance had tried to convince me. The mall had just opened the front entrance, the location I'd seen Black Onyx. His car wasn't in that spot when I first got there, and I wasn't in the mall but fifteen minutes. Even if he'd done his shopping that quickly, it didn't seem likely to me that Roman would've left through an exit other than the one where he'd parked. I wasn't quitting until I'd seen what I needed to see.

"Roman, look at this, honey! Isn't this the cutest little thing?" A woman's voice carried from around the corner as Lance and I were about to pass by.

"Yeah, I like this one, too. Which one you think we should get?" It was definitely Roman's voice.

I took a deep breath, slowly backed up and stepped from around the corner. "Frankly, I don't give a damn which one you pick. So, this is who you stayed with last night, huh? I can't believe I've allowed myself to get caught up in this trick bag again. Roman, you're so full of shit, you ought to be able to smell your own ass."

"Holiday, let's go. Don't get worked up in this store," Lance pleaded, pulling on my arm.

"Let me go, Lance." I jerked away. "This nigga shacked up last night with the bitch who had my house burned down. How low can you get, Roman? Just when I think you're sincere, you prove me wrong."

Roman stepped in front of Rachel, the woman from the Christmas party. "Holiday, you don't know that this woman had anything to do with having your house set afire. Lance, take her home, man. I'll be by to talk in a little while."

I spoke out before Lance could. "No. Don't try it, Roman. I don't wanna see you near my home. I'm through fucking with you and that's for real. You may as well get real cozy with your baby momma. It's over!"

Roman raised his voice. "What the hell do you mean? You told me it was over months ago. Don't try to come up in here acting a fool like we've been happy lovers 'til now. Go home. Shit, I'll talk with you later."

Lance spoke up for me. "Bullshit! I know you heard Holiday tell you not to bring yo' ass around, and you're gonna respect that."

Roman stood silent as he looked over to notice security approaching us. I, on the other hand, felt it necessary to say one more thing. "Ms. Rachel, let me shake your hand 'cause now my problem doesn't lie with you. It's with this asshole over here." Rachel stuck her hand out, and I firmly shook it as I continued to respond. "I always said I would shake the hand of the bitch who could steal my man. Congratulations." I was fuming, but I did well to finally walk off.

I heard Rachel screaming. "No. Let me go, Roman. She called me one too many bitches. I should've slapped her ass the first time she said it. She better keep walking." I looked back, and Rachel continued to yell though security had asked her to keep it down. "Don't worry! I'ma keep him real happy for ya," she said.

Roman did all he could to hold on to Rachel. If he had managed to let her loose, I would've just taken the ass whipping. I wasn't gonna harm her unborn baby. It was late-March, and I knew she was about to deliver any day. Lord knows, the last bit of drama I needed was going to jail.

Chapter Thirty-three

If You Didn't Know

As I headed out of the mall, I could hear Lance scurrying to keep up. He was one tired brotha by the time we made it back to the car. I left there swearing and talking to myself. Lance kept silent. I felt that he knew what was going on with Roman, but he would just continue to protect him. I was extremely pissed by the time we got back to my house.

"Lance, you can just leave. There's nothing you need to say to me now."

"So you still think I knew what he was up to?"

"I know you did. You're lying. It's done and over with! Stop your lying, Lance! He told you last night, didn't he?"

"For the last time, no! Holiday, even if I had talked to Roman, he knows not to put me in his mix. He's too worried it would give me an edge with you. Now, I'm just as smart as you are. When I saw his car in the mall parking lot, I figured he was with someone, but I wasn't about to tell you so you'd go and act a fool."

"It's just real crazy to me. It's amazing how you'll sit up there and defend him like that! It makes me sick!"

Someone began knocking on my door. I pushed Lance out of the way and headed to answer it. Lance spun me around by my shoulders and held on to me.

"Holiday, please, sit down and calm your nerves."

"Oh no! This better not be this trick at my door. I do remember telling him he wasn't invited."

Lance looked me in the eyes. "Holiday, sit down and let me get the door."

I didn't listen. I couldn't wait to confront Roman. I began screaming in his face the moment I opened the door. "Didn't I tell you not to come over here?"

"Wait a minute, Holiday. You're the one who's wrong. You are dead wrong!" Roman seemed just as angry as I was at the moment.

"Explain to me how so."

"Holiday, you don't know the story. You just jumped to conclusions before asking any questions."

"You were in that store buying baby things with the woman you said was not pregnant with your baby. Not to mention this female had something to do with a firebomb being thrown through my window while your ass was inside of the house with me! Now what kind of things should I have considered when I saw you with her?"

"Would you stop saying Rachel had something to do with that fire at your house? You don't know that she did. If I knew she did, her ass would have hell to pay. I've been going back and forth with Rachel for the longest, and the only way I've found to calm her down is to simply act as though I care. I've been calling her for the last few weeks to make it seem like I'm interested in her and the baby. Once the results are back from the blood test, she's gonna have to move on. I know that baby ain't mine. You have to believe me. I didn't spend the night with her either. I met with her this morning. That's all."

"Whatever. I really can't stand to look at either one of you though. Leave!" I felt the tears coming on, and I didn't want them to see me cry.

"Okay, baby girl. I'll give you some time. How about if I just check on you later this evening?" Lance asked.

"How about if we check on you later?" Roman seconded.

"It's funny how you seem to keep having selective amnesia. Holiday doesn't want you. Leave her the fuck alone." I was surprised to hear Lance cuss twice in one day.

"My boo hasn't said one time she didn't want me. She told me not to come over. Don't be putting mutherfucking words in her mouth." Roman stepped in Lance's face.

I grabbed their keys off the coffee table and threw a set at each of them. "Here. Get your shit and get out. You wanna fight? Fine. Get the hell out of my house and go squabble out there in the streets."

Though my reaction was not one that Roman and Lance may have wanted, they adhered to my demand of leaving my home. I peeked through the curtains to see if they were going to quarrel, but neither of them even so much as looked at each other, let alone fought. They both backed out of my driveway and drove in different directions.

Time was something I definitely needed. I was starting to feel consumed and swallowed again. I still felt I needed these two men in my life, yet I wanted them out of it as well. I began to do something I hadn't done in a long time. I started praying about the situation.

I hadn't talked to my girlfriend, Erika, in quite some time. After the way I'd treated her before I moved into my new home and joined another church, I couldn't blame her if she didn't want to talk to me ever again. I took a chance and called her anyway.

"Erika, it's me, Holiday," I said, solemnly enunciating my words.

"Hi, how are you? You sound down and out."

"I need to talk. You told me once you'd be here for me if I needed you, and now is the time."

"Holiday, I *am* here. Are you going to be okay? Do I need to come where you are?"

I sighed before I answered. I really wanted to ask her over, but I also wanted to be alone. "No, I can talk to you on the phone."

I filled Erika in on the latest with the guys and me. She gave me some advice, but she mostly listened. I don't know if she was afraid to comment or if she was just really speechless. It didn't really matter, though. I just needed someone to talk to. I wasn't ready to call home and give Renee another reason to be disappointed in me. Furthermore, I was too embarrassed to talk to my momma. I figured this wasn't the sort of thing to share with her anyway, so I told Erika. I also let Erika know she could be the "mouth of the south" if she wanted, but my God would be the final judge of me. She apologized for what she'd done and reassured me she wouldn't share this information with anyone.

A couple of months went by and Erika and I still didn't

communicate as often as we had before Lance and Roman came in the picture. It bothered me, but only because I made it a point not to associate with a lot of women. Erika was my only girlfriend in Memphis. Lance and Roman were my only male friends. I guess it would be fair to say this was another reason I felt I couldn't let go. I had a phobia about being lonely, and I loved my career in Memphis too much to go back to Charlotte.

One Saturday morning, my doorbell rang. I had my heart ready and set to give Lance a piece of my mind for showing up so early for the third time unannounced. I didn't bother looking to see who was standing outside. I tightened my robe and swiftly pulled the door open. It was Roman.

"Boo, what's yo' man's name?" Roman brushed right past me, waving a piece of paper.

"Huh?"

"I said what's yo' man's name? Boo-yow! Peep this out!" He handed me the paper.

"Zero probability that this child could be produced by Mr. Roman Broxton." Surprised by the results, I looked at Roman and smirked. "Hmph. So you weren't lying to me, huh?"

"Naw. I told you I used a condom," Roman said.

"Well, I guess this is congratulations to you, but you really didn't need to bring this for me to see. I'm no longer your woman."

"Yes, you are. We're just going through some rough times right now, but you are my woman."

"No. I'm not, and I'm gonna have to ask you to leave now."

Roman began to stutter. "W-w-why? Who? Who's here?"

"No one, Roman. I swear to you, no one besides Crystal. I don't want her to awaken and find you here. Please leave."

"I'll leave, if you say my name first," Roman said as he began to dance. "Say my name. Say my name. C'mon, boo, say my name," he chanted, doing a silly-looking impression of James Brown's footwork.

"Why do I need to say your name? Just leave, Roman."

"Un-uhn, boo. That ain't it. Say my name," he chanted and danced.

I looked around to see if Crystal had come into the living room, but I didn't see her. Though we were alone, I was totally embarrassed by Roman's behavior, and I knew the only way to get him to leave quickly would be to do as he'd asked.

I whispered, "Rome."

"What is it? Let me hear you say it again. Say my name," Roman said, continuing his fancy footwork.

I looked around once more then spoke out. "Rome."

He stopped dancing and took his paternity result from me. "Thank you. Now you gon' learn to believe your man," he said, leaving out of my house.

Roman may have gotten off easy that time, but I was almost certain there would be more baby momma drama in the future for this man.

Chapter Thirty-four
Tastes Like Cake

Erika loved my new house. The first time she came over we drank strawberry margaritas and talked for a couple of hours to make up for old times. I told her about the outcome of Roman's paternity test. She seemed to be elated for him. We were on the subject of Roman and Lance almost the whole time. She wanted to know if I felt better about Roman now that I knew the baby wasn't his. She also wanted to know who I loved more, Roman or Lance.

"Listen, I'm not in a situation where I have to make a decision one way or the other. I wanna get to that level though. I just can't see me making that crucial choice between Roman and Lance right now. I try to keep them both from thinking I may want to start over with them though. I know it seems like I'm sending mixed signals to each of them at times, but it's just something I'm still praying about. No matter what I do, I just don't seem to know the answer."

"Well, I can tell you what it seems like to me."

I could feel a sermon coming on. "What?" I asked her, but I didn't really care.

"It seems like you just don't want to let go. I think you're afraid of seeing them happy with someone else."

"What? Oh, you mean like seeing them with another woman?"

"Naw! Another man." Erika laughed. She felt like making jokes. "No, I'm just teasing. Of course another woman."

"Yeah. That's some of it. How can you tell?"

"I don't mean any harm, sweetie, but during this entire conversation, you've sounded selfish. You're sorry for the drama that occurs, but you don't wanna do anything to end it all."

"Now that's not true. Hell, you just don't know how I'm stressed," I said in defense.

"Apparently not stressed enough," Erika stated, repositioning herself to look me in the eyes. "Holiday, Roman has given you several tickets to move on. Instead of using them, you've made excuses to cling to him. Why?"

"The thought of Roman possibly being the father of Rachel's baby tore me up inside. We had talked about plans of him being a family man in *my* world. You don't know the thoughts Roman and I have shared. He and I both have done things to screw up the potential for us to be a couple again, and it's hard to sit back and watch him offer the same happiness he had given me to another woman. Yes, it hurt me to think that Rachel would be the one he'd be good to."

"Roman would only give that woman as much grief as he has given to you. He's not gonna change. You need to quit believing he will."

I stood to fix me a drink. "Erika, you've never listened to Roman. He has a great heart. He means well most of the time."

"When you get finished defending him, Holiday, Roman is the same no-good man you and I use to discuss a couple of years ago. Oh, and don't let me forget to add the word *crazy* to his title." Erika chuckled.

"It's not funny, Erika. He does have some issues. He's literally becoming a nightmare for me, too."

"Then, I don't see how you could be so in love with him."

"I don't know if I'm in love with him anymore. I just know I care a great deal for Roman. I guess you can classify it as love."

I offered Erika another strawberry margarita, but she declined because she hadn't finished her second one. I, on the other hand, had finished my glass and was ready for a fifth drink in less than two hours. Our talk of Roman and Lance had caused me to drink far more heavily than Erika. Concerned, she suggested I let the fifth one be my final glass.

"I'm going to ask you one more question and then I'm going to leave this topic alone. I think the subject is really bothering you 'cause you're drinking a little more than I can ever remember," Erika said, taking my glass and setting it on the coffee table.

"Whatcha wanna ask me?" I slurred my words as I spoke.

"How about Lance? You still haven't answered that question. Do you love him?"

"Yes. I can definitely say I love Lance. Simply because his demeanor has never changed. He's not gonna give me grief, and he loves my dirty drawers. I know he genuinely loves Crystal, too. He goes out of his way at times to make her happy. I don't tell Lance how much I care for him 'cause I haven't discovered if my feelings are strong enough to let Roman go. Now is that whatcha wanna hear?"

"See! That's what I'm talking about. That's not fair, Holiday. You're being totally unfair to these two men."

"Well, I guess you think I just need to suffer and let them go, right?"

"At least one of them, honey. Stop holding these men captive."

"But if I try to tell them I don't want to see them anymore, they just try even harder to remain a part of my life. Both of them."

Erika stood to fix her third drink. "Hanging around you with all this drama is gonna turn me into a drunkard," she said, pouring the margarita mix. "I know Roman has been with at least one other woman since being with you. What about Lance? Do you know if he has any dirt?"

I gave her a look 'cause her question sounded pretty ridiculous. "The only thing I can think of is once before I'd asked Lance for space and he tried to give it to me by seeing someone else for a minute. My coworker told me she'd seen him out to lunch with another woman. I never saw him with the broad, but I questioned him about her. He said he was never intimate with her and all she managed to do was show him she wasn't me."

Erika plopped down on the sofa. "Hmph! And you believed him, right?" Erika's expression was saying, "whatever!"

"Yeah. Lance knows he doesn't have to lie to me. He doesn't always volunteer information, but when he can tell I know the truth, then he'll admit it."

"Holiday, you have a serious problem on your hands. Don't try to make it seem like you're so innocent. Remember this? 'I just wanna make them see I do have it going on.' You wanted to show them a side of you they hadn't seen before. Well, you've succeeded."

"Oh, now it's all my fault, huh?"

"No, but you've contributed to the problems you're having with them."

"I've already owned up to that. I never said I was innocent. I'm sorry you've perceived me to be saying so, but I do know I'm not innocent in everything."

We talked and talked and talked. Finally, the doorbell saved me. I got up and answered the door. It was Lance as I'd expected. He had called earlier and said that he'd be over in a little while to help Crystal with her pre-algebra assignment. I didn't mention to Lance that Erika was over 'cause he wasn't coming to keep me company. Erika was well aware of the fact that I'd been keeping in touch with both Roman and Lance, so I knew she wouldn't be surprised by Lance's visit.

When I opened the door, Lance was looking back at Erika's car. He came in, and I wondered why he seemed so surprised to see her. Then I thought he must've remembered that my last words about Erika weren't so kind. I never told him we had made up our differences. He kissed me on the cheek and then threw his hand up at Erika to speak before taking a seat.

I went to sit on the couch next to Erika, but Lance called me before I had a chance to get over there. I was shocked to hear him ask me to sit next to him.

"Hey, I've missed you these last few days," Lance said, embracing me then planting the sweetest kiss on my lips.

I looked over at Erika and she put on sort of a smirk by keeping her lips pressed and only raising one side of her mouth, then she shrugged. I didn't know how to respond to Lance with her sitting there. I was feeling a little tipsy, and I'd been open about everything else with Erika, so I decided to take advantage of the attention Lance wanted to give me.

"I've missed you, too, Lance," I replied, gazing into his hazel-colored eyes.

Lance's scent was insatiable, and it made me feel more gratitude for him holding me so closely. I wished I could melt deeper into his grasp, but I knew he was already holding me as firmly as possible. Though I hadn't expected Lance to be so loving, I was proud he was. At least his actions could serve as affirmation to Erika of how I said Lance felt for me.

I tried to get up, but Lance pulled me back down, almost in his lap. "Un-uhn. Where you going?"

I sat in an awkward position, halfway on Lance's lap. "Lance, you didn't come to see me. You came to help Crystal with her pre-algebra, remember? I'm going to let her know you're here."

Lance pulled me comfortably onto his lap. "Can we just have a few more minutes?" he whispered, nibbling on my ear and rubbing my back.

"Lance! No. I have company." I got up from Lance's lap. "Crystal, Mr. Lance is here," I yelled.

Lance stood to meet Crystal as she entered the great room. Erika and I smiled as we noticed Lance giving Crystal a warm embrace. They headed to the kitchen table to study.

"Look, I'm getting ready to let y'all have this. I'll see you later, Holiday." Erika jumped up real quick and reached for her purse.

"Erika, what's wrong? You don't have to go." I followed her to the door.

"Yes, I do. Y'all have fun."

Erika's abrupt decision to leave made it obvious something had upset her. I went into the kitchen to speak to Lance.

"Something's wrong with Erika. She sure left out of here all of a sudden," I said.

"Really? Well, are you mad that she's gone or something?" Lance looked as if he really didn't care.

"What? Why are you sounding rude?"

"I don't mean to be rude, but last I heard was that the two of you weren't friends anymore. Now all of a sudden she's sitting in your great room drinking tea."

"Lance, it was strawberry margaritas, and you're not sounding too nice. Before you continue, let me remind you Crystal's sitting right here at the table."

"I wasn't gonna say anything mean. C'mon, Holiday, you know me better than that."

"Oh, well. My company is gone so I guess I can turn in early."

"Or, you can sit right here with Crystal and me to learn a thing or two about pre-algebra," Lance stated, winking at me.

"Fine. What are we working on?"

I didn't care all that much that Erika had left. I knew I could just call her later and apologize for whatever I had done to upset her—if I had done anything at all. Erika's patience seemed very short for no good reason at times, so I figured this must've been one of those moments.

Lance didn't stay over too late since it was a school night for Crystal and the next day was work for both him and me. We hated for the evening to end, but we said our good-byes and made plans for the weekend.

Chapter Thirty-five
If It's Good for the Goose

I couldn't wait until I got off work the next day to call Erika. Although she had done way more to me in the past to hurt my feelings and wouldn't ever be the first to make amends, I still felt it necessary to contact her. I wanted our discussion to wait until we'd both gotten off our jobs because I wasn't certain she would have a lot of time to talk while at work. Despite what the two of us had gone through and the distance in our friendship, I cared a lot about Erika's feelings.

I tried to reach Erika several times on the ride home. All of my attempts failed, but I left several voice messages for her to return my call. While I waited to hear from her, I went to take care of a few bills and to pick up some ice cream. My phone began to ring while I was standing in line at the checkout stand. It was in my purse and I thought I wouldn't be able to get it in time. I fumbled with putting my purchases on the counter, dropping the bucket of ice cream on the floor, and even spilling things out of my purse. In spite of what I had to go through, I managed to answer the call.

"Rome, what's up?" I huffed after I checked my caller ID.

"Nothing, boo. What's up with you? You sound out of breath."

"I'm okay. Just picking up some ice cream for Crystal."

"Is that right? I didn't want anything, boo. Kinda just wanted to hear your voice."

"Cool. That's sweet of you, Rome. Listen, I need to go."

"What you got going on tonight?" he asked, disregarding my comment.

"Hey, I've got plenty of homework to do."

"Speaking of homework, isn't Lance supposed to come over and help Crystal with hers tonight?"

"Oh yeah, that's right! But I don't know where he is right now. I've already called him and left a message, and anyway, how did you know?"

"I heard him telling someone on the phone."

"Mmhmm, and you were just dippin'." I laughed.

"Boo, you're laughing, but you're right. Whenever I hear Lance call your name, I listen whether he's talking to me or not."

"You've got some serious issues, Roman, but I can't entertain them right now. I'm on my way to pick up Crystal and then I'll try to call Erika again. She's been on my mind all day," I said with the phone to one ear while paying the cashier for my groceries.

"What's up with that, boo?"

"Nothing. You know. Girl stuff."

"Okay, well y'all handle that. I'll try to talk to you later," Roman said just before hanging up.

I had been unsuccessful with reaching Erika again. Once I got home, I checked my answering machine and saw I didn't have any messages, so I went back to my master tub to make me an early bubble bath. Crystal and I had stopped to get burgers and fries for dinner, so that part was out of the way. Lance was coming over to help Crystal with pre-algebra again, so I didn't have to worry about staying up to assist her. I had gotten ready for an early night in bed, then Lance called.

"Lance, I've been calling you. I just wanted to make sure you remembered Crystal needs help tonight."

"Yes, baby girl, I remembered. I'm heading that way now."

"Good. It's been a long day at work, so I'm about to crash. Crystal knows to listen out for you though. Will that be okay?"

"What? You're not gonna get up and let me see you?"

"I have on my night clothes. If I do, Crystal will wonder what's really going on."

"Baby girl, that's messed up. You're gonna let me come all the way over there and I can't see you?" He made me feel guilty.

"Okay, when I hear the doorbell, I'll just cover up and come to the great room for a minute. Is that okay?"

"I guess that'll do."

"Alright, I'll see you then." I hung up the phone with Lance and put on my robe.

Two minutes later my phone rang back. I wondered what Lance had forgotten to tell me. I ran over to answer it and discovered it was Erika.

"Erika, what's up, girl? I've been trying to call you today. Did you get my messages?"

"Yeah. I got 'em. What's up?" Erika was being short with me.

"No, that's what I want to know from you. What's up? You left here yesterday acting all funny and everything. And right now, you really don't sound too enthused to be talking to me. Are you tired or something?"

"No, Holiday, I *do* need to talk to you."

"Okay. What's going on?"

"Holiday, if you were wondering whether I left because of Lance's visit, the answer is yes." Erika's voice was somber.

"Why? Did we offend you in any way?"

"Holiday, I really don't want to tell you this, but I have to. I was the woman having lunch with Lance."

My lower jaw dropped. I had only thought Rachel Clark broke my face, but this time I was absolutely certain my face was broken because for a few seconds, I couldn't say a word.

"Hello? Are you still here?" Erika couldn't tell if I had hung up the phone.

"Erika, no! Tell me you didn't just say what I thought you said."

"He's been lying to you, Holiday. We've made love before, and it's been more than once."

My tears came instantly. Like some type of reflex or something. I never thought I'd see the day when I'd get my own payback for playing between two best friends.

"Oh my God! Oh my God! Tell me you're lying, Erika. Tell me you're lying!"

"Holiday, it's the truth. I didn't want to tell you, but it's been hard keeping it from you."

I dropped the phone and continued to cry with my hand over my mouth to muzzle the sound. I didn't want Crystal to hear me. I didn't know how to be strong in a situation such as this. I never saw it coming.

I picked up the phone and heard Erika asking for me.

"Hello? Holiday? Are you there?" she asked.

"Erika, you're supposed to be my girl!"

"Holiday, I didn't go looking for Lance. We had a chance meeting at Piccadilly's for lunch. He saw me standing in line and asked me to join him. We talked about you for a bit, and we decided to keep in touch. Things just kind of happened from there."

"Oh my God!" There wasn't anything else that would come to mind.

"See, this is why I've kept this so long. I knew you'd be hurt. No matter how much you say you want Roman and Lance out of your life, I've discovered the truth. You really don't."

"Now looky looky. You were Miss Goody-Goody." I mocked Erika for once making me feel like I was scum. "You dogged me about what I did with the two men, and now you've stabbed me in the back. Don't ever say what you won't do, Erika! That shit has come back to haunt you, and at my expense!"

"I want to apologize, Holiday, but I'm afraid you won't accept it."

"Then don't apologize 'cause that just means the shit ain't sincere! I don't want no half-ass apology!" A sense of anger had set in. "How could you sit in my house all that time knowing what you had done and not tell me? And how do I know you're not lying anyway?"

"I wanted to tell you, but I couldn't find the words. I was just hoping to be able to convince you that neither man was right for you then just maybe you'd leave them alone. And as for me lying, well I could go there and tell you how he was in bed, but I won't. I will tell you he just left here, and he's on his way over there to help Crystal with her homework."

I shook with anger and pain. I literally sat on the edge of my bed trying to control the tremors. I was angry enough to fight.

I heard the doorbell ring. More anger set in. Thank God I had the sense to realize my baby was in the other room and I didn't want to act a fool in front of her. I tried hard to wipe my tears and headed to the great room with my cordless phone to my ear.

Once I stepped around the corner into the great room, I stood at the entryway and just stared at Lance with the phone up to my ear. He spoke, but he didn't step toward me. He knew from the look on my face and the phone up to my ear something was definitely going on.

Lance sat on the couch next to Crystal and tried to focus on her as she began speaking to him and turning the pages of her pre-algebra book. He kept trying to play off his guilt by just continuing to answer the questions she asked. He'd look up at me with concern on his face and glance right back down. My eyes were filled with bitterness, and it was too hard for him to ignore my voice as I spoke firm and short with Erika on the phone.

"I'm sure Lance has made it over there by now."

"Yeah," I answered.

"Well, I'd appreciate it if you don't let him know it's me on the phone."

"Whatever, Erika."

"Holiday, Lance and Roman didn't let you totally destroy their friendship. They can still work together and everything. I think you and I shouldn't let a man come between us either. Can we still be friends?"

"Well, I don't see how," I replied.

"Oh you gonna be a fucking hypocrite?"

"I tell you what, don't call me again," I calmly told Erika just before hanging up on her.

I stood there, propped against the doorway at the hall entrance for about five minutes, staring at Lance. He would attempt to look up at me, but he couldn't maintain eye contact. He appeared as if he didn't know whether to run or hide. When I couldn't stand the sight of him anymore, I walked off, leaving him there to finish tutoring Crystal. He soon had Crystal ask me if he could come back to my room and speak with me. I couldn't sleep, so I agreed to talk.

"I guess Erika called, huh?"

"Lance, I know what you're thinking, but there's no way I'm going to accept this." I remained calm. There wasn't any need to act a fool when I knew it was over.

"Holiday, I've already told you I was trying to get over you. We weren't together then."

"So you go and get the next best thing to being with me, my girlfriend? Way to go, Lance."

"I'm sorry it sounds strange, but when I saw her in that restaurant, that's the way I felt."

"Yeah, but did you have to go and sleep with her? She's bragging about how it happened more than once."

"Baby girl, that's a lie. She wanted me to have sex with her, but I couldn't. There wouldn't have been any feelings attached to it. You know I don't waste my time like that. Erika only said she and I were intimate to hurt you."

"I don't know if I believe you, Lance. You were at her place before coming here tonight. I called you several times and couldn't get an answer."

"Erika called me at work today, even after I asked her to stop phoning me. She said we needed to talk. I finally agreed, and when I got over there, she didn't want anything. She was only talking about missing me coming around. I told her then that I love you and I've come too far with you to mess up now. She lied and told me she wouldn't tell you anything about us ever going out, but I guess she got angry and changed her mind. I'm sorry if she feels used in any way, but that really wasn't my intent."

"So, you really thought you could have a relationship with her?"

"No. I don't know. I mean . . . baby girl, I was missing you. I don't know what else I was thinking."

"I don't even know how to trip hard with you, Lance. I know that I brought a whole lot of everything on myself, but I will say that at least now, I know it's over."

"What? Baby girl, you know I love you. You can't give up on us like that!" Lance pulled me close to him.

"I'm sorry, Lance. I just can't take any more of you and Roman. It's too much drama involved with keeping it together. I wish you the best, and I wish Roman the best."

My heart was aching. I didn't want to let either man go, but I had to use the open door to get out. Lance had never stood up to me until this day. He really let me have it.

"You know what, Holiday? This is some sorry shit you're pulling on me. If you want Roman, you can be with his ass. After all the crap I done took off you, I make one little mistake and you're through with me?"

"One little mistake? Lance, you slept with my best friend."

Lance raised his voice. "Were you there?"

"I didn't have to be," I yelled back.

"That's not what I asked you. Were you there?"

I didn't answer him. Lance's chest was heaving up and down as he began to breathe faster, and his face got harder with anger.

"I can't believe you gon' believe a bitch-ass friend over me. I've done nothing but try to love you. I've stuck by and waited to see if you'd ever realize I'm the better man, but every time I feel you've got enough proof to have an answer, you conveniently overlook it. You never intended to choose, did you?"

"Lance, I-I love you."

"Don't go around the question, Holiday. Were you ever going to choose?"

I sighed and tried to control my voice level. I didn't want Crystal to be alarmed of an argument between Lance and me. "Yes. I wanted to choose you. Why do you think I'm so hurt about you and Erika?"

Lance was heading to the door, then he turned back. "Would you stop! Stop with the Erika thing 'cause

I didn't have sex with that woman. You, on the other hand, did continue to sleep with my best friend during the same time we were intimate."

"I haven't been intimate with anyone in a long time though, Lance."

"Well, what do you want, a cookie? You've played around with my feelings for more than two years, Holiday. I've tolerated Roman's shit for your sake."

"For my sake? How so?"

"Oh, now you don't remember asking me to ignore Roman's foolishness, huh? The man has fucked with me nonstop, but all you cared was to keep him out of jail. My truck has been tampered with—" Lance tried to explain.

"We don't have proof he—" I wasn't allowed to complete my thought.

Lance raised his hand in a silencing motion, cutting my speech. "Shhh! You don't wanna go there, Holiday. Trust me. Now is not the time to defend Roman."

Lance sucked in his jaws and clenched his teeth so tight I could see their imprint on the sides of his face. The hostility in his eyes paralyzed me. A dead silence fell over the room. I dared not to say another word.

Lance finally spoke out. "As I was trying to say, my truck has been tampered with, someone kept placing prank calls to my mother about my well-being, and my job has been jeopardized more than once. Don't stand there and tell me you feel Roman didn't have anything to do with these occurrences."

I played it safe by keeping quiet. I felt the same as Lance about all those mishaps, but my reasoning for asking him to spare Roman was because I cared for

Lance, too. He could've gone to jail, lost his career, or even gotten hurt trying to take matters into his own hands. Lance didn't see it this way. He felt I was only looking out for Roman.

I stood silent, waiting for Lance to continue.

"I'll always love you, Holiday, but if you aren't serious about being done with me, then I am for real about us being done and through with each other. I'm the one who can't take any more of the drama. I'll find a woman who can love me back."

I let Lance walk out on me, and I cried a river. Although I knew this was only a symptom of me getting back what I had dished out to Roman for cheating with his best friend, I wasn't willing to let the escapade go on. I plainly understood that what goes around comes around. And now that it was back around, I could see the whole picture clearly. It was time for me to release the key I'd been using to keep their hearts on lockdown.

When I told Roman about the blow-up between me and Lance, he was pissed. He felt that since he hadn't done anything, I should be willing to continue seeing him. He did admit, however, knowing about Lance and Erika's lunch date. Roman said he didn't mention it to me because he never had any real proof there was something serious between them. Regardless, it felt like a big burden off my shoulders to finally release the two men.

I knew when I hung up on Erika that evening, it would be the last time we ever talked. I was glad I had a new home church. At least, I wouldn't have to see her anymore.

Chapter Thirty-six
Rome Wasn't Built in a Day

Now, I shouldn't have to tell you that Roman wasn't going to accept me leaving him. He was very upset with Lance, and he was even more upset with me. I kept threatening to report him to the phone company, and he didn't want that to happen. BellSouth is strict against harassing phone calls. Roman knew this because one of his friends from college isn't allowed to have service with BellSouth anymore because of placing prank calls to his baby's momma's house. Threatening to report Roman prevented him from dialing my home from his place and even from his own cell, but he got smart and started calling from pay phones. I just stopped answering unless it was the double-ring feature I had added, so I'd know it was Crystal on the line. Roman would fill my voice mail daily.

Work wasn't necessarily a safe haven either. I had to tell my assistant to screen all my calls. It was getting to be very annoying to have to dodge Roman like that. Luckily my superiors didn't know what was going on with the phone calls. It would've been extremely embarrassing to have to explain this man was stalking me. I couldn't help but wonder what was going on with Roman. I thought he'd never been mentally unstable, but he sure was beginning to act like it. I wondered if I drove him insane. After the way Lance told me off, I felt guilty of a lot of things. I also wondered what I had done to make Roman feel he couldn't let go of me.

Roman caught me coming out of my office building on several occasions. "Holiday, I just need to speak with you for one moment. Please. I'm asking you for just a moment," he pleaded one day.

"Roman, please. You're really starting to scare me. What is going on with you? Once upon a time, the man I knew named Roman Broxton was a playa. He didn't have to chase women. Women chased him. He also took advantage of the fact that numerous women wanted him and that they didn't mind sharing him. So tell me, is this a game for you or what? I'm tired, Roman. I'm just real tired." I talked to him as I walked through the parking garage to my car.

"Okay, boo, listen. I know I've done my share of dirt. And we've been through some real trials. I realize that, but I want us to go back to the life we started out trying to have. Remember how sweet it was for us in the beginning? We can have that back. We can have that back, boo. Lance . . . well he fucked up. He just fucked up. Can't you see that this is the opportunity for you and me to make our thing sweeter?"

"I can't, Roman. You betrayed me first. I know that from past experience, I'll never love and trust you the way a man deserves. I discovered what you and

Lance had to offer just about the same time. When we had our thing going at first, yes, I cared for you deeply, but our hearts weren't quite ready yet. The time we shared after I started seeing Lance set me up to be in love with you. You started going way out, above and beyond to prove how strong your feelings were for me. Unfortunately, Lance was doing the same thing. I just got too caught up with all the affection you guys were giving me, and I sort of lost myself. I'm no longer dedicated to all the things in life that should matter—I don't care for this new me at all. I have to let go, and I'm sorry, but I have to let go of both of you. I wish you well, Roman." I opened my car door and got in.

"Holiday! Holiday! Wait, boo, don't leave. I need just one more minute. Please. Just one more minute," Roman yelled through my car window, but I cranked up and backed out of my parking spot.

I left him standing there because he was too pitiful. I couldn't handle that. It put too much guilt on me. He could've been playing with my emotions then, but I wasn't trying to find out. I had plenty of compassion for him, but I couldn't let him see it. That brief talk with Roman caused me to go home and remember things when it was just us. Our thing was shaping up to be pretty good, but I also recalled that I didn't start all of this. Roman met some woman at the office in Jackson, Tennessee, and forgot he had a woman at home waiting to hear from him. Then he came home trying to lie. It worked for a minute, but I had to bring out the old Holiday Simmons who could see some things that had slipped right by me, like the fact that he didn't bother to call me back at all the night he asked Lance to take me out. Roman's normal routine was to speak with me every night before we went to bed. This was a dead giveaway. Rome never passed up a chance to call me to say good night.

Lance was still hurt as well, but I managed to maintain a kosher relationship with him. Well, a phone relationship that is. I refused to see him when he'd ask. I had begun to learn myself more, and I knew that seeing Lance would bring back feelings that I'd been trying to harbor. I just couldn't do that to myself. I had come a long way with suppressing my feelings. I knew better than to stir things up again.

By late May, I had begun to feel better about myself. The one thing that had been difficult to shake was the feeling of needing a man in my life. I had experienced more than two years of attention from Roman and Lance. I was having withdrawal symptoms. I knew I wasn't going to call either gentleman, though. I had recently convinced Roman to give me some slack by telling him I was considering moving back to North Carolina in order to get some peace. He said that he would back off some—at least until I realized I still wanted a life with him. I wondered who the heck he thought he was. He hadn't been able to predict my every move before, but he still seemed convinced I'd come back to him one day. Hmph—some nerve!

Chapter Thirty-seven
My Sunshine Has Come

One Friday evening, Crystal and I decided we were going shopping. We went to the Hickory Ridge Mall first, and then we decided to go out to the Wolfchase Galleria to find a pair of Tommy Hilfiger shoes she'd seen in Dillard's. As we were walking through the mall, a very fine young man walking toward us on the opposite side of the mall gave me full eye contact until we were no longer facing each other. I didn't look back because I didn't want to give the gentleman any mixed signals. I was afraid he'd think I wanted him to say something to me. I wanted him to stop and speak, but I just played it off and spoke warmly as we passed by.

"Mommy, I saw how you were looking at that man," Crystal said.

"What? What are you talking about?"

"Uh-huh, Mommy, I saw you. You were looking at that man like you wouldn't mind giving him your phone number."

"Well, what does it mean if I want him to have my number?"

"It means you wouldn't mind getting to know him and maybe having him as a boyfriend."

"Who told you that a woman peering at a good-looking man has to mean she wants his phone number?"

"Mommy! I'm in junior high school. Nobody had to tell me that."

"Okay, Ms. Junior High School, you just make sure you don't be giving your number to any boys."

"I don't want a boyfriend. That's for grown people. I have a while to go before I'm an adult," Crystal stated as if I didn't know.

We found the shoes Crystal had admired, and we asked the associate to find her size. I also saw a pair of shoes I had admired and asked to try them on. After I had taken a seat and pulled the sandal out of the box, a handsome baritone voice spoke.

"Allow me," the man said, reaching for the sandal. "May I?"

"By all means, yes." It was the man from out in the mall.

"My name is Derek Michaels," he said, placing the shoe on my foot.

"I'm Holiday Simmons, and this is my daughter, Crystal."

"Hello, Crystal. You have pretty good taste in shoes, huh? I like those Hilfigers," Derek said.

"Thank you," Crystal replied.

"You have nice taste in shoes as well, Ms. Simmons,

or is it Mrs. Simmons?" he asked, looking for a ring on my left hand.

"I'm not married. I've never been married. And Crystal's father and I are not together. Just thought I'd throw that one at you. It was probably your next question."

"Beautiful, smart, quick on your feet—I like that. So, then do you mind if I ask you out sometime?"

I looked over at Crystal, and she was smiling and nodding. "Go right ahead. Ask me," I said.

"I'd like to take you out sometime, get to know you a little bit, and hopefully your daughter, too. May I give you my number?" he asked, pulling out a receipt to write on.

"Sure. Maybe I'd like that." I opened my purse for an ink pen.

"Do you have a number where I could reach you, Holiday?" Derek asked as he wrote down his number.

"No."

"No?" Derek looked up at me in confusion.

"No. But, once we talk some more and I determine if you're worth it—maybe." I smiled to break the seriousness.

"Fair enough. Just be sure to call me. Crystal, make sure your mother gives me a call, okay?" Derek said as he slowly walked backward, away from Crystal and me.

"Yes, sir," Crystal replied.

"I'm not going to take up any more of your time with Crystal, so I hope to hear from you later, Holiday Sim-mons," he said as he turned to walk away.

Derek Michaels was about six-foot-one. His flawless, milky bronze complexion smoothed over his baldhead with no variation in tone. The way his clothes complemented his body told me that he had to be ripped in all the right places. While his perfectly straight white teeth could make me comfortable with a simple smile, his dreamy ebony eyes could almost cause hypnosis from a basic glimpse. The man was fine.

I didn't rush home to call him, but I wanted to. You know the games women play. Let some time go by before we make that first call. Well I tried and I tried, but as soon as Crystal was in bed, I called that man. Derek Michaels had been heavy on my mind ever since I met him. We had a very pleasant talk for about half an hour, then he was very gentlemanlike and suggested he let me get to bed since I had to be up early to take Crystal to her tae kwon do lesson. Before we got off the phone, we made plans to see each other the next day.

I met Derek down on the river walk shortly after dropping off Crystal. I invited him along for my run, so he came dressed to sweat. He had on a gray muscle shirt and a pair of navy shorts with a skintight pair of biking shorts under them. This was the first time any man had taken me up on the offer to run with me.

I could tell Derek wasn't accustomed to doing five miles, so I suggested he sit nearby until I finished. He refused and kept running.

"Whew! That was invigorating. And after all of that rain we had the last couple of days, I can't believe how nice it is today," I said as we walked to cool down.

"Oh yes. It has turned out to be a pretty decent

day." Derek was out of breath, but he managed to get his statement out.

"I'm glad you decided to meet me down here. You really didn't have to run with me. You know that, don't you?"

"Yeah, I know, but I wanted to see you again. Besides, running is something I need to get back into doing anyway," Derek said, huffing.

"By the way, one reason I made the suggestion is because you already look like this is something you do regularly."

"I hit the gym. Not a ten-mile marathon."

"We only did five, Derek."

"Well, it feels like ten," he said, laughing.

We were approaching my gym bag I had left under a tree. "There's my bag. I brought us both some water," I said. We picked up my bag and kept walking.

"So, Holiday, I know we learned quite a bit about each other last night over the phone, but one thing I didn't have the chance to ask you is how'd you get a name like Holiday."

"People are starting to ask me that a lot lately. I was born on Christmas Day."

"No. Get out of here!"

"You seem surprised. What? Did you expect me to have a birthday like Halloween or something?"

"No, that's not it at all. I'm just kind of wondering how you dealt with that growing up. Did you get two presents on Christmas from everyone?"

"No, just my parents and occasionally my grandparents."

"Does anyone ever call you Holley?"

"If they tried I'd bite their head off."

"Ooo, why?"

"My name has meaning, and most people who've met me already know this," I said as we passed some benches.

"Here's an empty bench. Would you like to have a seat?" Derek asked.

"Sure. We have an excellent view of the river."

"Holiday, how is it that an attractive, got-it-going-on woman like yourself manages to be single right now? I almost didn't turn around in the mall because I just knew you had a boyfriend at least. How is that?"

"Oh, you don't want me to go there!"

"Oh yes, I do. I'm just having trouble understanding it."

"Well, I don't have to tell you how men are 'cause you are a man. Most men soon take my kindness for weakness, so it just never manages to work out."

"Are you looking for something permanent right now?" he inquired.

"Derek, I'm not gonna even lie to you. I honestly don't know. I think I should be interested in pursuing something permanent, but I don't know if that's what I want. I've just let go of a relationship, and it may not be good for me to jump into another so soon."

"Well I can understand that, but I'd still like to be able to take you out sometime. Friends can go out and have a good time, too, you know?"

"Yeah, I know. Boy, do I know!"

Derek and I decided to plan a date that same night. Crystal invited two cousins to stay over, so I knew she wouldn't mind me stepping out. Shaundra and her older sister, Katrina, were ecstatic about spending the night. Katrina was sixteen, but she enjoyed hanging with the younger girls because they looked up to her and liked it when she'd teach them things. She taught them chants, cheers, the latest dances, and even how to beat the Pac-Man game on PlayStation 2. Crystal and Shaundra really loved it when Katrina was around.

I called Derek to ask him if he'd mind meeting me down at Isaac Hayes in The Peabody Place. He seemed excited that I had called back to ask him, and he agreed to meet me. I got out the old trusty black dress I'd worn so long ago when I first went out with Roman and Lance. It still fit like it was made for me. I pulled the same stunt with my hair that I'd pulled on Roman and Lance. Derek met me in the mall with my hair pulled up, and when I met him at the river, I had it pulled up then, too, so I decided to catch him off guard and let my hair flow. He didn't recognize me sitting at the table, so I went over to the hostess desk to meet him.

"Derek, I was waving at you. We're seated over near the stage."

"Holiday, you look beautiful. I didn't recognize you with all of this hair." Derek looked stunned as he walked with me back to our table.

"I hope you don't mind, but I asked for nonsmoking."

"Oh, that's great. I'm not a smoker either," Derek said, smiling.

"Well I took the liberty of ordering me a drink while waiting for you, but I'm sure the waitress will be over to take your order soon," I said.

"That's fine. I'm not in a hurry. I just got here,

and from the looks of it, I'm not gonna want to leave."

"Oh, you'll leave. You don't have to go home, but I'm sure they're going to put you up out of here," I said jokingly.

"I like that. You've got a sense of humor, too. Well, I'm just saying I'm extremely proud to be the one to accompany you tonight. You look fabulous!"

"Thank you, Derek. I'm impressed with how great you look as well."

We had a great time at Isaac Hayes. The food was scrumptious, the band was great, the service was outstanding, and the overall atmosphere was superb. It was everything I had expected.

We left the restaurant around eleven. We decided we were going to take a late-night walk down Beale Street to see what it had to offer. We were down there for another two hours. I was having the time of my life. Derek was a breath of fresh air. I didn't think about Lance or Roman one time while I was out with him. He knew how to keep me talking to him by asking a lot of questions.

"Tell me something. What made you call me last night? Most women would've waited until some time next week."

I laughed and thought, *If only you knew.* "Well, I guess I kind of liked your style."

"What do you mean? I didn't know I had one," he said, being sarcastic because he was busted.

"Oh, c'mon. You practiced that style. First, you come at me with a suave approach by asking to put the sandal on my foot. Next, you say some kind words to my child. Somebody's taught you how to warm a woman's heart. Then, you tried to figure out whether

I'm married, single, or dating with the, 'is it Ms. Simmons or Mrs. Simmons?' approach. You handed me your home phone number, office number, cell number, and email address, all on a receipt from a store that showed you have exquisite taste. Then, you tried to impress me by being adamant about not taking up any more of my quality time with Crystal, and lastly you recited our names just before you left to ensure me that you'd paid attention. Smooooth! I liked it!" I said to him with a chuckle and a convincing smile.

"You are smart. Just as I had suspected. A man can't pull anything over on you, Holiday."

"So, now you know. I guess you've learned, but I still like your style."

I knew that night I would see Mr. Derek Michaels again. I didn't expect to meet anyone as charming as him so close to my breakup with Roman and Lance, but I was very happy I did. I made up my mind to definitely take it slow with Derek though. I knew I wasn't ready to be serious, so I figured the slow approach was the best one.

As soon as I made it home, all the security I felt with not having thought one time of Lance or Rome was flushed down the drain when I checked my voice messages on both phones. Rome had left several disturbing messages on my cell, and Lance had called a couple of times as well. I turned my ringers back off, put on some Jill Scott, and sat in my Jacuzzi for nearly an hour. I was not about to let the Lance-and-Roman saga get the best of me that night.

Chapter Thirty-eight
Read My Lips . . .

A couple of weeks went by and I had gone out with Derek two weekends in a row. I was starting to really like him. I wish I had met him before I started getting serious with Roman and Lance. Maybe I wouldn't have had so much stress. Derek was actually a good guy.

The more we talked, the more I learned about him. He loved children; however, he didn't have any. He said he'd always wanted a daughter. All the plans he spoke of as far as a future included Crystal and me. When I'd ask about us doing certain things together, he'd decline unless I would include Crystal. He said that Crystal was a part of my package and unless she was away with her father or other relatives, then there was no excuse for excluding her from our activities. I was very surprised by this. Most of the men I had come across since Darius never included Crystal unless I asked them. Lance was the first to offer to spend some quality time with her.

The next plans we made to go out were on a Saturday. I wasn't ready for Crystal to be in his company. Crystal was too smart about Derek. When she saw me looking at him in the mall, she already knew what type of thoughts I was having, so I couldn't lie to her like I did about Roman and Lance. Crystal had also become accustomed to Lance helping her with her pre-algebra assignments. Not having him around anymore was kind of tough for us both to deal with, so I didn't feel that suddenly bringing Derek into her life would be healthy. Derek understood perfectly when I explained the situation to him. He wanted to hear more about Lance, but I wouldn't talk about him or my past.

Roman called me on the Thursday before my date with Derek. He wanted to know if he could see me on Saturday, but I declined, making the excuse that Crystal and I had some shopping to do. I had only answered his call because Crystal was trying to study and Roman was ringing both my cell and home phones nonstop. When one line would quiet down, the other would begin. I tried to keep the conversation as short as possible, but Roman never wanted to accept no for an answer. It became very difficult to get him off the phone as he began to make threats.

"I just don't see how you can say that you ever loved me and you can refuse to see me—even if it's just for one minute. If I show up on your job, you treat me as if I'm a stranger and just about jog to your car." Roman was smart enough to know I didn't want to be bothered, but he didn't let it faze him.

"That's because when I get off work, I'm in a

hurry. You don't need to keep popping up on my job, trying to see me before I get to my car. You have my cell phone number. Call me and ask if I'm busy and if I'll meet you somewhere. It'll save you a lot of time and keep you from getting your feelings hurt."

"Holiday, how am I gonna ask you something if you won't answer your phone? I know you look at the caller ID. Come on now, boo!"

"You don't know what I do, Roman."

"Oh, I know what you do. I know plenty about what you do."

"And, what is that supposed to mean?"

"You just better not go anywhere with that nigga this weekend," he said adamantly.

"What?" I didn't know from where this was coming.

"You heard me. You just told me you couldn't see me Saturday because of plans with Crystal. You better had been telling me the truth. I'm not accepting anything else, especially not for you to go see that Mr. Clean-looking mutherfucker. Tell his muscle-head ass you've got plans this weekend—with me."

"Roman, you're sounding real silly right now. How do you know who I'm seeing? It's none of your business anyway. I'm getting ready to hang up if you don't stop talking foolish."

"I'm foolish? I tell you what. You can hang up. Don't go out with that mutherfucker Saturday! If you do, you'll be the foolish one. I've already said it: you better not go out with him Saturday!" Roman hung up on me.

Roman would say things from time to time, trying to put fear in my heart, but for him to know about Derek, he'd definitely been following me again. At times I had known Roman to just talk sometime to see if he could get me to do what he wanted, so I didn't fear his words that day on the phone. I did, however, take extra precaution just in case. I called Lance for assistance.

"Hey, Lance, we need to talk," I said just after he answered.

"What's up?" Lance's tone was dry.

"Roman called here not too long ago acting stupid. He knows I've been going out with someone on the weekends, and he's not too pleased. I know you may not want to help me, but I need you to do me this one favor."

"Like what?"

"Will you hang out with Roman Saturday? Try to keep him away from my house when my date arrives to pick me up."

"Holiday, you're right when you say I might not want to help you. Do you ever stop to think about some of the things you require of me?"

"You're not required to do anything, Lance. I know that of everything I've ever asked, this is pushing it, but I have no one else to turn to. You seem to be the most levelheaded between you and Roman. You've easily cut your losses with me and moved on. I was just hoping you wouldn't mind helping me out as a friend."

Lance blew into the phone. "I'll help you this one time, Holiday—not just because you've got me twisted. I know Roman can be foolish, and I don't want him to hurt you."

My mouth flew open. "Has he been talking about that or something?"

"Oh yeah, he's been talking real crazy to people

about you lately. I met some of our mutual friends at a bar one night, then Roman showed up. He wanted to ramble on and on about how you never really gave him a fair chance at a relationship. I tried to convince him to move on. My advice to him has been to allow you to call him when you're ready. Roman's having a really tough time dealing with you not wanting him in your life."

"Lance, what have I done? What makes Roman so crazy for me?"

"Baby girl, you have to remember what kind of women Roman was use to dealing with before he started seeing you. You're the first real woman worth having to him. He could easily let go of the others. They weren't half the woman you are when it came to intelligence, independence, stability, and a loving heart. Roman could see through those women."

"Is this your synopsis, or has Roman said this?"

"It's something we've both discussed. You're a woman who's worth holding on to. That's what the struggles between Roman and me have been about. Not the power and the principle of it like you think."

"Lance, there are a lot of women out there worth holding on to. Roman doesn't have to act a fool with me. You've even moved on."

"Is that how you see things? As hard as it's been, I've backed off, but only because I love you enough to respect your wishes. If you really think a life without me is what will make you happy, then I'm all for it. That's exactly what I want to see, you happy."

"Lance, you make me feel guilty when you put it that way. I love you, and you're right. I really don't know what I want, but don't I deserve a chance to try and find out?"

"Absolutely, but I can't make Roman see it that way. He's a different man than I am."

"Well, Lance, if you'll just do this for me this one time, I promise I won't ask you anymore."

"Where's this man taking you?"

"I was thinking of doing something downtown. Maybe Beale Street again."

Lance sighed and responded, "Okay, then I'll take Roman down to the casino with me—if he'll go. Hanging out with me will be the last thing Roman expects for me to offer."

"The casino will be perfect, Lance. By the way, have you known that I've been out with another man all along?"

"I've known ever since Roman first saw you."

"The thought of him following me like that scares me."

"He's been following you on the weekends, so from now on, you may want to plan your activities during the week. He knows your routine. He figures you won't go out during the week."

"Oh my goodness. This is serious. When did he tell you all of this?"

"Roman wasn't exactly talking to me. One of our mutual friends told me. It's gonna be okay, Holiday. I'm just gonna keep talking to him. Try not to stress."

Lance's words convinced me to keep my date with Derek on Saturday. Roman tried to call me on Friday, but I didn't feel like the aggravation. I didn't answer the phone. Of course I got several messages on the voice mail, but I would delete them as soon as I heard his voice. I was determined I wasn't going to let him bring my spirits down on my day out with Crystal.

* * *

Saturday came, and Crystal was going to a sleep-over at her classmate, Monica's house. Monica had invited Shaundra to come along, too. Crystal having her cousin there as another familiar face made me feel better about her staying over. I went in with the girls to speak with Monica's mother. We discussed the girls' activities and games for the evening. I had to be sure there weren't scary movies in the plan because Crystal didn't handle watching fright films very well. Crystal gave me a kiss, and I told her to call if she needed me.

I went home to prepare for my night. I called Lance to be certain he'd had a chance to talk to Roman about going out with him for the evening. He confirmed he had and said he would pick Roman up about six o'clock. That would give them plenty of time to head to the casino before Derek was scheduled to pick me up at seven. Everything was working out as planned.

Derek was on time, and I was running late. I was still getting ready when he rang the doorbell. I had a little trouble for some reason deciding what I wanted to wear. To Derek's surprise, I answered the door in my robe. Once I offered him a seat, I had a chance to see his attire for the evening. This gave me a pretty good idea of how I'd be most comfortable for the night. I went and put on my favorite white pantsuit. Not only was it beautiful, but it also took me out of my norm of wearing black. The jacket had silver beads embedded around the collar, and the blouse had the same accessories sewn in neat designs on it. I wore my sterling-silver jewelry and my two-toned silver-and-white pumps. Once I stepped back into the great room to meet Derek, his mouth dropped open in sheer amazement. I'd succeeded at making a man speechless once again. It felt pretty damn good, too.

Chapter Thirty-nine
The Madness Continues

On the ride downtown, Derek and I discussed going somewhere to dance and do karaoke. Derek mentioned a place in the Whitehaven area that wasn't familiar, but I agreed to go. I knew Roman and Lance were at the casino, so there was no worry. Derek seemed very comfortable with me. I liked being around him as well. We rode to the Whitehaven area talking and listening to Sade's *Lovers Rock.*

"I didn't know you were a Sade fan, Derek."

"Yes. I've been listening to this woman since back in the day," he replied.

"So have I. Her voice, her lyrics, her music period can just mellow me out."

"You're telling the truth there. I can come home from a hard day at work, turn on Sade, and everything is all right."

"Yeah, I know. I can do anything to her music.

Cook, clean, read, sleep, you name it. There's not much I can't do listening to Sade."

"Make love."

"What?" He caught me off guard with that one.

"Make love. Can you make love to her music?" Derek inquired.

"I have. I don't know if I will again."

"Why is that?"

Lance came to mind. "The one time I made love to Sade's music was with someone who's still very special to my heart. I'll have to be sure I'm over him before I test those waters with someone else." Now I was really reminiscing. "Can we change the subject please? I don't want to think about that right now."

"Sure. I don't mind. Sorry. We're about to pull up to our destination anyway."

The place seemed too crowded, but I didn't want to hurt Derek's feelings so I told him it was okay. I chose the locations of the last couple of times we went out. He selected this one, and I didn't want him to think I was a snob or that he didn't have good taste when it came to picking spots.

The dance floor was kind of small, and the tables were too close together, but I just grinned and tolerated it. Derek got up and sang, "Three Times a Lady." I didn't feel it was the appropriate song to be singing to me. He didn't know me like that. But again I just grinned as if everything was okay. He was an excellent singer. I could understand then why he had chosen to bring me to a karaoke bar. He wanted me to see his skills. Kind of like I did when I recited my poetry during open mic night at Precious Cargo.

Derek's voice did impress me, but I wished he'd chosen another song.

Derek stepped back to our table and kissed me on the lips. Oh, I knew then he had to be showing out for somebody or just plain old trippin'! He could tell by the look on my face that I wasn't happy with him doing that, so after he sat down he looked me in the eye and apologized.

I tried to continue to tolerate the entire night, but after Derek mentioned making love to Sade's music, I was having a tough time enjoying myself. I opened my purse to check my phone for missed calls. I wondered if Lance or Roman had tried to call me. Lance had indeed tried to reach me, and he left me a voice mail.

"Baby girl, I hope you get this message and call me back. I stopped at a service station pretending I needed to buy some gum so I could talk to you in private. There has been a very serious accident on Highway 61. The traffic is extremely backed up, so we're headed back to Memphis. Don't worry, we won't come downtown or anywhere near Beale Street. You just try to have a nice time and we're going to go somewhere, anywhere away from your house. Once you've made it in, let me know. Talk to you later."

My heart skipped a beat. I immediately dialed Lance's cell phone, but he didn't answer. I dialed it again, and I got the voice mail. I told myself not to panic. I knew the night with Derek would be a total wreck if I sat there worrying about Lance and Roman's whereabouts. I told myself, *There are tons of things to do in Memphis tonight. I'm pretty certain they won't come down here.* I put my phone back in my purse and continued to sip on my margarita.

Five minutes later, I looked up at the door and who's showing their IDs, getting ready to enter? Roman and Lance. Okay, this was the time to panic. They didn't see me right off. They were looking around for somewhere to sit, but all of the tables were full. Derek excused himself to the restroom, then I took my cell out and dialed Lance's phone. I could see it lighting up on his hip, but he didn't have the ringer on. Finally, after numerous tries, someone sitting at a table told him his phone was flashing. When Lance finally answered, I tried to whisper and wave to get his attention.

"Lance, I'm over here at a table near the rear window."

"What?"

"Go in the back to the bar, and I'm gonna try to sneak out of here."

"Oh, okay. I gotcha," he said.

I saw Lance pull Roman to the back bar with him. Once Derek returned to our table, I could tell he detected something wrong. He frowned as he questioned my nervousness.

"Is everything okay?" Derek asked.

"Huh? Ummm, yeah. Ummm, no. Derek my ex is here, and I believe he'll start trouble. Do you mind if we leave?" I got up to put my jacket back on.

"Okay, if it makes you uncomfortable. It's not a problem."

We headed to the door, and I looked toward the bar on the way out. Roman had his back to us so he didn't see us leaving. Once we got outside, the night air hit me in my face, reviving me. Before getting out of there, for a moment I sort of lost myself. Anyway, we had to walk down the side of the building to get to Derek's car. I happened to look up as we headed to the back of the parking lot. My attention had been drawn to a huge window at the end of the building. I was walking on the side nearest the window, so when I looked in, staring right at me from the bar was Roman and Lance. I watched Roman jump up from a barstool and charge toward the door like a madman. I yelled for Derek to run, but he kind of stood there looking at me in shock.

"Roman! Roman! Stop! Derek doesn't even know you. Don't do anything stupid!" I yelled frantically as he charged toward us.

"What did I tell you, huh? What was the last thing I said to you before I hung up the phone Thursday night? Huh?" Roman was enraged. He held me up by my shoulders as he questioned me.

"Man, why don't you let her go?" Derek said, stepping toward Roman in my defense.

Lance wasn't having it though. He backed Derek up, away from Roman and me. "Look! Stay out of this. I'll handle Roman. I'm not going to let him hurt her." Lance then turned to Roman. "Come on, Roman. Let her go, man."

"Hell no. She's bringing her ass with me. I'm taking you home, Holiday," Roman said.

I managed to jerk away from Roman and screamed for dear life. "No! Stop, Roman! Let me go!"

"Leave her the fuck alone!" Derek tried stepping toward Roman once again.

And again, Lance backed Derek up. "Look, man, take your ass to your car and wait! I said I got this. I'm not gonna let him hurt her!"

"You ain't going nowhere with him!" Roman said as he picked me up and began to carry me to Lance's truck.

I kicked and screamed, and it was my luck that this hole-in-the-wall place Derek had taken me to didn't have any real security. At least not the licensed kind with a badge and a gun. People began piling up to watch what was going on. No one would help at first. I guess Roman's rage had paralyzed everyone. Derek went over to his car to watch 'cause Lance wouldn't let him get within two feet of us.

"Lance, man, open the door!" Roman was still holding me as if he was cradling a screaming and kicking baby.

"Roman, put her down, man! She doesn't wanna go with you! Man, let her go!" Lance insisted, trying hard to loosen Roman's lock around me.

"Roman, damnit! Put me down!" I kicked and shook one last time, hard enough to make Roman drop me.

Yeah, he dropped me. I had dirt and oil and everything else all over my once beautiful white suit. I had lost a shoe. And there were scuff marks all over the one shoe I somehow managed to keep on. Once I was on the ground, I started to cry. I had never felt so defeated in my life. Lance came to pick me up, and Roman went to look for Derek. I didn't want Roman to do anything to hurt Derek, so I asked Lance to leave me alone and go stop Roman. Derek probably could've held his own, but judging by the way he had let Lance back him up, I wasn't taking any chances.

Lance caught Roman and pulled him back toward his Escalade. I tried to run around them toward

Derek's car, but Roman caught me and put me in a headlock.

"So, you gon' be hardheaded. You gon' act like I ain't said nothing to you, huh?"

"Rome, please, you're hurting me. Stop it. Lance, help me." I was in so much agony.

"Holiday, I'm trying. Roman, man, let her go! The owner just told me he's called the police. You don't want that type of trouble, man. Let's go!" Lance pulled on Roman's arms to relieve some of the pressure from my neck.

I tried bargaining with him. "Rome, please! What do you want me to do?"

"Come ride with me!" he said as he kept a death grip around my neck.

"Rome, I came with Derek. It wouldn't be right for me to leave with you. You wouldn't want me to do that to you."

"I'm not him. I'm Rome! Fuck that nigga! Now come on!"

"I can't!" I cried even louder. I knew I was defeated.

Lance called back to Derek for help. I believe some of the bystanders were tired of watching how pathetic I was, so a few of the men also came to help Lance. Once they had gotten Rome's grip from around my neck, they held him and told me to run. I was so dizzy from all the blood rushing to my head that as I ran, I fell and hurt my knee. I made it to Derek's car, and we sped away. Looking back as we drove away, I discovered Roman darting to get into Lance's Escalade. I didn't worry that they would follow us 'cause Lance was driving, and I knew I had time to make it home.

On the way home, Derek asked me about what

had just happened. I hadn't planned to talk about Roman with Derek, but I knew I owed him an explanation. The only man he'd heard of was Lance.

"Derek, Roman is a deranged ex-boyfriend."

"No kidding. I can see that, but where does he fit in?"

I took a deep breath. "Roman and Lance were best friends and former coworkers of mine. I don't care to go into any more details, but yes, I did have a relationship with both of them at one time."

"At one time? Meaning once upon a time or at the same time?"

I looked out of the window as I spoke. "At the same time. I couldn't choose between the two, so I let them both go."

"Whoa. I don't know what to think," Derek replied.

"You don't have to say anything. This is my problem, and I see now I need to give things time to cool down before pursuing a relationship with anyone," I further explained.

"Roman doesn't frighten me, Holiday. Is that what you're worried about?"

"I'm convinced now that he will not only hurt me, he'll hurt any man with whom I come in contact. This is not your decision, Derek. I'm sorry. I'll keep your number though."

Derek wasn't pleased with my decision, but he respected it. It bothered me to have to stop seeing Derek because of Roman's foolishness. I felt imprisoned at times. When I wanted to go out, I couldn't. There was a possibility that Roman would be lurking.

Lance called me while I was in the bathtub and said he thought Roman might be on his way over. He had just taken Roman to his house, but he didn't go

in. He got in his car and drove off. I jumped out of
the tub and got dressed. I asked Lance to stay on the
phone with me awhile to see if Roman would show
up. As soon as I heard the doorbell, my fright returned, and I asked Lance to come over. He hung up
with me and headed to my house.

My refusal to open the door only aggravated
Roman more. He stood outside kicking and beating
and yelling through the door. It was a little after nine
o'clock. In my neighborhood, everyone was quiet
and in the house by dark. This really embarrassed
me. I told Roman someone was going to call the police, but that didn't make him leave.

Lance made it over, and I heard them arguing outside. Roman was swearing with all the strength of his
lungs. I only talked to them through the shut and
locked door. Soon, all I could hear was Lance's voice.
Whatever he was saying to Roman, it had begun to
break him. Soon Lance told me I didn't have to
worry anymore. I peeked out of the window and saw
them both driving away.

Sunday morning, I still had my stiff neck from the
chokehold and headlock Roman put on me the
night before. Still paranoid, I peeked out of every
window, looking for signs of his presence, but I didn't
see him. I don't know what Lance said to calm Roman
down, but I'm forever grateful.

Chapter Forty

Must Be a Dream

"Crystal, what do you think you'd like to do this summer? You know school will be out in another month."

"I don't know, Mommy. I just know I don't want to go to another one of those boring summer camps. I'm getting too old for those. I really hated the last one. All they did was baby-sit us. They didn't let us swim or anything. Maybe you can enroll me in one of those performing arts or a cheerleading program. What do you think?"

"Perhaps I'll look into all of that. I do know your father would love for you to come to California for the summer."

"Mommy, you'd let me go?" Crystal was surprised at my mentioning California.

"I've been thinking about it."

"That would be great, Mommy! Please think about it! I'm gonna see if Shaundra can go, too."

"Ah-ha. Now, that's not a bad idea. At least then I

wouldn't have to worry about you being bored out there."

"Come on, Mommy! Bored in California? I don't think so."

"You don't know anything about California, little girl."

"I know that it looks pretty on television, and it has to be more fun than Memphis."

Crystal was very excited about the idea of going to California with her dad. Although he and I had our differences, Darius was very loyal to his daughter. I could appreciate that very much. We talked over the phone and made the final plans for Crystal to go stay with him.

I also spoke with Derek Michaels, the man I thought would be my sunshine before the night Roman acted a fool at the karaoke bar. I let him know that, although he had been a perfect gentleman, things in my life still weren't right for dating. I told him that I wouldn't throw his number away, and when I felt I was ready, I'd give him a call to see if he was still available. He tried to understand. He had some buts and what ifs, but he eventually told me he understood.

Lance was being the perfect gentleman I'd asked him to be. He didn't call unless I asked him to. And he didn't try to pop up unannounced. I was very pleased with the way Lance was handling things. He told me that in the back of his mind, he was telling himself this breakup was just temporary. That's how he was able to deal with it so well.

Rome, on the other hand, continued to have a tougher time. He was constantly calling me, leaving messages, and showing up unannounced. I would drive down the street for lunch and while waiting at a drive-thru, I would see his car parked across the street. He'd sit and watch me from a distance all the time. I was beginning to wonder how this man got any work done. Every time I'd go out for a drive, he'd call my cell phone.

"Hello, Holiday Simmons. You have one unheard message." This was my voice mail.

"Yeah, Holiday! I see how you gon' treat me, boo. You could've answered the phone. How you gon' look at the caller ID, see that it's me, then not answer the phone? See, that's the shit I'm talking about right there. Okay, you wouldn't pick up at the red light at Union Avenue and Third Street, but I'm gon' see what you'll do when you get up there to the light at Poplar Avenue." This would happen almost every time I'd go out for lunch.

I got to the point where I no longer wanted to leave the office at lunchtime. No need in me trying to go out with coworkers either. Roman would only harass me in front of them. I knew better than to set myself up for embarrassment like that. When my coworkers would ask me to go out for lunch, I'd turn them down, stating I needed to catch up on some paperwork.

Roman was smart enough to know he was annoying me, but not quite smart enough to know he was only pushing me farther and farther away from him. Sometimes I felt I still cared for him and others I thought I hated him. The hatred grew from being weary as the result of the aggravation he was giving me, like the annoying calls to my workplace.

"Ms. Simmons, you have a call on extension 557," my assistant said, buzzing my office.

"Thanks, Ms. Dodson." I answered the line without thinking. "Hello, this is Ms. Simmons. How may I help you?"

"I'd like to take you and Crystal to dinner tonight if you don't mind," Roman said.

"Roman, I'm busy."

"See what I'm saying. And you wonder why I don't call before I show up."

"Roman, I'm serious. I've got a lot going on today, and I can't talk right now."

"Great. I'll see you this evening then. Bye," Roman said and hung up.

It only got worse, and I had to have company security to walk me to my car. Roman's temper was escalating, and I didn't want him to catch me off guard in the parking garage.

One beautiful Friday afternoon in May, I stood looking out of my office window contemplating whether I would go out for lunch. For some reason, our only security officer wasn't at work, so I was a little leery about leaving the office. But then, I thought, *What the hell! Just go! Roman is not that crazy. The man just thinks he's in love. He doesn't want to kill you.* I grabbed my purse and headed to my car.

I looked over both shoulders and trotted to my Benz. I couldn't believe the coast was actually clear. The day was so beautiful I couldn't resist relishing it. After lunch, I put on my sunglasses and rode around for a minute. The clean, crisp breeze blew my hair, which I had chosen to wear down in an attempt to make myself feel better. It was sort of symbolic of me releasing stress. Once the heat began to rise on the leather interior of my car, I rolled up the windows and turned on the AC. I managed to spend a couple hours out without a sigh from Roman.

I parked my car and got out, once again looking over both shoulders. Upon making it to the door of my office building, I no longer felt threatened. A sense of peace came over me for having such a marvelous lunch and a breath of fresh air afterward.

I had an abundance of work. I'd usually take the bulk of it home on Friday to finish up before Monday, but this particular day, I had declined to do so. Crystal's cheerleading squad was having its final competition that weekend. I didn't want my mind to be bogged down with work, so I finished as much as I could and left the rest.

I left out of the office around five. Crystal was expecting me pick her up from cheerleading practice by six. I knew I had plenty of time, so I had planned to surprise her with some Angel Food Butter Pecan ice cream, her favorite. She'd been asking for it all week.

As I sat in my car adjusting the radio station, I heard a tap on the passenger side window. I was startled to see Roman peering at me.

"What? You scared the hell out of me, Roman," I yelled through the glass.

"Open the door, boo. I wanna talk to you."

"No, Roman. I have to go pick up Crystal. I don't have time right now."

"It will only take a minute. Come on, open up," he said.

"Roman, I've told you I can't," I started, but he wouldn't let me finish.

"You're not getting ready to keep telling me no,"

he stated, walking around the front of my car, toward the driver's side.

I immediately shifted the car in reverse and looked behind me to back up. Just before I had a chance to totally get out of my parking spot, Roman met me as I began shifting gears, and put his fist through the window. The glass shattered with such force that I lost all focus. I sat there in shock for a few seconds before he reached into the car and began choking me. I gasped for air and prayed that someone from the office would come out to the garage. It may not have been but a few seconds with his hands around my throat, but it seemed like minutes. Something told me to put the car into drive and drag his ass through the parking lot. As soon as he saw me reaching for the gearshift, he let me go and moved back from the car. I sped off like a crazy woman.

I had been parked on the upper level of the garage. I sped down and around those curves as if I was driving in the Indy 500. Normally, I'd have to let the assistant at the exit shack see my badge, the company's preventive tactic for car theft, but I just broke right through the gate without looking back. My only agenda was to get away.

Before I decided to slow down a bit, I looked in the mirror to be certain I had lost Roman. My heart was doing about a thousand beats a minute. I really feared for my life. Roman had snapped. He was stalking me, and I felt like I was in a bad nightmare. I couldn't believe my life had come to this.

While driving, I called Lance and asked if he could pick up Crystal for me. After explaining the situation, he advised me to call the police. Crystal had a key to get in the house, but I asked Lance to take her to his place, and I arranged to pick her up from there. I called Crystal's cheerleading director to let her know Lance would be providing Crystal with transportation home.

The questioning and paperwork went on down at the precinct for a couple of hours. The police told me I'd have to go downtown to the Criminal Justice Center on Monday morning to make further complaints. I was discouraged by this news. This meant I would have to come up with an excuse to give my boss so that I could discreetly take care of this situation. Roman was causing me to go through all kinds of unnecessary changes.

This chaos made me very nervous about going home. I didn't want to leave the police precinct, but thinking of Crystal calmed my nerves. I knew I would have to hold it together for her. I couldn't leave her with Lance overnight, but I didn't want to take her home either.

While I headed to Lance's place, I rehearsed what I'd say to Crystal about the broken window on my car. I came up with, "Sweetie, someone broke the window in the parking garage. The guard wasn't on duty today, so he didn't see who did it, but I still had to go to the police precinct to report it." You see. That wasn't totally a lie. It was actually the truth, just sugarcoated a little bit.

As I continued to drive toward Lance's, I continued to check all the mirrors and rehearse my line to Crystal. Upon approaching my destination, I spotted Roman's car at a stop sign. I picked up my cell phone and called Lance. Before he could answer the phone, I made a U-turn in the street to get away from Roman. He began to follow me at full speed.

We were in a residential neighborhood, and the two of us were driving at speeds of up to eighty miles per hour. Lance was on the phone with me trying to talk softly and remain calm for Crystal's sake. I hit all the residential streets, trying to lose Roman. It seemed I wasn't going to be able to shake him.

"Baby girl, what street are you on now?" Lance asked.

"Ummm, I think this is near Crump and Valley-dale." It was hard for me to remain calm.

"Okay, try to stay in that area. I'm coming to look for you. Just let me put my shoes back on, then I'll call you when I get to my truck."

Lance left Crystal at his house and came to look for me. Before he could find me, Roman bumped the side of my car, just beyond the back door. My car spun then came to an abrupt stop. At first, Roman revved his engine up as though he was going to ram into me, but then he shifted his car into park, opened the door, and started walking toward me. Roman's face was fixed with permanent fury. My car was still running, so as he got closer, I drove over a sidewalk and onto a resident's lawn to get around him. Roman immediately ran back to his car and followed me.

My cell phone began to ring, and I answered it hysterically. It was Lance. He was assuring me he was on his way to help. He also asked me to call the police and make them aware of my location. We hung up, and I pressed the number eight key on my cell. I had programmed 911 in case of an emergency.

"Please help me," I yelled when the 911 operator came on the line. "I'm in my car, and I have a deranged ex-boyfriend chasing me at full speed in a residential neighborhood."

"Calm down, ma'am. What's your name?"

"Holiday Simmons."

"Ma'am, try not to yell. Tell me your name again, please."

"It's Holiday Simmons. It's kind of hard to calm down when a man is chasing you through the streets of Memphis."

"What's this man's name?"

"Roman Broxton. He's driving a black Lexus, and I'm in a white Mercedes-Benz. Hurry. He's crazy."

We must've been driving around like madpeople for another five minutes before Lance caught up to us. I had been ducking, dodging, and weaving from Roman for more than thirty minutes. My adrenaline was still pumping. I felt Roman was going to kill me, and I wasn't ready to die. I just kept thinking about Crystal.

Lance tried several times to get his vehicle between Roman's car and mine. I'm not sure exactly what Lance had thought this would do, but he had been unsuccessful. Roman would manage to get his Lexus back behind my Benz to ram it again, every time. Soon the police were able to join the pursuit. This didn't make me feel any better, though. Roman was unrelenting. He was oblivious to the police and kept up this dreadful chase.

After saying a prayer, I slowed down so Roman could ram me in the back once again. I hoped this would cause him to crash into me hard enough to break his rampage. It worked. His car came to a halt, but he had knocked my car into the side of a house.

The impact startled me a bit, and it was sort of hard to shake off. After coming to my senses, I opened my car door to run. A bit dazed, I leaped out of the car, hitting the ground. I felt certain Roman was headed to get me, so I tried frantically to get up. I heard the wailing of the sirens, and blue lights nearly blinded me as I tried to focus. I looked over and noticed Roman standing with his hands in the air. The police bombarded him with guns drawn. More officers rushed over to my aid.

Before anything could stop the chase, Roman, Lance, and I had been making tracks all across people's lawns. We tore down fences, destroyed gardens, and knocked over mailboxes. I wasn't proud of what we'd done, but I was very glad to be safe. No one was in the home I crashed into, and I wasn't seriously hurt. I ended up with minor bumps and bruises and extremely sore muscles. Roman's vehicle was mangled, but he wasn't hurt either.

Roman was put in jail for the weekend on charges of driving under the influence of alcohol, wreckless driving, and vehicular assault. I knew there wouldn't be any judges hanging around on the weekend to set bail for him, so I felt safe attending Crystal's competition that Saturday. Lance helped me out with transportation. He went to Crystal's event, and he refused to let me rent a car. Lance allowed me to use his truck to take care of all my business. Crystal thought that I'd been in a car accident, and I didn't tell her any differently.

Roman wasn't supposed to contact me after he made bail, but remember this is Roman I'm talking about. He continued to call me as if he had every right to do so. He touched base with me on my job, shortly after his release. My assistant didn't recognize his voice.

"Ms. Simmons, pick up on extension 545 please," she said.

"Hello. This is Ms. Simmons. How may I help you?"

"I wasn't going to kill you. I just wanted to scare you. I realize now it wasn't the best way to handle my anger." Roman was calm as he spoke.

"Yeah, a few nights in jail will make a lot of niggas think rationally. I guess you aren't any better than the rest of 'em. I've come to the conclusion your ass needs mental help!"

"Boo, I didn't mean to cause any harm. Did you get hurt?"

"So you didn't mean to put that death grip around my neck in the parking garage, huh? Roman, fuck you! I've been downtown this morning to put a restraining order on your ass. Be looking to get your papers soon!"

"What did you go and do that for? Don't you know they'll serve me on my job?"

"Oh well, you should've taken time to think about that before you had me playing cat and mouse with you through people's lawns. You're sick, Roman. Stop calling me." I hung up on him.

He called me that whole day at work. I also had to change my other phone numbers again. This made it difficult for him to reach me other than on my job. I had my calls screened at work from that point on. He didn't bother to show up on my job anymore. He knew that could get him caught. So, for a brief moment, I was Roman-free.

Chapter Forty-one

Crazy with a Capital "C"

School was out, and Crystal was delighted to go to California. Shaundra's mother did agree to let her go with Crystal to visit Darius for the summer. I took the girls shopping for clothes. They were running around that mall like they were on some kind of shopping spree that would only last for an hour. We were in and out of each store. The girls didn't even want to try on the clothes they'd picked. I had to force them to do so. Their excitement had gotten the best of them. There was no need to hurry, but the girls sure acted like there was.

They picked some of everything to take to California—matching outfits, shoes, sunglasses, swimwear, and anything else or which they could think. Once we left the mall, I told Crystal we were done 'cause they had enough stuff to last the entire vacation. I figured if they needed anything else, Darius would buy it.

The time came for me to take the girls to the airport. This was Shaundra's first flight, and Crystal's first one in a few years. I was more nervous for the girls than they were for themselves. Their adrenaline kept them pumped up from the time they had gotten up until the time they stepped foot onto that plane. I couldn't wait for Darius to call me and let me know they'd made it.

After speaking with the girls later that day, I learned they both had enjoyed the flight. They still seemed overly excited, and I wondered when and if it would begin to wear off. It made me feel good to know my baby was happy and this was something she wanted to do.

A week later, I started getting prank calls. The person would wait for me to say hello then hang up on me. I knew this wasn't Rachel Clark, Roman's almost and could've been baby momma. I had run into her at the mall a few weeks earlier, and we were very cordial to each other. I was amazed at how much her baby had grown, and I admired how beautifully she had dressed him. We talked about how much drama I'd been through with Roman, and she was thankful her baby wasn't his child. She said she didn't know she was already pregnant when she and Roman slept together, which was why she thought she was pregnant by him. Well I had already figured it out. Sometimes it happens like that. Rome is known for being a smooth talker. Hell, he wooed me when I thought it couldn't be done. That didn't make Rachel or me a slut. Just women with feelings.

The prank calls kept coming. Of course I figured they were from Roman. I knew it would be a matter of time before he found a way to get my new phone number. I took the phone off the hook at night to keep him from calling and hanging up on the answering machine while I was asleep.

Roman didn't try to say anything to me for a few weeks. I had a strong feeling I needed to be worried, though. I knew if Roman was quiet, then something was on his mind. The silence from him was good, but it also made me want to call him and ask what was up. I just knew Roman had something up his sleeve. He soon confirmed my suspicion with a phone call.

"What's up, boo?"

"Roman, how did you get my home number?"

"Why are you worried about that? You can't ask me how I'm doing first?"

"Okay, how are you?"

"I'm fine. I just wanna see you, though."

"Roman, you know you're not supposed to see me. You're not going to see me."

"I'm not supposed to, or I'm not going to? Make up your mind. Which one is it, boo?"

"Are you outside of my house?" I headed to look out the window.

"Do you see me outside of your house? With your scary ass. I know you looking out the window."

"Okay, Roman. I'm not supposed to be talking to you. We will be going to court next week, and I don't wanna have to tell the judge you've been harassing me again."

"Tell the judge whatever you want, Holiday. See, now you're pissing me off. You made a nigga fall in love with you, showed me how real you can be with a man, then you just wanna snatch that shit right out from under me. It ain't happening, boo. I still got mad love for you, baby."

"Roman, why don't you go talk to your father or

something? I'm sure he'll have some very encouraging words for you right now. You just need someone like your father to remind you it's okay to move on, that's all." I finally stepped away from the window, confident Roman was nowhere near my house.

"Then what is it you need? You need something. Playin' with a nigga's heart ain't normal. Do you feel you were right in playin' with my emotions the way you have?"

"I'm sorry you feel that way. I didn't mean to give you the impression I never cared. I promise you, you'll get over it."

"Are you trying to be smart with me? I didn't call you for this shit."

"Roman, I'm going to excuse you this time 'cause you're drunk, but don't call here."

Before I could get that last sentence out, everything went dark. My television, my lights, and all the power I had going in the house were completely shut off. Panic came over me. I ran to the window, surprised by what had happened. All the houses on the other side of the street still had power. I looked out of a side window, and all the houses on my side had power, too. Roman's car was nowhere to be found.

"Boo, you ain't talking. What's up?"

"Roman, why are you doing this? Turn my lights back on, please."

"Yeah, now you want to be nice, huh? I knew you'd change your tone. *'Roman, turn my lights back on, please',*" he said, mocking me. "What else you got to say? Huh? You ain't got nothin' else to say?"

"You know what? This ain't even cool. I know you done lost your mind now. Quit playing. Turn my power back on."

"Quit playing? You still think this is a game? What you gon' do? Your alarm system is disarmed, and the police can't get to you fast enough." Roman laughed like a madman.

I looked over at the keypad to check for my back-up system. I discovered it had even failed. Realizing Roman was right, I attempted to reason with him. "What do you want from me?" My voice trembled.

"Your heart, bitch! If you won't give it to me, then I'm just gon' take it from you. You won't love another man with that one," Roman threatened.

"I'm not trying to love anyone else. I just want to be by myself, Roman. Why won't you understand that?" I felt helpless so I started crying.

"Cry, bitch. I don't give a fuck about you crying. You need to cry. Do you know all the fucking tears I done shed over yo' ass, huh? Do you?" Roman taunted me.

I couldn't answer him. I fell to my knees in horror. I felt Roman had come to kill me, and there was nothing I could do to prevent him from doing so. The more I cried, the more Roman continued to harass me.

"Naw, you don't know. You don't know 'cause you never take time to find out what's in my heart. You don't give a fuck about the pain I've been going through."

"Roman, yes, I do. You keep trying to make me be with you, but I can't. You should give me time to do some things I need to do, then maybe I can see you, okay? Now, you're drunk, so just go back home, and we'll talk tomorrow."

The phone went dead. When I tried to call back out, it didn't work. I ran to my cell and dialed 911. I kept looking all around the house, trying not to breathe too loudly. I wanted to hear from which direction Roman would be coming in the house if he tried. The operator wanted me to stay on the line and keep talking with her, but I was too nervous to do so. I needed total silence so I could be keen on hearing any little noise in the house. I asked the dispatcher not to ask me too many questions, but she said it was a requirement. I hung up on her out of fear.

Shortly after hanging up, I felt more alone and uneasy. I still hadn't heard any strange noises other than my neighbor's dog barking, but I ran to hide in my walk-in closet anyway. I called Lance and whispered the situation to him. He told me I didn't have to talk, to just stay on the line with him as he was on his way over. I took long, easy breaths—making almost no noise while inhaling or exhaling. My neighbor's German shepherd began to bark even louder. We had a privacy fence that separated our houses, so I knew this dog couldn't see over the fence, but his bark sounded strange. It was ten o'clock and that dog never so much as whimpered unless his masters were out playing with him. During those times, his bark would be friendly, not the harsh, deep-pitched tone I heard.

The police made it and told me that Roman was long gone. There was no sign of him trying to force his way into my house, but footprints were left in the soft ground just outside my bedroom window. It had rained earlier that evening, so Roman managed to leave his tracks in my yard, as well as in my neighbor's lawn, coming and going over the fence. The German shepherd must've been asleep when Roman came across the fence the first time. I didn't remember him barking then.

The police told me they were going to see if they could find Roman, either at his house or roaming the streets. I figured he probably wouldn't remember doing the things he had done. Intoxication does that to most people.

Lance spent the night with me. I was too frightened to stay by myself, and even with Lance there, I was still afraid to go to sleep. He tried everything he could from holding me to kissing me on my forehead to staying up until I fell asleep, but I couldn't. I just couldn't.

"Baby girl, I promise you, nothing's going to happen to you. I'm here. I'll be damned if I let something happen to you while I'm here. Do you see this nine?" Lance showed me his gun. "When Roman sees that Escalade out there, he'll know not to step foot into this house," Lance said convincingly.

"I just can't help it. I'm just really disturbed. My mind can't rest."

"Baby girl, you're trembling. I don't like that. I want you to trust me. I want you to feel safe with me. Do you feel I could let something happen to you?"

"No."

"Then do me a favor. We don't have to go to the bedroom. If you're more comfortable with us sitting here in the great room on the couch, we can. I just want you to lie back on me and relax. Close your eyes and think of something pleasant. The power is back on, and you have someone who loves you very much right here with you. You're gonna be fine."

Well after he said all that, I did try to relax. Since the power was back on, this meant that my alarm was reactivated. With this in mind, I tried to get some sleep. I had to be at work the next morning.

I managed to drift off into a deep sleep for about thirty minutes, but I couldn't doze longer than that. I kept waking up from nightmares. I was lying on Lance's chest, and each time I jumped out of my dream, he felt it. Sleeping on the couch with our clothes on was difficult anyway. I had the great room well lighted, and this didn't help me rest any better. Lance put up with all of this for me. To say I was grateful would be an understatement. Just by being more attentive to Lance, I had come to learn even more about what true love is and what it can put a man through. Lance's love was beyond anything I'd ever been use to, and I realized I wanted to offer all of me to him. However, I just wasn't ready to say it.

Chapter Forty-two

Can't Stop, Won't Stop

The morning sun had come up, and Lance and I had only a few winks of sleep. I called in to work and so did Lance. He wanted to go home to take a shower and to change clothes, but I wasn't about to let him leave me alone. I rode with him, and I even sat in the bathroom with him while he showered. Lance asked me to join him, but the only clothes I had were the ones I still had on from the day before, so I declined.

We left and stopped at a coffee shop to get breakfast. I told Lance before we went in that I wasn't going to be able to eat, but he ordered for me anyway. When we got back to my house, he played doctor and told me I had to eat something. He heated the eggs, sausage, and grits up in the microwave and fed me as if I were a baby. Upon receiving the first forkful, I leaned back on the couch with my eyes closed.

"C'mon. Open up. It's gonna be good. You'll see. Just open up for me," Lance said.

"Damn! I can't tell if you're talking about the breakfast or something else."

"Well, in that case, either or, whichever you prefer," he said, smiling. His smile eased the mental strain I was feeling as well as heated my soul. I was ready to give in and make love to Lance, but I ate my breakfast instead.

I asked Lance to come into my bedroom with me while I showered. I had begun to feel comfortable enough to trust that Lance was going to look out for me. The long, hot shower did me some good, but I still didn't feel relaxed enough to sleep. Lance was yawning all over the place, but he hung in there for my sake.

The phone company had come out and repaired my phone lines just after I had gotten out of the shower. They said that it wouldn't be any charge to me since I had been paying for insurance and protection on my services. Great news to my ears.

I got a call about eleven o'clock that morning from my attorney's office. I had called her once the police left my place the night before and left her a voice mail about Roman's latest actions. Attorney Jenkins said she'd gotten my message, and she did some investigating that morning. She found out that the police picked up Roman late the night before and that he would be held until our next court date the following Monday. I was elated.

I gave Lance the wonderful news and told him that he could go to my room and lie down if he wanted. He refused to do so unless I went with him. I agreed, but I had to do my own investigating on Roman's whereabouts before I could be totally comfortable going to sleep. I called the Criminal Justice Center and asked if they were holding Roman Broxton, and I gave them his birth date. The rep ran down a list of charges they were keeping him on, then she told me if they decided to release him, I would get a call first. She didn't have to say any more. I hung up that phone and dove into my bed. Lance and I slept the whole day away.

We woke up around nine to the sound of my telephone ringing. I had turned the ringer up high in case I slept too hard.

"Hello?"

"May I speak to Ms. Holiday Simmons?"

"Speaking."

"Ms. Simmons, I'm calling to inform you that we're releasing Mr. Roman Broxton on his own recognizance."

"How could you? He violated the restraining orders. He should be in jail until the next time we have to be in court."

"No, Ms. Simmons, I'm showing you filed the papers for a restraining order, but he couldn't be served. He must've dodged the sheriff somehow when they came to serve him the papers."

"Then how come my attorney didn't tell me this?"

"I don't know that, ma'am. When is your next court date?"

"Next Monday."

"Well if he shows up for court Monday, maybe they'll serve him there. I don't really know what will happen with that. Are you afraid he'll try to come back over there if we release him?"

"Yes. I know he will."

"Well, I'll make note of this in the system. When the officials get ready to release him, they'll see the notation, but I have to tell you, this may not stop Mr. Broxton's release."

"You mean to tell me you release criminals at night?" I was dumbfounded.

"Yes, ma'am. We only have so much room down here, and depending on what the offender has done, he may be allowed to sign saying he'll return for court, then we'll let him go. All I can say is call the police if Mr. Broxton comes back over. If he has to come back down here tonight, he's not leaving any time soon."

"This is so unfair. I can't believe this. All right. I hear you."

"Thank you, Ms. Simmons. I hope you have a good night."

"Me, too, ma'am. Me, too." Out of frustration, I almost hung up in her face.

I explained to Lance what the jailhouse representative had told me, and that was it for the rest of a good night's sleep. I kept calling every thirty minutes to see if Roman had been released. Finally about eleven, I was told he was free. That night for Lance and me was almost as bad as the one before as far as sleep went. I felt so emotionally drained. Lance had toughed it out with me, though. We would catch a wink here and there, but that was all.

I had too much work to do to call in again, so I pushed on. I went to the office without a drop of makeup on. My associates knew something had to be wrong 'cause although I would sometimes come in without eyeliner or mascara, I never showed up without my liquid foundation and lipstick. I didn't have bad skin, but when I didn't wear my foundation you could tell the difference. I didn't look as revived. I just told them I wasn't feeling well.

I prepared myself to have an argument with Roman that morning. I knew he couldn't let the opportunity go by without calling me at work, where his calls couldn't be traced. Every time the phone rang I expected it to be him. Lance advised me that morning to try to avoid Roman's calls and that if I had to speak with him, to be cool and listen to whatever Roman had to say. Never in my wildest dreams did I ever expect the man to show up on my job. My assistant, Ms. Dodson, didn't recognize Roman because he had shaved his head. She phoned to let me know I had company.

"Ms. Simmons, your morning client is here to see you," Ms. Dodson said.

"Is it my nine o'clock appointment, Mrs. Thurston from The Domestic Paper Company?" I asked Ms. Dodson.

"No, it's a man. I'll ask him for a name if you need me to."

"Yes, although I believe it may be Mr. Wimbleton from Good-All Beer Incorporated. He's running a little behind for our eight-thirty appointment."

"Alright, let me check for you." Ms. Dodson briefly put me on hold. "Yes, he is Mr. Wimbleton from Good-All Beer."

"Great. Send him in. I'm going to pull his file right now."

I turned my back to browse through my file cabinet of newly assessed clients. I could feel a presence, though, even with my back turned. Then I heard the door close. Thinking it was my morning client, I wasn't alarmed.

"Good morning, Mr. Wimbleton. Have a seat if you will. I'm looking for your file right now. Are you doing all right this morning?"

"Yeah, I'm fine. How about you?" Roman said rather calmly.

I turned and looked at Roman with wide eyes. I just knew he had come to do me in. We stood and looked at each other for an awkward minute before I could finally speak.

"Why are you here, Roman?"

"Relax. I'm not here to hurt you. I just wanted to see you. You look terrible though. Like you're stressed out or something. Where's your makeup? Why didn't you pull your hair up better than that today? I've seen you dress way better than that. What's wrong witcha?" Roman's voice was so cool and relaxed.

"You've got a lot of nerve. I am stressed, Roman. You're the one who's causing the stress."

"Boo, I'm surprised at you. You shouldn't let anyone get under your skin this way. I'm the one who's been to jail and everything. And you see, I look great this morning. I haven't let anything bring me down. I've even got a new style. You like the baldhead?"

"Roman, get out."

"I will. But just a minute. What I really wanted to say to you this morning is I may have acted a damn fool the other night, but I wasn't gonna hurt you."

I gave him a sarcastic reply. "Yes, you were very convincing of that by turning off my electricity and cutting my phone lines. Yeah, I knew then you weren't going to hurt me."

"I'm serious, boo. I was drunk, but I wasn't that damn drunk. I told you I just be trying to scare you."

"Yeah, well you don't mind if I still take precautions, do you? No matter what you say, I'm going to always take you seriously. I just ain't in the mood for all these games you want to play, Roman."

"You don't have to worry about it anymore. I'm through with that stuff. I don't need to keep going to jail. I have a career to think about. Hopefully I'll just get a slap on the wrist next week when we go to court. You need to tell the judge you aren't afraid of me. That may work."

My assistant interrupted us with a knock on the door. She said there was a man out there who said he was Mr. Wimbleton. She gave Roman the stare-down. I told her to give me a few moments then she could invite my client in.

Roman began to back up toward the door. "Well, I'm sorry for taking up your time, but you take care of yourself. On the next occasion we meet, I'd like to see you with that glow you use to have. I'm through with all that craziness, so you can relax."

My assistant rushed into my office to apologize and explained Roman had lied to her about his identity. It had been a while since she'd seen him and all she knew was that his face looked familiar.

Roman's surprise visit put me on the defense again, so I called Lance and talked to him about moving in with me for the summer. He made sure it was what I wanted 'cause he said he wasn't going to be dragging all of his things back and forth. I assured him I wanted him to stay with me, and he packed enough things so he wouldn't have to go to his house for anything but to make sure his home was okay. I let him use the extra closet and dresser space in the guest bedroom. His presence gave me a sense of contentment.

The judge put Roman on probation, gave him some community service, and some anger management courses. He also stuck him with that restraining order and told him that if he violated any of his orders he would serve the full amount of suspended time attached to the probation. Roman left the courtroom fuming, although he couldn't understand he had done this to himself. I didn't feel sorry for him. He was lucky his driver's license wasn't suspended for drunk driving. Roman didn't see luck in it at all.

Chapter Forty-three
The Script Done Flipped

By late June I began to feel sensually alive again. Lance had been living with me for about a week, but I wouldn't touch him. He was a perfect gentleman as I expected he would be. We slept in the same bed, and I believe that he must've sensed that I only wanted him to hold me at night.

Roman wasn't bothering me anymore, so this allowed me to be comfortable in my surroundings and with my life. I could think clearly and I must add, more wisely. I had one of the finest men I had ever come across in my life living with me, yet in the whole week he had been there I couldn't bring myself to make love to him. I told myself that wasn't rational thinking at all. Lance was in fact, a man. And a mandingo at that. Enough said.

While wrapping up at work one evening, I began to come up with creative ways to entice Lance. Not that he needed persuasion, but after all that he had gone through for me and with me, I wanted to show him a little appreciation. I continued with planning the even-ing, and I called Lance to see if he could tell me a definite time he'd be home.

"What's going on, baby girl?" he asked after realizing it was me on the phone.

"Oh, I was calling to see if you knew how late you would be working tonight."

"Well actually, tonight is a good one. I was only gonna work a little longer 'cause you said you were going to the grocery store when you get off. I can wrap it up now if you have something you'd like me to do."

"No. I'm still planning a visit to the store, and I want to make a quick stop at the mall before I come home."

"That's cool, baby girl. Do your thang! Just let me know what time you'd like me to be there."

"Will you meet me at the house about eight o'clock tonight?"

"Eight? That's kind of late, isn't it? It's only a quarter to five now. I don't have that much wrapping up to do here."

"Well, I told you I wanted to go by the mall. I'll try not to be long, though."

"What about dinner? Do you want me to pick something up so that you won't have to cook?"

"No. Just get you a snack, but I want you to wait and have dinner with me."

"Okay, then I'll see you tonight. Later, baby girl."

I fixed that lie right on up. I'm glad he fell for it 'cause what I really had in mind was to pick up some essentials from the grocery store for dinner and a little sumin'-sumin' extra from Sassy Loraine's. I went and found the perfect little seducing piece. It was a

sheer black full-body suit. It had the French maid
black-and-white headpiece and bow tie, with the
cutest little matching apron. Now this left very little
to the imagination because the backside would still
be out, and the top was exposed. This little number
also had easy access. There was a huge opening in
the crotch so Lance wouldn't have to undress me if
he didn't want to.

I made it home in time to whip up Lance's favorite
meal. He loved southern fried steak, smothered pota-
toes, corn on the cob, green beans, and my southern-
style sourdough bread. I had already prepped the
dough the night before for dinner, and when I remembered that while still working, it gave me the
idea to cook everything else he was so crazy about.
And for dessert . . . well, I'll talk about that later.

By a quarter to eight I called Lance on his cell to
be sure he was en route to the house. When he confirmed, I took off the robe I'd left on after my shower
and put on the French maid outfit. I started his bath
water in the Jacuzzi. Of course, I had to add the bubbles. What good would it have been if I didn't accen-
tuate it with candlelight and soft, sensual bubbles? I
left the light off in the bedroom 'cause there was a
little sumin'-sumin' extra on the bed for him.

I had already eaten a bite before Lance got there.
I nibbled here and there as I prepared the dinner.
This was Lance's night, and I planned to spend it
spoiling him. With that in mind I had a couple of
drinks before he got home.

When I saw the headlights of his Escalade pulling
in the driveway, my nerves escalated. I knew Lance
wasn't expecting any of this, so I couldn't wait to see
his reaction once he walked through that door, took

a whiff of the aroma from the kitchen, and ogled my costume.

The key jingled in the lock while I stood just a few steps away filled with anxiety. Lance opened the door and paused before taking any farther steps into the house. Caught off guard, he gawked at my half-naked body, widened his eyes, then quickly turned to close the door.

"Baby girl, you don't have any clothes on," Lance said, pleasantly surprised.

"Yes, my king! I have on clothes. But only the kind you like," I said seductively.

"Yeah, transparent ones!" Lance said as he took off his suit jacket and started toward me. "May I have a kiss?"

"If you wish. This is a night of making all your dreams come true." Before I could finish speaking, Lance planted a slow, loving kiss on my lips.

"Do I smell southern fried steak? Sourdough bread?" Lance asked.

"Yes. Would you prefer to eat dinner now or have your bath first?"

"Damn, baby girl, you gave a man some hard choices. I guess I'll eat first."

"As you wish. Come this way, my king."

I led him to the formal dining room. The chandelier had been dimmed. As Lance stepped into the dining room, he noticed I had only set the table for him.

"Aren't you going to have dinner with me?"

"No, my Nubian king. A good servant doesn't sit to have dinner before her master. She brings his food and serves it to him. May I feed you, my king?"

"Only if you'll sit and feed me so that I may look into your eyes."

"As you wish," I responded.

I went to fetch his dinner plate along with a bottle of white wine. As I stood over him pouring into his glass, I looked down and observed him staring up at me. He began to loosen his tie and collar. I quickly set the wine down and said, "Oh no, my king! You mustn't do that. I am your servant. Please allow me." He looked up at me while I was taking off his tie and shook his head.

"You never cease to amaze me. This morning I didn't know what to think of you and what you wanted. Now this evening, I have to tell you, I'm beyond impressed. I just hope I give you all you need tonight."

"Oh no, my Nubian king! You mustn't worry about me. This is your night. A night of making all your dreams come true." I picked up his fork and began to feed him.

In actuality, I had said to Lance he didn't have to worry about me 'cause I knew him. I knew he'd be proud to hear me say this, but I also knew he'd let it go in one ear and out the other.

"Dinner was great. Now do I get dessert?" he asked twenty minutes later.

"Yes, my king, but I'd like you to wait until I've given you your bath, if you will."

"That'll be fine."

As I led him by the hand to the master bath, I could feel Lance watching my ass, so I made sure I put a little extra switch in my walk. He asked me if I was going to turn on the lights in the bedroom, and I told him I preferred not to until he'd had his bath.

The water was still hot 'cause I had set the temperature before giving him dinner. As Lance stepped down into the water, he let out a pleasant sigh.

"Oh, baby girl, I don't know how you're gonna get me out of this water. This feels so good," he said, moaning.

"Stay in as long as you like, my king. We have all night," I replied, rubbing Lance's back.

Lance closed his eyes and relaxed. "Holiday, everything has been going perfectly, but there's just one thing that I want you to do for me."

"What's that, my king?"

"I understand this is supposed to be my night, but I just want you to be a little understanding when I feel the need to flip the tables on you."

"As I've said, this is your night, but I will allow you to do as you please with me."

"Good, then in that case I'm ready to be washed." I managed to suppress laughter and just nodded.

I washed his body, and he oooed, aahed, and oohed as I bathed him. His moans were turning me on so much, I wanted desperately to get into the water with him, but I sent his sensual moans to the database in the back of my mind, so they could easily be replayed in his absence, if necessary. Lance let me know when he was ready to get out of the tub, and I dried him off. I left the bathroom so I could prepare for our bedroom scene.

I lit candles as far as the bedroom was wide. When Lance walked out of the bathroom, the mood was set. I had made up the bed with my black satin sheets. I sprinkled a little Issey Miyake powder under the sheets and pillowcases. This was the fragrance he loved for me to wear. I didn't forget the rose petals, either. These were a must. Since they are used as symbolism of royalty, and on this particular night he was my Nubian king, it would've been a shame to leave them out.

He stood in the doorway of the bathroom smiling. I wiggled my finger, beckoning him over to the bed where I made him sit. I went and turned on the CD I'd made earlier.

I began to dance seductively to "Cupid" by 112, "So Anxious" by Ginuwine, and "Etcetera" by R. Kelly. As I sensually danced for him, I took off the headpiece, necktie, and apron. With all the twisting, swaying, and kicking I'd done, Lance managed to discover the opening in the middle of the body suit. He kept reaching to feel me between my legs and patting me on my ass as I danced.

I had placed another glass of wine on the nightstand for him, so while he was caught up in all the emotions of me dancing, he kept picking it up to take a sip. After the music stopped, I put on a mix CD of slow songs then went to the refrigerator to get his dessert.

Dessert was a banana split with mostly caramel and chocolate toppings. I went over to Lance and began spoon-feeding him. He wanted to return the favor, so I let him, then I got up to get a blindfold to cover his eyes. I didn't want Lance to see what was coming next.

I had some extra caramel sitting on the nightstand, so after blindfolding him I took some pieces of fruit from the banana split and poured the caramel over them. I made Lance eat the fruit from my fingers. Once I was satisfied with watching him as he ate, I poured the remainder of the caramel from the con-

tainer all over his body. I began to slowly lick the
caramel off his chest. Once I had enough of the
sweetness in my mouth, I went on to share it with
Lance. I kissed him long, hard, and passionately before deciding to lick his entire upper body. His moans
kept me hot and horny. I skipped over portions of his
body that were still sticky with caramel and went
straight for his penis. I slurped and sucked the caramel,
making sure he wouldn't be able to compare me to
any other woman when it came to this type of erotic
pleasure. When he motioned he'd had enough by trying to pull my head up, I wouldn't let go. He moaned
louder, his toes curled, and his body trembled.

"Now that was lowdown, baby girl. You knew I couldn't
take anymore. You just had to see a brotha with the
quivers, didn't you?"

"I just wanted to make certain that my king was
satisfied."

"Well, that I am. Come here. I want to taste you,"
Lance said.

I didn't deny my king his request. Since he was already lying on the bed, I just climbed on top of him
and sat on his face, the best move I could've ever
made. Lance paid me back for not letting go of him.
When I'd had enough, he put an unbreakable grip
around my waist that held me to his face. We both
had to take a breather after that one.

The CD was still going, and "Moments of Love" by
Art of Noise started playing, putting us both right
back in the mood to get riled up again. Lance flipped
me over and got on top of me. He sucked my titties
straight through that sheer body suit until my nipples stood straight out, hard as rocks. I wouldn't allow
him to stop. I can only describe it as a great sensa-

tion, causing me to scream for more. Once Lance was ready for something different, he tore that body suit off me. I didn't mind 'cause I knew exactly what I had coming.

The next morning, we were both late for work. Oh, we got up on time, but waking up to the smell of the pillowcases and seeing me lying there naked made Lance want another round. There was no way I could reject this man after glimpsing his erection and watching him lick his lips as he turned me over. We went from the bed to the floor to the shower. I believe his agenda was to make sure I'd think about him the rest of the day.

Lance gave me a call at work. We reminisced on the night and morning we'd just shared. I started to wonder if I had created a monster. I also had begun to think maybe I really did want to share a life with Lance. I admired his meekness toward Crystal and his unrelenting fight to prove his love for me. It also pleased me that Lance cared enough to be my protector during my time of need. I began to flash back on the special times he and I had shared, and I realized the quality was genuine. I could finally see what I couldn't before. Lance had always been the better man for me. I felt closer to him than I had before. I also gained more appreciation for Lance, but I still couldn't share my love for him just yet. I wanted to be sure the good sex between us didn't just have me wrapped up.

Chapter Forty-four

Peace Unreal

I had been talking to Crystal every other day. I longed to speak with her more, but she made me feel guilty by accusing me of not trusting her father to take care of her. Although I believed Darius would be there for Crystal, I was use to having her closer to me, and I had a tough time dealing with her being so far away. I spaced a day between each time I called, forcing myself to cope with her absence.

For a few more nights, Lance and I lived in peace, but that Friday all the serenity came to a head. Lance and I were lying in the bed half dressed when we heard a loud bang then glass crashing to the floor. We both sat straight up in the bed. The alarm sounded, and Lance told me to stay in the bedroom until I heard him say it was safe to come out. The phone began to ring, and I almost didn't answer it because I was worried about Lance. It was a gentleman with the alarm company asking if I needed help. I explained I wasn't sure 'cause my boyfriend hadn't come back into the bedroom yet to let me know that everything was okay. The operator suggested I let him dispatch the police, so I did.

I was relieved to finally hear Lance call out to me. I went to meet him in the great room and discovered one of the side windows smashed out. I knew it would just be a matter of time before Roman would strike again. I couldn't believe he actually had the patience to wait as long as he did.

The police took a report and told me to call them back if I needed them. They said they'd also patrol the neighborhood to look for signs of trouble. I tried to reactivate the alarm system, but I kept getting an error signal that the window location was not secure. I helped Lance prop the window to fool the security system to think it was closed. Rigging the house alarm was all I could do in order to feel safe besides taking the police at their word of doing an occasional drive-by.

Lance stayed up with me. I wouldn't let him turn on any music or the television because I wanted to be able to hear every small sound. We just sat there for about two hours, whispering in the dark.

All of a sudden, we heard a noise from the kitchen, like the door was crashing in. We jumped up off the couch and turned in the direction of the crash. I anxiously stood and waited to see someone step into the great room. Lance slowly walked toward the opening that led to the kitchen, pointing his gun.

"Baby, be careful." I whispered.

"Holiday, it's Roman! Get down!" Lance yelled back to me just before the gunshots began.

* * *

Have you ever been so frightened that your mind goes into a state of confusion? I heard Lance tell me to get down, but I kind of froze, not knowing what to do. I didn't know if I still had a heart in my chest. I felt it fall after hearing the first gunshot. I was so scared. All I could do was scream and holler. I finally jumped behind the couch. By this time the alarm was blaring. The phone was ringing, and I was unable to answer it. I knew the alarm company would automatically dispatch the police.

More shots rang out. There is no real way of explaining how I felt. Still, even to this day, that moment is indescribable. The only thing I knew to do was pray the gunfire would cease. It seemed like forever before the shots came to a halt. I heard what sounded like someone trying to reload, so I slightly rose from my shield to take a peek. I couldn't see Lance, but I saw Roman coming from behind the coat closet door, aiming his gun. I figured Lance was out of ammunition, and I feared for his life. A quick burst of adrenaline came over me, and I jumped from behind the couch yelling and screaming. I dove on top of Roman before he could get a good aim at me.

We wrestled with his gun for a few seconds before Lance came to help me. Roman and I both had our hands on the gun. The struggle went on longer than I expected. Lance and my strength were no match for a crazy man. Roman managed to get control of his gun, so Lance and I both began to scoot away from him. As we slid away from Roman, he aimed his gun and fired at Lance. The blast of the weapon was so strong, my eardrums popped, leaving a muffled echo of the sound in my head. I saw the blood oozing from Lance's shoulder as he lay there motionless. I felt my heart fall once again.

Roman turned toward me. I didn't have time to stand. I could only continue to scoot away from him while he kept walking closer to me, trying to get a better aim. Little did he know that Lance had regained consciousness and was slowly inching toward the end table drawer where he'd previously hidden another gun. I kept wishing for Lance to hurry up.

Roman decided he had a farewell speech for me. I was almost relieved because I was hoping this would give Lance some time to collect himself.

"I loved you with everything I had in me. And I told you, if you can't love me, then you won't love anybody else."

"Roman, think of how upset this is going to make Crystal. Why would you take her mother from her?" I asked in a frenzy.

"That ain't my kid. Did her mother think of how upset she was making me when she refused to let me back into her life? No. I don't wanna do this to you, boo, but right now I feel I have no choice."

I made the terrible mistake of looking around Roman to see what Lance was doing. Roman turned and spotted Lance. Before Lance had a chance to shoot, Roman fired at him, and Lance fell to the floor once again. I screamed, using all the air I had in my lungs.

Roman stood a minute looking at Lance on the floor. He then turned and took aim at me. I raised my arms to my face, and that's when I heard the shots go off. So many shots, I couldn't count, but I didn't feel a thing. The shots stopped, and I looked up to see what was going on. Roman had a startled look on his face. He fell to his knees and gazed in my eyes without blinking. After holding that position for a few seconds, Roman raised up, stood on his feet, then quickly fell to the floor, tossing his gun a few feet away. Startled, I looked up and saw Lance sitting on his knees with a blank expression. He was still holding the gun used to shoot Roman.

I called out to Lance, but quickly discovered something was terribly wrong when he didn't respond. The blank look remained on his face until he, too, had collapsed onto the floor. I screamed in horror.

I frantically jumped up, running to Lance's aid. He was unconscious and barely breathing. I picked up his head and placed it on my lap and cried for him to wake up.

"Lance, baby, c'mon. You can't die on me. You just can't die. I love you. C'mon, baby. Wake up."

I carefully placed Lance's head back onto the floor then attempted to get up to make sure help was on the way. I felt a dull pain in my side that prevented me from rising. I looked down and discovered I had been shot. I wanted so badly to reach the phone, but I couldn't. I collapsed on Lance and slipped into semi-consciousness.

Chapter Forty-five
What You Don't Know

I had been in the hospital for quite some time before I awakened from my coma. My surgeon, Dr. Donovan Chambers, is a very intelligent and respectable doctor. I had to have reconstructive surgery on my liver in order to remove the bullet. Upon hearing of my improvement, he came in the next morning to check on me. I wanted to bombard him with questions, but I was still too weak to speak. It was tough just lying there, not being able to verbally respond.

I learned that after Darius's sister had heard of the incident that occurred at my place, she quickly came running. She called my parents, which troubled me. I worried that the news of me being shot would give my mother a heart attack. My parents did need to know though. They asked Renee to take time off work to drive them to Memphis. Renee didn't hesitate to do so.

Early one morning I overheard Dr. Chambers and Renee whispering.

"Dr. Chambers, how is she doing this morning?"

"She's not looking too good, Ms. Hamilton. One of her lungs is in danger of collapsing. At least that hasn't happen, so I don't know if you really need to alert the rest of the family."

"Her parents are elderly and I'm not so sure they'd be able to handle this type of news. Mr. and Mrs. Simmons were so elated to see Holiday come out of the coma the other day. I gave them today off to rest at the hotel while I spend time with Holiday," Renee said.

"I've been extremely proud of the way she's been up and talking for the last few days. I was beginning to think that she would actually pull through all of this," Dr. Chambers responded.

My mind had shifted into another gear. I wanted to respond to them, but I felt I needed to hear more first.

"So are you saying she's not going to make it?"

"Ms. Hamilton, I'm saying pray. And keep talking to her. We need to learn why she, after a few good days of improvement, has begun to physically fight against her survival."

"I see. Last night she did seem a little distant. She even asked me not to hold a conversation with her. I just thought she needed to rest, but then she turned her back to me and gazed at the wall."

"Yes, but this didn't just begin last night. I've noticed through my talks with Ms. Simmons that her comments are lacking self-worth. We need to figure out a way to help her have a fighting chance. If that lung collapses, this means double work for the other one and will put a tremendous strain on her heart as well."

Renee sighed and responded tearfully. "I don't know what I'm going to say to her parents when I call them at the hotel."

"Continue to tell them what you have been. I'm going to do everything within my ability to improve her condition. Come and take a walk with me to the front desk for a moment. I have a few suggestions I think may help."

After I could no longer feel their presence in the room, I opened my eyes and lay there thinking about what I'd just heard. To be honest, Dr. Chambers was right. I was fighting against my survival with a dreary spirit and a lack of self-love. I'd had long thoughts of how Crystal was deserving of a better mother than me. I thought of how ashamed of me she would be upon her return to Memphis, and I wondered what I'd say to justify the deadly events.

I waited for Renee to return to the room. She had been out in the hallway for what seemed like forever before she stuck her head around the door to ask me if I'd be mad at her for allowing one visitor into the room.

"One visitor like whom, Renee?"

"Well, she says she feels really close to you, and I think you ought to see her."

My mind wouldn't allow me to think, but I had only hoped it wasn't someone from work. I wasn't ready to see my coworkers. "Okay, I'll see just one visitor."

Renee stepped aside. In walked my former friend, Erika Peebles. She had swollen red eyes and a face shielded by sadness. She stood three feet away, with her bottom lip trembling as she fought hard not to let tears flow. Moved by the sight of her, I couldn't speak. I raised my hand instead to beckon her to come in.

Erika swiftly walked over to me and put her arms around my neck. "Holiday, I'm so sorry. I'm sorry, sis. I've wanted to come before now, but I was afraid you would reject me. I love you," she cried. Warm tears streamed down her cheeks.

"What gave you the courage to come now?" I whispered in her ear.

"I truly care for you. I should be here for you."

I formally introduced Erika and Renee. The two of them had more of a conversation than Erika and I did that day. The only reason I have for this is maybe it was because Erika felt awkward trying to mend a friendship given the timing, and Renee probably sensed I just didn't have a lot to say to Erika.

Before Erika packed up to leave at the end of visiting hours, she took advantage of the time to share some things on her heart she felt necessary to say.

"Holiday, I know we've gone through a lot, but I've never stopped loving you. I can honestly say you've been a better friend to me than I have been to you. I'm hoping you will forgive me. A part of me has been jealous of you, and a part of me wanted to even be you. I guess that's why I couldn't offer all the right advice without being so hard on you. Maybe that's even the reason I could rationalize betraying our friendship so many times. But, my sole reason in coming here today is to ask for your forgiveness and to be able to tell you you're the sister I always needed." Erika stood over me and stroked my hair as she continued to speak. "I don't know if this is the right time, but I need to tell you that I lied about the intimacy between Lance and me. Lance loved you too much to be involved with me on that level. I apologize for the deception and hurting you the way I did with that lie. I shouldn't have waited until something like this occurred before I would come and confess. I feel like crap for having been so immature. I never knew how much you meant in my life until I lost your friendship."

Erika and I had tears streaming down our faces as she spoke. Filled with emotions, I was unable to speak. I did, however, squeeze her hand.

"Thank you for not sending me away today, sis. I'm going to let you get some rest now. Just hurry up and get better, okay?" Erika kissed me on the cheek and waved as she exited my hospital room.

I could tell Renee and the nurses were moved by Erika and my emotions, but they all did an excellent job of withholding their feelings. I thought of Erika and the good years we'd shared. Then I thought of Roman and Lance and how they both had recalled having a great friendship. Thinking of Roman and Lance again put me back into the same slump I had been in. Definitely not the state Dr. Chambers had hoped for me.

Chapter Forty-six
The Day of Reckoning

"How about today, Dr. Chambers? Is she doing any better?" Renee inquired, the following day. She still worried a little more than I wished.

"She's improving. She's definitely improving. The test results are all looking positive. We've just got to somehow keep her on this upward trend."

"Well, I'm just grateful. That's about all I can say right now. I'm sending the praises up," Renee said.

Later that morning Erika visited me again. After two weeks of seeing the same faces, it was sort of refreshing to see someone else to help keep my mind off why I was in the hospital.

Erika and I talked about Memphis. She also told Renee how she and I had met several years before. It was amazing how she recalled the events just as I had remembered. Erika couldn't stay long. She had an engagement she couldn't break. I almost didn't want her to leave, but I understood she had to. Soon after Erika left, I turned over to take an afternoon nap.

* * *

"This room is absolutely beautiful!" Dr. Chambers said, stepping into my room. He was admiring all the flowers that had been sent to me. "Oh, I'm too loud, aren't I? I didn't know she was asleep."

"Well, it doesn't look as if you've awakened her. I think it's okay." I wondered if Renee and Dr. Chambers had an eye for each other. He was starting to come to my room a little more frequently. "She has very loving coworkers and church members who have filled this room with such beauty," Renee said.

"Wow! Who sent these odd-colored roses? They're beautiful, but there isn't a card attached with them," Dr. Chambers stated.

"They are different, but enchanting. I'd been thinking all this time they're sort of lavender colored," Renee said.

"Well maybe they came from a church member. This just looks like the work of a clergyman to me," Dr. Chambers said.

"No, Dr. Chambers, I disagree. I think only someone very special in her life could've sent something so rare and beautiful."

"Then why do you suppose this person didn't include a card?"

"Now that, I can't answer. I can only tell you she's loved in Memphis by many, judging by the number of flowers and cards in this room."

"Oh yes, I will agree with that. These flowers nearest the window are from her job. And this bunch is from her neighbors. And these . . ." Dr. Chambers didn't finish his statement.

"But who would send such beautiful roses and not

send a card with 'em? These had to have cost a fortune. Lavender-colored roses! How about that?" Renee said, interrupting Dr. Chambers.

"Silver." My mouth was as dry as the Sahara Desert as I spoke to them.

"Holiday? How are you feeling since taking a nap?" Renee asked.

A great fatigue had come over me, but I didn't want to express this to the doctor. "I'm okay."

"What, honey? What did you say?" Renee inquired.

"Silver. The roses are silver," I replied, ignoring her original question.

"Honey, you have a whole roomful of flowers now. Do you like them?"

"Yeah. There are enough flowers in here to just go on and have a funeral. Who sent me silver roses anyway?"

"We don't know. There isn't a card. Have you ever gotten silver roses before, or do you know who would send them to you?"

I nodded. "But it couldn't have been him, though."

"Ms. Simmons, you seem to be feeling so much better this evening. You still have a long way to go, but I'm amazed at your improvement," Dr. Chambers said later that evening.

"You've forgotten how long I've been here already. Two weeks in this place is enough motivation to wanna get better. I'm ready to get out of here," I replied.

"C'mon now, Ms. Simmons. We're not all that bad in here, are we?"

"No, but I'm not use to being down like this."

"Well I have to just say I admire your wit. I don't know if I could be so strong if it were me in this situation. You keep hanging in there, Ms. Simmons. I'll be back shortly," Dr. Chambers said just before leaving the room.

Although I tried to display a sense of humor and a desperate will to live for Dr. Chambers and Renee, my sullen heart had been impossible to mask. I continued to pretend I was holding it together.

Renee asked me if I felt well enough to let her French braid my hair. I allowed her to because I didn't have to get up. This made me feel so much better about my appearance. I shouldn't have been surprised that Renee would want to help me feel as wonderful as possible. The mirror she passed me confirmed my good thoughts. As I looked at my reflection, Renee joked I resembled a little schoolgirl. I did have sort of an innocence that accompanied the hairstyle.

Dr. Chambers returned to the room with one of the best smiles I'd seen in a long time. He complimented my hair and made small talk with both Renee and me.

"So, Ms. Simmons, what I'd like to know is when you plan to be out of here."

"I don't know. Why? Are you bringing bad news or something?"

"No. Actually you're doing pretty well. I'd like to see you out of here as soon as possible, but I can't give any definite dates."

"Then, why are you bringing it up?" I put on one of my joking voices, but gave him a serious face.

"Well, I'd like to aid in your recovery as much as I

can, so if you have any ideas, I'd like to hear them. I'd just like to hear anything you may have on your heart to say."

"Dr. Chambers, I don't know. You're the doctor. You need to tell me what I need to get better."

"Well first, let me ask you this: Have you taken time to think about what happened the night you were shot?"

My sullen heart gushed like a raging river that had just been released by a broken dam. I closed my eyes and twisted my face, confirming I indeed had something very bitter on my mind.

"Are you okay, Ms. Simmons?"

I wanted to ask him to leave me alone, but instead I just shook my head. My eyes burned, and I wailed out to him, sounding like a woman with a broken heart. "Why are you doing this to me? This is not the way to help me feel better. I've already spoken to the police about everything I can remember."

"Yes, Ms. Simmons, but I feel like there's a grieving process you haven't gone through. You haven't asked any questions about that day or the other parties involved."

My voice trembled. "What is there to ask? Oh, well maybe there is something I should ask. How about this question: Am I even worthy of living? For the past two weeks I've had no other option but to stare at these same four walls and the mass of cards and flowers that accompany them. The anxiety I'm feeling is only adding to the thought that I should be dead. Every time that door opens, I get a whiff of what really should be fresh air. But instead it's the stale smell of blood and corrosion, which is a constant reminder that I now have the death of one too many people on my hands. And it was all a result of love."

Renee and Dr. Chambers looked as though I had surprised them with this response. There was an awkward silence in the room until I went on to speak again. "I may as well have died because I feel so dead on the inside right now."

Dr. Chambers gave me a perplexed look and slowly walked closer to me. "Ms. Simmons, I don't know if I'm following you correctly. From what I understand the detectives to say, there were only three people in the house."

"Yes, that's right. The perpetrator, Roman Broxton, and my boyfriend, Lance Ferrell. I could hear the EMTs working to try to save Lance's life, but then I also heard them say he was a goner." I paused and took a deep breath. "Lance died, too. He was everything to me. Only I discovered it a little too late." My voice faded as I choked back the tears.

"Lance? I'm sorry, but did you say Lance Ferrell?" Dr. Chambers questioned.

I locked eyes with the doctor. I was surprised to hear him say Lance's name as if he knew him. I swallowed hard and answered, "Yes."

Dr. Chambers took his hands out of his pockets and then gave me that familiar perplexed look I had seen a few moments before. "I need to take care of some business, Ms. Simmons. I'll be back to check on you later." He then turned and left my room.

I wondered what I had said to make Dr. Chambers walk out on me. It bothered me even more that he hadn't satisfied my curiosity of why he had sounded as if he knew Lance. I wished I hadn't talked of Roman and Lance and the tragedy that occurred at my house. That dreadful day was stuck in my mind, and I wanted to release it through poetry, but I was afraid my own words would be destructive to my soul. Bitterness toward myself ruled my conscience. I began to cry uncontrollably. Renee had been on the phone when she heard me cry.

"Holiday, are you okay?" she asked, hanging up the phone.

I couldn't answer her. I had begun to long for Lance, and I detested the thought that I would never share more time with him. Flashbacks of the good times should've made me feel better, but instead they made me cry harder because I felt he and I needed another chance to make more memories.

"Holiday, I know Dr. Chambers has forced you to begin a grieving process with talk of the day you got shot, but I think it will do you good to let some of it out." Renee cuddled behind me in my bed. "Do you need anything?" she asked.

"I think I need to be alone. Please call my parents and ask them not to come here today. I really need some space," I cried.

"Sure. I can go to the hotel with Mr. and Mrs. Simmons for the night. I'll ask the doctor and nurses to keep an eye on you. How does that sound?"

"Fine," I whispered and dried my tears.

Renee left as she promised. I turned over in bed and gazed at the floral imprints on the wall.

Dr. Chambers returned to my room late that evening. I wondered why he had worked so late, but before I could ask him, he blurted to me with excitement.

"Ms. Simmons, I know you're trying to get some rest, but I have some wonderful news for you," he said, gasping for his breath.

"What is it? You sound as if you ran in here to talk to me."

"Oh, I did. I was so excited when I received the news I couldn't wait on the elevator. I ran three flights of stairs."

"Okay. Well, tell me the news."

"When you mentioned that your boyfriend, Lance Ferrell, had died, I couldn't believe it. I remembered hearing on the radio he had survived and was taken to the Regional Medical Center for treatment. I just received confirmation he is in fact alive and doing pretty well."

"Dr. Chambers! I can't believe what I'm hearing. Are you certain you have news about the right man?"

"Yes. That's why it took me so long. I had to be sure before I brought the news to you," he said.

"Wow! This is excellent. Can I see him? Is he well enough to visit me?"

"Hold on now, Ms. Simmons. I've been told Mr. Ferrell has been released from the hospital, but due to possible upcoming trial dates, his attorneys have restricted him from seeing you."

"What? The police know Roman broke in on Lance and me. I don't understand the problem. Lance and I did nothing wrong." I began to weep.

"Ms. Simmons, the only reason I told you is because I thought you'd be happy. I didn't mean to make you cry. I do know that Lance wishes to see you as well, but due to conflicting evidence found at the scene, suspicions are raised as to whether Mr. Roman

Broxton continued to pose a threat to either of you before he was shot."

This just didn't make sense to me. "Say what? No . . . no . . . no . . . I watched Roman shoot Lance and then try to kill me. He broke into my home for crying out loud! What more threat does there have to be?"

"Mr. Broxton was found lying face down, gunned in the back more than two feet away from both you and Lance Ferrell. To make matters worse, neither of you are telling the same story, and *your* fingerprints were found on the gun said to be owned by Mr. Broxton. It was also named as the weapon by which he was shot. Authorities are questioning the events of that night."

"This can't be! This just can't be happening to me," I cried, shaking in disbelief. "The police think I killed Roman, huh? That's not what happened."

"Mr. Broxton's gun was lying at your feet," Dr. Chambers said, reaching for my hand. "Is there a chance you could've forgotten some crucial elements of this tragedy?"

"No! Oh, how I wish I could, but the answer is no. How do you know all of this anyway? The investigators haven't questioned me in such an accusing manner."

"I made several phone calls trying to reach Mr. Ferrell, but during one of those attempts, I was placed on the line with one of his attorneys. I was given limited information at that time."

Dr. Chambers's words had become more than I could bear to hear. I began to scream, begging him to leave me alone.

"I'll let you have the rest of your evening to your-self after I send a nurse with your medication. Please try not to stress, Ms. Simmons." Dr. Chambers turned to leave.

"Sure. At least now I know Lance is alive."

Around ten o'clock that night, the hospital was calm. Dr. Chambers hadn't returned or sent a nurse as he had stated, so I knew he must've gone home. I couldn't sleep, so I picked up the remote to turn on the television. I clicked to every channel at least twice and couldn't find anything worth watching. I wished I hadn't asked Renee for space because I really needed her company then. There was so much I wanted to talk about. Thoughts of what Lance was doing at the moment entered my mind.

I wondered how Lance was feeling and if he blamed me for anything. Just when I had begun to think my nightmare had ended, I was faced with a challenge to prove Lance's and my innocence. I longed to tell him he was my king and I loved him. Chances of me getting to share my thoughts with him soon were looking slim.

I turned over to try to doze, and then the silver roses grabbed my attention. *Lance sent them to me. He didn't include a card because of his lawyers.* I began to laugh and cry. This was the first time since being in the hospital that I felt so revived.

I heard the door to my room open, but I was too lazy to turn back again. I remembered a nurse hadn't come to check on me in a while, so I assumed it was time for my medication. I called out to her.

"Is it time for my antibiotic or is it that nasty liquid stuff Dr. Chambers prescribed for me?" I asked.

"Neither," a man said.

I was startled by the familiar tone, and my heart skipped a beat. I quickly turned to see the face that owned the baritone voice. My suspicion was confirmed as a six-foot, red-eyed, raging maniac hovered over me. Roman Broxton had come to finish me off.

His head was clean shaven as I had remembered him last, but he had also grown a goatee. Dressed in green hospital scrubs and a white lab coat, Roman had managed to walk past the front desk and into my room.

"Don't bother screaming, boo. No one will hear you in time," he said, muffling my mouth with his hand.

For so many years, I lived to love, but I could never get it back. My father didn't care. My baby's daddy cared even less. The one man I knew had the same feelings for me as I had begun to own for him almost lost his life. Not even in my wildest dreams had I ever thought so much tragedy would enter my world.

As I lay muffled, panting, with tears streaming down, I looked in the eyes of the man who would in just moments begin to claim my life. I prayed for mercy.

EXCERPT

I Don't Wanna Be Right
March 2006

Chapter One
A Man Scorned

Maybe if I hadn't been the cause of Momma's death things would be differently for me today. There isn't a soul in this world who can replace Ma. Well, there is just one woman who closely measures up. Holiday Simmons, the woman I've grown to love more than any other, is like a breath of fresh air. But now the time is drawing nearer to the day that just as my mother had to die, I will claim Holiday's life.

Upon the first day of meeting Holiday, I knew there was something special about her. Her long legs are the sexiest pair I've ever laid eyes on. They're toned and they totally complement the rest of her well-fit body. I've always been in love with Holiday's smooth brown complexion and her satin-black, Indian-looking hair. The days I'd see her let it flow were few and far between. Holiday has eyes that give new meaning to the word *ebony*. Although they're the blackest of black, they give off enough light to brighten every man's heart. And there is so much more beneath her. I've never been able to just put my finger on all that lures me to her, but there is an attraction I feel toward her that goes far beyond her beauty.

Holiday could somehow manage to get me to understand her reasoning in life. Just about everything she'd say to me would make sense. But, for any other woman, I wasn't trying to hear all of that noise. Hell, I'm a man! My mother was the *only* woman who could just totally have my attention. For the most part, all I'd meet were the chicken heads and gold diggers anyway. And, who could replace my mother? No one! At least not in my eyes.

Momma passed from sugar diabetes when I was just a kid. Although the family counselors kept telling me it wasn't my fault, Dad made sure I knew it was. My mother never suffered from the disease until she became pregnant with me. For several long agonizing years after my birth, Momma stayed strong and endured the sugar attacks before her body finally succumbed to all of its woes. Just a kid, the only thing I knew to do was call for help during that last episode. When my father made it home, he only had time enough to see the paramedics lift Momma's lifeless body, which had become locked in a fetal position, stiffened by all of her pain. Once the EMTs had placed her onto the gurney, I stepped over to have a peek at her. I couldn't understand that she was actually dead. Just as her body had stiffened into an odd form, her face remained in a painstaking frown. The tears she'd shed were dried up, leaving long ashy-brown streams running down to her chin. This is my last memory of Momma because I couldn't bring myself to hover over her coffin at the funeral. Instead, I sat in the pew with my arms folded and chin buried deep in my chest. Even with my eyes squeezed shut, the heap of tears managed to pry through them and soaked onto what I had considered at the time to be my best Sunday shirt and tie.

For years, on the anniversary of Momma's death, I had to listen to my father explain to me that if Momma hadn't talked him into having a child when the understanding between them had been that he never wanted anymore, she'd still be alive. He was satisfied with only having my half-sister, Sharonda, in their lives. Dad says he never meant to get Sharonda's mother pregnant—especially since she was someone he could never respect anyway. I'm not sure why. But in spite of those feelings, he did take care of my big sister.

I came to learn that Momma had been envious of the relationship between Dad and Sharonda, so she talked him into allowing her to offer him that same bond with a child she bore for him. The illness started shortly after finding out she was pregnant and never went away. Neither did my father's ill feelings toward her death.

Dad said there would never be another woman to take Momma's place, and he meant it. Every woman he'd bring home was purely for his sexual satisfaction. He'd tell them they meant something to him, but he didn't treat them that way. After I started dating, he made sure he drilled into my head that there wasn't anything out there the quality of my mother. I figured why waste my time on falling in love with anyone? Listening to Dad tell me Momma was as good as they come, I knew he'd told the truth about nothing else being out there because my mother, the best of the best, was dead.

Once I got into high school, a brotha was cut in all the right places, had that naturally wavy hair all the girls liked, and kept a good-paying job, too. At lunchtime, girls who would offer me their lunch money would surround my table. At first it was cool, but then it got old. I had my own money. I couldn't understand why that didn't register in their minds. All I wanted was to eat my lunch and rap with my homeys for that thirty-minute interval, but those girls made it extremely difficult.

The rest of my life continued to go a little something just like that. Women continued to make me feel like I'm the cream of the crop when it comes to the African-American male gender. Years and years of that kind of shit only convinced me it must be true. Hell, just about anything I'd pull on these women they were willing to take. Just because I'm a good-looking brotha with some education and a little change in my pocket. The cars I drove and the clothes I wore spoke for my wallet size. Some women can't seem to look past that kind of shit, and for a woman to offer me what I want, how I want it, and when I want it, that's a lot of pressure for a man like me.

Getting out of college and landing a serious position at New Vet Life Insurance had no significant effect on my attitude toward life. The women behaved the same as anywhere else I'd worked, and as long as they were giving, I was a willing recipient. I came to expect it from all the ladies, but working in the midst of Holiday Simmons proved my thoughts otherwise.

Holiday is a classy black lady with all of her priorities in the right perspective. She was the only woman in the office who didn't seem to have the same attraction for me as the others. I really don't believe it was anything like the fact that I'm not her type, because my boy Lance would get sweated by almost every woman in the office, too. He's the total opposite in height and complexion as me, but Holiday wouldn't look at him twice either.

I'd come on to her and she'd give me that "nigga please!" look, twisting her mouth sideways and tilting her head to the side. Something about that stubbornness kept me coming back, though. Sure, I knew she was a good girl and a classy lady, a whole 'nother breed from with what I'd been use to dealing, but deep down, Holiday was the kind of woman with whom I really wished to someday settle. I didn't try to pressure her too much, but I think I used a detrimental approach to gaining her attention. Since we had to work so closely, I would share my personal experiences about women with her. I told her how I hadn't had any complaints in the bedroom. Then, I told her how I had this one and that one craving me in the late-night hours and exactly what they'd do for it. She absorbed all of this for a couple of years before finally letting me know she'd never have a man like me. We were in the privacy of her office, but her words still embarrassed me.

"What do you mean you'll never have a man like me?" I asked, outraged at her thoughts.

"I didn't stutter! Can you understand plain English?" Holiday could be so stern with her responses.

"Holiday, I'm a good-looking brotha, highly educated, and it doesn't hurt that I have a little bit of change in my pocket. What is the problem?"

"Am I supposed to be impressed?"

She had clearly scratched my ego. Now that's twice. I chose not to answer her because I really didn't know how. She continued, "Yeah, you've got all that going on for you, but I look at how you view women. If a man can't respect a woman like he'd respect his mother—and it's obvious *you* can't—then he's not in my league."

"Ouch, boo, that hurts!"

"Boo? My name is Holiday! Don't you forget it." She locked eyes with me, and she didn't blink.

"Now see, you'll let my man Lance call you baby girl. What's wrong with me giving you a pet name?"

"'Cause that's exactly what boo is, a pet name. I'm not a dog or a cat. And coming from a player like you, it never feels like a compliment anyway," she said, folding her arms.

Holiday was working on scratching my ego for the third time, so I tried to soften things after she finished explaining. "I'm sorry, Holiday, but the truth is I only mean it as a compliment when I call you boo."

"Then how about waiting until you do something to give me a newfound respect for you as a man before attempting to call me that again?"

Oh yeah, she did it! She definitely touched my ego for the third time. Except this time she didn't just scratch it, she put a big gash in the muthafucker. I couldn't let her know it, though. That would be against all principles and rules of a playa!

"A'ight, Holiday. No doubt I will do that, but it is okay to call you Holiday, isn't it? Or should I call you Ms. Simmons?"

She looked up at me again while continuing to organize the paperwork on her desk and said, "Just Holiday will do fine." Again, she didn't blink.

I didn't know what kind of man Holiday was messing around with at the time, but I really didn't care. All I know is that she had some ways on her that could really blow my mind. I hadn't met anyone like her before and the atmosphere around her was so refreshing.

Holiday had to leave New Vet Life because the company had become a hindrance to her ability to be promoted in the industry. I didn't want to see her go, but this is just another example of her wit and motivation with keeping her priorities straight. A big turn-on for me. My best friend Lance was equally as impressed with Holiday.

I decide not to tell Lance how much I was attracted to Holiday in the beginning. To Lance, all I've ever been is a player, exactly what I wanted him to think. I've never allowed my homeys to see any other side of me. The softhearted men I know come off like punks, but my boys with all the game, I can give the utmost respect. My father was a playa—before and after Momma's death, and he is the wisest man I know. He'd spend a little money on women, but not much. Hell, it's gotta be the reason why he's sittin' on overload in his bank account now, and why he hasn't had his heart broken before. It's because he didn't waste time with relationships and caring too much for women. This is one of the wisest things I've ever observed from my father. If only I'd done the same.

Chapter Two

Keepin' It Real

I called Holiday to see if she would let Lance and me take her out for a celebration of her new job. She had been at the new company for several months by then, but for some reason she kept avoiding my requests to take her out. I missed her, and just because she was working for a new firm didn't mean we couldn't remain close. I couldn't tell what was going through her head, but I just couldn't give up on trying.

After Lance and I had finally convinced Holiday to join us for a night out, we hung up the three-way phone conversation and I called Lance back.

"Lance, what's going on, man? Do you think she'll call us back to cancel again?" I pondered.

"Naw. I think she's for real on this one. Something's telling me she'll actually go through with her promise this time."

"I wonder what's got her so stubborn. You think she's fucking anybody? Usually when a woman is tough like that, it's because she needs some dick in her life." The fact that Holiday could downplay a couple of good-looking guys like Lance and me made me wonder what was up with her.

"Oh, I wouldn't know if she's seeing anybody right now, but I do know she's been through hell and high water with her past relationships. She even sounds a little bitter at times when we've talked about her experiences."

"Well what she gon' do? Hold it out on the rest of us brothas? She needs to let the past be the past. I hate to sound insensitive, but what the last man got to do with me?"

"The last man ain't got jack to do with you or me, Roman, but of course, I've never come on to her before. She probably only knows I find her attractive and that's all."

"So would you ever have a woman like Holiday?" I was trying to see what was going through my boy's head.

"Oh yeah! The sista's got it going on, but what you have to remember is that Holiday knows too much about our personal affairs. We've exposed all of our business to her for years. And for that reason, she ain't going."

"What the fuck you talking about she ain't going? Where is she supposed to be going?"

"On a roller coaster. You know full well like I do that after knowing what she does about us, she'll never take interest in either of us."

I wondered who the hell Lance thought he was to tell me I could never get a woman like Holiday. He must've forgotten for a brief moment who I am. I'm Roman Broxton! I ain't known a woman unattainable for me. Lance knew this. We've been friends for a little more than four years, ever since coming to the company for training at the same time. Lance knows me better than my own father. I just couldn't understand how he could omit the fact that I've gotten every woman I've ever wanted. I didn't stay with any of them for long, but this was the way I had intended for things to be. Holiday was a little bit more difficult to reach than other women I'd come across, but to say she was unattainable only made me more dogged about getting her.

As for that roller coaster shit, I never tried to tell any woman how she should feel. They all knew in advance that the possibility of being with me for an extended period of time was slim. I never hid the fact that I didn't want a relationship. I made sure I let every one of them know what type of man I am and whether or not I was seeing someone else at the time. If they were willing to deal with that, then they could hang with me. If not, then oh well! It was only their lost.

I didn't waste any time going to the barbershop to prepare for my first night out with Holiday. Looking my best was important. She hadn't seen me in several months by then, and I felt I needed to make a lasting impression on this woman. After all, I was determined to make her go back on her word of not ever being my lady.

After getting groomed, I sat around the shop and rapped with Lance and some of my old college buddies. Several years before, I had introduced Lance to my barber, Mr. Charles Brown. He is an older yet wiser brotha than the rest of us. Mr. Brown had us all sitting around listening to some of his stories of how things use to be when he was growing up. Even once we'd gotten out of his chair, my homeys and I— Carlos Wright, Anthony Stewart, and Lance—remained to listen until the last one of us had been cleaned up.

"Mr. Brown, you tryna tell me that you use to rake *and* bag the leaves from your neighbor's lawns for just twenty-five cents a bag, and I'm supposed to believe that?" Anthony asked, frowning in disbelief.

Mr. Brown was in the middle of shaping up Carlos's fade. He cut his clippers off and began to shake and wave them at Anthony as he responded. "Son, I was ten years old. Let's see, then the year must've been around 1959. None of you cats were even thought of then, let alone being born! I wonder how you can even make that doubtful face. You ain't ever been on my level to be able to tell me, as you cats say, what's really going on!"

We all responded in mockery toward Anthony. "Oooooh!" The barbershop rang like there was an all-male chorus holding out on a whole note, all in unison. Anthony, a six-foot-four, former college basketball player, stretched his legs out in the chair he was sitting in then threw his head back and shook it in disagreement. We all sort of chuckled until Anthony could come up with a response.

"Mr. Brown, I respect you and everything, but there is no way you can fairly say I ain't ever been on your level. I have an associate's degree in business and a bachelor's degree in psychology. From what I understand, all you have is a piece of paper that licenses you to cut hair. Sounds like to me you ain't ever been on my level."

The barbershop rang out once again with another tune from our unintentional male chorus, but this time, we added a little bit of whispering behind it. Mr. Brown took about another five seconds to finish up Carlos's fade then he cut his clippers off. Indefinitely. He asked Carlos to get up and sit over in one of the waiting seats then walked around to the front of the barber's chair and sat down. He locked eyes with Anthony, then brief whispering began just before Mr. Brown opened his mouth to speak. I shushed everyone, trying to get complete silence because I didn't want to miss a word.

"Son, pay close attention. I'm only gonna teach you this once." Soft whispering began to escalate, but I quickly shushed the barbershop once again so Mr. Brown could finish. "In 1959, the cost of living wasn't even a fraction of what it is today. I had eleven dedicated neighbors who would allow me to service their lawns every week. These yards were approximately twenty-by-fifteen feet, which means I could expect to stuff at least four fifteen-gallon bags for each lawn every time. I hope you listening 'cause I said every time. Every time—that's once a week, eleven clients, and four bags per lawn at twenty-five cents a bag. Now, I see some of y'all scrambling your brains tryna figure it out, so I'll gon' and tell ya that I made a minimum of eleven dollars a week. That's forty-four dollars a month promised to me. My momma's rent was $112 a month for our two-bedroom shotgun house. This meant that four times that year, I could pay the rent for Momma and still have twenty dollars to add to my savings. At the end of the year, I had a total of eighty dollars to do whatever I wanted. Do you have any idea of what eighty dollars could get you in 1959, Son? Huh? Do you?" Anthony just stared at Mr. Brown. The whole room remained silent. Mr. Brown continued on with this life lesson. "Well, I haven't been as fortunate as you to be able to go to college, and as a matter of fact, I know plenty of people who haven't had that same blessing, but in this case, this is when you learn to use what you got. Now, don't stop listening yet 'cause I ain't finished teaching you." This time, no one whispered. Instead, we only drew in closer to Mr. Brown because his lesson was all starting to come together. "Ten years old with eighty dollars, you'd think I'd blow it on junk, but I didn't. I learned that this was what a little hard work could get ya, so I continued on with the same path. As the years went by, economy changed and I was soon able to increase the cost of my labor as well as pick up more paying clients. In 1969, I was twenty years old and still unable to attend college due to lack of funds, and I refused to quit helping my mother out financially. So, I dipped into my savings and enrolled in a local barber school. After getting my license, I took it over on Jackson Avenue to a white male's house, along with the rest of my savings, $7,369. This man was about forty years old or so. Said he needed to move to another city by the end of the month. I gave him every penny of my life savings. By the time I left his house, I had the keys and the title to the building you all are sitting in today. So don't tell me that just 'cause you done went and got that piece of paper you like to call a degree that you better than me."

The male chorus rang out once again. Someone

even yelled, "Go 'head, Mr. Brown! That's telling 'im!" I have to admit I was pretty proud of the way Mr. Brown had explained things, too. I didn't want to add to my boy's shame, so I just smiled and nodded at Mr. Brown when Anthony wasn't looking.

"Well are you trying to say that a good education doesn't matter since you can make the same salary I do without any degrees?" Anthony questioned.

"No. You doubted the fact that I'd service my neighbor's lawns for so little money. I merely tried to show you it did make sense. I wasn't sure of what type of education you had before you told me. Had I known, I would've assumed in the time spent getting those two degrees someone would've taught you how to do your math. But, I can see they didn't."

Mr. Charles Brown tore Anthony up. I bet he wouldn't try to openly belittle anyone else. I almost felt sorry for my boy. It must've been hard faking embarrassment. He tried to act as though Mr. Brown hadn't said anything, but I caught him in a daze every once in a while until we had left the shop.

About the Author

Alisha Yvonne is a rising new voice in the world of African American fiction. She has recently landed a two-book-deal with the more popularly-known, Urban Books LLC, a Kensington Publishing imprint. Lovin' You Is Wrong releases July 2005.

Alisha is a member of several online literary groups, including R.A.W.SISTAZ Book Club, Black Writers United and APOOO411. She is President of the R.A.W.SISTAZ Memphis Chapter Book Club, and she is an avid supporter of local anti-domestic violence charities.

Visit Alisha online at *www.alishayvonne.com* or email to *author@ebonyliterarygrace.com*.